Dick Donovan

Tracked to Doom

The story of a mystery and its unravelling

Dick Donovan

Tracked to Doom
The story of a mystery and its unravelling

ISBN/EAN: 9783337393977

Printed in Europe, USA, Canada, Australia, Japan

Cover: Foto ©Andreas Hilbeck / pixelio.de

More available books at **www.hansebooks.com**

TRACKED TO DOOM

THE STORY OF

A MYSTERY AND ITS UNRAVELLING

BY

DICK DONOVAN

AUTHOR OF "THE MAN-HUNTER, "WHO POISONED BETTY DUNCAN?"
"THE MAN FROM MANCHESTER, "CAUGHT AT LAST!"
"A DETECTIVE'S TRIUMPHS," ETC.

A NEW EDITION

London
CHATTO & WINDUS, PICCADILLY
1893

CONTENTS.

CONTENTS.

TRACKED TO DOOM.

CHAPTER I.

THE TRAGEDY AT ST. JOHN'S WOOD.

It was a fervid July night. The scene London, and the hour near twelve o'clock. The roar of the vehicular traffic was dying down, for the theatres had emptied some time before, but the restaurants and public-houses were still doing a roaring trade, while the streets were full of bustle and life, for the stagnant and heated atmosphere induced people to linger and chat and smoke in the open air rather than hurry to their homes.

In one of the by-streets off the Strand was the stage-door of a popular theatre. Up to half-an-hour before this the theatre had been packed from floor to ceiling with an enthusiastic audience, to witness the first production of a new burlesque. A young, good-looking, and popular actress had taken a leading part in it. She had been favourably known to London for about a year. Up to that time she had been playing in the provinces, and had come to London a stranger and unheralded, but made her mark immediately. Her professional name was Vesta Florence, and from every photographer's shop-window portraits of "Miss Vesta Florence, the popular burlesque actress," stared one in the face. She was a blonde, with wavy, golden hair and a remarkably pretty face. Her figure was faultless, and she had a sweet, musical voice. Although about twenty-four, she seemed little more than a girl, for she was *petite* and child-like in her manner.

In the by-street where the stage-door was, a man promenaded up and down with an air of impatience and irritability. He was in evening-dress, and wore a thin Inverness-cape over his frock-coat. He had been in the front of the house, but when the performance ended he went round to the stage-door and inquired of the porter how long Miss Florence would be before she was ready to leave, and was told perhaps half-an-hour or three-quarters. He was a dark man, of about medium height, with a full moustache and no whiskers, while his hair was cropped close. His face was tanned with sun and weather, as if he had travelled abroad a good deal, and his dark, restless eyes seemed to bespeak a passionate, vindictive, and fiery nature. Now and again he glanced nervously at the stage-door, looked at his watch, then resumed his walk, but never going many yards away from the door, and he eagerly scanned the face of every one who came out. Presently the door swung open again; a gleam of light shot athwart the pavement, and a clear, ringing voice exclaimed to some one inside—

"Good-night, dear. Good-night, all."

Then there was the rustle of a silk dress, and a young woman came forth. It was Miss Vesta Florence, and she was about to get into a hansom-cab that waited at the edge of the pavement for her, when the man who had been promenading up and down strode up, seized her by the arm, and hissed into her ear—

"So, Mary, we meet again."

The mere utterance of the name "Mary" and the sound of the man's voice startled her, and as she turned round and looked at him she exclaimed, in low tones—

"My God! you here?"

She was very pale, and evidently greatly agitated.

"Yes," he answered, with a cynical smile. "You didn't expect to see me?"

"No," she faltered. "But come away from this spot, for goodness' sake."

Telling the cabman to wait, she moved down the street, the man in the Inverness-cape by her side. Then she turned to him, and with evident emotion and distress, said—

"What has brought you back? What do you want?"

"To your first question, business has brought me back. To your second, I want you."

"No, no!" she answered in a pleading voice. "You cannot have me; you must forget me. You must go away."

He laughed a cynical laugh again—a laugh that was suggestive of a cold-blooded, sneering disposition, and he said—

"I must go away, must I? No, my sweet Mary; not this time."

She glanced around her nervously, and said—

"Oh! don't let us loiter about, or we shall attract attention."

"Very well," he answered. "Not that I care, but I am hungry and want some supper. You will sup with me?"

"Anything," she said; "but let us go from here."

He led the way to the cab, handed her in, and telling the cabman to drive to a well-known hotel in the neighbourhood of Piccadilly, took his seat beside her.

Arrived at the hotel he ordered a costly supper, including white wine, sherry, and champagne. He did full justice to it, though she ate but little. Her pretty face wore a look of woebegoneness, and now and again tears welled to her eyes, as though some great trouble was on her mind.

"Why don't you eat?" he asked.

"I can't," she answered curtly.

"Why not?"

"Because you are here," she remarked savagely.

He laughed again.

"You are still the pretty devil of old," he said carelessly. "But perhaps I shall be able to take some of the devil out of you." Then he called for the bill, and when it was brought he said to her—

"As I hear you are making a fortune with your acting, you can pay for this."

Without replying, though her lip curled with scorn, she drew forth a well-filled purse and gave the waiter the money for the bill.

"What are you going to do now?" her companion demanded.

"I am going home," she said.

"Where is your home?"

"Why do you ask? What has it got to do with you where I live?"

He shrugged his shoulders and coolly lighted a cigarette.

"I should say it has much to do with me," he replied. "Any way, I am going with you."

"No; for Heaven's sake, no! You cannot; you *must* not!"

Then, as she saw that the attention of some other people in the room had been attracted to her, she whispered—

"Don't drive me mad! Let us leave this place at once. Remember I am well known."

They went into the street, and he hailed a passing cab and helped her in.

"Where shall I tell him to drive to?"

After some hesitation she gave an address at St. John's Wood; thither they were driven. And when St. John's Wood was reached she stopped the cab at the corner of a road and alighted, followed by her companion. She paid the cabman and dismissed him, then said peremptorily to her companion—

"You must leave me here."

"Why?" he asked, in astonishment.

"Because my husband will be at home, and there will be a row."

"Your husband!" he exclaimed as he seized her by the wrist, so roughly and cruelly that she cried out and said—

"Leave go. You hurt me."

But he did not leave go; he was excited and chafing with passion. He put his face close to hers, and between his teeth said—

"You lie! I don't believe you. But if you are married, I'll make your life a hell!"

"You've done that already," she answered bitterly, as she wrenched herself free from his grasp, and showing spirit and determination. "You may do your worst now, for I will defy you."

She sped away from him, and entered the gates of a house some little distance down the road. When he had recovered from his surprise he followed, but by that time she had disappeared. The house was a detached villa, standing in a small garden, and on the gate, painted in black and gold, was the name "Linda Villa."

The man noted this, and for some moments stood irresolute, as though he could not make up his mind what to do. But at last he turned on his heel and walked quickly away.

A week later, at about half-past two in the morning, five men alighted at the gate of Linda Villa from two hansoms. They were all smoking—all in evening-dress; while their husky voices and unsteady gait suggested that they had supped not wisely, and had looked on the wine that was red.

"Come in, chappies, and have the final," said one of the men, who evidently lived at Linda Villa. He was of medium height, dark-complexioned, with close-cropped hair, a full moustache, and dark, restless eyes.

"No, no," they all said; "it is too late. It would be a shame to disturb your wife at this time of night."

"Oh, nonsense! Come in," urged the man.

"Not to-night, Ricardo," answered one of his companions, who were also neighbours. "We'll look you up on Sunday evening."

"All right," answered Ricardo. "Don't forget that's an appointment. Well, good-night."

The friends shook hands and parted. Ricardo unlatched the gate of Linda Villa and staggered to the door, which he managed to open after much fumbling with a latch-key. Then he entered the house and closed the door behind him.

About a quarter of an hour or twenty minutes later there was a flashing of lights in the house; the street-door was flung violently open, and Ricardo, in slippered feet and with pallid, scared face, rushed out hatless, tore down the road for about a hundred yards till he reached a house on the door of which was a brass plate bearing the inscription, "Dr. Wilkinson." He rang the night-bell violently, and succeeded in arousing the doctor, who, in response to Ricardo's urgent request, returned with him to Linda Villa, and was taken to the dining-room, and this was what he saw :—

On the couch lay a woman. Her left arm was bent, and the hand, tightly clenched, rested on her bosom. Her right arm was stretched at full length; the hand, also tightly clenched, was resting on the floor. The right foot was also on the floor, but the left knee was drawn up. The face was distorted, the eyes bulging out, the tip of the tongue protruding from between the blackened lips, the nostrils dilated. The whole attitude and the distorted features told of agonising suffering.

The woman was Vesta Florence, the burlesque actress and the wife of Eugène Ricardo. She was quite dead. Her beautiful fair hair was disarranged, part of it hanging over the pillow of the couch. The front of her dress was open at the top, and round her white throat was a silk handkerchief, folded into a narrow band, but quite loose. With that handkerchief, however, Vesta Florence had been strangled; for there was a livid mark, corresponding with the handkerchief, all round the throat.

"She is dead," said Dr. Wilkinson, after a very brief examination. "She has been strangled."

"Yes," answered Ricardo, seeming very confused and bewildered. "I found her so."

The doctor looked at him with an incredulous expression. Three or four scared servants in dishabille had crowded into the hall, and were peering in at the doorway. He looked from Ricardo to them, as if expecting them to give him some explanation. But they spoke never a word.

"Well, I can do nothing," he remarked. "Your wife

is quite dead, and has died of strangulation ; and I don't think she can have strangled herself. It seems to me a case of murder, and it is my duty, therefore, to give notice to the police. If you have the key of the room, let me have it, so that I may lock the door, and prevent the body being touched and the things from being disturbed."

He was told that the key was in the door, so he turned it in the lock, took the key with him, and hurried off to the nearest police-station, where he reported that he believed a dreadful murder had been committed at Linda Villa.

CHAPTER II.

WHEN the news was spread that Vesta Florence, the
public favourite, had been murdered in her house at
St. John's Wood, the excitement was intense. No
murder of modern time had aroused Londoners as this
one did. Apart from the woman being so well known
as an actress, the crime was shrouded in mystery.
And, by the papers, the public learnt for the first
time that Vesta Florence was a married woman, and
the wife of Eugène Ricardo. The evening papers
also announced that Eugène Ricardo had been placed
under arrest on suspicion of having killed his wife.

The subject of the murder was the one topic of
conversation for hours. Business men on the way to
the City discussed it. In trains, in 'buses, and at
public-house bars it was talked about. Men on
'Change forgot stocks and shares for the moment to
speak feelingly of the strange murder of "poor little
Florence." If the Prime Minister or the Prince of Wales
himself had suddenly died, the attention of London could
not have been more strongly concentrated on the event
than it was on the death of Vesta Florence, the actress.

That afternoon a gentleman, whose white hair and whiskers and lined face told that he had long passed the meridian of life, drove in a cab from the City to a house near Clapham Common, where he alighted and rang the door-bell with nervous agitation. In a few minutes the door was opened by a neat maid in white apron and cap.

"Is Mr. Sugg in?" asked the visitor, with some manifestations of anxiety, as if he feared that Mr. Sugg might be out.

"Yes, sir," was the answer. Whereupon the gentleman seemed relieved. "Come in, please. Who shall I say wants him?" as she showed the gentleman into the front parlour.

"Glindon is my name," was the answer.

The maid withdrew, and in about five minutes Mr. Sugg entered the room, and Glindon shook his hand cordially.

Calvin Sugg was a remarkable man, physically, facially, and mentally. By profession he was a detective, and he had made himself famous almost throughout Europe. It could truly be said of Mr. Sugg that he had been born for his profession; and nature seemed to have embodied in him the ideal detective. Although he might have been considered somewhat short in stature, his wonderfully well-knit frame spoke of great powers of endurance as well as great strength, both of which he possessed in a striking degree.

His hands, shapely and flexible, were joined to wrists

B

that seemed to be all sinews. His general physical appearance was suggestive of the athlete trained to a point of absolute perfection. His face was a study. The features, though somewhat small, were regular. He had soft, blue eyes that in repose were dull; but once let the man feel interested in anything, and those eyes blazed out like living coals, and had such a steady, piercing gaze that it was not many men who could look fixedly at him.

Deep nerve-lines extended from the nostrils to the corners of the mouth, and two thought-furrows between the eyes not only gave one the impression that he was capable of great concentration on any particular subject, but had a will that nothing could break down. He was clean shaved, the better to enable him to adopt various disguises, at which he was known to be an adept.

He was slightly bald, and his hair was iron-grey, which made him look older somewhat that his years, which were about forty-four. He had a soft, clear voice that was very pleasant, but somewhat struck a stranger as being a little incongruous when contrasted with his build—a build that one is apt to associate with a deep, even a raucous voice.

His mental gifts were in keeping with his other qualities. There were few things, in a general way, he did not know something about. He spoke at least six languages fluently, and had a good knowledge of several others; while his memory for detail, dates, and minutiæ was simply astounding. He had been instrumental in tracking down some of the most notorious criminals of

the age.   So that, if he was the criminal's horror, he was
the law's pride; and hidden away—for a retiring modesty
was not the least conspicuous of his many conspicuous
qualities—he had innumerable medals and souvenirs of
all kinds that had been presented to him by different
Governments for service rendered.

But Calvin Sugg never boasted, never talked of his
own power, and had as sympathetic and as kindly a
heart as ever beat in man's breast.   He used to say
sometimes, when in a jocular mood, that nature had
given him a detective's brain but a woman's heart.

"Well?" he said, as he shook his visitor's hand.
"It must be something urgent and important that has
brought you here, Mr. Glindon."

"It is, it is," answered Glindon.   "Of course you've
heard of the murder of Ricardo's wife, Vesta Florence?"

"Oh yes."

"Have you received any instructions in the matter?"

"No.   I understand that the Scotland Yard people
have put Peter Grierson on the case."

"Ugh!" exclaimed Mr. Glindon, with an expression of profound disgust; "Grierson is a fool.   Now,
look here, Sugg: you know that Ricardo has been
arrested?"

"Yes."

"According to what the papers say, however, the
murder is surrounded with the deepest mystery, and
that there is no evidence at present against Ricardo.
In my own mind I am sure the wretch is guilty, and I
want you to bring the crime home to him.   You must

do this, Sugg; you must. And if he should be convicted, then indeed I shall breathe freely and live again."

"Mr. Glindon, what is the strange power that that man exercises over you?" asked Sugg, with the pointed emphasis that he always gave to any question that interested him in an unusual way.

"Do not ask, for I cannot tell you," answered Glindon, with a look of keen distress in his face, which was careworn and anxious. "But if you can bring this crime home to him you will relieve me of an incubus. Take the case up on my behalf, and rest assured that your guerdon will be no mean one."

"Don't mention that," answered Sugg. "When I saw the account of the murder I was, of course, greatly surprised, and intended to call upon you to-morrow."

"Well, you see, I could not wait. I was too anxious and too impatient, and I resolved to come out and see you. If Ricardo really murdered his wife, he must not be allowed to escape for the want of evidence, and there is no living man so capable of getting that evidence, if it is to be got, as you. You will try, won't you?"

"Yes," said Sugg, after some reflection. Then he asked, "Did you know Mrs. Ricardo?"

"No."

"But you knew that Vesta Florence was Ricardo's wife?"

"No, I did not even know that. It is two years, nearly, now since I first commissioned you to watch the

man, and for some time you have not reported anything to me."

"True; because I had nothing to report. However,
I will do what I can in this business, and call upon you
in a few days."

"Do, do; and leave no stone unturned to convict
Ricardo."

"But supposing that he did *not* murder his wife?"

"I cannot suppose any such thing, Sugg. I believe
there is no crime under the sun that he would not
commit. He is an incarnate devil."

"That may be true, and yet he may not be responsible
for this crime."

"Don't harass me with these doubts, there's a good
fellow," said Mr. Glindon irritably. "I know the
man and you don't. However, I must go now; but
I shall hope to see you in the course of a day or
two."

Mr. Sugg wished his visitor good-night, and they
parted; and when Sugg was alone he mentally asked
himself—

"What is the link, I wonder, between Ricardo and
Glindon, and why should Glindon wish to see Ricardo
hanged? Umph! Perhaps some day it will come out,
but at present I don't know that it is my business to
discover it. I do not like to interfere in other folks'
concerns if I have no interest in them. Every man has
his skeleton, and poor Glindon is no exception to the
rule."

Four days later Calvin Sugg, in fulfilment of his

promise, called upon Mr. Glindon at his place of
business in the City. Mr. Glindon, still looking very
anxious, very troubled, and very careworn, received him
in his private room, and betrayed his great anxiety by
the way in which he asked the question—

"Well, Sugg, what success?"

"In accordance with your request, I have left no
stone unturned, and I am bound to confess that the
murder is one of the most mysterious crimes I have
ever been called upon to investigate."

"Yes, yes; but you discovered something?"

"Yes, I've discovered several things."

"And you have no doubt that Ricardo is guilty?"

"On the contrary, I haven't the slightest hesitation
in expressing my conviction that he did not murder his
wife, and that, when he is again brought before the
magistrate, he will be discharged."

For a moment or two Mr. Glindon presented the
appearance of a man who was stunned, and he gazed
at the detective with a look that was like a look of
reproach.

"But, Sugg," he exclaimed at last, "you are surely
mistaken."

"Oh, dear, no," answered Sugg, with the air of one
who knew that his words were absolutely indubitable.
"I tell you that Ricardo did not murder his wife, and
yet the man who did seems, strangely enough, to have
borne a strong resemblance to Ricardo."

"What man? What man?" gasped Mr. Glindon
hoarsely.

"A week before the murder," continued Sugg, "a man in evening-dress and wearing an Inverness-cape inquired for Miss Florence at the stage-door of the theatre. The stage-door porter knew Ricardo, and thought for a moment that this man was Ricardo, but soon saw that he was mistaken. When Florence left the theatre, and was about to get into a cab that was waiting for her, the man accosted her, and they seemed to have an altercation. They subsequently drove to an hotel in Piccadilly and supped, and afterwards were driven in a cab to St. John's Wood.

"From that point all is shrouded in mystery. On the night of the murder Vesta Florence drove home from the theatre as usual; and the cabman says she was alone. She reached her residence between twelve and one, and let herself in with a latch-key. None of the servants were in the habit of sitting up unless Ricardo was at home. He had gone to a dinner on this particular night, and the servants were in bed. They heard nothing and knew nothing until aroused by Ricardo frantically ringing the bell, and he himself rushed out for Dr. Wilkinson.

"It was a quarter to three when Wilkinson arrived, and he says in his evidence that the woman had been dead then from an hour to an hour and a half. Consequently she must have been murdered soon after she got in. Now, Ricardo did not arrive home until half-past two, as proved by friends who were with him and parted from him at his gate. The mysterious murderer has for the time escaped. The coroner's verdict is,

'Wilful murder against some person or persons unknown.' Ricardo is to be brought before the magistrate
to-morrow, and as there is not a tittle of evidence
against him he will be discharged."

"And then—and then?" muttered Glindon, speaking
rather to himself than addressing his visitor.

"And then," said Sugg drily, "the murderer must
be hunted down. There are two things that, I hope,
will ultimately enable me to bring him to justice. The
first is this silk handkerchief. It is of the finest Tussore silk, and though large, as you see, it will pass
through a wedding-ring. With that handkerchief Vesta
Florence was strangled. The Thugs of India used
to strangle their victims with handkerchiefs exactly
like this one; for it is readily twisted, and is as strong
as steel wire. The second thing is this ring, a massive
gold signet-ring. It slipped from the finger of the
murderer, and was found on the couch where the
dead woman lay. You will note that on the stone
is engraved the unusual device of a skull and cross-
bones."

Mr. Glindon examined the handkerchief and the
ring with some manifestations of curiosity, and yet,
so to speak, in a mechanical way. And then he said
again—

"And you believe Ricardo innocent?"

"I am certain he is. But I am going to find the
murderer."

Mr. Glindon showed that he had lost all interest in
the subject now, and Calvin Sugg soon took his leave.

And when the merchant was alone he paced up and down, pressing his hands to his head like one who was sorely troubled, and he murmured audibly—

" Fate mocks me ; even Heaven turns its face away, and the torture I suffer is the torture of Tantalus."

CHAPTER III.

THE PRIORY.

In one of the most beautiful parts of Richmond, Surrey, and commanding a view of that really wonderful panorama of the Thames, which even prejudiced foreigners have admitted to be unique of its kind, stood The Priory. It was an old house that had undergone restoration at the hands of a modern architect, who, being less of a vandal than most of his contemporaries, had preserved all the picturesque features of a bygone age.

The building itself was spacious and commodious, and its external walls in places were covered with mantling ivy; while over the main entrance a magnificent specimen of wistaria had been carefully trained, and in the season of its blossoming it was a feast of beauty for the eye capable of appreciating the glory of nature as displayed in flowers.

The house stood in about eight acres of ground, where nature, in unkempt wildness, had been allowed to blend so cunningly with the primness of art as to produce an effect that was at once charming and delightful. In one part was a miniature lake, on which floated a genuine Venetian gondola; and in another was a sylvan glade, where, beneath the deep um-

brageous shadow of the tall trees, one could wander
knee-deep in ferns and flowers, and, in the silence and
seclusion that reigned, find it difficult to realise that he
was within a few miles of the roar and passion of the
world's mightiest city.

Everything connected with The Priory seemed to
have been ordered and arranged with an exquisite
taste, in which the keen observer might have detected
the feminine mind—the mind of a woman of culture,
but with the instinctive eye for beauty. Internally
the same influence was made manifest even in a more
marked degree : colour and harmony were there blended
with faultless taste. Wealth displayed itself with a
lavish hand; but it was not with the vulgar obtrusive-
ness that is often a marked feature in the expenditure
of your rich parvenu.

Most certainly vulgarity found no abiding-place in
The Priory. There was nothing there suggestive of
"sweet bells jangled, harsh and out of tune." And
with such a home it seemed difficult in the extreme
to disassociate human happiness in its most exalted
aspect. Surely under that favoured roof sorrow could
find no resting-place, save such sorrow as kindly hearts
and generous natures must ever feel for those on
whom fortune smiles not, and to whom the way of
life is a *Via Dolorosa*, thorny and sad with the moans
of suffering.

But as the fairest fruit has oft a canker at its core,
so in the heart, as it were, of this beautiful home lay
a gnawing worm, and over the roof-tree hung a dark

and impenetrable cloud of sorrow.   But that sorrow,
whatever it might be, does not seem to have touched
as yet the fair, sweet girl, who, with beaming eyes and
expectant face, stands in the threshold of the main
doorway, watching with undisguised eagerness the ap-
proach of a young man who, with elastic step, is hurry-
ing along the carriage-drive, which extends from the
doorway in a straight line for over a hundred yards,
through an avenue of superb chestnuts.

It is summer-time, and summer's many voices fill the
air, while the brilliant sunshine falls from an all but
unclouded sky, and throws a coruscant splendour over
the landscape.

The young man wears a light suit, and he carries
over his arm a dust-coat, which seems to indicate he
has come off a journey. He hurries up the steps of
the doorway, and in another moment he and the young
lady embrace each other tenderly, and that embrace
declares them lovers.

She is the daughter of the house—Muriel Glindon,
upon whom life sits very lightly yet, although her
twenty-fifth year has almost drawn to its close. A
gown of soft, diaphanous material clings in graceful
folds to her slim but well-shaped figure.

From her gloved arm depends, by its ribbons, a large
garden-hat, which she has just removed for coolness'
sake. A mass of nut-brown hair is coiled gracefully
about her head, and its rich, warm colour throws into
relief, and contrasts pleasantly with, the decided blue
of her eyes and the clear red-and-white complexion,

which is so suggestive of healthy open-air life. Even a cynic who had vowed to hate all his kind must in common honesty have pronounced Muriel Glindon a charming woman.

Her lover, Raymond Penoyre—for lover he was—could give her some months, perhaps—not more—in seniority, for he was as yet in his twenty-sixth year. He was a graceful, gentlemanly fellow, well set up, with a manly bearing and a sapient expression beaming from his dark face. In striking contrast to her, he was as dark as a raven.

"Why, Raymond dear, whatever has made you so late?" Muriel exclaimed, when they had embraced each other with unconventional heartiness. "We have waited luncheon, and I have been on the look-out for you so long that I had quite begun to despair."

"Poor little woman!" he said laughingly, as arm-in-arm they entered the hall. "The fact is, Muriel, I missed the first train, and had to wait an hour."

"Oh, you naughty boy! But there, I forgive you," she said sweetly, as she relieved him of his coat, hat, and stick. "And now let us go in to luncheon, or aunt will be quite cross."

They proceeded down the passage, and entered a charming room, the long French window of which commanded a view of a splendid lawn, that was bounded by a bank of rhododendrons, now a blaze of variegated colour. In this room luncheon was set, and as the young couple entered, a sedate, matronly lady rose and warmly shook Penoyre's hand.

"Come, young gentleman," she said pleasantly, "we shall have to take you to task."

"You must forgive me, Mrs. Romanoff," he answered. "I have already explained to Muriel that I missed the train and had to wait an hour."

"What! a lover and miss a train! Oh, fie, fie!"

"Nay, do not be too hard upon me," he laughed. "My sisters are to blame; they would insist on my trying over some new duets with them."

"There, there!" said the lady, "make no excuses;" and ringing the bell, she bade the servant serve the luncheon.

Mrs. Romanoff was a childless widow, her husband, a Russian, having been dead about fifteen years; and since then she had lived with her brother—Muriel's father and a widower—as the mistress of his house. She was dependent upon him, for her husband had left her penniless. She was a lady-like, cultured woman, verging on sixty, with a pensive expression of face and a certain sadness in her voice, as if in her heart she had some stifled regret for something missed and lost for ever.

But whatever her feelings were, she uttered no complaint, and, outwardly, was contented and cheerful. When the luncheon was ended, and after a brief chat, she said, as she rose—

"Now I must leave you young people to look after yourselves, for I have some housekeeping affairs to attend to. I know you will excuse me."

Of course, the young people were quite willing to do

this, and Muriel suggested they should spend an hour
in the gondola on the lake, to which Raymond readily
assented. As they went forth into the hall a young
woman was just descending the stairs. She stopped
and spoke to Muriel.

"You are going out, Miss?" she asked in English,
but with a pronounced foreign accent.

"Yes, Ita. I shall not take my lesson this afternoon;" and having secured her hat and sunshade,
Muriel, beaming with happiness, tripped down the steps
followed by Raymond, who had paused to light a cigar.

The young woman addressed as Ita—Ita Prokop
was her name—was a Russian. She had been in Mr.
Glindon's service close on two years in the capacity
of a teacher of languages for Muriel. She was a short
and stout young woman, about her pupil's own age;
not good-looking by any means, but with a strongly
marked face, a sallow complexion, a suspicion of a
moustache on her upper lip, and eyes that were keen
as an eagle's, as dark as sloes, and which seemed to
watch one from under overhanging brows with an
apparent innate fierceness.

The "hour" on the lake stretched to nearly three
before Muriel and Raymond thought of returning.
It was very pleasant there, dreaming and drifting;
watching the many birds, if they had eyes for aught
but themselves, that had their haunts among the
sedges; and listening, if they were not deaf to all
other sounds save their own voices, to the whispering
wind as it seemed to woo the trees lining the banks.

At first Raymond assumed the character of tl gondolier, and he sang a stave or two, in a cultivate musical voice, of a Venetian love-song. But present he found the heat too oppressive, or the sculling t laborious, or Muriel's person too irresistibly magneti for he took his place beside her, and his hand foui her hand, and ever and anon his lips met hers.

It was a pretty picture—an idyll—a summer poer that told of human bliss. But as in the garden Eden the serpent lurked, so in the future happine which these two mortals pictured for themselves w. to come a serpent, whose name was Sorrow.

CHAPTER IV.

THE FALLING OF THE SHADOW.

MR. IVAN PETER GLINDON was a general merchant in the City of London, his place of business being situated in Leadenhall Street. His principal transactions were with Russia, but he had connections with nearly all the civilised parts of the globe. He was reputed to be " as wealthy as Crœsus," and men envied him, while his charming daughter had been sought by all sorts and conditions of fortune-hunters. But no one had found favour in her sight, or had been countenanced by him, save Raymond Penoyre.

Mr. Glindon had been born in Russia, though of English parents. His mother and father had gone to that country immediately after their marriage, his paternal grandfather having been in the Russian trade. Of that marriage three children were born. One died in infancy; the other two, Peter and his sister, lived. The parents were not particularly fortunate in their transactions. The father died at a comparatively early age, and his wife did not long survive him. The daughter married a man who was in the Russian Government service, and she went with her husband

C

to Siberia, where he had an official appointment, and there she passed many years of her life.

During her absence Peter married, but Mrs. Romanoff never saw her sister-in-law, who was killed by an accident while travelling in the Ural Mountains. She knew there was a great deal of mystery in connection with that marriage, but her brother would tell her nothing. He was a young man, and though he had a flourishing business, he sold it almost immediately after his wife's death and proceeded to London, where he established himself, and soon began to prosper.

Some years later he married a second time, his wife being an English lady of good family. The only issue of the marriage was Muriel, who had but a very faint recollection of her mother, who died when the child was scarcely seven.

When Mrs. Romanoff became a widow, she, at her brother's request, took up her residence with him at the time he bought The Priory at Richmond, and she had since been a mother to the girl and the keeper of his house.

Mr. Glindon was a tall, gentlemanly man, on the wrong side of sixty. His hair was silvery white, and silvery whiskers fringed his oval face, which might have served an artist as a model for brooding grief. A dark melancholy seemed to have settled there, and seldom, if ever, did a smile light up the darkness.

In the City his name was one to conjure with; for no one would have dared to breathe a syllable against his integrity, while his commercial astuteness had

placed him in the very front rank of business men.
Honoured and respected; with, as it seemed, almost
boundless wealth at his disposal; with a daughter who
was the joy of his heart, and whose warm affection for
him displayed itself in a thousand ways, he ought to
have been, inferentially, one of the happiest of men.
For he was full of generous impulses, had a heart that
melted to charity, and he gave with a liberal hand;
and yet he seemed a prey to some dark, brooding sorrow,
that made his life all but unbearable.

Troops of friends he had, but he all but shunned
them; and such enjoyment as he was capable of ex-
periencing he found in solitude in his beautiful home
at Richmond.

Both his sister and his daughter had tried to lift him
from the gloom into which he seemed for ever wrapped,
but their efforts had been fruitless. They had filled
his house with all that art and refined taste could
suggest, and though he expressed his gratitude, he
displayed no interest. He loved to ramble about the
grounds alone, or to shut himself up in his small but
well-stocked library.

Whatever the cause of his grief was—and that there
was a cause was obvious—he kept his secret well. He
was a mystery even to those who watched his coming
with joy and sighed when he departed. To his beautiful
daughter he was passionately attached. Her word was
law in the house; her wishes were granted almost before
they were expressed. In regard to those affairs that
are supposed to lie nearest a woman's heart he had

allowed her a free hand. He had said to her years
before, when she had just touched the verge of womanhood—

" Muriel, you are beautiful, and probably will be rich;
therefore suitors will seek you eagerly. But I, as your
truest and best friend, ask you not to let your heart go
out to any man until I know him."

To this request she had been unswervingly loyal;
but up to the time of meeting Raymond Penoyre,
she had, as it seemed, steeled her heart against all
comers.

She first saw Raymond at a picnic to which she had
been invited by some friends. He had, as many others
had done, sought her acquaintance, and became a guest
at her father's house. Mr. Glindon took kindly to him.
He did not hesitate to say he admired his frankness,
his manliness, his freedom from the cant and frivolity
which seem so characteristic of the modern young man.
And so between Raymond and Muriel love had grown,
and Mr. Glindon had said no word that was calculated
either to encourage or check it.

Raymond Penoyre's wooing, however, had not found
favour with his own family. They were people who
boasted of an aristocratic descent. His father, Sir
Ralph Penoyre, had been for over thirty years in
the Consular Service, and had spent most of his life
abroad, but had retired in broken health, with little
more than his pension to live on, and with his family
had settled down in Windsor. Raymond, who was
the youngest of four sons, one of whom was in the

navy and the other two in the army, had been educated for the Civil Service, but up to the time that we meet him he was still waiting for "a good appointment."

He had, however, distinguished himself as an artist —for he had a passion for art—and some of his pictures had already attracted attention. But while his father preached to him the necessity of "marrying money," seeing that he would inherit nothing but "an honoured name," he gave him to understand that he would countenance no one who could not boast of "good lineage." His parents did not regard Muriel Glindon as coming within this category ; and though they did not exactly snub her, they treated her with such studied reserve on two or three occasions when she had visited them at her lover's request, that it had made her very unhappy.

But Raymond had told them that if he could win Muriel he should do so, and make her his wife ; and his mother had been kind enough to say that, as the young lady was an heiress, they might in time be able to overlook the painful fact that she represented a family of traders. This annoyed Raymond, but as he was very fond of his mother, he allowed the unkind remark to pass without comment.

Some few days before we meet the young couple at The Priory, Raymond had asked Muriel if she would be his wife. Her answer was, "Yes, dear, subject to my father's approval." So it had been arranged between Muriel and Mrs. Romanoff that he was to come to The Priory on this particular day, and that evening after dinner he was to put the all-important question to Mr. Glindon. Muriel had not the slightest doubt as to what the answer would be. She knew that her father liked Penoyre, and that, if it was her wish to marry him, that wish would not be opposed.

Mr. Glindon nearly always came down from the City by the five o'clock train when he went to his business, which was about four days a week, and he dined at seven. If there was company, which was often the case, except the people were old and familiar friends, he took his dinner alone, and afterwards he would shut himself up in his library. Those who were comparative strangers to him called this eccentricity; some even went so far as to say it was boorishness. But his sister and daughter knew it was neither the one nor the other.

It was due to the fact that he could take no part in the merriment and enjoyment of his guests, and rather than be a drag upon them in any way he preferred the solitude of his room. His hospitality was unbounded, but he left the dispensing of it to Muriel and Mrs. Romanoff.

On this eventful evening Mrs. Romanoff had taken care that there should be no other guest present but Raymond. Mr. Glindon was used to him, and Penoyre never tried to draw his host out, as the saying is, and refrained from talking to him when he saw that he wished to be silent. Mr. Glindon generally asked if there was any one to dinner, and did so on this evening.

When he was informed that there was no one but Raymond, he said he would join the family party. When his daughter welcomed him as was her wont, she thought that he seemed unusually depressed, and anxiously asked him if he was not well.

"As well as usual, my dear," he answered, "but a little fagged. It's been sultry and oppressive in the City to-day; perhaps that has something to do with it. I ought to have telegraphed to you to send John up to the station with the gig, but really I didn't think of it."

Although The Priory was nearly three-quarters of a mile from the station, he preferred to walk in fine weather. He said that the walk did him good after being "stewed up in London all day." In bad weather the coachman met him either with the brougham or the dog-cart.

He greeted Penoyre cordially when he went down to the dining-room, and inquired how long he had been there.

" I was here in time for luncheon," answered Raymond.

" Ah, you've been amusing yourself since then to your heart's content, I suppose ? "

" Well, sir, I've spent a happy and delightful afternoon——"

Mr. Glindon sighed, and a look of pain swept across his face, as though the remark had revived in his brain some memory of the long ago, when *he* knew what happiness and delight meant. But he made no reply, and Raymond continued—

"And—and I want to have a few words with you after dinner, if you will kindly give me the opportunity of doing so."

Again Mr. Glindon seemed to be troubled and pained, but he answered in a quick, nervous way—

"Very well—very well; I'll see."

During the dinner the master of the house appeared to be strangely depressed and preoccupied, and he took his food in a mechanical way, as if he derived no pleasure from it, and was hardly conscious of what he was doing.

Muriel could not be blind to this, and was much concerned; and when she got the opportunity she said to her lover—

"Raymond, don't say anything to papa to-night. He is not well, and I am quite anxious about him."

Of course Raymond readily assented to this; but when the dinner had ended he was left without any option in the matter, as Mr. Glindon requested him to join him in the library, and the young man complied with the request. As Glindon sank into a capacious and softly cushioned chair, he leaned back, put his hand to his forehead, covered his eyes, and said—

"Now, Raymond, what is it you have to say?"

"I will be brief," was the answer, "for it is an occasion when, I think, the fewer words the better. It is of Muriel and myself I wish to speak. She is essential to my happiness, and she tells me that I am essential to hers. We love each other, and I want your consent to her becoming my wife."

"Have you spoken to her on the subject?" asked Mr. Glindon, with a sigh.

"Yes, sir."

Mr. Glindon rose from his chair. He seemed to be weak and suffering. He rang the bell, and when the servant came, he told her to send Miss Muriel to him.

"Muriel, my darling," he said when his daughter entered the room, " Raymond tells me he has asked you to be his wife."

"Yes, papa."

"God knows," Glindon continued, with moving pathos, "I have your happiness at heart, and would make many sacrifices, even that of my life, to ensure you an unclouded future. But I have something to say to you both — something that will astound you — something that almost chokes me as I try to utter it."

He put his hand to his throat, as if he literally felt some sensation of choking. His voice was husky; his eyes bleared with the tears that had gathered there. He was standing by the chair with his left hand resting on the back of it, and paused in his speech as if his breath had failed him.

Naturally both Muriel and Raymond were alarmed and distressed, and suddenly, with a cry of anguish, Muriel sprang forward and threw her arms about her father, over whose face a deadly paleness had spread, while he seemed to become faint and to stagger as if he were about to fall.

CHAPTER V.

RAYMOND also went to Mr. Glindon's assistance, but the merchant, with what appeared to be a supreme effort, recovered himself, and said, in a voice that painfully told of mental suffering—

"Forgive me for this exhibition of weakness. The fact is, I—I feel almost as if my heart was torn in two. But there, a man must face the foe, and should die with defiance on his lips. You ask me, Raymond, to give my consent to your marrying Muriel. You say you are essential to each other's happiness. That is the dream of love, but will you still think the same thing when you are man and wife?"

"Oh, yes, yes!" cried Raymond and Muriel, in chorus.

"All lovers say that. But supposing, Raymond—supposing that, when this dear girl has become your wife, some great disgrace were to fall upon her name—a disgrace that should cause the world to point at her, and scoff at her, and shun her as a leper—would you still cling to her, still love her?"

Raymond, who had taken a seat in a chair in obedience to a sign from Glindon, rose up at this as if with

some sudden impulse of uncontrollable energy, and exclaimed, as he threw his arm round Muriel's waist—
" Ay would I, or may God forget me ! "

"You are a noble fellow," answered Mr. Glindon, " for I believe that you are sincere, and, with a man like you, honour is above price, and impregnable against the assaults of scorn and uncharitableness. Come here, Muriel." His daughter went to him, and he took her hand. " You ask me to give you this woman for your wife," he continued, still addressing Raymond. "If I do so it will be with a firm confidence that I am giving her into the keeping of a man who will cling to her, who will cherish her, who will honour her. But you have told me that you are dependent upon your father, and you expect, and have a right to expect, that I shall dower her well. You think, as all think who know me, that I have wealth, and, having but one child, my wealth will descend to her. I have wealth. I can count my wealth by tens of thousands ; and yet, Raymond Penoyre, I tell you solemnly and before God that, if you marry Muriel, you will marry a pauper."

Raymond visibly started as this was said, and he looked puzzled no less than distressed. Muriel threw her arms round her father's neck as she exclaimed—

" Papa, papa, what do you mean ? Why do you talk in riddles like this ? "

He disengaged her arms, and answered—

" I thought my language was plain. I tell him that, if he marries you, he will marry a pauper. I mean that you will be a penniless bride; that I, your rich father, can give you nothing——"

"But papa——"

"Hear me out. You have been brought up in luxury, nurtured in the lap of ease, and affluence has surrounded you. But you must leave all this for your husband's sake; and what think you people will say? The tongue of scandal, the tongue of envy and malice, the tongue of idle gossip, will ring in the air, and your happiness will be blighted, your peace of mind poisoned."

"Mr. Glindon," said Raymond gravely, taking a step nearer to where Muriel stood looking scared and bewildered, and speaking as a man may speak whose resolution is as firm as rock—"Mr. Glindon, I must believe that you are talking in all seriousness, and with a full sense of the responsibility of your utterances. But again I ask you to give me your daughter for wife, and I will take her, and honour, cherish, and cling to her, though she passes from your house without a second gown to wear. Scandal may wag its tongue and slander spit its venom, but it will affect me not; it will never cool my love."

Mr. Glindon seized and grasped the hand of Raymond and wrung it. But for some moments he could say nothing; emotion choked him. He seemed to be wrestling with some great shadowy feeling that crushed his manhood and weakened him. At last he spoke; but his voice was shattered, as it were; its resonance had gone; it was hollow and tremulous—

"If you have both weighed the consequences of the

step you wish to take, and thoroughly realise what I
have told you, I oppose no obstacle. I know that what
I have said is pregnant with mystery, but let it be so;
seek not to solve it, for I can give you no solution. My
lips are sealed. Not for my own sake, God knows, but
for this fair child's sake."

He laid his trembling hand on his daughter's head,
and she sank sobbing on his breast.

"Let this painful scene close," he added, struggling
to conceal his feelings. "You now know what lies
before you. But be not precipitate. Do nothing
rashly. Dwell upon what I have said, and in a
month's time, Raymond, tell me if you are still of
the same mind; and I must charge you, as a matter
of honour, to let your parents know. Now go, leave
me; I would be alone. But one last word, Raymond
Penoyre. God has made no honester woman than my
daughter. She is gifted with a fine nature and a heart
so sensitive that it would shiver to atoms were it sub-
jected to neglect, deceit, or cruelty. Honour this gift
of God, therefore, as you honour your own soul."

"I will," was Raymond's only answer. But no man
ever uttered "I will" as he uttered it who did not
mean what he said.

Muriel wanted to speak, but her father again expressed a desire to be alone, and they left him. Then
the will-force that had upheld him during the ordeal
no longer exerted itself, and, with a sob, he sank into
his chair, and covering his face with his hands, he
wept. The tears of a man fall not lightly, and it

must have been a strangely powerful emotion that could move him to such an outward expression of grief.

Presently he grew calmer, but he still sat there, and his careworn face wore a pitiable look of abstraction. He sat staring into space, his cheek resting on his hand.

From this room a double door of plate-glass opened into a splendid conservatory that was filled with palms and exotic plants. At the end farthest from the room a door gave access to the garden, and another door opened into a passage that communicated with the back part of the premises.

Now, had Mr. Glindon not been so absorbed he might have noticed, if he had turned towards the conservatory, a pair of dark, glittering eyes that seemed to be watching him. They were the eyes of a woman—a woman with a swarthy, sinister face; and as she stood there, half concealed by the great overhanging leaf of an African palm, she was suggestive of some fierce wild jungle animal on the alert for prey. Perhaps it would have been a mere fanciful imagination that would have thought this.

But one thing is certain, whether she meant ill or whether she meant well, she was there clandestinely, because that conservatory was almost sacred to Mr. Glindon and his daughter. It was one of the few things in which he seemed to take an absolute interest, and the magnificent plants it contained were tended by Muriel with the most loving regard and care. Of the servants, no one but the head-gardener was ever allowed to enter the place, and he always had to go to Muriel for the key.

The three doors were opened by one key. Muriel kept possession of this, and her father had a duplicate. Therefore, it was obvious that the dark woman had no business there, and, being there, she was as obviously watching him. But he was all-unconscious of the fact as he sat brooding over his grief.

Presently there was a gentle tap at the door of the room, but he did not hear it. It was repeated, but still he was deaf. Then the door opened. Muriel Glindon glided in, and fell on her knees at her father's feet; and at that instant the watching woman in the conservatory quickly withdrew, until she was hidden from sight amongst the palms. And, as the only light in the conservatory was that which reached it from the gas burning in the library, there was not much fear of her being discovered, unless some one entered the place; but, even then, she could have concealed herself amongst the thick foliage and escaped observation.

Mr. Glindon was aroused from his semi-unconscious condition by the presence of his daughter.

"Muriel, my child," he said, "what are you doing here?"

"Oh papa," she murmured, "I am so concerned—so unhappy about you! For long and long your sad and sorrowful face has troubled me; and I have felt sure that you have something on your mind that you are concealing—some terrible and corroding secret that is wearing your life away. Whenever I have spoken to you in the past on the subject, you have turned the matter off; but what has taken place to-night is a revelation, and confirms my worst fears. I am your daughter—your loving and dutiful daughter. Confide in me ; make me your confidante. Who can be better fitted to give you consolation than I am? And, if you wish it, much as I love Raymond, I will not leave you. I will not be his wife——"

"No, no, my darling; no, no. You must make no such sacrifice on my account," her father said quickly.

"But, papa, do let me comfort you! Do tell me what your sorrow is! Remember, I am not a child now, but a matured woman. Let me share your burden with you, for it breaks my heart to see you so unhappy—to know that your life is so darkened."

"Muriel, my beloved girl, I cannot tell you," Mr. Glindon faltered, speaking with difficulty, as if he had some constriction of the throat. "While I live, it is better that you should remain in ignorance. Perhaps I am a moral coward, but I cannot help it. Bear with me as I am. I am an old and broken man—older far than my years, and the dark shadow of the coming end lies heavy upon me. Before you is life; and though I feel sometimes as if I could not pray for myself, I pray for you, and I ask God, and plead to Him as only a broken-hearted father can, that He will bless you, and give you that peace of heart and contentment of mind that is beyond price.

"Raymond Penoyre is a good fellow, and a man of honour.

"I am glad, therefore, that you have brought your wooing to a climax, and that he has asked you to be his wife. And since he agrees to take you as a penniless bride, my mind is so far relieved, while the day that sees you his wife will be for me a relatively happy one. Gossips will be busy for a time, but you will live the gossip down. I have been able to make some small provision for your aunt, and she will have the wherewithal to live in a plain and secluded way until, in the fulness of time, her years are complete. As for Raymond, I have no fear for him. He will make his way. He has a head on his shoulders, and he is not the man to grovel in the dust when there is honest work to be done. But there, there! you must not fret like that" —she was sobbing bitterly, with her head pressed to his breast. "Come, my child, be brave! It has relieved my mind considerably to be able to speak to you as I have done. Henceforth we shall understand each other better. And see——"

As he said this he raised her gently, and rose himself, drawing her arm through his and walking to a large, handsome escritoire. Here he drew a bunch of keys from his pocket, selected one, and opened the flap of the escritoire. Touching a secret spring, he caused a panel inside to slide back, revealing a drawer. This he opened with another key, and took from it a small, almost square packet, done up in white paper. It was tied round with a piece of narrow blue ribbon, the

D

ribbon being sealed with wax to the paper in sever(
places and stamped with his signet.

"Read that," he said, pointing to something writte
on the outside of the packet; and as he held
so that the light fell upon the paper, she read alou
as follows :—

"On my death this packet is only to be opened by my daughte
Muriel, when and where she likes. Under no circumstances ar
on no conditions is any other hand but hers to break the seal
And in the event of circumstances, at present unforeseen, arisii
which would prevent her exercising this right, the packet is
be committed to the flames and utterly destroyed. Any oi
failing to comply with this solemn injunction will be guilty
a crime that Heaven itself will punish.

"Ivan Peter Glindon."

"What is the paper, papa?" Muriel asked betwee
her sobs.

"The story of my early life and the secret of m
sorrow," he answered, with a deep sigh. "It is wel
perhaps, that you should know what is here writtei
for it will explain much that is mysterious; but it ca
only be when I am dead. *When I am dead,*" he r(
peated slowly and with lingering emphasis. "An
now go to your bed, for the hour is late; and when
have smoked my usual cigarette I too will retire."

Muriel's heart was too full, her brain too confuse
with a dozen conflicting thoughts, for her to ask an
questions or pursue the conversation further, so sh
tenderly embraced her father and left him.

For some moments he stood with the packet in hi

hand, but at last restored it to its receptacle, then locked the escritoire.

To this little scene there had been a witness all unknown to Muriel and her father.

That witness was the dark woman in the conservatory, who had waited and watched!

CHAPTER VI.

A MIDNIGHT MYSTERY.

MR. GLINDON usually went to the City about ten o'clock, but on the day following that eventful evening he remained at home to luncheon, though he ate but little. He looked wretchedly ill and haggard, and both his daughter and sister were greatly distressed. They wished him to remain at home all day and rest, but he said—

"No; I have important matters to attend to, and must go to town for a couple of hours at least. But I tell you what we will do. I want a change, and we will go down to Eastbourne for two or three weeks. You ladies can make all arrangements. It would be better, perhaps, if you were to run down to-morrow and see if you can secure a small furnished house. We will take a couple of servants, and tell John he can take down the pair of bays and the brougham. There now, I hope you are satisfied."

They were more than satisfied, they were delighted, for they could never get him to go away even for two or three days at a time. He stuck to his business far too closely, making an excuse that it afforded him distraction. They knew that he sadly wanted change and rest, and his proposal, therefore, was peculiarly gratifying.

Of course, Muriel had not been able to conceal from her aunt that something unusual had taken place on the previous evening, but it was not until her father had departed for the City that she told her about the extraordinary statement he had made ; and she appealed to her aunt to clear up the mystery.

But the lady shook her head sorrowfully, and while the tears gathered in her eyes she said—

" Alas ! my child, I cannot do that. All that I know is, that there is some dark and terrible shadow on his life, but what it is I know not. He has told me nothing, and when in the past I have sought for an explanation of his grief, he has become angry. I associate it, however, with something that occurred in Russia when he was a young man. But what that something was I have no idea, except it was in connection with his first marriage."

" You never knew papa's first wife, auntie, did you ? "

" No. During the time he was courting her, and for some time after her death, I was in Siberia with my husband. He never told me anything about her, not even when he was first married. However, it is no use trying to worm his secret from him. He only gets irritated when questioned. If Raymond is willing to take you as a penniless girl, why should you make yourself unhappy about things you cannot alter ? I am sure Raymond will prove a good husband, and will carve his way in the world."

Muriel felt more comforted after this little conversation with her aunt, while the arrangements that had
to be made for going away gave her mental occupation.
With the approval of her aunt, she wrote off at once
to Penoyre, asking him to accompany them on the
morrow to Eastbourne; and when she had fulfilled
sundry little household duties, she put on her sunshade
and sallied forth into the grounds with Ita Prokop, as
was her habit, in order that they might talk together
in two or three different languages.

Mr. Glindon was an exceedingly good linguist himself, and he was anxious that his daughter should
have the same accomplishment; but she already spoke
French, German, Italian, and Russian, and Ita was engaged merely for the sake of keeping her in practice.
In fact, the girl had been taken into the service partly
out of charity; for she had gone to Mr. Glindon saying
that she had been brought to London by a lady, who
had treated her badly and discharged her penniless,
and as she mentioned the names of several people in
Russia with whom Mr. Glindon was well acquainted,
he employed her, thinking she would be an agreeable
companion to Muriel.

As the two young women strolled about the grounds
Muriel told her in Russian about the proposed sojourn
in Eastbourne, whereupon Ita asked quickly—

"And am I to go?"

"No, I think not. Papa didn't say so, at any rate.
Besides, I don't see the necessity for your going."

"No, of course not; and I am very glad, because I

do not want to go." And there was an expression in her face that seemed to indicate she spoke no mere words, but really was glad.

In accordance with the arrangements, Mrs. Romanoff, Muriel, and Raymond went off on the following morning to Eastbourne. Muriel's letter had brought Penoyre from Windsor by an early train, for it would have had to have been something very extraordinary that would have prevented him availing himself of a day's outing with the woman who was dearer to him than all the world.

It was a glorious day—one of those perfect days that even our fickle English climate can sometimes give us. No reference was made to the events of the preceding evening; and, perfectly happy in each other's presence, Muriel and Raymond did not give way to forebodings or useless sorrow.

They were fortunate in being able to find a house that exactly answered the requirements—admirably situated, comfortably furnished; a two-stall stable and coach-house, and plenty of accommodation. So a bargain was made, the place engaged for a month, and everything settled, and the three returned to town delighted with their success.

At first Mrs. Romanoff suggested that she should be left at home to take care of the household, but her brother would not hear of this. He said that she needed change as much as he did. Besides, she would be wanted to chaperon Muriel. This argument was decisive.

It was, therefore, arranged that part of the house was to be shut up, the rooms locked, and the keys given into the charge of the under-housekeeper; and when the servants had received their final instructions, the family departed for their seaside quarters.

Mr. Glindon seemed to have recovered his spirits —that is, in a relative sense, for his haggard face still wore the same look of abstraction and sorrow that it had worn for years. But his daughter and sister did all they could to try and wean him from himself, though, it might be said, without success.

The second week of their stay Raymond Penoyre went down to Eastbourne as their guest for a few days; and Mr. Glindon made it evident that the young man's company afforded him gratification and pleasure. He had become warmly attached to him, and spoke quite cheerfully of the time when he would welcome him as his son-in-law. His faith in Raymond was whole, and he firmly believed that in placing his daughter's happiness in his hands Muriel's future was secured. And her happiness was the one thing he lived for—the one thing that made life at all bearable to him—for no father could have borne a stronger affection for his daughter than he bore for her.

At the end of a fortnight it was evident that the change had been beneficial to Mr. Glindon. He certainly looked better, and he was less gloomy than usual. But just as those near and dear to him were beginning to express their gratification for this a great shock fell upon them, and to explain what that shock was we must return to The Priory.

It had been one of those uncertain days, climatically speaking, peculiar to midsummer in England. The morning had come in splendidly fine, but by noon the sky was overcast, and soon after thunder and lightning rent the air, while the rain fell in a deluge. This condition of things continued for some time, until the thunder sullenly growled afar off. The rain ceased, but sheet-lightning flashed at intervals along the horizon for many hours. The night closed in gloomy and murky. The earth seemed oppressed by the heavy mass of thunderous clouds that obscured the sky. The air was stagnant; and never the gleam of a star broke the inky darkness.

The hour was near midnight, and the inmates of The Priory had retired to rest. The house stood in a lonely situation; but every precaution had been taken to guard it against burglary. Now, however, a man climbed a high fence at the bottom of the lower garden. He chose this mode of ingress, no doubt, to avoid the lodge gates. He made his way through the shrubbery, and walking as if his feet were shod with wool, crossed the lawn to the garden-door of Mr. Glindon's special conservatory, where he crouched down and waited.

In a little while there broke on the still air the sonorous boom of the church clock as it solemnly tolled midnight. Scarcely had the last vibration died away, when the conservatory door opened, and a

woman peered cautiously out. The man rose and
greeted her. He entered the conservatory, and the
door was closed. Then he lighted a dark-lantern
he carried with him. The door leading into Mr.
Glindon's library was already open, and the man and
woman passed in, then paused and listened.

But nothing was stirring; the house was silent as
death. The man handed the woman the lantern while
he went down on his knees, and with some pick-locks
endeavoured to open the escritoire. It was not an
easy job, but at last he succeeded with the aid of
a long, thin chisel, which he used as a lever.

When the flap was opened, the woman, who evidently
knew the secret, pressed the spring that caused the
panel to slide back, revealing the drawer where Mr.
Glindon kept the story of his life. The lock of the
drawer was also forced, and then the man drew forth
the packet Glindon had shown to his daughter. This
packet was evidently the sole object of the man's
burglarious entry; for, having secured it, he placed it
underneath his waistcoat next his breast, and tightly
buttoned his coat over. His purpose fulfilled, he left
the dark-lantern and the chisel on the floor, kissed
the woman, uttered some whispered words to her, and
hurried out into the darkness of the night, leaving the
conservatory door open.

When the morning came, and the servants descended
to their duties, they found, to their alarm, that the house
had been entered during the night. But nothing had
been touched save the escritoire, and nothing stolen, so

far as they could ascertain. To them the whole affair was shrouded in mystery; and the housekeeper in charge despatched the following telegraphic message to her master :—

"House has been entered by burglars, and your escritoire broken open, but so far as we can ascertain nothing is missing. Will you please return at once ?"

CHAPTER VII.

DID HE ACCUSE HER UNJUSTLY?

THE effect of the receipt of the telegram was like that of an electric shock on Mr. Glindon. He reeled; his arms fell powerless by his side; he sank into a chair, and remained motionless, speechless, dazed. It so happened that Muriel was with him at the time, and without reading the telegram, and thinking her father had been seized with apoplexy, she screamed, which brought Raymond and her aunt on the scene.

"Fly, Raymond, fly, dear, for a doctor!" exclaimed the distracted girl, as, falling on her knees, she began to chafe her father's hands.

But it was not apoplexy that he was suffering from, and he managed to stammer—

"No, no; don't get a doctor. Give me some brandy."

This stopped Raymond just as he was in the act of leaving the room. The brandy was administered, and had a revivifying effect. Then the stricken man pointed to the telegram, that had fluttered to the floor.

Muriel picked it up, and when she had read it she also turned pale and displayed alarm. But quickly recovering herself, she said—

"After all, papa, there doesn't seem to have been anything stolen, so why concern yourself so much?"

"Girl," he said, quite sternly, "there is more in this matter than you dream of."

Both his daughter and sister were terrified by his manner and words, but did not deem it prudent to press him for an explanation in his then frame of mind.

Mr. Glindon decided to start for town by the next train, which left at twelve o'clock, and he said he would go alone; but Muriel overruled this. She insisted on accompanying him, and he yielded. It had previously been arranged that Raymond was to leave for his home the following day, as his family was going into Wales, and he was to go with them. But he determined now to anticipate his departure from Eastbourne by a day, and return with Mr. Glindon and his daughter, while, in conformity with her brother's wishes, Mrs. Romanoff was to remain at Eastbourne, and he promised to be back in a few days.

And so they parted; and all the way back to town Mr. Glindon seemed distressed in an unusual way. Naturally anxious to learn all about the robbery, Raymond went down to Richmond with Glindon and his daughter. On arrival at The Priory Mr. Glindon soon found that his surmises were correct, his worst fears realised. The sole object of the thief had been to secure the packet, and the object had been achieved.

At first he did not tell his daughter this, and, consequently, she was greatly puzzled to understand why he was so stricken with grief. For, as far as she comprehended then, nothing whatever had been taken away, and she shared the opinion of the servants that the thief or thieves had been disturbed in their operations, and had decamped without accomplishing their task.

But, later on in the day, when Raymond Penoyre had taken his departure for his home at Windsor, Muriel came to the conclusion that she did not know all, and that there was some potent cause for her father's distress. So she went to him, and expressed her feelings that he was holding something in reserve.

" Yes," he answered; " there is something—a something that to me is of dreadful importance. The packet I showed you the other night—the packet containing the papers written for you, and you only —it is that that has been stolen."

" Father ! "

" Ay, child, you may well seem surprised."

" But who could possibly have known of that packet being there, and what object could the thief have had in stealing it ? "

" Ah ! the latter part of your question must remain unanswered—at any rate, for the present. As to who could have known of the packet being where it was I am in the dark. I thought that no living soul save myself was aware of the existence of the manuscript until I showed you the packet a fortnight or so ago. But its loss has made me a desperate—a terribly desperate man ! "

He spoke as a desperate man; and his manner was

in accord with his words, for he was excited, and there was a look of stern, dangerous determination in his eyes.

Muriel's frame of mind can easily be imagined. She was mystified no less than sorrow-stricken; and though she dared not give utterance to such a thought, she began to seriously think that her father's reason had given way. She tried her best to soothe him, and partially succeeded, for she had great influence over him, and when he had grown a little calmer she said—

"Papa, do you think that any one else in the house but myself could possibly have known that you kept the story of your life in that drawer?"

"I tell you, girl, I am in the dark on that point. But there is one person, and one person only, against whom my suspicions point."

"Tell me, dear, who that person is," she said softly and persuasively.

"It is Ita Prokop."

Muriel uttered a half-suppressed cry of surprise as she echoed the words—

"Ita Prokop!"

"Yes. I have long thought that this woman has displayed an unwonted curiosity with regard to my movements. On several occasions she has annoyed me by abruptly disturbing me in the library on the plea that she wanted some information about something or somebody in her native country. Until now I have attached no importance to all this; but now it presents itself to me in a different light, and I believe that Ita Prokop is a spy—a traitress."

"But in whose interest, and why?" asked Muriel, scarcely able to speak for surprise and anguish.

"There again I cannot answer you. You must be content to let this matter remain a mystery for the present. I confess that I may be doing Ita a wrong; but what is indisputable is, that the paper I intended for no human eyes but your own has been stolen. Whoever has stolen it has done so with a terribly sinister motive, and with a view to wield a tremendous weapon against me. But now it shall be war to the death!"

He ground his teeth as he spoke, and displayed anger that was altogether unusual, for he seldom got angry.

"Oh papa, papa!" exclaimed his daughter, "why do you talk in such riddles? Why not pour out your troubles to me, your loving daughter, who yearns to comfort you. Clear up this fearful mystery, whatever it is. It will be better for us all, and you will be a happier man."

"No," he answered, in hollow, raspy tones. "I have told you before that I cannot do that; but I have a weapon in my own hands, and, as God witnesseth, I will use it."

He had become so excited and agitated that Muriel decided it would be unwise to pursue the subject further then. It was certain there was some deep and impenetrable mystery, but she could not make the faintest guess as to its nature. What she felt, and what she was painfully conscious of, was that never until then had she known what it was to be truly unhappy. Now the sunshine of her life was clouded over, and she was like one who gropes in the dark with danger all around.

Presently she asked her father, with a nervous shrinking, what he was going to do in the matter.

"I am going to send for Calvin Sugg, the detective, and I am going to question Ita in your presence," he answered; and in accordance with that determination he rang the bell and ordered the servant to send Ita to him. A few minutes afterwards she entered the library.

"You want to see me, sir?" she said timidly, looking curiously from him to her pupil and back to him again, as though amazed that she should have been sent for.

"Yes, I do," he answered gruffly. "I want to ask what *you* know about this robbery."

"Me!"—opening her eyes wide and putting up her hands in an attitude of profound wonderment—"me!" she repeated. "How should I know anything about it?"

"It is not for me to tell you *how* you should. What I believe is, that you do know; that you have had some hand in it."

"Oh!" screamed Ita, as she rushed to her young mistress and threw her arms about her, as if she wanted her to protect her from the stern, angry man, who seemed trying to read the very thoughts of her brain. "Is your father out of his mind that he dares to say such a thing as that?"

Then she suddenly sprang up and faced him, her dark face red as a blood-red rose, her dark eyes flashing forth fire, her bosom heaving, her lip quivering with emotion, her clenched hands pressed hard down against her hips, her whole body rigid. She was the very incarnation of anger and scorn.

"Sir, you are a villain!" she hissed, with that sibilant emphasis an angry Russian woman knows so well how to employ. "You want to blast my character—to take away my reputation. But you must not do it, for, though I am a stranger here, I will go to the law with you."

"Oh papa!" interposed Muriel, as the tears ran down her cheeks, and twining her arms lovingly about his neck, "I am sure you are doing Ita a wrong by entertaining a suspicion against her."

"Yes, Miss," put in Ita, "he is doing me a cruel, cruel wrong, for I am innocent—quite innocent; and it is cowardly of him to try to ruin a poor girl's character. I am a foreigner here, with no friends; but your English law is just, and it will protect me."

She could say no more, but broke out into hysterical sobbing; and Mr. Glindon, like one already distraught, put his hands to his head and exclaimed—

"My God! my God! I shall go mad!"

It was a distressing and terribly painful scene, and his pallid, haggard face and twitching muscles indicated too surely the anguish of his mind.

Muriel went to Ita and kissed her on the forehead, trying to soothe her, and she said—

"Go, Ita dear; leave the room. Papa is so stricken with grief that he is scarcely conscious of what he says. You know that he is the soul of honour and goodness, and would not wrong any living soul wittingly."

"Then he must withdraw his words and make me an apology," sobbed out Ita in a broken, jerky way.

"Yes, yes; I am sure he will do that if he thinks he is wrong. But leave us now, leave us, there's a good girl."

Thus urged, Ita took her departure, sobbing bitterly, and then Muriel went to her father again. He was sitting in his chair, with his face buried in his hands. She knelt down beside him, and in her sweet, loving way said—

"Do try and calm yourself, papa. You will be very ill if you give way like this. And I am sure you are wrong in suspecting poor Ita."

"Perhaps I am—perhaps I am," he moaned. "And yet—and yet——"

Whatever his reservation was he did not speak it, but suddenly changing his tone and manner, as if with a supreme effort of will called forth for a purpose, he said, with a display of self-possession as he took Muriel's head between his hands as she knelt before him, and kissed her on the forehead—

"Sometimes, dear, that which in our blindness we think the cruellest fate is often meant for our good. I will try to think that it is so in the present case. At any rate I will set you right now. And Raymond Penoyre, when he takes you to wife, shall take riches with you. But mention nothing of this; keep your own counsel. It were better so—better so."

If Muriel had thought before that her father's reason was going, she felt convinced of it now. For surely no man in his right senses could talk so strangely and enigmatically as he did. Less than a month ago he had told her she would go to her husband penniless; now he spoke of her having riches. And as she further reflected, it struck her that what he had told her about the packet being the story of his life was perhaps but the invention of a mind unhinged by constant brooding over some real or fancied wrong. His love of solitude and his habitual melancholy seemed further proof that her fears were well grounded.

She resolved, therefore, that she would lose no time in seeking the advice of the family physician and telling him what she thought. By her father's request she left him alone now.

And when she had gone he rose and paced the room in agitation. Then suddenly he stopped, and muttered fiercely—

"Yes, it shall be done now! I have been goaded into madness, driven to bay, and now I will turn and rend my enemy!"

Presently he sat down and wrote some letters. When they were finished he sealed them, and resolved to post them himself. The terrible fears of his daughter that his mind had gone made her watchful and alert, and when she heard him open his door she followed him to the hall.

"Where are you going to, papa?" she asked anxiously.

"To the post, dear, with some letters."

"Can I not take them for you?"

"No; I will take them myself."

This unusual course seemed a further piece of evidence in justification of her fears, and so she put on her hat and went with him.

The letters were duly posted, and Mr. Glindon despatched a telegram to Sugg asking him to come down by the next train. Then Muriel suggested a stroll in the park, which her father consented to, and he seemed the better for it.

That evening Mr. Calvin Sugg arrived at The Priory, and had an interview with Mr. Glindon in the library. They had not met since Sugg called at Glindon's office in London about the murder of Vesta Florence; that was twelve months ago. And so far the detective had not unravelled the mystery of that murder, which had taken its rank amongst London's undiscovered crimes.

Mr. Glindon gave his visitor the details of the robbery, and told him that he had suspected Ita Prokop of having had something to do with it.

"Of course," he said, "there is more in this robbery than appears on the surface. It is part of a vile conspiracy to blast my life and send me to my grave before my time. But these papers must be got back if possible, and my hopes of their recovery are placed in you."

"What is the nature of the documents?" asked the detective.

"I cannot—dare not tell you," replied Glindon, the question bringing back all his old distress.

The detective shrugged his shoulders as he remarked—

"Well, you know you place me at a disadvantage if you don't give me the information I seek. It's very much like working in the dark." He then inquired what were the grounds of suspicion against Ita, and Mr. Glindon told him what he had told his own daughter.

The result of the interview was, that Calvin Sugg was to remain at The Priory for a day or two as a guest and watch Ita. Nobody in the house but Glindon and Muriel knew that Sugg was a detective, so that his presence would not arouse suspicion.

That night, when Mr. Sugg retired to his room, he pondered a great deal over the mystery which seemed to surround Mr. Glindon's life; and he had to confess to himself that he could not at that moment suggest any plausible theory to account for it.

But suddenly an idea seemed to flash upon him, and he wondered if there was any possible connection between the murder of Vesta Florence and the theft of the documents from Mr. Glindon's desk? On the face of it this might have seemed a far-fetched theory.

But Calvin Sugg knew from long experience that in dealing with human crime the seemingly impossible often lay nearest the truth.

CHAPTER VIII.

Mr. HILKIAH THORNE was a lawyer with offices in the Inner Temple. He had practised law for thirty years or more; and at the time we introduce him he was an exceedingly well-preserved man of about fifty-five. His portly figure and florid, jovial face might be taken as an indication that both life and the law agreed with him. In his business he had been a remarkably successful man, and had had for his clients some of the most conspicuous members of the upper ten. It was said in the Temple that Hilkiah Thorne could be more silent than the Sphinx, so far as the business of his clients was concerned. The secrets that were locked up in Hilkiah's brain were many and strange. Indeed, he had been mixed up with some of the most thrilling and romantic cases of the day. But what he knew he kept to himself; and not even his dearest and most intimate friend could have got information from him he did not feel justified in parting with.

To this, probably, combined with his acumen as a lawyer, he owed his extensive business—a business that was the envy of a large number of his colleagues. An even-tempered man, and of cool and calculating disposition, he allowed nothing to ruffle him. The motto that guided him seemed to be *Dum vivimus vivamus.* Most certainly he drank of the wine of life and eschewed the drugs. Blessed with a good digestion and having epicurean tastes, he loved the pleasures of the table.

Having a fund of anecdote and good stories at his command, and being a brilliant *raconteur* to boot, his company was much sought after; but Mr. Thorne was no less choice about his companions than he was about his wine and cigars. It wasn't every man who said, "Come and dine with me, Mr. Thorne," who could secure him, and in his feasting he knew how to exercise a wise discretion. Therefore, not only as a business man, but as a companion, he was widely respected, and he was looked upon as one of the staunchest of friends.

Mr. Thorne lived at Upper Sheen, where he had built himself a charming house, known as "The Crags." He was blessed with an admirable wife, and two sons and three daughters. Fortune, therefore, seemed to have smiled upon him with her benignest smile, and nothing that could give a pleasure and zest to life had, apparently, been withheld from him.

Amongst the letters that Mr. Glindon went out to post in company with his daughter was one to Mr. Hilkiah Thorne, and that gentleman sat in his office reading it the morning after. The lawyer had transacted Glindon's legal business for many years, and for a long time the two men had been very intimate. It might be said they were neighbours, for The Priory and The Crags were only about two and a half miles apart. Thorne was a frequent visitor at The Priory, and he was one of the few Mr. Glindon seemed to take any real interest in and to derive any pleasure from. A hale, jovial, hearty fellow, Mr. Thorne presented a striking contrast to Mr. Glindon, with his brooding, melancholy disposition, and any one not knowing the links between them might have wondered how it was that Thorne tolerated Glindon's company.

The letter referred to, being marked " Private " on the outside, was not opened by the head confidential clerk, as was the case with other letters, but was laid on Mr. Thorne's desk in his private room. It was worded as follows :—

"THE PRIORY, RICHMOND.

" MY DEAR THORNE,—I am almost distracted. The devil has been at his work again, and this time with remarkable success. But it has had one effect : it has made me defiant and desperate, and now I am determined to do what you have so long urged me to do, and I will break the chain that has so long kept me chained in a pit of darkness. I intend to execute a will leaving everything I may die possessed of to my beloved girl. I want you, therefore, if convenient, to come here to-morrow night to take my instructions and prepare the necessary draft, and I will execute the will as soon as possible, for fear I should change my mind. So pray do not delay.—And believe me, ever faithfully yours, IVAN P. GLINDON."

Mr. Thorne put the letter down, gave expression to a meditative " Umph ! " and for some moments toyed with his quill pen, biting the end of it, and resting his left index-finger on his temple—a habit he had when particularly thoughtful.　Presently he touched his bell, and a boy entered.

"Send Mr. Beck here."

"Yes, sir."

Five minutes later Mr. Beck entered the chief's room.

Mr. Perley Beck was confidential clerk, and had been in Mr. Thorne's service for something like five years; but though he knew a good deal in connection with his master's business, there was a good deal more that he did not know, for not even to his confidential clerk did Mr. Thorne impart all his secrets.

Mr. Perley Beck was a young man in the early thirties, fair as to complexion, with a light, drooping moustache, and a mass of blond limp hair.　He had blue eyes, small and deep set, but apparently they were not very strong, as he habitually wore glasses. His dress, carefully trimmed nails, and slightly lisping drawl were suggestive of the dandy, the man about town, the "sporting gent," the dangler after women.

Perhaps Mr. Beck was none of these things, but his appearances were against him.　On the other hand, Mr. Thorne knew his men, and it was much in Beck's favour that he occupied the position he did.

"Beck," said his employer, "I am booked for the dinner of the Incorporated Law Society to-night, am I not?"

"Yes, sir, you are."

"Can I get out of it, do you think?"

"I don't see how you can, as you are to take the vice-chair."

"Umph! that's awkward. And to-morrow night I am to take the chair at the Law Clerks' Benevolent Institution dinner. Well, look here; just write a few lines to Mr. Glindon acknowledging receipt of his letter, and saying that I will be with him on Friday evening at eight o'clock without fail."

Perley Beck withdrew, and Mr. Thorne occupied himself with other matters.

In about an hour he went out to make a business call upon a barrister in the Temple Gardens, and a few minutes after he had left, Mr. Perley Beck re-entered the room and searched about the desk for something. The something he wanted was Mr. Glindon's letter, and having found it, he read it, and a curious smile came over his rather vapid face. Then he put the letter back in its place and left the room, locking the door again after him. The door was always kept locked when the master was absent, and Perley Beck was the only one in the office, besides Mr. Thorne himself, who had a key.

Presently Mr. Thorne returned, and subsequently he put Mr. Glindon's letter in a tin deed-box marked "*re* Glindon," and of which he himself kept the key. Then he occupied himself about other business, and for a time Glindon passed from his mind.

Mr. Thorne was a punctilious man about his engagements—indeed he was about most things—and so at eight o'clock on the Friday evening he presented

himself at The Priory. He had walked over from
East Sheen, for he was fond of walking, and never
neglected to walk when he got the chance, for he
had a dread of growing too corpulent. It had been
a very dull, blustering day, very much like a late
autumn day, and there had been frequent showers
of rain, which had soaked the ground and given a
delightful freshness to the country.

Mr. Glindon welcomed his friend with great heartiness, and as the two men went to the library Thorne
said—

"You are looking a little better, I think, than you
were when I last saw you."

"I don't know that I am better in health; but since
I have come to the resolution about the will I seem
lighter in my mind."

"Of course you will," said the lawyer cheerily.
"You should have taken my advice and done it
long ago. But what has brought about this change
in your views?"

In answer to this Mr. Glindon related the story of
the robbery, and the lawyer listened with a grave
countenance.

"Umph!" he exclaimed; "it's strange—very strange.
But these machinations against your peace and happiness must be stopped. The fact is, you have been
far too sensitive—far too sensitive! You should have
set your enemy at defiance and braved public opinion.
But you wouldn't take my advice, you know."

"Well, well! don't be severe," said Glindon, with

a shade of irritation in his tone. "Better late than
never; and I am going to do it, so I hope that will
satisfy you."

"You say that you accused Ita Prokof of having
had a part in the stealing of your papers?" the
lawyer remarked reflectively, tapping the ends of his
fingers together as his elbows rested on the arms of
the chair, while his head was thrown back and his
eyes were fixed on the ceiling—an attitude he often
assumed when very thoughtful.

"Yes."

"And she denied that, of course?"

"Yes."

"Would you mind my putting a question or two
to her?"

"She has left," answered Glindon. "The following morning she came to me, and was very abusive,
threatening me with an action for slander and all
sorts of things. As I thought perhaps I had done
her a wrong, I apologised; but she said she would
not stay in the house another day. So I paid her
her wages, and she took herself off."

"So, so!" muttered Mr. Thorne. "Well, I'll keep
an eye on that young lady. She may be dangerous.
I will tell Sugg, the detective, to work up her past
history. She'll have to be pretty cute and cunning
if she baffles Sugg, for I don't think Old Nick himself could do it. But, come now, let us to business,
for I want to be home by ten, as my wife has some
company, and I said I would make a hand at whist."

"The fact is," answered Glindon, "I have already communicated with Sugg, and he came down here. Of course when Ita left he left too, and he is going to watch her. Sugg's a cute fellow and may get at the bottom of this infernal business."

"I hope so—I hope so," said the lawyer thoughtfully. "But come, give me pen, ink, and paper, for I must get back by ten."

Agreeable to this request, Mr. Glindon opened his escritoire and provided the lawyer with writing materials; then dictated to him the terms of a will, in which he left an annuity for life to his sister, and the rest of his property to his daughter.

When the draft was finished Mr. Thorne carefully folded it up and put it into the breast-pocket of his coat, saying that on the morrow the will should be prepared, and that Glindon could call at the office to execute it.

The business being settled, and the lawyer having partaken of a glass of sherry and a biscuit—declining a pressing invitation to stay to supper—rose to depart.

"How are you going?" asked his friend.

"Oh, shanks' pony, as usual."

"Let me drive you over in the dog-cart."

"No, no, dear boy, thank you. I prefer to walk. You know that."

"Very well, then, I'll go part of the way with you. A walk will do me good."

They descended to the hall, and Mr. Thorne looked into the ladies'-room, where Muriel was entertaining a young lady friend. He chatted for a few minutes with them. Muriel, when she heard that her father was going out, told him not to be long, and he said he would be back in about half an hour. So she kissed him, and he and the lawyer left the house.

It was a squally night, moonless and dark, but with stars here and there displaying themselves where the clouds parted. The two men passed through the lodge gates, and for some distance their road was parallel with Mr. Glindon's grounds, which were separated from the road by a ditch and a grassy bank surmounted with an oak fence, while behind that again was a row of trees. It was a lonely road, but sparsely furnished with lamps. Where the grounds ended another road crossed the one they were on, and here there were two lamps, one on each side of the way.

When Mr. Glindon and the lawyer emerged from the lodge gates they were not aware that a figure rose up from the ditch, without a sound, and followed them silent as death itself. It followed them like their shadow, and no sound came from its footfalls.

When the two men reached the cross-roads they stopped to say a few words preparatory to Glindon turning back. The figure that was following also stopped, and disappeared into the ditch, whence, in a few moments, issued a tongue of flame ; and an echoing report went up to the watching stars, and cried, "Murder!" for Mr. Glindon reeled, threw up his arms, and then pitched on his face.

Bewildered and startled by his friend's fall, the

lawyer scarcely knew what to do; but he moved away a few yards, as if impelled by fear, and at that moment there was another tongue of flame, another report, and Mr. Thorne sank to the ground with a stifled cry.

Then from the ditch a man sprang out. He was enveloped in a long coat or cloak, and his face was concealed by a mask; while on his feet, to deaden the sounds of his footfalls, he wore list shoes. He ran forward to where the bodies lay, stooped down, and examined Mr. Glindon for a moment, then passed on to the lawyer and rifled his pockets. That done, he rose, fled away as if he were a veritable shadow, and the darkness swallowed him up.

Then all was silent again. The stars still watched; the night-wind sighed mournfully amongst the trees, and in its sighing seemed to say, "Murder! Murder!"

CHAPTER IX.

AFTER the terrible deed no one passed along the road, until a policeman, tramping his round, and never dreaming of murder, came across the two bodies, lying a few yards from each other. The position of the bodies was suggestive of death, and the blood on the ground, as revealed by the light of the bull's-eye, cried out with dumb eloquence that murder had been done.

Naturally the man was aghast, for it was too evident that there had been a tragedy. But presence of mind and action were needed, and the man showed that he possessed the one and was equal to the other; for, having satisfied himself that it was a case of urgency, he set off at his topmost speed for the house of a doctor—Dr. William Blewitt, who lived about a quarter of a mile away.

Dr. Blewitt—who bore a high reputation, having been for many years consulting physician to one of the great London hospitals—was just sitting down to supper when the policeman made known his discovery, whereupon the doctor slipped a case of surgical instruments into his pocket, put on his hat, and hurried to the scene of the tragedy. He at once recognised Mr.

Glindon, whom he pronounced to be stone dead. The other gentleman he did not know, but he found that life was not extinct in him.

"Run, Smith," said the doctor, addressing the police-man, "to the lodge gate at Mr. Glindon's grounds, and get assistance. And, look here, tell the people to keep quiet; I will go and break the news to Miss Glindon. Poor thing, poor thing!" he added sympathetically; "it will drive her mad."

Before going to execute his orders the policeman blew his signal-whistle two or three times, which brought another constable to the spot. The lodge-keeper at The Priory and the gardeners were soon on the scene, and further aid was forthcoming from other houses. And when Dr. Blewitt had carefully noted the exact position of the bodies Mr. Glindon was borne to the lodge, and the lawyer was taken to the doctor's house.

The medical eye detected at once that it was a very serious case, and a wound at the back of the head just behind the right ear showed how the injury had been caused. It was unmistakably a gun-shot wound, and there could be little doubt but that the brain was injured.

The doctor at once despatched his man-servant, post haste, to requisition the services of a colleague, a surgeon, who resided in the neighbourhood; and this gentleman went at once to Dr. Blewitt's house, where a critical examination was made of the sufferer, who was, of course, quite insensible. The opinion arrived at was that a bullet was lodged in the posterior lobe of the brain

and that, though a desperate case, it was not necessarily a fatal one. It was arranged that the surgeon
should remain with the lawyer and do what was
necessary with a view to preserving his life, while
Dr. Blewitt went down to The Priory and broke the
terrible news to Muriel.

Dr. Blewitt was an elderly man of high scientific
qualifications who had rendered eminent service to his
profession. He had been well acquainted with Mr.
Glindon, and had been in the habit of visiting The
Priory, both professionally and as a friend.

When Miss Glindon heard that Dr. Blewitt was in
the reception-room and wished to see her a shock
ran through her and made her feel faint, for she
had already got into a nervous state by reason of her
father's prolonged absence, and she was just thinking
of putting on her things and, accompanied by a
servant, setting out in search of him. The fact, therefore, of the doctor being in the house seemed ominous,
and, filled with alarm, she hurried to the room, looking
pale and scared as she came into the doctor's presence.

Her hand trembled as she took his, and she exclaimed, "Oh doctor! what has brought you here?"
thereby showing that she had some dreadful fore-
shadowing of the coming event.

Dr. Blewitt was a kindly, sympathetic man, and
could not but feel a little unnerved as he saw that
the shock to her must necessarily be terrible.

"Well, my dear," he began, "you must not excite yourself; but the fact is there has been an accident——"

"To my papa?" she exclaimed interrogatively, and not waiting for him to finish his sentence.

"Well—yes; but——"

"Oh doctor! don't keep me in suspense," she moaned out impetuously. "What is it? What has happened?"

"Now, my dear child," he said, with paternal solicitude, "you must be brave and calm. Sometimes it seems as if Heaven smites us with terrible severity; but, as frail mortals, we should submit ourselves into God's hands with perfect faith, and He will give us strength and comfort."

Muriel by this time had broken out into a passion of hysterical weeping, but she managed to articulate the words, "My father is dead; your words and manner tell me so."

"The truth cannot be concealed, my dear lady. Your father has been suddenly struck down. But you, as his only child, as his sole representative, while feeling your sorrow, as a true woman should, must not forget that you owe a duty to yourself. Therefore be brave, and try to think that all that befalls us is God's good work, and that He chastens us for our benefit."

Having said so much, Dr. Blewitt felt that he had said enough for the time, and he knew that the outburst of furious grief would have to exhaust itself before the poor girl would become calm. It was, perhaps, unfortunate that her aunt was away; but, with thoughtful solicitude, he sent a message to a neighbour, whose daughter was very intimate with Muriel, asking that the young lady might come and

stay with the stricken girl, and administer the comfort
that a woman knows so well how to administer in the
hour of bitter anguish. Then he prevailed upon Muriel
to go to her room.

He next proceeded to make inquiries amongst the
servants, and learnt that the gentleman who had been
with Glindon was Mr. Hilkiah Thorne, of The Crags,
East Sheen. The doctor had the body of Mr. Glindon
carried into a lower room, where he made an examination, and determined that the unfortunate man had
been struck under the left shoulder-blade by a bullet,
which presumably had injured the heart, as there was
evidence that death had been all but instantaneous.

Of course it was too late then to do anything more
that night; but as soon as possible the following morning a telegram was despatched to Mrs. Romanoff requesting her to return at once; and the under-housekeeper also took upon herself to telegraph for Mr.
Raymond Penoyre, who lost no time in reaching The
Priory; and his feelings, when he learnt the facts, may
be far better imagined than they can be described.
Mrs. Romanoff also arrived soon after midday, and was
for a time prostrated with the shock that the news
caused her. But recognising how much depended upon
her in this terrible trial, she brought all her fortitude
to bear, and did what she could to comfort Muriel.

The house was truly a house of tears, for the dark
shadow of the mysterious and ghastly crime lay heavy
upon it, and there was no one under the roof who
was not more or less affected. The blow had fallen

so suddenly, so unexpectedly; it pointed to some deep and devilish motive, and was as inexplicable as it was terrible. No wonder, therefore, that Muriel, in the light of recent revelations, should be almost maddened with suspense and anxiety, no less than with heart-breaking sorrow for her cruel loss. But Raymond's presence afforded her some measure of comfort, and helped to sustain her under the burden of the affliction.

In the case of Mr. Thorne, Dr. Blewitt resolved to do everything that human skill and modern science could suggest to save the lawyer's life; for, apart from humane motives, there was the hope that if he recovered consciousness he might be able to throw light where all was now dark and obscure. He therefore sent an urgent message to his friend, Sir Wilfred Weir, the well-known specialist in the treatment of wounds and brain injuries. And at great inconvenience Sir Wilfred went down at once to Richmond; and he, Dr. Blewitt, and the local surgeon met in consultation.

After a most thorough and crucial examination of the patient, the eminent specialist thought, having regard to Thorne's splendid constitution, that he would live, though there would probably be permanent brain injury, which might take some peculiar form, such as entire loss of memory. He also said that no attempt could be made for some time, if at all, to extract the bullet, which was evidently lodged in the brain, and he strongly recommended that the lawyer should be removed to a London hospital, where he could be watched and every attention given to him.

To this latter suggestion Mr. Thorne's family would not accede. They preferred to have him in his own home, and said that every possible attention would be given to him, and Dr. Blewitt was requested to take him under his care. As it was not considered safe, however, to remove him then, it was decided that he should remain at the doctor's house for a week at least.

Turning now to the legal aspect of the tragedy, it was considered to be one of the most mysterious crimes that had startled the metropolis for a long time, not excepting the murder of Vesta Florence, the actress, whose cruel death was still unrevenged. Of course, the social position of the two gentlemen and the fact that they had not been robbed served to enhance the mystery; and people asked one another what the motive of the crime was. But this was a riddle by no means easily answered. Some said it was a mere act of vengeance directed against Mr. Glindon, and that Thorne had been shot by mistake; others, that it was the work of some tramp or loafer, whose sole object was robbery, but that he had been disturbed and frightened off before he could accomplish his purpose, so far as the robbery was concerned.

But there was one person who took a very different view. That person was Calvin Sugg, the detective. He knew that there was some dark and, apparently, unfathomable mystery in connection with the late Mr. Glindon's life, and he felt sure that if he could but find out what that mystery was he would have the key to the problem.

As soon after the murder as possible Sugg went down to Richmond and inspected the spot where the tragedy had taken place; and aided by the description given to him by Dr. Blewitt and the constable who first discovered the bodies, he made a most careful drawing, and came to the conclusion that the fatal shot had been fired either from the ditch or from behind the fence on the top of the bank—that is, from Mr. Glindon's garden.

But he put the latter theory on one side as untenable from the fact that a pistol had been used and not a gun. This was proved by the *post-mortem* examination of Mr. Glindon's body. It was found that he had been killed by a revolver bullet which had penetrated the heart. Now it was found by actual experiment that it would have been very difficult for any one to effectually use a pistol from behind the fence: firstly, because the fence was high; and, secondly, because the foliage was very thick.

The conclusion, therefore, was that the murderer had been lying in wait in the ditch, and the particular spot where the crime was committed had been chosen because the lamps there enabled the murderer to see and mark down his victims. This argued that he must have been an exceedingly sure shot with a revolver, and, by deduction, one accustomed to use that weapon.

But there was one other point that set Mr. Sugg pondering deeply: it was, that the murderer must have known that his victims would pass along the road that evening. How did he get that information?

CHAPTER X.

MR. SUGG had to confess to himself that he was confronted with as hard a problem as it had been his lot to have to deal with, and in working out a theory of the crime there were two things that appeared to him absolutely certain. The first was, that the murderer was well acquainted with Mr. Glindon; and, secondly, that he had some potent motive for wishing his death.

And there was a third point that, while less certain, was, nevertheless, probable: it was, that there was some connection, some strange link, between the murder of Vesta Florence, the actress, and of Ivan Peter Glindon, the merchant.

Sugg was not the man to be daunted by difficulties, however insurmountable they might seem; and he registered a mental vow that as long as he lived ae would never rest, never abandon the work, until he had unravelled the dreadful mystery. Although he made a most careful examination of the road and the ditch in the vicinity of the murder, he found nothing that was likely to prove a clue. There was distinct evidence in the crushed grass and marks in the mud that somebody had been concealed in the ditch about twenty yards from where the gentlemen stood; and there were also imprints of either a golosh or a slipper without heels.

That was all the detective had to go upon for the present, and his next step was to seek an interview with Mrs. Romanoff. But the fact of that lady having been at Eastbourne on the night of the tragedy disqualified her from giving any particulars that might have been of value, and Muriel was so ill that it was not deemed advisable to question her for the present.

The coroner's inquest having been held, and no new facts being forthcoming and no arrest having been made, a verdict of "Wilful murder against some person or persons unknown" was duly returned, and Mr. Glindon was laid in his last resting-place in Kensal Green Cemetery. He had often expressed a wish to be buried there, and his wishes were duly respected. Muriel was too prostrated to attend her father's funeral, and her condition was such that Dr. Blewitt, who had taken her under his care, gave strict orders that she was to see no one save her near relatives and Raymond Penoyre, and under no circumstance was the tragedy to be referred to in her presence. This prohibition prevented Calvin Sugg from questioning her as he desired to do.

Raymond Penoyre proved himself most devoted to the unhappy girl, and she did not hesitate to confess that his presence and kindness afforded her an infinite amount of consolation and comfort. His mother and sisters did her the honour of calling upon her, and displayed a great deal of fussy sympathy.

Mrs. Penoyre was a very grand dame, and shared with her husband the notion that, though they were restricted in their means, they were undoubtedly conspicuous members of the *haut ton*, and that the little world in which they moved would be the poorer without them. Their object in choosing a residence in Windsor was, as Mrs. Penoyre herself expressed it, that they might "at least breathe the refined air of royalty," and be "as far removed as possible from the *canaille.*" They ought to have taken for their motto the saying attributed to Cæsar, "Better be first in a village than second in Rome," for they liked to be considered leaders, not followers. Of course, all this was very contemptible, and it was saying much for Raymond that he did not share his parents' silly prejudices and equally silly vanity.

When Mrs. Penoyre returned home after her formal visit of condolence to Muriel she said to her son—

"The Priory is certainly charming, exceedingly charming, but Muriel is very commonplace, and so dreadfully plebeian in her tastes. Notwithstanding that she is heiress to a fortune, I can scarcely reconcile myself to your making her your wife. But I think the first thing you should do is to try to instil some refined and aristocratic notions into her. It is a duty you owe to your family and yourself."

"By the way, Raymond," put in his father, "do

you know how Glindon's affairs are likely to turn out? I suppose, any way, Muriel will have a very tidy little dot?"

Now, it will be remembered that on the eventful evening when Raymond had told Mr. Glindon he wished to marry Muriel, Glindon said if he did marry her he would take a pauper, as Muriel would be a penniless bride; and he charged Raymond to make the fact known to his father as a matter of honour. The lad was certainly not wanting in honour, but he had most certainly shrunk from telling his father what he had been charged to tell him. He knew that if he did so his home life would be wretched, and as he was resolved to have Muriel, whatever her financial state might be, he did not see that there was any necessity to tell his people the truth until the last moment.

However, since the murder a new complexion had been put upon matters. Men die, are buried, and forgotten, but their affairs, so far as they affect their relatives, have to be looked after, for the living cannot be sacrificed to the dead. Therefore, it became necessary that somebody should inquire into the deceased man's affairs, and Mrs. Romanoff took upon herself to do this. She knew that her brother had frequently said that he could only leave her a small annuity, and next to nothing to his daughter. This had always been a riddle that she could not read, though, as a matter of fact, she did not attribute serious import to it; for she was aware that his business was exceedingly prosperous, and The Priory was considered a very valuable property.

If, therefore, Muriel was not his heir, who was? Now that he was dead, the answer to the riddle would be forthcoming; and she placed herself in communication with Mr. Thorne's manager, knowing that Thorne had been her late brother's confidential legal adviser for many years. The manager was a Mr. Robert Sulcoates, and he lost no time in waiting upon the lady with the information that, so far as he knew, Mr. Glindon had died intestate. At any rate, he was sure that Mr. Thorne had no will of Glindon's in his possession; and there was nothing in Mr. Glindon's deed-boxes at the office in the nature of a disposition of his property, with the exception of a legally drawn up document by which he arranged that on his death three per cent. consols yielding two hundred per annum were to be transferred to her. He had made no documentary disposal of his property in any shape or form to his daughter; but as she was his only child, she would, of course, take everything. And Mr. Sulcoates added that he should be glad to receive Miss Muriel's instructions as soon as possible with regard to the business in the city. His own advice was, that it should be continued, as Mr. Glindon's right-hand man was quite capable of carrying it on on her behalf.

Naturally, Mrs. Romanoff was delighted when she learnt that her niece would get the property after all, and she lost no time in imparting the pleasant news to Muriel, who in turn told Raymond, saying to him one day—"Well, Raymond, if you still think that I am essential to your happiness, I shall not be a pauper bride altogether, as poor dear papa told you I should be. For it seems he has left no will, and, of course, legally, everything comes to me, I am so glad of this for your sake, dear; for, after all, money is very essential in this world. I know nothing about the affairs yet, but aunt says she is sure I shall be very rich."

Raymond did not attempt to disguise from her that he considered this very gratifying news; but he gave her distinctly to understand that he would have married her though she had been penniless.

It will thus be seen that he was in a position to answer his father's question in a manner that could not be otherwise than gratifying to that gentleman; for though Mr. Penoyre—being greatly under his wife's influence—pretended to endorse that lady's opinion that Muriel Glindon was plebeian, he nevertheless considered it a most excellent thing that his son should become owner of The Priory and of a goodly number of thousands a year to keep up the dignity. Even in Mr. Penoyre's eyes money could gloss over a good many defects in rank and birth.

"Yes," said Raymond to his father, "I understand that Muriel will get everything."

"Have you any idea what it will tot up to?"

"No."

"Well, it will be something handsome, no doubt. You are a lucky dog, and I congratulate you. We shall be able to introduce Muriel into society and get her presented at Court. No doubt that will tend to reconcile your mother to the marriage."

"Oh, I dare say it will," answered the lady, with a sigh. "But still, I wish Raymond had chosen a person of quality for his wife. But there, I suppose we must take life as it comes to us, and make the best of it. We cannot get all we desire in this world."

Whatever Raymond might have thought of the mercenary views held by his parents, to say nothing of their hypocrisy, he kept his thoughts to himself. He had no desire to quarrel with either his mother or father, and that is what it would have come to if he had opposed them in any way. He saw Muriel through a lover's medium, and to him she was perfect. And whether she was poor or whether she was rich, whether lowly or nobly born, it could make no difference in his regard.

About a week after that conversation with his parents he was at The Priory. He had been in London on business, and called on his way home, being in time for luncheon. Muriel, although still very poorly and very nervous, insisted on going in to luncheon, as there were two visitors besides Raymond. They were the clergyman of the church she attended and the late Mr. Glindon's business manager. Before this meal was finished a card was handed to Muriel. It bore the name "IVAN GLINDON," and the servant who handed it to her mistress said—

"The gentleman says, Miss, that he must see you on a matter of the highest importance."

Muriel read the name, "Ivan Glindon," again and again. She was puzzled, bewildered. What did it mean? Who was Ivan Glindon? She had no idea that she had a relative of that name, therefore her surprise was natural.

Her first impulse was to show the card to her aunt, but the presence of the visitors checked her from doing that. As soon as the luncheon was over she excused herself, and went to the reception-room, where the stranger was waiting.

Ten minutes later the bell of that room rang violently. Alarmed by the unusual ringing, Mrs. Romanoff and Raymond rushed to the room, which adjoined the dining-room, and, to their amazement, they beheld Muriel lying on the floor insensible, while bending over her and chafing her hand was a dark-complexioned man, with a full moustache and dark, rather restless sort of eyes. He was a man of medium height, with a spare figure and naturally pale and nervous face, and thin drawn lips that are said to be inseparable from a cold-blooded, deceitful, and selfish nature.

CHAPTER XI.

A REVELATION.

THE stranger arose and bowed politely.

"Miss Muriel has fainted," he said. "Perhaps, madam, you will have her conveyed to her room." This to Mrs. Romanoff, who again rang the bell for the servants.

"What is the meaning of this, sir?" asked Penoyre peremptorily, and glancing anxiously from the stranger to Muriel and back to the stranger again.

"It means that the young lady has fainted, as I have already stated," answered the stranger loftily.

"I see that for myself. But why has she fainted, and who are you?"

"She will be able to satisfy you herself on the first point, I have no doubt, when she recovers; and she already gives signs of recovering. I must take the liberty of answering your second question by asking another. Who are you, sir?"

Penoyre was annoyed, but tried not to show it, and drawing out his card-case he handed a card to his questioner.

"Thank you. 'Mr. Raymond Penoyre, Stoneycroft, Windsor.' That tells me that you are Mr. Raymond

Penoyre, and that you live at Stoneycroft, Windsor.
Interesting so far as it goes, but it doesn't inform me
by what right, here, in this house, you question me."

The irony and ill-concealed sneers of the speaker
were extremely irritating to Penoyre, but he kept his
temper and said coolly—

"As you are an utter stranger to us all, I have a
right to demand to know who you are."

"Without recognising your *demand*, you shall know.
There is my card."

Penoyre took the card and read the name that had
caused Muriel so much surprise, and turning white and
red by turns, he gasped—

"Ivan Glindon!"

"Ivan Glindon!" echoed Mrs. Romanoff, turning
from the couch on which Muriel had been placed,
and under the influence of sal volatile and fanning was
already reviving.

"Yes," answered the stranger; "that is my name."

"What relation are you, then, to the late Mr.
Glindon?" asked the lady.

"I am the son of the late Mr. Glindon."

"The son!" cried Mrs. Romanoff, as she literally
staggered and clutched the head of the couch for support, while Raymond stood dumbfounded and could
say nothing. "I was not aware," continued the lady
faintly, "that my brother had a son."

"Indeed! Well, perhaps not. My father was peculiar,
and had his own reasons, no doubt, for concealing the
interesting fact. But it is true, nevertheless, and I

have all the documentary evidence to prove it. Since you refer to the late Mr. Glindon as your brother, you are, of course, my aunt. Permit me, therefore, to greet you, and say how glad I am to make your acquaintance."

He put out his hand and made a movement as if he would have kissed her. But the lady held back; she showed no pleasure at the revelation, and no desire to become more familiar with her new-found nephew. She drew herself up, and said, with dignity of expression and manner—

"It is not for me to say, sir, that I doubt your statement that you are the son of the late Mr. Glindon— that is, of course, by his first wife. But I may be permitted to inquire how it was Mr. Glindon never spoke of you, never told me of your existence; and only now that he is dead do you appear on the scene."

"Really, my dear madam," answered Glindon, with a light laugh of scorn, "you cannot hold me responsible for your brother's, my father's, eccentricities. Although his lawfully born son, he never displayed any affection for me. And though he knew that I was anxious to make the acquaintance of my half-sister, he told me that I was not to visit the house."

"Why?" asked Mrs. Romanoff, with flashing eyes and in an angry tone.

"To answer that monosyllabic question would take up too much time, and it seems to me that it is not opportune now to do so," answered Glindon, with studied emphasis.

"It occurs to me that a good deal of explanation is

needed," chimed in Penoyre, unable longer to keep silent.

"The explanation, sir, shall be given at the proper time, and to those who are entitled to receive it," answered Glindon indignantly. "But you have not yet told me what your position is in the household, Mr. Raymond Penoyre."

Raymond was about to speak, when Mrs. Romanoff answered for him.

"Mr. Penoyre is the affianced husband of your half-sister. He was received here in that position by your late father, and was your father's friend."

"Oh, indeed! Well, I am glad to know Mr. Penoyre."

Here Glindon held out his hand again, but Penoyre refused to take it.

"Well, upon my word," exclaimed Glindon, "this is a pretty reception for a fellow to meet with. My sister faints when she learns who I am, my aunt refuses to acknowledge me, and my sister's future husband insults me by declining to shake hands with me. So be it," and Glindon shrugged his shoulders contemptuously.

Then he added, with a look of significance and with marked emphasis in his tone—

"Perhaps you will be glad enough, sooner or later, to accept my friendship. But you will have to solicit it when you want it."

"Mr. Glindon," answered Penoyre firmly, "I have no desire to be rude, nor to wound your feelings in any way; but your unexpected appearance here has taken us all by surprise, and as we know nothing of you—not even your existence was known to us—and as the late Mr. Glindon must have had some very powerful reason for not making known that you were in the world, I have a right to assume that he did not deem it fit that you should be known to his family. Therefore you can hardly expect us, at present, to rush into your arms."

Glindon's dark face reddened with kindling anger, and there was a gleam in his eyes which was indicative of a passionate nature.

"You speak very glibly and flippantly of *us* and 'his family,' as though you were one of the family," he said with a sneer. "Perhaps I may suggest that you confine yourself to the first person singular. The ladies, I have no doubt, will be able to speak for themselves."

By this time Muriel had quite recovered, and sitting up on the couch, she spoke.

"Mr. Glindon——" she began.

"Pardon me," he said, "but surely, as my half-sister, you might call me Ivan."

"Mr. Glindon," she repeated, without deigning to notice his interruption, "your unceremonious and unexpected intrusion here——"

"Intrusion!" he exclaimed.

"Yes, intrusion! I say your unexpected intrusion has caused a painful scene. May I suggest, therefore, that you withdraw and give us time to recover from the shock and the surprise, and to think over the matter? Or, if you prefer it, I will stay and listen to anything you have to say, providing you allow a friend who is in the house to be present."

"Who is your friend?" asked Glindon brusquely.

"My late father's manager, Mr. John Jessop."

"Oh, yes, I shall be very glad to see Mr. Jessop," said Glindon quickly; "as I shall have to come into business relations with him, it is as well we should become acquainted."

"I think, dear," said Muriel, addressing her aunt, "that you and Raymond had better retire and leave me and my—me and Mr. Glindon alone for a few minutes. And when I ring the bell, you might ask Mr. Jessop to be good enough to come here."

Mrs. Romanoff and Penoyre both offered some objection to retiring, but Muriel said firmly, "I must ask you to gratify my wish in this respect; I have a reason for it."

The argument was conclusive, and they retired. Then Muriel stood up, and facing Glindon, said with considerable energy and firmness—

"I cannot doubt that you are what you represent yourself to be, my half-brother, and the son of my dear, beloved father, whose blood still cries aloud for vengeance on his cruel slayer. But before you can expect me to greet you with a welcome, or display any sisterly affection for you, you must tell me something of your history, and why my father concealed from me and my aunt your very existence, for let me assure you that he never breathed a word to me that I had a brother living."

"Muriel—may I call you Muriel?"

" Yes, certainly, if it pleases you."

" Well, Muriel, I am quite prepared to satisfy you on all points. Your questions are natural and justifiable. I was born and brought up in Russia, and have not been very long in this country. At quite an early period of my life my father ignored me."

" Why ? "

" Because, he said, I was wild."

"Surely it must have been something far worse than mere wildness, as I understand the term, that could induce your own father to ignore you."

" Perhaps it was," answered Glindon. " I was placed at a school in Moscow, where they treated me badly, and after a time I ran away, which gave great offence to my father, and he was very unkind to me. Then he placed me in a school in St. Petersburg, where I remained five years. But being young and foolish, I got mixed up in a conspiracy in which a number of students took part. The conspiracy was discovered, and I, amongst others, was arrested and imprisoned, but was released in the course of six months. My father then gave me a considerable sum of money, about ten thousand roubles, and told me he would have nothing more to do with me. As I still lacked wisdom I fell in with some sharpers, and soon lost my money by gambling. After that I lived I don't know how for years, and all applications to my father failed to elicit any response."

" And during those years did you keep yourself honest and upright ? "

"I did many things during those years that I fain would forget and I bitterly regret. But it can serve no purpose for me to enter into details. The past is past. Let it go. It were better forgotten. During all that time I knew nothing whatever of my father's affairs—did not know that he was married; did not know that I had a sister. At last I came to England and found him out."

"And why did he not bring you here? Why did he keep your existence a secret?"

"My father—your father—*our* father, that is, was peculiar——"

Muriel did not like this remark, and said warmly—

"You have no business, sir, to speak of my father disrespectfully. To me he was the most loving, gentle, and indulgent of men. He tried to make my life perfect in its happiness, and it would have been so could I have seen the dark cloud lifted from his dear face. If he was *peculiar* to you, as you are pleased to term it, it was because you must have given him serious offence. I know that he had some terrible weight on his mind, some strange secret that cankered his whole existence, and from what you have now told me, I cannot but infer that you had much to do with darkening his life."

Glindon shrugged his shoulders with what seemed to be an habitual expression of cynicism, for a sneering smile accompanied the shrug, and he answered—

"Well, look here, Muriel; I have been frank and open with you, and told you as much as I think you ought to know. And allow me to say that I think it a great pity that you should seek to pick a quarrel with me at the very commencement of our acquaintance. I certainly had a right to expect that you would show some joy at seeing me and display some affection."

"Pray don't mistake me," she replied. "You say you have been frank and open. This is a matter upon which I have a right to form an opinion for myself. I, at least, will be frank and open with you. I can express no joy at seeing you, because I feel none. Nor can I display any affection, for I feel absolutely convinced that you must have treated your father, my father, very badly, or he would never have cast you off."

"Very well; you can hold to that if you like. I would be your friend, but you are trying to make me your enemy. That is neither politic nor sensible. The same blood flows in your veins as in mine, and blood is thicker than water. You are a handsome young woman, and one that a brother might be proud of. I offer you a brother's love, a brother's protection, but you meet me in a spirit of antagonism before we have been acquainted an hour. However, perhaps we shall become more attached when we are better acquainted. It may be as well now if you will allow me to see Mr. Jessop."

"One word first," said Muriel. "As you remark, the same blood flows in our veins, and, as far as I can see at present, it is a matter of regret to me that it is so. Perhaps I do you a wrong. God forbid that I should do so, but I cannot forget that my father kept the knowledge of your existence from me. And for that there must have been some terrible reason. Until you can satisfactorily explain to me why he did so, we must be strangers in all but name."

Again the shrug of the shoulders, again the bitter smile, as Glindon made reply—

"As you will, Miss Glindon. You are proud now, but perhaps your pride may have a fall. *Nous verrons!*"

She did not answer him, save it was with a look of contempt that flashed from her bright eyes; but ringing the bell, she asked—

"Do you wish me to remain during your interview with Mr. Jessop?"

"I think perhaps you had better do so."

A knock came to the door, and in reply to her "Come in," Mr. Jessop entered.

Half an hour later Muriel joined Raymond, who was pacing up and down impatiently on the terrace in front of the house. She was pale and agitated, and her eyes were suffused with tears. Laying her hand on his arm she said in an emotional tone—

"Raymond, my father was right when he told you that if you married me you would have a penniless bride."

CHAPTER XII.

CHANGED FORTUNES.

"I UNDERSTAND you, dear," he answered. "You mean that if this Ivan Glindon is your father's lawful son he is the heir to the property. But don't trouble yourself unnecessarily. He has yet to prove that he is the son. He may be an impostor, for aught we know."

"Alas! he has given too certain evidence that he is no impostor, so far as his claim to be my father's son is concerned. Of course, he will have to satisfy the law on the point, but I feel convinced that he is what he represents himself to be."

"Well, Muriel, darling," said Penoyre, as he lovingly toyed with her fair hand, "as far as I am concerned, you know that I do not care a pin whether you have money or not. If you are penniless, my people, of course, will object to my marrying you, but what do I care for that? I am no longer an infant, either legally or actually, and I shall claim the right to act and think for myself."

"Ah, dear!" sighed Muriel sorrowfully, "you must not talk like that. You are morally bound to respect the wishes of your parents, and under no circumstances would I be a willing party to your taking any step that might give offence to your father and mother. No, Raymond; a dark shadow has fallen upon us, and I am realising now that life is hard and bitter, and the human heart full of wickedness. I know that you love me, and for me to separate myself from you is to turn my life into a living death. But a woman knows how to suffer and be silent——"

"Oh Muriel——"

"Nay, dear; hear me out. A man may deeply feel a disappointment in love, and suffer keenly for a time. But in this respect, at least, the man's nature is more elastic than the woman's. He has a thousand ways of distracting his mind that she has not, and sooner or later he recovers, sees some other face that charms him, and remembers his first love no more, save as a dream he has dreamed."

"Muriel," cried Penoyre, with an expression of anguish, "do me not the injustice of thinking me capable of ever forgetting you. Supposing that every member of my family went down on his or her knees and uttered a malediction on me, it would not prevent my marrying you if you are willing to become my wife. You cannot, surely, have forgotten that on the eventful evening when I spoke to your father, and asked him to consent to our union, he said that you would be dowerless. What was my answer? I said that though you had not a second gown to wear I would take you!"

"You did, dear."

"I am quite aware," he went on, and having painful recollections of that interview with his mother, when she declared that only Muriel's fortune could ever reconcile her to the girl whom she referred to as a plebeian, "that the wish of my mother and father is that I should marry somebody with money. But when the wishes of parents are opposed to the happiness of their children, the children are justified in resisting them. At any rate, I repeat now, with stronger emphasis than ever I have done before, if that is possible, that I'll marry you or no one, even though we have to live at first in one room."

Muriel was very greatly touched, and in spite of her efforts she could not conceal her emotion. She remained silent for a little time, and when at last her voice came to her she said, with deep pathos—

"I am fully convinced of your love and devotion for me, and in this dark hour of my bitter sorrow that knowledge upholds me. It seems to me now, however, that the world can offer me no joy. My father's cruel death, and the unsolved mystery connected with his life and his murder, have shattered my dreams and turned me into a hard, stern woman——"

"Tut! Muriel, darling; you must not talk like that."

"I talk as I feel, Raymond; and I am convinced now that I have a stern and terrible duty to fulfil. Ivan Glindon told me a little while ago that, though legally he was the heir to everything, he would provide handsomely for me. But think you, Raymond, that I would accept one penny-piece from the hands of this man, relative though he be, until I have learned the story of his past life, and what is the terrible reason that caused my father to disown him? I shall go from this dear home, where I have passed so many happy, happy years, with a fixed and unalterable purpose. That purpose is to devote the rest of my

life, be it long or short, to trying to solve the mystery
of my father's sorrow."

"But, Muriel," cried out Penoyre, in an agony of
distress, "what good can that do? Why should you
offer up yourself as a living sacrifice to a phantom.
Your father is dead; better to let his secrets be buried
with him."

"No," said Muriel, with a display of sternness that
astonished her lover. "No; that cannot be. Ivan
Glindon has aspersed my father's memory; he has
hinted that my father's honour was sullied, and until
I have proved this innuendo to be false, if false it
be, I shall not rest. I am aware that my dear father
himself hinted at something in his career that might,
if it were known, subject me to the scandal of evil
tongues. The story of his life he had written for me.
But that story has been stolen, and the person who
stole it must and shall be discovered, for I cannot
believe that my father could have been guilty of any
serious offence. His sensitive and upright nature
caused him to exaggerate some mere social sin. At
least, that is my belief; and could the stolen papers
be recovered, the truth from the man himself would be
known. At any rate, I will believe nothing that any
mortal being can say against my father, unless he can
produce the most indubitable documentary evidence."

"Your sentiments and purpose are noble and grand,"
said Penoyre. "But let me, as your husband, aid you
in carrying this purpose out."

"No, dear; I will never marry while there is the
suspicion even of a stigma on my father's good name."

"Is that your unalterable determination?" Raymond asked, in a broken voice.

"It is."

"Then a blight falls upon my life," he answered sadly. "To possess you I would have sacrificed everything—friends, home, prospects, ay, even the hopes of Paradise——"

"Hush, Raymond; you must not speak like that."

"I will speak like that!" he exclaimed, with fiery energy. "I would have defied Heaven itself could I have gained you. But since you are determined to wreck my life I know not what lies before me. A desperate and reckless man can always find Lethe somewhere. I will seek for it."

"Ah, dear!" moaned Muriel, turning her pale face to his and clinging to his arm; "you are talking thoughtlessly and foolishly, and as a man is apt to talk if his love affairs go not smoothly and just as he wishes. But in calmer moments, and when you have reflected, you will think differently. You are too noble, too upright, too philosophical, to become either desperate or reckless. It is weak men only who give way to despair and who ignore, or affect to ignore, the responsibilities of life. No one has any right to sully or destroy God's great gift because, in his blindness of heart, he thinks that his life is not quite what it ought to be. I love you, and no other man can or shall win my love. But I owe a duty to my dead father's memory, and until that duty is done I cannot, in justice to you and in justice to myself, become your wife."

Raymond Penoyre was greatly cut up. He could

not conceal that fact. This disappointment to him was terrible. Perhaps he was weak, but it must be remembered that he was young; he was enthusiastic, and with the hopefulness of youth he had reared magnificent air-drawn structures that had toppled now about his head and, as it seemed to him, entirely crushed his hopes.

A little later he parted from Muriel, not in anger, but in bitter sorrow, and with a feeling that between him and her had come a barrier that nothing could ever remove. If youth is capable of rising to great heights of hope, it is also capable of sinking to great depths of despair. And Raymond Penoyre went forth with a sense of being plunged in a darkness into which no gleam of hopeful light would ever more penetrate.

From whatever point of view Muriel's determination is looked at it was a noble one, and reflected great credit upon her. She felt that between her and her new-found brother there could not possibly be any true affection—at any rate, so far as she was concerned—and she neither knew the art of dissembling nor could she act the hypocrite, and she preferred poverty and hardship to luxury and ease so long as the dark mystery surrounding her father's life remained unsolved.

Ivan Glindon had but little difficulty in clearly establishing his identity. He was born in the town of Yarensk, in the province of Vologda, in Northern Russia, and was the lawful son of Ivan Peter Glindon and his wife, Jessie Glindon, *née* Pestrowitch. And as his father had died intestate he was his lawful heir.

He offered to make a settlement on Muriel, but she proudly refused to accept anything from him.

It was a bitter wrench to go forth from that dear home, where she had been so happy, and where she had dreamed her entrancing dream of love. But there was no help for it, and she tried to resign herself uncomplainingly and with patience to the inevitable. But the struggle was, nevertheless, very great, very painful. It seemed as if the fires of her youth had all burnt out and only the cold grey ashes remained; and the idols she had so lovingly cherished had crumbled into the dust. She and her aunt established themselves in a small and unpretentious house in Fulham. It was a great change from the luxury and beauty of The Priory, but they made no complaint, and in order to be independent of her aunt's slender income Muriel set to work to endeavour to get some music and language pupils. Raymond Penoyre had gone abroad. The change in Muriel's affairs had made his life unbearable at home, for he persisted in declaring that he would never marry any one if he did not get Muriel. This " obstinacy " greatly offended his people, and they said so many bitter things about the poor girl that he could not endure it. He therefore went out to a brother who occupied a vice-consulship in one of the West India islands. Previous to his departure he had a very affecting and tender interview with Muriel, and just before going on board the steamer that was to bear him away he wrote the following note to her :—

" My beloved Muriel,—We are drifting far apart, and God alone knows whether in the future our tide of affairs will bring

H

us together again. To me all seems dark and drear, and it is impossible for me to be cheerful in this hour of our parting. But on my heart is engraved your image, and the woman is not born who can efface it. Farewell! It is a hard word to utter, but it must be said, even though its sounds are like the clanging of the iron door of a tomb, which shuts us for ever and ever from all that we have loved, from all that has made our lives endurable. Once more, farewell! The Lord watch between thee and me when we are parted one from the other."

Amongst those who, in Muriel's changed fortunes, showed her true and devoted friendship was Calvin Sugg, the eminent detective. His sympathies were very real, and his friendship took the practical form of offering her for her use a considerable sum of money which he had saved; it is, perhaps, needless to say it was gratefully declined. But in Sugg, Miss Glindon felt that she had a genuine friend, a wise counsellor, and a trusty confidant.

During the time that had elapsed since the murders of Vesta Florence and Mr. Glindon every endeavour had been made by Sugg to bring the criminals to justice, but so far he had not been successful. Although, on the face of it, it seemed almost absurd to suppose that the one crime had any bearing on the other, Sugg was firm in his belief that there was some strange connection between the two, and he never allowed his hope of being successful sooner or later to unravel the mystery to waver in the slightest degree. Of course, there were those who did not hesitate to say harsh things of Sugg; for, unhappily, every successful man in this world makes enemies. Envy and jealousy exert a powerful influence over the human heart; and it was said of Sugg that he had been baffled at last, and that the confidence which the authorities and the public reposed in him was misplaced.

This sort of criticism had no more effect on Calvin Sugg than a hailstone has on the back of a crocodile. His only reply was—"I am not the only man who has failed. Others besides me have been employed in both cases, but have made nothing out of them. Besides, my failure is only temporary. As sure as the sun shines in the sky, I'll solve the riddle some day."

It is very probable that at the time he said this Sugg spoke only from a firm belief in his own abilities and faith in his star, which hitherto seemed to have served him so well. No man could do impossibilities, and Sugg laid claim to no superhuman powers. But the faculty of solving problems in connection with human wicked-ness was very strong within him, and he declared this problem was not going to baffle him—that it was not beyond his capabilities.

One day, some months after Muriel had left The Priory, Sugg was seated at breakfast in his own house at Clapham. Having partaken of his meal with a good appetite, he lit a cigarette, dropped into a luxurious easy-chair, and opened out his morning *Standard*. He continued to peruse the paper for some time, turning from page to page; but suddenly a change came over the placid expression of his face; his eyes blazed out with the light of an eager interest, and crushing the paper in his hand with nervous energy, he sprang to his feet and exclaimed—"By heavens! a clue at last!"

CHAPTER XIII.

A HUMAN PHENOMENON.

It is necessary to make an apparent digression here in order to explain the nature of the clue that Calvin Sugg believed that he had got hold of.

A good many years before the period at which this story commences, there was living in a strange, isolated, and old-fashioned house, situated near Northallerton, in Yorkshire, a Mr. Sylvester Parmiter, together with his housekeeper and two children, a girl and a boy. For a long, long time Mr. Parmiter had lived in Dutch Guiana, as a coffee and cotton planter, and was supposed to have accumulated money. He had married a Dutch lady, the widow of a brother planter, and she bore him a son and a daughter, both of them being born in the town of Paramaribo, on the banks of the river Surinam. When the children were aged respectively twelve and fourteen, the boy being the younger, Mr. Parmiter realised his estates and sailed for England.

At this time he was a widower, his wife having been dead three or four years. Mrs. Parmiter's death was not only sudden but suspicious, and it was said that she had been poisoned by a very deadly herb which grows in Guiana, and produces death in a few hours. As Mr. Parmiter and his wife were known to have led a cat-and-dog life, and he had been heard to say that he wished she would die, he was charged with having murdered her. The fullest investigation was made, but no evidence being forthcoming, the charge had to be abandoned. Notwithstanding this, the general feeling was that he had done his wife to death; but he denounced the accusation as a lying and wicked calumny, and in spite of the odium he stayed on in the colony for some time in defiance of public opinion. At last, however, his health began to break up, and his children were also suffering, so he turned his back upon the colony for ever, and settled down in his native county of Yorkshire.

He bought a small estate which had been in the market for quite twenty years. It had got a bad name owing to its being the scene of a fearful tragedy. People said it was haunted and accursed, and so it fell into neglect and ruin. It was situated on rising ground and commanded extensive views over the moorlands. The house was an irregularly built place surrounded by dark fir woods. When Mr. Parmiter took possession of his property it might have been described as the very home of melancholy. The woods had become almost impenetrable jungles; the gardens were choked up with dank weeds, and the house was a windowless ruin. The price asked for it was so ridiculously small that Parmiter was tempted, in spite of the evil repute attaching to it. He executed the necessary repairs in order to make the place habitable; but with the exception of clearing away some of the weeds from the garden, he allowed the land to remain as it was.

Somehow the man and the place seemed suited. He

himself was a brooding, melancholy man, without any
interest in life, apparently; and soon it began to be
whispered about that he was a confirmed opium-eater,
and was constantly in a dazed condition through his
unfortunate habit. His two children, Katrina and
Jäel, the boy being named after one of his wife's relatives, seemed in a fair way of being totally neglected,
when their father engaged a housekeeper to look after
them. She was a sensible woman of about forty, and
her name was Margaret Jenner. Mr. Parmiter showed
so little interest in his affairs that the housekeeper was
allowed full control of everything, and she soon showed
that she intended to rule the household with an iron
hand. Katrina Parmiter at this time was a pretty
girl, but very delicate, and seemed to wither up in the
bleak, cold climate which was such a marked contrast
to the country of her birth, and where she had passed
fourteen years of her life.

Jäel, her brother, on the other hand, was apparently
a robust lad. He was well built, dark-complexioned,
and he had small glittering eyes that proclaimed a
cruel and cold-blooded disposition. Nor did his eyes
belie him. From his infancy almost the boy had
evinced a cruelty of disposition that was absolutely
phenomenal. As evidence of this, on one occasion,
in Guiana, he was playing with a small dog, a great
favourite of his father's, when the animal accidentally
bit him. He was then a mere child, but so enraged
was he that he heated a piece of steel wire and deliberately burnt out the dog's eyes. Then, while the poor
animal was suffering excruciating agony, he suspended

it by its tail to a cocoa-nut tree, where it hung for many hours, until it was devoured alive by the formidable red ants which infest Guiana.

On another occasion an old negro on his father's plantation offended him, and the lad caught up a hoe used for hoeing coffee-plants, and hurled it at the negro's head. It struck the old man on the forehead, inflicting a serious wound from which he never recovered, but died two months later from erysipelas, the result of the wound. On hearing of his death the boy laughed and said—

"The black brute will never annoy me any more."

This innate cruelty of disposition was a source of grave anxiety to all who had anything to do with him, and it was the means of causing Mrs. Margaret Jenner, his father's housekeeper, to evince an unconquerable dislike for him. The youth reciprocated this as such a youth was likely to do, and he promised to make her life unbearable. She therefore told his father that unless he exercised some control over his son she would have to leave. But Mr. Parmiter was too listless, too wanting in energy, and too besotted with his opium habit to bestir himself to any extent. The climate of Guiana had shrivelled up his liver and made a wreck of him. However, he said that Jäel should be sent to a good strict boarding-school, and he commissioned the housekeeper to look out for such a place.

Now, it was an extraordinary thing, a psychical problem in fact, when considered in connection with the boy's natural cruelty, that he was passionately attached to his sister, and seemed almost to worship the very ground she walked upon.

She was the one being, and the only one, who was capable of swaying him, or who had the slightest influence over him. He disliked his father and hated the housekeeper. When in a passion he had been heard to declare over and over again that his mother had been murdered by his father, and that some day he would be revenged for it. He professed to have been fond of his mother, and in spite of the fact that not a vestige of evidence could be got to justify the suspicions entertained against Mr. Parmiter, the boy persisted in declaring that his mother had been murdered. Sometimes, in a sudden outburst of energy, Mr. Parmiter had severely flogged his son, but it had no effect, and he had at last, in sheer despair, given up trying to control him. Katrina, however, seemed able to influence him by a look, and it was through her that he consented to go to a school the housekeeper had discovered in the neighbourhood of York, and where it was hoped that discipline and moral training would effect an alteration for the better in his nature.

Subsequent events proved that these hopes were not likely to be realised. At any rate the reports that were sent from the school were far from encouraging. He was described as a "singularly wayward and stubborn boy, with a hard, cruel nature, and apparently cannot be affected by fear." At last he was expelled from the school as absolutely incorrigible. It was said that he had a clever head, and was capable of deep and earnest study if he would only give his mind to it; but his moral nature appeared to be absolutely diseased or warped.

It was singular, however, that on his return home he seemed to change to some extent; but this change was no doubt due entirely to his sister. Her health had become more delicate; in fact, she was now a confirmed invalid, but was so gentle, so patient, so uncomplaining, so sweet in manner and temper, that the people who knew the two used to say that she was an angel, while he was a devil. Another school was now found for him, and she induced him to go to it. It was situated in Lancashire, and for nearly three years young Parmiter remained there and made some pretence of studying hard. It was his father's desire that he should go up to Oxford, but those who were responsible for the boy's training said it would be useless, for he had no application, and apparently no ambition, and it would be a perfect waste of money to send him to college.

During this time Jäel Parmiter had developed into a showy, good-looking man, with a flippant manner of speech, and a cold, cynical style that seemed out of place in one so young. It was a remarkable fact that he never spoke of any one kindly except his sister, and at last he received a summons to return home immediately, as she was dangerously ill. When he arrived, it was to find that her case was hopeless. She was in the very last stage of decline, and the doctors said her death was only a matter of days.

The effect of this announcement on such an extraordinary nature as Jäel's may be imagined. It seemed

to frenzy him, and he uttered curses against heaven
and earth.   But the dying girl calmed him, and on his
knees, and with his hands clasped in hers, she made
him promise her that he would never marry.   And
when he asked why she wished to exact such a
promise, she said it was because she knew he was
not fitted to be a husband, and he would wreck the
life of any woman he allied himself to.   At first he was
not disposed to give such a promise, but her influence
was too strong, and she made him vow solemnly that
he would respect this, her last request.

A few days later she was dead.   It seemed then
as if nothing on earth could give Jäel comfort.   For
two days he disappeared, and spent most of his time
wandering about, half distracted, in his father's woods.
Utterly wanting as he was in religious sentiment and
in a sense of moral obligation to an omnipotent Power,
he sought not for consolation where most young men
would have done; and when he returned home he was
sullen, misanthropical, and irreverent.

For six months following his sister's death he
abandoned himself to a moody, morose silence, and
he seemed to take a positively fiendish delight in
torturing animals.   Mrs. Jenner was afraid of him,
and was always glad when he left the house.   About
this time an old merchant friend of Mr. Parmiter
called upon him.   The friend had been for some years
settled in Russia; and the result of the visit was, that
he made an offer to take Jäel into his business in
Russia.   He knew nothing of the young man's disposition, otherwise the offer might never have been

made. As it was, to the housekeeper's intense delight, no less than to his father's surprise, Jäel consented to go.

He was absent for three years, but he only remained with the merchant six months. What he did during the other two years and a half was a mystery. One thing was clear—he had come back in a state bordering on destitution, and his father, who was then in very feeble health, relieved his necessities.

Two years passed, and Jäel Parmiter continued to idle his time away, spending most of it from home. But during the time an event occurred which was destined to affect all his future life, and what that event was will be told presently. At last Mr. Parmiter, who had long been suffering acutely, died. He left his son a sum of three hundred a year only, and he gave his housekeeper, Mrs. Margaret Jenner, a life interest in his house and estate at Northallerton, with power to her to let it as she might deem fit. On her death it was to be sold, and the proceeds divided amongst some nieces and nephews.

As may be supposed, this disposition of the property caused great offence to Jäel, who had counted on succeeding to everything, and it was not calculated to produce in him anything like reverence for his dead father's memory, while the dislike that he had always displayed for Mrs. Jenner became more bitter, more intense. However, as she was in an independent position now, she was not likely to allow him to trouble her long; and so he removed from his father's house everything that belonged to him, and went forth into the world again.

CHAPTER XIV.

A RIDDLE.

WHEN Jäel Parmiter was at school in Lancashire he made the acquaintance of a family named Rees, who resided near Liverpool. The family consisted of the father and mother, two sons, and three daughters. They were hard-working and highly respectable people, and held in high repute in the neighbourhood in which they lived. Mr. Rees was a builder by trade, and the sons assisted him; while his wife and their daughters kept a stationery and fancy shop; so that the family, altogether, were in an easy and comfortable position. They were church-going people, and took a lively interest in all that concerned the welfare of those less fortunately situated than themselves.

It may seem difficult to understand how it was that Jäel Parmiter managed to obtain a footing in such a family; for, young as he was, he held views with regard to religion that were well calculated to shock orthodox people; while his unsentimental, cold-blooded nature and his innate fierceness were not qualities calculated to win the affection and esteem of such people as the Rees. He must, therefore, have played the hypocrite and dissembled with consummate art and skill to have deceived them as he did.

The youngest daughter, and the flower of the flock, was Mary Clara Rees. At this time she was only a child, but she was gifted with extraordinary intelligence, vivacity, and good looks. She also gave promise of a voice, so that her father had been induced to send her to study music and singing under a celebrated Italian professor resident in Liverpool. She was then barely fifteen, but her precocity led people to think she was several years older than that. She was a blonde, with a wealth of singularly fine golden hair—hair that seemed, in very truth, to be threads of spun gold.

Over Jäel Parmiter this young lady exercised an irresistible fascination, young as she was, and young as he was. The attention he paid to her could not escape the vigilance of her parents; but they, believing him to be well connected and of most honourable intentions, offered no opposition. At last it came to this: Jäel asked Mary if, some day, she would marry him; and she said she would, provided her parents were willing.

Soon afterwards came the death of his sister, and, anomalous as it may seem, Jäel respected the promise he had made to her when she was on her deathbed; and it was this promise, no doubt, that caused the gloom and moroseness that characterised him during the subsequent months. He did not keep away from Mary Rees during this period, and she and her friends sympathised deeply with him, believing that his melan-choly was due entirely to the loss of his sister.

Before leaving for Russia he had an affecting interview with Mary, and made her promise that she would be true to him. During his absence in Russia many affecting letters passed between the young couple; and it was a testimony to his consummate art of deception that, during all this time, he managed to blind her as to his true character.

When Jäel returned from Russia Mr. Rees was dead, and there had been a considerable change in the fortunes of the Rees family. Securities which were thought to be good during his lifetime were proved, after he was dead, to be worthless, and the family were thus reduced to comparative poverty. Mary by this time had developed into a most attractive young woman; and there is little doubt that her beauty and accomplishments would have enabled her to have married well. But she remained true to Parmiter, and when he returned she expected that he would make her his wife without unnecessary delay.

He, however, had no intention of doing this. Had his dying sister never exacted that promise from him, there is no telling what he might have done. As it was, he had no intention of losing Mary Rees. Her charms had enthralled him too deeply. It would be an outrage on the very name of love to say that such a man as he was was capable of love. His selfishness was too intense to permit him to love any human being; indeed, he loved nothing that moved on the face of God's fair earth, upon which he himself was an excrescence, a blot on nature. He had the miser's greed for money, but the spendthrift's desire to part with it as soon as he got it. To enjoy his worthless life after his own peculiar fashion was all he lived for. To gratify the tastes of the hour; to give no thought to the morrow; to never utter a prayer for the welfare of his hereafter—such was his existence. And yet this strange man, this moral monstrosity, was enabled so to play upon the feelings of the beautiful and pure-minded Mary Rees that she fled from the protection of her brothers and placed herself under his. Let us seek not to learn how he accomplished his purpose. There are depths in human nature that escape the scrutiny of even the most painstaking student. A woman who truly gives her heart to a man is too often blind, alas! to her own interests and welfare. Jäel Parmiter had certainly succeeded, in the most perfect manner, in blinding Mary; and when at length her eyes were opened, she discovered, with horror, that the idol she had fallen down and worshipped had cloven feet, and the fruit she thought so fine was bitter ashes in her mouth.

For some time she endured his coldness, his neglect, his scorn, for scorn her he did. Having succeeded in dragging her down into the depths, he scorned her for her weakness—at least, he would have justified his scorn by saying that she was weak. There was no wonder that she became desperate. At the age when to most women life is an elysium and full of rich promise, she found it a veritable Tophet; and the future seemed to stretch out before her as a dark and thorny way. And this man, who had so dazed and fascinated her, now filled her with a loathing that she could not conceal.

Not the least remarkable phase of the unhappy connection between this man and woman was the fierce jealousy he evinced. Although he declared to her over and over again that he did not love her, he was never-

theless jealous to a degree that almost made him mad.
Not that she gave him any just cause for jealousy, but
such a man would imagine he saw a cause where none
existed.   At any rate, he watched her with a vigilance
that added another torture to her now miserable life.
And he used to say, with an emphasis that indicated he
was capable of carrying out his threat, that rather than
let another man possess her he would kill her.   Times
out of number did she try to soften his hard nature,
to change his cynicism, to develop in him some moral
regard for the feelings and thoughts of others, but
her efforts were all useless.   He outraged her womanly
nature ; he mocked at her efforts ; he insulted her by
saying that he was in strict accord with the Turks when
they said that woman was simply a toy for man's sport ;
that she had no soul, and ought to have no feelings.   It
was, indeed, a bitter, bitter awakening for poor, gentle
Mary Rees ; and yet she tried to be patient.   Gentle
she certainly was, and she used every effort to make
him comfortable.

At last her release came.   Jäel Parmiter had been
spending an evening with some roistering friends,
when a dispute arose, and something that one of the
party said so enraged Parmiter that he knocked the
man down with such brutal force as to seriously injure
him.   Jäel very speedily realised that he had placed
himself in a grave position, and in order to escape
the penalty of his act he resolved to fly from the
country.   He told Mary that he was going, but did
not tell her why ; nor did she trouble herself to inquire,
though she very soon came to know of it.   For a long

time she had gone in mortal fear of him, and, therefore, she was not likely to experience any regret that the hour of her deliverance was at hand. He cautioned her to be true and faithful to him as she valued her life, and said that in a little time he would send for her to join him.

So he took his departure, and went to Russia again. When he had gone Mary drew a great sigh of relief; and in her heart she prayed that she might never again look upon his face, for the very thought of him begot in her a shudder. And yet the remarkable influence he had exercised was not quite dead, and she still feared him; and it is possible that under the influence of that fear she would have followed him had he so commanded; but he did not, and she breathed freely.

At this point we must for the present leave them both, but it will be necessary later on to take up their history again, and follow it to its end. And now the reader, perhaps, will be disposed to ask, What connection is there between this story of Mary Rees and Jäel Parmiter and Calvin Sugg's exclamation that he had discovered a clue? The cause of Sugg's exclamation was the following advertisement which he read in the *Standard* :—

"To JEWELLERS, PAWNBROKERS, AUCTIONEERS, COLLECTORS, CURIO DEALERS, AND OTHERS WHOM IT MAY CONCERN.—Lost or stolen, a curious antique massive gold ring, set with a large blood-stone, on which is engraved a death's-head and cross-bones. As the ring is a family heirloom, and greatly prized by its owner, a reward of twenty pounds will be paid for its restoration.— Address, IVAN GLINDON, Esq., Rutland House, Hyde Park Corner, London."

CHAPTER XV.

THE PUZZLE BECOMES MORE ABSTRUSE.

WHEN Ivan Glindon came into full possession of his father's property he let The Priory at Richmond, as he preferred to live in town, and he chose as his residence Rutland House, Hyde Park Corner. It might, without exaggeration, be described as a noble mansion, and the rent demanded for it was in keeping with the accommodation it afforded and the aristocratic neighbourhood in which it was situated. Apart from the heavy rent, the outlay necessary to keep up such an establishment was very great; but expense seemed to be no object to Mr. Glindon. For when his late father's affairs came to be wound up they turned out even better than was anticipated. He still carried on the business, although he troubled himself very little about it, leaving its entire management in the hands of Mr. Jessop.

Notwithstanding his wealth and grand house, Mr. Glindon did not succeed in obtaining a footing in society, although he strove hard at first to get himself acknowledged by his wealthy and aristocratic neighbours. But he had come there without any credentials. Moreover, it was widespread that there had been some-

thing very shady in his past history; and so the door
of the houses he would have liked to enter were closed
against him, and he was looked upon as one who
somewhat detracted from the high-toned respectability
of the neighbourhood.

As if to revenge himself for being thus snubbed,
Glindon entertained people whose very presence tainted
the atmosphere of that select region; at least so the
neighbours thought. But Glindon showed now that he
was utterly indifferent to their views or opinions. His
doctrine was, that he lived in a free country, paid his
way, and therefore had a right to do as he liked. Notwithstanding his income was said to be a very handsome
one, it seemed as if he took every means to dissipate it
as fast as possible, and he became known as a frequenter
of all the racecourses in the country; and the majority
of his companions were horsey men—men about town
—men whose histories would not bear looking into.

Mr. Ivan Glindon had tried very hard to get his
half-sister to be friendly with him, and had urged
her to preside over his household. But she had not
only resolutely declined, but frankly said she regarded
him with aversion, until at last he lost his temper, and
told her, though she was starving, she should never
have a penny-piece of his money.

She was not affected by that, for she had reconciled
herself to her changed position, and she preferred to
work for her living rather than accept anything from
the hands of one whom, though a relative, she could
never respect.

The day after Calvin Sugg had read that advertisement in the *Standard* which led him to believe that he had found a clue he made his way to Rutland House. He did not know Ivan Glindon personally so far as he was aware of, and he did not think that Ivan Glindon knew him. Nevertheless, with his habitual caution, when the flunkey who opened the door to him inquired his name, he declined to give it, merely requesting the servant to tell his master that a gentleman had called with reference to a matter of private business.

So Sugg was kept standing in the hall for some time, until the servant came back and showed him into an elegantly furnished room, and said that Mr. Glindon would see him shortly. The "shortly," however, proved to be a good half-hour before the door of the room opened and Ivan Glindon presented himself.

As the two men came face to face they each started with surprise; for in Glindon the detective recognised Ricardo, the husband of Vesta Florence; and Glindon recognised Sugg as the man who had been engaged in trying to unravel the mystery of Vesta Florence's death.

"This is a revelation," Sugg exclaimed, fixing his keen eyes on Glindon, as if trying to read his very thoughts.

Glindon showed signs of some confusion and was more than usually pale. But he quickly recovered himself, and, with a jerky little laugh, said—"Possibly it is, Mr. Sugg; for I don't think we have come across each other since that strange affair in St. John's Wood."

"No," returned Sugg, still watching the other with

that fixed gaze which was one of his marked characteristics; and self-possessed as Glindon evidently was, he winced before it. "No, we have not," continued the detective, "and it seems to me some explanation is needed."

"Oh," exclaimed Glindon, with an assumed air of indifference, "the explanation is simple. My late father and I never hit it. Of course, you don't expect me to go into my history and give you all the details of my past life."

"If I were to wish you to do so, would you do it?" Sugg asked pointedly.

"No, certainly not. Neither you nor any one else have any right to make such inquiry. I was charged with my late wife's murder, and it was proved conclusively that I had nothing to do with her death. Consequently I was a victim of the law's blunders."

"Possibly," remarked Sugg sententiously.

"Possibly!" echoed Glindon angrily. "What do you mean? Do you mean to say that you think I killed my wife?"

"I am perfectly certain that you did not," answered the detective coolly.

"Thank you." This sarcastically. "I need scarcely say that, in the face of its having been proved that I am quite innocent, any one daring to hint to the contrary would render himself liable to an action at law, and I assure you I would spare no expense in prosecuting my traducer to the bitter end. He could expect no mercy from me."

"No more than you might expect mercy if you were proved guilty of that or any other crime," returned Sugg, with peculiar emphasis on his words.

"Just so," answered Glindon with a bitter sneer, and seemingly not affected by the pointed remark. "But now, Mr. Sugg, will you kindly tell me to what I am to attribute your visit?"

"Yes, I will do so; but I should like first to ask one or two questions, and I will venture to say it is to your interest that you should answer them."

"Fire away, then," said Glindon tartly, as he proceeded to roll a cigarette.

"How was it you lived in St. John's Wood under the name of Ricardo?"

"Oh, that's easily explained! The old man——"

"You mean your father," put in Sugg correctively.

"Very well; my father, then," was the snarling reply. "He made me an allowance on condition that I changed my name."

There was an expression on the detective's face which seemed to indicate that he did not believe that statement; but he asked another question.

"I happen to know that the late Mr. Glindon was greatly embittered against you. Indeed, I should not be guilty of exaggeration if I were to say that he hated you. *Why did he hate you?*"

"Were you well acquainted with my father?" asked Glindon, becoming a little confused and uneasy under Sugg's searching glances.

"I knew him fairly well."

"It's a wonder, then, that he didn't tell you himself why he hated me."

"Mr. Glindon was a singularly reserved man, and never talked about his affairs."

"No, I should think not." This with a coarse, sneering laugh. "He knew better than that. My father didn't choose to own me, although I was his lawful son. But as he did not tell you the cause, I fail to recognise your right, sir, to inquire into it, and, flatly, I refuse to tell you."

Glindon looked as though he had scored a point, though Sugg was not in the least degree disconcerted, but said coolly—

"Very well; perhaps some day I shall find out. Now as to the object of my visit. You advertise for information about a ring, which, from your description, would seem to be a very peculiar one."

"Yes. Do you know anything about it?"

This question was asked with a display of anxious eagerness, and a deadly pallor spread itself over Glindon's face; while the cigarette he was smoking fell from his lips on to the carpet. He stooped to pick it up, but seemed to take an unreasonable time to do so. These things did not escape the keen eyes of the detective, and he waited until he could look Glindon full in the face again before he answered the question. Then—

"During the inquiry at the time of your wife's death I heard something about that ring——"

"Why was it not mentioned in the evidence, then?"

"Oh, there was no necessity to mention it. It was

considered that it might afford a clue to the murderer of Vesta Florence, and therefore we deemed it advisable, in the interests of justice, to keep the matter secret."

"But it has not proved a clue," exclaimed Glindon, with a triumphant little laugh.

"True; it has not done so up to the present. But still, it may do so yet. Now tell me, please, did this ring belong to you?"

"It belonged to my wife, and she wore it."

"Did she wear it at the time of her death?"

"Probably she did, but I am not sure. She did not wear it constantly; only occasionally."

"When did you miss it?"

"After I was released from custody and when I came to examine her things."

"Did you make any inquiries about it then?"

"I did not."

"Why?"

"I did not think it was worth while doing so."

"Why have you advertised for it now?"

"I have advertised on behalf of a member of her family who sets great store upon the ring, and is prepared to pay any reasonable reward for its restoration."

"Will you give me the name of that member?"

"No, I will not; and I deny your right to poke your nose into my affairs. Now tell me, have you got the ring?"

"I decline to answer that question at present. This much I will tell you, I know where it is."

Mr. Glindon was greatly annoyed and irritated, and he displayed this as he remarked—

"It seems to me that you are making a fool of me; and no doubt you think you are very clever and very sharp, and all that sort of thing. But let me tell you this, Mr. Sugg, whoever has the ring is in unlawful possession of it, and since, according to your own showing, you know something about it, I shall hold you responsible for its return."

"And supposing I decline to give you any information."

"Then I will see what the law can do in the way of compelling you. I suppose the fact is you found the ring at the time you were making inquiries about the murder."

"I acknowledge that your guess is right."

"Very well, then, since you can have no possible interest in retaining it, you must restore it to me."

"There I must differ from you. I have a very strong reason for retaining it."

"What is your reason?"

"It will yet enable me to track down the murderer of Mrs. Ricardo, and possibly—*probably*—Mr. Glindon's murderer also."

Ivan grew deadly pale again, and said savagely—

"Humbug—bosh! You fellows are nothing if not suspicious. But in this case you are making a mistake and an ass of yourself at the same time. I am the owner of the ring, and you must restore it to me."

"I shall take time to consider the matter," answered

Sugg. "In fact, I may as well say that unless you furnish me with indubitable proof that the ring really belonged to your late wife, I shall not restore it."

"That's all right," said Glindon sharply. "I will consult my lawyer in the matter, and see what he can do."

He struck a little silver bell that stood on the table, and in a few moments a man-servant entered.

"Show this gentleman to the door," was Glindon's order.

Calvin Sugg rose from the chair he was occupying. He was not in the least disturbed by Glindon's rudeness and abruptness. But, with a slight inclination of the head, he remarked—

"We shall meet again, Mr. Glindon."

Then, without another word, he followed the servant down the hall and left the house.

When his unwelcome guest had gone Glindon ground his teeth and stamped his foot and muttered—

"Curse the thing! What a fool I've been!"

And Mr. Sugg, as he wended his way across the park, seemed to be peculiarly pleased with himself, and he thought—

"I've got hold of the end of the thread, and I'll unravel the skein as sure as I am a living man."

Perhaps Sugg was right, though it did not seem very clear just then how he was going to do it.

CHAPTER XVI.

THE LITTLE HUMPBACKED MAN.

ALTHOUGH the detective was under the impression that he had got hold of a thread that was likely to lead to important results, he had had to own to himself that his interview with Glindon had given the puzzle the appearance of being a little more intricate. The discovery that Ricardo and Glindon were one and the same was certainly startling, and it established pretty clearly that Glindon was an adventurer. Indeed, when the late Mr. Glindon gave Sugg instructions about "Ricardo," he was described as an adventurer, and Glindon had said—

"This man is a scoundrel, but he has a certain power over me, and I cannot openly quarrel with him. I believe him, however, to be capable of almost any wickedness, and wish you to shadow him; for, sooner or later, I am sure he will break the law, and then I may get him into my power."

For some time Sugg carried out these instructions, but though Ricardo led a somewhat fast life, he was no worse in that respect than tens of thousands of other men who, in a general way, were considered highly respectable. Ricardo was idle; he was dissolute.

and his associates were, for the most part, a shady lot; but he did not break the law. Then came the murder of his wife, and at first it seemed almost a certainty that he was the murderer; but Sugg had satisfied himself by the most exhaustless inquiry that he was innocent of that dreadful crime.

But now came the strangest part of the whole business. Ricardo proved to be Ivan Glindon, and Ivan Glindon was the late Mr. Glindon's son; and now, long after the murder, he was desirous of recovering the ring which, by inference, had belonged to the murderer, and had slipped from his finger on to the sofa while he was engaged in his ghastly work. That was the theory that Sugg had constructed; and now, on leaving Glindon's house, he asked himself again and again if that theory was altogether wrong.

It could not be denied that there was a possibility that Vesta Florence had worn the ring on the night of her death; but the ring was so large in circumference, so massive, and so conspicuous altogether, that it was hardly likely to be worn by a woman. At any rate, if Vesta Florence had been in the habit of wearing it, it could hardly have escaped the notice of people whom she moved amongst and associated with daily.

Consequently, Sugg proceeded to make the most careful inquiries amongst the actors and actresses employed at the theatre where Vesta Florence had fulfilled an engagement during the whole time she had been in London, but not one could recall the ring to mind. That she wore two or three diamond rings, and also one set with opals and brilliants, was well known and remembered; but the signet, with its emblems of mortality, nobody had seen. Now, was it not reasonably certain that, if she really had been in the habit of wearing so remarkable a ring as the one Sugg had in his possession, some of her companions would have noted it?

He therefore came to the conclusion that the statement Glindon had made to him was false.

"Now, what was the motive that prompted the statement? Was Glindon, after all, the murderer of Vesta Florence?"

The question naturally came into Sugg's mind, but he dismissed it; for, on the clearest possible evidence, it was proved that Ricardo, on the night of the crime, was dining with some friends at a well-known Regent Street *café*, the object of the feast being to celebrate the success of one of the friends, who had netted a large sum over some races. Therefore, unless Ricardo had a dual personality, he could not have been at Linda Villa and at the *café* in Regent Street at one and the same time.

All the circumstances of the case indicated that the criminal was the man who had met her at the stage-door of the theatre, and driven first to Piccadilly with her, and afterwards to St. John's Wood. Singularly enough, the stage-door keeper, the cabmen, and the waiters in the hotel where the stranger and Florence supped gave a description of the strange man which tallied pretty accurately with Ricardo, and yet the *alibi* in Ricardo's case was conclusive.

Clever as he was, and used to dealing with complicated human problems, Calvin Sugg was conscious that he had got one now that defeated him, so far as he could see then; and the revelation that Ricardo was Glindon, and that Glindon was anxious to recover the ring, heightened the mystery. Until, suddenly, it dawned upon the detective that Ricardo and the man who killed Vesta Florence might have been acquainted. It was certainly a startling theory, but one that opened up all sorts of possibilities; and Calvin Sugg, as a student of human nature, knew that anything was possible in connection with human wickedness.

All these various points revolved themselves in Sugg's busy brain for many days, and he worked out an entirely new theory of the murder of Vesta Florence and the murder of Mr. Glindon, and he was more than ever convinced now, since his visit to Rutland House, that there was some connection between the two crimes.

And there was one who, if he could but speak, might throw considerable light on the subject. That one was Hilkiah Thorne, the lawyer, who still lived, although his mind was a complete blank. His case had been regarded as such an extraordinary one that it had attracted the attention of some of the most eminent men of the day; and Dr. Blewitt, who still had charge of the case, had been overwhelmed with suggestions and advice. But he and his friend, Sir Wilfred Weir, followed their own plan; but though they had proved beyond doubt that the bullet was embedded in the lawyer's brain, they had not dared to attempt its extraction.

The wound, therefore, had been allowed to heal, and Thorne had almost recovered his wonted physical health. But mentally he was a wreck, or, rather, he had become a little child again; for all that he had ever learnt, all that he had ever known, was entirely forgotten. Though there was this difference between him and a child: he had no power of acquiring knowledge. Sir Wilfred Weir was of opinion that unless the bullet could be extracted his condition would not alter, and he might live for many years, though his life would be an entire blank. On the other hand, any attempt to get at the bullet would almost certainly prove fatal.

Calvin Sugg was fully aware of the peculiar phase Thorne's injury had taken, and he felt sure that locked up in that benumbed brain was some secret that would prove invaluable in helping him to unravel the mystery with which he was confronted. But, having regard to the opinion of so eminent a specialist as Sir Wilfred Weir, it seemed almost hopeless to expect that the secret would ever be told. Now, however, that he had found out that Glindon and Ricardo were the same person, he resolved to call at Mr. Thorne's office in the Temple and have an interview with Robert Sulcoates, the manager.

Mr. Sulcoates was not in any sense of the word a communicative man. He hailed from the North beyond the Tweed, and seemed to be endowed with a much larger proportion than usual of that caution which is supposed to be an attribute of his countrymen. Suspicion, too, which is another trait of the sons of Caledonia, was his in an exaggerated degree, and the two things had been schooled and cultured by his legal training.

"I really am not in a position to give you any information about Mr. Thorne's affairs," was his answer to Sugg's preliminary inquiry.

"But probably you are aware that the late Mr. Ivan Peter Glindon was acquainted with Ricardo, who was charged with the murder of Vesta Florence?"

"No; I was not aware of it."

"But Mr. Thorne was."

"Ah! I know nothing about that. Mr. Thorne did not make me the repository of his secrets. My position is, and has been, that of general manager of the purely commercial department, and Mr. Thorne has never honoured me with his confidence so far as the affairs of his clients are concerned."

"Well, perhaps you can tell me whether, on the night of the murder, Mr. Thorne went down to The Priory on legal business or not?"

"No, I cannot; but perhaps his confidential clerk could."

"Who is his confidential clerk?"

"His confidential clerk *was* a young man named Perley Beck."

"Is he in?"

"No; he has left. He threw up his situation without any explanation some months ago."

"Do you know where he is to be found?"

"I do not. I know nothing at all about him."

Mr. Sugg was disappointed with the result of his visit and somewhat annoyed at Sulcoates' curtness, though he was careful not to display his annoyance. As there was nothing more to be learnt, apparently, he took his leave.

He descended the stone stairs—Mr. Thorne's offices were up two flights—in a very thoughtful frame of mind, and when he gained the entrance doorway he stood there for some minutes pulling his ear, as was his habit when in a very meditative mood.

And as he stood thus somebody came along the passage, touched him on the elbow, and said, in a peculiarly squeaking voice—

"Mr. Sugg, could I have a word with you?"

And turning quickly round, the detective beheld a strange-looking, little humpbacked man.

K

CHAPTER XVII.

STRANGE INFORMATION.

THE humpbacked man who had accosted Sugg was a somewhat remarkable person. He was almost a dwarf, and had long pendulous arms, and a pale, cadaverous face, and light-grey, dreamy, expressionless eyes.

"You'll excuse me," he said in a shrill or what seemed like a falsetto voice, "but you have been making some inquiries of Mr. Sulcoates?"

"I have."

"My name is Mobbs—Charles Mobbs—and I'm a copying-clerk in Mr. Thorne's office. But perhaps I had better not be seen talking to you here. Will you take a turn in the Temple Gardens for a few minutes?"

"Certainly," said Sugg, looking at the little man with eager interest. "And now, Mr. Mobbs," he said, when they had reached that part of the gardens where the fountain plays, "I'm at your service."

"Thank you," answered Mobbs deferentially. "You see, I'm not a very prepossessing individual, and I find it deuced hard to make ends meet on twenty-five shillings a week. But though Nature wasn't kind to me when she made me, I suppose I'm of some use in the world; any way I've got a pair of ears, and I've got a pair of eyes; and though I never says much, there ain't many things that come within range of my vision or sound of my ears that escape me."

Calvin Sugg began to look with still keener interest on the queer individual, whose appearance and manner of speaking suggested that he had a grievance against the world in general, and was glad of an opportunity to let off some of his bottled-up wrath.

"I've been ten years in Mr. Thorne's office; and I'm there from nine in the morning till five at night for twenty-five shillings a week. It ain't much, is it?"

"Well, I should certainly be disposed to say you earned your money, Mr. Mobbs."

"Of course I do. But it ain't that I want to talk about. I know that you are a detective, and I guess you've been seeing Mr. Sulcoates about the governor's case."

"Your guess is certainly not far wide of the mark."

"Have you got any clue, do you think?"

Mr. Sugg was rather amused at the blunt and pointed way in which the question was asked, but, with his habitual caution, he answered with another question—

"Will you tell me first what your object is in speaking to me?"

"Oh yes; I think I can give you a tip."

"Indeed!"

"Yes. Mind you, I don't say there's much in it, but I ain't blind, and I ain't deaf, and I ain't altogether a fool."

"I should be disposed to think you are very far from a fool," remarked Sugg, feeling that a little judicious flattery would not be wasted on Mr. Mobbs. Nor was it; for the little humpbacked man smiled sadly and said again, "Thank you," with that marked, deferential manner peculiar to a person whose life has been passed in a humble and dependent position.

"May I ask you to be brief?" remarked Sugg, wishing to bring Mobbs to the point, as he was evidently inclined to run off at a tangent, and pulling out his watch as a gentle reminder that time was flying.

"Certainly, certainly. Of course, what I'm going to say to you you'll consider as a confidential communication."

"Beyond all question of doubt I will."

"Well, now, do you know Perley Beck?"

"No; except by name."

"He was the governor's confidential clerk, but sharp as the governor was, I'm open to bet a week's salary that Beck was sharper."

"What do you mean?" asked Sugg quickly.

"Maybe I mean a good deal, and maybe I don't. It depends how you take it, and whether you think I'm a fool or not."

Sugg saw that the small man wanted humouring, and he answered kindly—"I have already told you that I think you are very far from being a fool."

"Thank you," repeated Mobbs, with the same deferential manner. "They think I'm a fool up in the office, though; and Beck once called me an unmitigated ass because I spoilt three folios of a deed I was copying. But I ain't so much an ass as Mr. Beck is a rogue."

Calvin Sugg's interest was increasing more and more.

"Indeed. Do you know anything against him?"

"Well, I know certain things which, as lawyers say, might be regarded as presumptive evidence, though it would probably be rejected as such in a court of law."

Mr. Mobbs was obviously tedious and unnecessarily prolix in his story-telling, so Sugg once more pulled out his watch as a gentle reminder, and observed, with much suavity—

"Would you kindly come to the point, Mr. Mobbs, for I fear I shall have to run away?"

The hint seemed to be lost upon Mobbs. In fact, he acted as though he had not heard it, and said—

"Look here, suppose we go and have a glass of ale and a sandwich."

Then he added quickly, as if he feared he might be misunderstood—"Of course, I'll pay for them."

Although the humpbacked man's loquacity was somewhat trying to the patience, Sugg was far too experienced to say anything that might be calculated to close his mouth; for was it not possible that he knew something that would prove of value in helping the detective to unravel the mystery with which he was confronted?

So, with a bland smile, he accepted the invitation, and the two men adjourned to a neighbouring tavern beloved of lawyers' clerks, copyists, and hangers-on. A seedy, wolfish lot all of them, with polished elbow-sleeves, down-at-heel shoes, and frayed trouser-legs.

As it yet wanted some time to the luncheon-hour, the bar was all but deserted, and having given the order for the sandwiches and ale, which he insisted on paying for in spite of Sugg's protest, Mr. Mobbs led the way to a snug corner where there was a small round-topped table and a form. It was not until Mobbs had finished his humble repast that he resumed the thread of his discourse.

"What I was going to say was this," he began: "Perley Beck was as sharp as needles, and though he was confidential clerk to the governor, I don't think the governor trusted him very much."

"But what has this got to do with the murder case?" asked Sugg, anxious to keep his companion from becoming discursive again.

"I'm coming to that," answered Mobbs in a tone that implied he intended to proceed in his own way or not at all. "Now, what was the name of Vesta Florence's husband?"

"Ricardo."

"Very well. Now, Perley Beck was well acquainted with Ricardo."

Mr. Sugg was all alert now, and the light in his eyes showed how keenly interested he was.

"Excuse me," he said, "if I ask you if you have direct evidence of that?"

"Of course I have. I've posted more than one letter for Beck addressed 'Eugène Ricardo, Esq., Linda Villa, St. John's Wood.' And one evening I had to take some papers from the office over to Mr. Beck's house. He lived in the Brixton Road, and from the style he kept up he might have been getting a thousand a year, instead of three hundred and fifty, which was his salary Just as I was leaving the house a cab drove up to the gate, and a man got out, and handed an awfully swell lady out. She made me stare, for she was as pretty a woman as I've ever seen. Beck came running down the gravel-path of his garden, and I heard him exclaim, 'How do you do, Mrs. Ricardo?' and then, to the man, 'Well, Ricardo, old fellow, how are you? I'm awfully glad you've come.' After I got away I puzzled my head to try and think where I had seen the lady, for her face was familiar to me; and then it suddenly flashed across my mind that she was Vesta Florence, whose portraits used to be in every photographic shop window. On the Saturday night of that week I had a shilling's worth of gallery at the theatre where she was performing, and I recognised her at once. About two months after that, Beck was much engaged with the governor one morning about something or other, and he came to me in a very bad temper, and slipped a little note into my hand without any address on it, and told me to take it to the theatre where Vesta Florence was performing, and to ask for her and give it to her into her own hands, and wait for an answer. I did so, and when she had read the note she said, 'Tell Mr. Beck I'm awfully sorry he can't come, and as I'm engaged this afternoon I shall not be able to see him.' When I told Beck this he swore and said some uncomplimentary things about the governor. Some time after that I was remaining at the office late one night to finish copying two mortgage deeds. Beck was there too, and just as I had finished my work a knock came to the door, and when I opened the door Ricardo was there, and he asked for Mr. Beck. As I had nothing more to do, I put on my hat and coat and took my departure, leaving Ricardo and Beck together in the office. Now, I ask you, Mr. Sugg, whether you think there is anything suspicious in what I have told you?"

Sugg had become exceedingly thoughtful, and appeared to be gazing away into vacancy, but the question recalled him to himself, and he answered—

"Eh? Oh—ah—yes! Well, that is, it's singular— very singular. But tell me, Mr. Mobbs, what sort of a man was Ricardo in appearance?"

"He was very dark, with small black eyes."

"Was he tall?"

"No; about middle height. He had a large moustache curled at the ends, and his hair was cut short."

"Was he stout?"

"No; rather thin than stout."

Sugg recognised the accuracy of the portrait, and though he did not give any outward indication of his feelings, he was deeply impressed with the important bearing this revelation might have on the case which he had in hand.

"Have you ever seen Ricardo since then?"

"No; and I don't know what became of him after the murder of his wife."

"You are aware, I suppose, that after Mr. Glindon's murder a son of his came forward and took possession of the estate?"

"Yes; I heard it talked about in our office."

"You have never seen Mr. Glindon's son?"

" No."

" You will be very much surprised to hear, then, that the man you knew as Ricardo is Ivan Glindon, and he has succeeded to all the late Mr. Glindon's property."

Mobbs' small eyes opened to their fullest possible extent, and his pale face was lighted up with unusual animation.

" Lor ! " he cried ; " you don't say so ! "

" It is true and strange," replied Sugg. " Now, do you happen to know what has become of Perley Beck ? "

" No ; he chucked up his situation soon after the murder, because, he said, he couldn't get on with Sulcoates."

" And you have never seen him since ? "

" No."

The two men sat silent for some minutes. It was clear that Mobbs had nothing more to tell. At last he said he must be getting back, and he rose to go. Sugg rose also, and they walked to the door together. Then the detective asked Mobbs at what address Beck lived in Brixton.

" Oh, he's not there now," said Mobbs.

" How do you know ? "

" Because two or three letters came to the office for him, and they were re-addressed to his house at Brixton, but came back marked 'Gone away.' "

" What became of those letters ? " asked Sugg, with more eagerness than he was in the habit of displaying.

" For anything I know they are in the office still."

" Look here," said Sugg, "if you can get them for

me without any one knowing about it, I will give you
a couple of sovereigns."

"I'll do it, if they are to be got hold of!" exclaimed
Mobbs, with an air of determination that he scarcely
seemed capable of a minute before. But two sovereigns to such a man was a large sum. "I can't get
out again, though, till luncheon-time—that is, one
o'clock. Be by the fountain in the court at that time,
and I'll come to you."

On this understanding they parted. It was then
half-past eleven, and Calvin Sugg was somewhat at
a loss how to get over the time, for though he had
plenty to do, he could not very well go away and get
back in time for the appointment; and his eagerness
to possess the letters caused him to feel indifferent
about everything else for the time being.

Of course, there was the possibility that the letters
were not of the slightest importance so far as he was
concerned, but in view of the information given him
by Mobbs, and which was undoubtedly of startling
significance, it was his duty not to let any chance
slip that promised ever so vaguely to throw light where
all was now dark.

And so he strolled along the Strand and came
back to Fleet Street; then proceeded leisurely to the
Temple, and by the time he reached Fountain Court
it was just one o'clock. But for fully twenty minutes
he waited before Mobbs put in an appearance.

"I had to wait until Mr. Sulcoates went out," said
the little man, "as I was not sure where the letters
were. I found them at last in the rack in Mr. Sul-

coates' room. You must promise me, however, that, whatever comes out of this matter, you will not say that I gave you the letters."

"You can perfectly rely upon my not doing so," answered Sugg.

Then Mr. Mobbs drew from his pocket an unsealed blue envelope, and handed it to the detective with the remark—"There are three of them in there."

Sugg opened the envelope and found three sealed letters, each addressed, "Perley Beck, Esq., c/o Hilkiah Thorne, Esq., Solicitor, Inner Temple, London, E.C." They had been re-addressed to Brixton, and then returned to the original address, marked by the Post-Office people in red ink, "Gone away"

"Are you going to open them now?" asked Mobbs, evidently a little curious to know their contents.

"No, not here." He placed two sovereigns in the hand of Mobbs, whose thin fingers closed greedily upon them, and he squeaked out—"Thanks, ever so much."

Then Mr. Sugg wished him good-afternoon, and going into the Strand he hailed a hansom, and told the cabman to drive to Clapham.

CHAPTER XVIII.

THE UNBIDDEN GUEST.

ALTHOUGH for some days after Calvin Sugg's visit to Rutland House, Ivan Glindon appeared to be troubled and uneasy, the feeling gradually wore off, and he recovered his wonted spirits. But he did not let the subject of the ring drop, for he wrote the following little note to Calvin Sugg:—

"SIR,—Referring to the subject of our conversation the other day, when you called upon me, I beg to say that I am prepared to pay you the sum of fifty pounds if you will restore the ring to me. This is a large sum, but the ring is an heirloom and greatly prized. I hope you will accept the offer; otherwise I shall instruct my solicitor to take action against you for unlawful possession."

This note had not the desired effect, for Mr. Sugg ignored it, and he hoped that Glindon would carry out his threat and commence an action. There is no doubt that Glindon had the law on his side in the matter, but, for reasons of his own, he did not show that he was in any hurry to avail himself of it. Perhaps his time was too much occupied in attending to his many guests, for it might almost be said that he kept open house, and what his guests lacked in quality they made up for in numbers.

But though life seemed to glide on so pleasantly in Rutland House, and its inmates appeared to be always in a whirl of gaiety and excitement, Mr. Glindon had his skeleton, as every one else has. It is necessary to say here that he had taken to himself another wife, who was as striking a contrast to Vesta Florence as it was possible, perhaps, for a woman to be.

The first Mrs. Glindon—or Ricardo—was a charming woman in every sense, with hair like threads of gold, a figure that was perfect, a face that was like a Madonna. Her successor was a coarse-faced woman, with hair as black as jet and almost like horse-hair in texture. Her hands and feet were large, and her body disproportioned without being actually deformed. She was sullen in disposition, and of a suspicious and jealous nature.

To this suspicion and this jealousy was attributable, no doubt, in a large measure the cat-and-dog life that the ill-matched pair led. She could not bear him out of her sight, and he could not bear her in his sight. She protested and vowed by many saints—for she was a Greek Catholic—that she loved the very ground he walked upon, and he was no less emphatic in his assertions that he hated her.

Let it not be supposed, however, that this man and woman, who were each playing a strange part in this strange drama of life, allowed their feelings to betray themselves in the presence of their friends. They both of them seemed to know the art of dissembling to perfection, and they could both act the hypocrite with consummate skill and ease, as if to the manner born. She was a Russian, like himself, and they had the advantage of being able to say many ugly things to each other without the fear of being understood by inquisitive servants ; for they would not have a foreign servant in the house, and Russian was a language that English servants were not likely to be acquainted with.

It is really no exaggeration of expression to say that Rutland House was a gilded hell. It was a noble mansion, filled with rich furniture, and there was a lavish display of the power of riches. The men and women who went there revelled in luxury, but the trail of the serpent was over it all. There was no innocence, no happiness. These men and women were what are generally termed "men and women of the world," which is another way of saying that the flowers of life are trampled and crushed in order that the passions may be enjoyed.

It has already been stated that Mr. Glindon having failed to pass the well-guarded portals which give entrance to the mystic region where dwells so-called "society," he had taken his revenge by gathering about him denizens of the murky purlieus of Bohemia. These Bohemians did not represent the brilliancy and the genius of Bohemia, but its passions and its sordidness. Now and again, though rarely, he did attract to his "at homes" an artist of note, a literary man who had made his mark, or an actor or actress of respectability. But these were quite the exceptions. An ill odour somehow clung to the place (figuratively, of course) which was antagonistic to true respectability. If one dare use such an expression without fear of criticism, it might be said that the frequenters of Rutland House were respectable blackguards; but let it be understood that the respectability was put on and taken off with the broadcloth and dressshirts of the men, and the silks and finery of the women.

Occasionally there were some brilliant assemblies in Rutland House; that is, brilliant so far as lights and flowers, gorgeous table decorations, fine dresses, and all the *ct cœteras* that are indispensable to a gay and festive scene are concerned. And there were laughter and song and revel, and the wine sparkled and ran red, and the rare fruits spoke of the sunny climes from whence they came. Many a ragged and shivering wretch passing at such a time may have turned wistful and longing glances to the well-lighted windows and sighed as he heard the boisterous laughter and the swelling music; but, after all, it was like a fair garden in which bloomed nothing but poisonous herbs and flowers, and he of the rags was more truly happy than any one of the giddy throng who tried in the delirium of life to forget that they lived.

It was on such an occasion as here described that a strange incident happened. It was the dawn of a new year—that is, it was early in January—and London was still keeping the New Year Carnival, and parties and balls were the order of the day.

Not to be behind their more aristocratic neighbours,

Mr. and Mrs. Glindon had issued invitations very extensively among their acquaintances for a dance. That very day a wild, blizzard-like snowstorm swept over London, bringing incalculable misery and suffering to thousands and thousands of the poverty-stricken and the homeless. But joy and sorrow, laughter and tears, mingle together, and those who had fat banking accounts and well-lined purses were barely inconvenienced by the storm. At any rate, it kept none of the invited guests away from Rutland House, and for a long time a string of cabs and carriages—for some of those Bohemians did manage to ride in carriages, though how they managed it would have puzzled themselves to tell—continued to bring the lucky ones to the hospitable mansion.

Mrs. Glindon was a spectacle in white satin and a barbaric display of jewellery, and the host really looked gentlemanly in his well-fitting evening-suit, his only adornment, with the exception of a diamond solitaire in his shirt-front, being a magnificent blood-red camellia in the lapel of his coat.

Any one judging Mr. and Mrs. Glindon from their appearance on this particular night might have been excused for envying them. They seemed to be the favourites of a kindly fortune and utterly without a care. Wreathed in smiles, the lady of the house was devoted to her guests, and must have felt more than rewarded by seeing how thoroughly they enjoyed themselves; while Glindon—like a little king of a happy realm—was surrounded with a group of fawners and flatterers, who vied with each other in trying to pay him the greatest homage.

It was all very pitiable, but it was all very human.

A little after midnight a man wearing a heavy top-coat, and with a woollen muffler round his neck, made his way up the broad steps under the portico and boldly rang the bell, as if he had been one of the most privileged of guests.

And when the flunkey, John Thomas, opened the great door the man said he wished to see Mr. Glindon.

"What's your business?" demanded John Thomas haughtily.

"What the deuce has that got to do with you?" was the prompt rejoinder, which had such an effect on poor John Thomas that he fairly staggered and seemed inclined to faint.

Taking advantage of this, the stranger stepped into the hall, closing the door behind him.

This audacious act quite took the flunkey's breath away.

"Look here," said the stranger peremptorily; "you go to your master and tell him that a gentleman wants to see him on important business."

John Thomas looked at the "gentleman" from head to foot, but whatever his thoughts were he kept them to himself, and managed to stammer out a request that the gentleman would give his name.

"Never mind my name. You do as I tell you."

Perhaps the stranger had the evil eye, and managed

to subdue the usually haughty and arrogant John
Thomas; for that important personage became as
mild and tractable as a poodle, and requesting the
stranger to take a seat on one of the antique chairs
that stood in the hall, he went off to find his
master.

But the stranger did not seat himself. He seemed
restless and uneasy, and paced up and down, pausing
occasionally to examine the pictures, the statues or
brackets, and the plants that were arranged in the
hall and on the stairs; and the sounds of revel and
music floated to him, while the aroma of many per-
fumes filled his nostrils.

At last John Thomas returned.

"Mr. Glindon desires you to send your name, or
he can't see you," said he, with an expression of contempt and scorn.

The stranger, with a gesture of irritation, pulled out
a pocket-book from his pocket, tore a leaf out, and
wrote on it—

"An old chum. You *must* see me. Dangerous if
you don't."

He screwed this up in a peculiar way, and
twisted it so that it could not be opened by the
flunkey.

"There," he said peremptorily; "take that to your
master, and look sharp."

The man did as he was told, and in about ten
minutes he returned and requested the stranger to
follow him. Then the stranger smiled like a man

who had won something. He was shown into the library, a rather make-believe sort of place. There were some real books there, but for every real book there were twenty dummies. No one in the household read much, and books were at a discount.

The stranger glanced round, and there was a sneer on his face. It wasn't a pleasant face, by any means; it was marked with dissipation, and was wicked in its expression. He opened his top-coat, revealing an under-coat that was frayed and shabby, and he placed his wet and greasy-looking hat on the table.

Then the door opened and Glindon appeared, and when he saw who the stranger was he grew deadly pale, and his eyes glittered with the fire of suppressed passion.

The visitor advanced a step or two and stretched out his hand, saying the while, with a certain gruff heartiness—

"Well, old fellow, how are you ?"

Glindon did not take the outstretched hand, but, positively glaring at his evidently unwelcome visitor, he said wrathfully—

"You do not expect me to say that I am glad you are here, do you ?"

CHAPTER XIX.

THROUGH DARKNESS AND TRIAL.

ALTHOUGH it often seems as if men made their own fate, Shakespeare gave expression to a great truth when he said, "There is a divinity that shapes our ends, rough hew them how we will." When Raymond Penoyre went out to the West Indies he took a very sombre view of life; and had he been endowed with less common-sense and had had less self-respect, he might have sullied his career by rash and reckless conduct.

To a youth who stands on the threshold of manhood and views the future through a roseate medium, love is the one absorbing thought of his life. Cynics may scoff and philosophers sneer, but the fact remains that there must be something wrong with a youth who does not feel that love is life, and that there can be no life without love. For is it not true that youth is a dream, manhood an awakening, old age a regret?

Nothing, therefore, can test a young man more than a love disappointment. It is true that it is seldom, if ever, that it has the same disastrous effect upon him as it has upon a woman. But certainly for the time being, unless he be devoid of all sentiment, it gives a bitterness to his existence which seems to make his life not worth living.

When Raymond parted from Muriel Glindon he was crushed, or at any rate he thought he was. It was so hard to have his bright hopes suddenly blighted, and the cup of nectar, that was just touching his lips, roughly snatched away and dashed to the ground. Up to that terrible day when the hand of a cowardly assassin struck Mr. Glindon down Raymond Penoyre had only seen the world from its brightest side. His home life had been without shadow or sorrow, and his love for Muriel was the crown of his happiness. The sudden change, therefore, was all the more terrible, and he went abroad with a shadowy wish in his heart that his days might end. He found great consolation, however, in the letters that Muriel sent him. They were always so full of good common-sense and rich in expressions of love for him. She carefully avoided mentioning her own great sorrow, and she counselled him to "hope and wait, to pray and work." He found it hard to wait and hard to hope, but work kept him from sinking into despair, and in the new sphere in which his lines were cast he found much to interest him.

The greater part of his time was spent in Kingston, Jamaica. The climate suited him, while the glowing skies, the brilliant sunshine, the magnificent foliage, and the turquoise sea aroused to enthusiasm his artistic instincts, and the efforts of his brush and pencil led his friends to predict for him a distinguished career as an artist.

When he had been away a little over a year he received a sudden summons to return home, as his father was stricken with dangerous illness, and was not expected to recover. Although Raymond took the next steamer sailing for England after the receipt of the letter, he arrived too late, as his father had been dead for some weeks. As a pension Mr. Penoyre had enjoyed ceased at his death, the family found themselves in straitened circumstances, and they had to remove from Windsor to a humbler abode in town, and the girls were compelled to try and turn their talents to account. It was a terrible blow to their pride, but pride availeth little where there is an empty purse.

As soon as ever an opportunity occurred after his arrival in England, Raymond went to see Muriel. The meeting was a very tender one, and forgetting her own deep sorrow, she expressed the greatest sympathy for him.

She had changed very much since he had parted from her. The girlish expression of face had given place to a grave, thoughtful, womanly one; and if she smiled, it was a smile of sadness rather than joy. She and her aunt occupied part of a small house at Fulham; and she had succeeded in getting together a number of pupils, whereby she was enabled to be independent of her aunt's income.

As Raymond now was entirely dependent upon his

own exertions for his living, and as his prospects.were good, for he undoubtedly had talent, and his friends were willing to help him to turn them to good account, he urged her to become his wife. He used the old, old argument that ardent lovers have ever used. He told her that with her by his side to encourage and stimulate him he would do great deeds, but that without her his life would be a purposeless one.

"You must not say that, Raymond," she answered, "you are too noble and too sincere to let your life become purposeless. Remember that, before you went away, I told you I would never marry until the mystery surrounding my father's death was cleared up."

"But, Muriel," he exclaimed imploringly, "that may never be."

"True, dear; it may never be, as you say. And yet I am far from hopeless. Indeed, Mr. Sugg is more sanguine than ever, and only a few days ago he expressed a very confident opinion that he would yet succeed in bringing my father's murderer to justice."

"But these detectives are always sanguine, or, at any rate, profess to be so," urged Raymond. "They don't like to have to own to defeat. I am afraid, however, too long a time has elapsed for the mystery to be solved. If Sugg couldn't do it at the time, he is not likely to do it now."

"I think, dear, you do him an injustice," said Muriel gently, and yet with some reproach in her tone. "I feel sure, myself, that where Mr. Sugg has failed no man would have succeeded. But, any way, I do not like to hear anything said against him; for he has been kindness itself to me, and has kept me from sinking into black despair."

"I don't wish to say a word against him," answered Raymond, "and I am sure I am very grateful for the kindness he has shown you. But I think, having regard to the utter uncertainty of his succeeding in the task he has set himself, that you and I should study our own interests and happiness, and unite our destinies; for love that is sundered can only be provocative of misery and distrust."

"It may be so, Raymond," she answered quietly, but with touching sadness; "and if you really think so, would it not be better for you to forget me?"

"Forget you!" he cried, with a warmth of expression that he had never displayed towards her before. "How can I forget you? Do you suppose that my love for you is a mere sham or shadow?"

"No, I do not," she answered decisively.

"Then why wish me to give you up?"

"Ah, Raymond! you are unjust. I have expressed no such wish. Do you suppose that a woman finds pleasure in torturing her own heart? When I look back to the bright and happy days I spent with you at The Priory, I feel as if I should go mad. You won my love then, and you hold it still. No one else in this world can ever possess it. That love has sustained me in my awful sorrow, and in the darkness in which I have been so cruelly plunged it has been the one ray of light that has given me hope and led me on."

"And yet you refuse to become my wife?" he said, with just a touch of irritability.

"I do, in your own interest," she answered.

"Well, upon my word, Muriel, that is a paradox. How can it possibly be to my interest? On the contrary, your refusal makes me unhappy and miserable."

"Let us agree to differ, dear," she replied. "At any rate, my decision is unalterable, and yet my love for you is stronger than ever. But Heaven forbid that I should be a bar to your progress in any way I repeat again that it is better, perhaps, that you should endeavour to forget me. The world is before you, and you can go forth to seek fame and fortune. You are a man, and can fight the battle of life untrammelled; but my sphere is limited, and I seem at present to have but one duty, and that is to endeavour to clear up the mystery about my father. To me he was all that was noble and true; but my half-brother aspersed his memory and uttered dark hints against his honour. And I cannot forget, nor can you forget, that my dear father himself hinted at something that might set the tongue of scandal wagging. The fact that he kept the existence of my brother from me proves that the something he hinted at was not a chimera. How, then, could I, in justice to myself, become any man's wife while this mystery is unsolved? It would be like a millstone round my neck, an incubus upon my life; and should at any time a disagreement arise between me and my husband, I should be liable to be reminded that there was some dark stain upon my father's honour."

"Do you suppose, Muriel," asked Raymond in amazement, "that I am capable of ever throwing that into your face?"

"I do not say that you are—I do not hint that you are—but I am morbidly sensitive on the matter, and the stand I have taken I shall maintain."

"So be it," exclaimed Penoyre, with a great sigh. "All I have got to say, then, in the matter is, that your love does not equal mine."

He was much cut up, and his emotion showed itself in his tremulous voice and tearful eyes.

She was not less affected, but she made a brave struggle to control her feelings; for she was afraid that, if she gave way in the slightest degree, she would break down altogether. It was a terrible trial to her—an ordeal that only a brave and really noble woman could have gone through as she was going through it.

"I will not contradict you, Raymond," she answered; "your own conscience will do that. But I do ask you, beg of you, not to press me any further in the matter. I believe honestly that it is more to your true interests to give me up. Somewhere in the world you will find a brighter and happier woman than I am, who will be to you all that a wife should be. I have had my day. The fair fruits that seemed to be blossoming for me have suddenly fallen withered at my feet. From the light of the high noonday sun I have been suddenly plunged into darkness, and times have been, of late, when I have wished that the grass was waving above

my grave. Perhaps it is impious, but when we are
weary we cannot help longing for rest."

He could constrain himself no longer. All the
emotion and sentiment of his nature was aroused,
and with a cry that burst involuntarily from his lips,
he caught her in his arms.

"Muriel—Muriel, you must not talk like that!" he
exclaimed. "You are as yet only in the morning of
your life, and before you lie many bright and happy
years. Forgive me for what I have said. I know how
great, how strong, how pure your love for me is. I
have been impatient; I have been harsh—ay, even
cruel; but find some excuse for me, dear. My love
for you is no passing fancy. It has grown and
strengthened day by day and month by month since
I first saw you. Both our fortunes are changed, and
we find ourselves face to face with the world, and
we must make our future. But I neither shrink nor
tear. I shall work cheerfully and honestly, and make
a bid for fame. It may pass me by, but what of
that? I shall find good work to do, and my life shall
be neither aimless nor useless. But since we have to
climb the hill, let us breast it together. Give me the
right to shield you. Let me have the proud privilege
of protecting your good name. Become my wife, and
let us find our happiness in each other's presence."

His touch and pressure broke down her strength,
so far as her self-control was concerned, and she was
now sobbing bitterly. She was a womanly woman,
after all, and yet her very weakness was her strength;

and when he again urged her to say "Yes" to his pleading, she answered—

"I love you, Raymond, and am proud of the love you give me, and yet I must be firm; I must not yield in my determination. It is better for you that I do not, although you do not believe it, and cannot see it in that light. To me it is an awful, a heart-rending sacrifice to have to refuse your request. But it must be—it must be. I must be cruel only to be kind."

He turned from her with a sense of disappointment that no words could have adequately expressed, and though he tried hard to keep back the tears, they would flow. It was surely not weakness, for it proved the depth of his feelings.

At this moment Mrs. Romanoff entered the room, and was naturally surprised to find her niece and Penoyre both in tears.

"What is the meaning of this?" the lady asked, thinking there had been a quarrel.

Muriel threw her arms about her aunt's neck, and sobbed out—

"Oh aunt, I am so glad you have come! Raymond urges me and presses me to become his wife; but I must not, cannot yield to him. He thinks me cruel and unkind, but tell him that I am not so."

"No; she is wrong," cried Penoyre, turning round impetuously, his face red, his eyes dim. "I could not possibly think that of her. But I cannot recognise the necessity for delaying our marriage."

"And yet the necessity exists," said Mrs. Romanoff firmly. "I know the views my niece holds, and I am in entire accord with them. We are under a deep shadow at present, and until the shadow passes away she would not be wise to marry. You are both young yet, and can afford to wait. And do not forget, Raymond, that a true man best proves his strength and devotion to duty by patience and firmness."

"It shall be so, then," answered Raymond, with a sigh. "I *will* wait, and if aught that I can do will help to lift the shadow from off your lives, I will do it."

Muriel braced herself up with an effort, and going from her aunt to Penoyre, she took both his hands in hers, and looking into his face, she said—

"Your words are words of comfort to me. To him who waits the triumph comes. Our days, surely, cannot always be dark, and after sorrow's night the day dawns."

CHAPTER XX.

THE seedy stranger who had arrived so inopportunely at Rutland House on the night of the ball was lacking neither in impudence nor self-assurance. It was not less certain that he was by no means a welcome guest. Nevertheless, he made himself at home. His raiment, on the night that he arrived, was not such as would have enabled him to appear with dignity in the ballroom. But, indeed, he had no desire to do so.

"You promised me," said Glindon, "when you went away that you would not return."

"I did; but in this life we are all creatures of circumstance. The fact is, I am hard up——"

"Hard up!" exclaimed Glindon in surprise.

"Yes. Don't look so struck. The cards are responsible for it. I knew, however, that I should always find a friend in you; so here I am."

"But not to stay, I hope?"

"That depends. You seem to have exceedingly comfortable quarters here. However, I am not unreasonable, and I have a proposition to make when you can devote a little time to listening to it. What I want now is a comfortable bed, a good supper, and a blow-out of fizz. I don't want to disturb your arrangements or startle your guests. So fix me in a room by myself and I shall be all right. When I've had some supper I shall sleep for twenty-four hours right away, for I've travelled all the way from Vienna with scarcely a wink. Now, don't scowl at me, you know, old chappie. I've been a good friend to you, and you must be a friend to me."

"But I have already done all that I promised to do," growled Glindon angrily.

"You have, dear boy, handsomely. But I tell you I've fallen on evil days, and cannot sink while you are afloat."

The result was, a very snug and comfortable room was allotted to the stranger, who partook of a substantial supper, which was more than moistened with a plentiful supply of champagne, for which he seemed to have a decided partiality.

He did not sleep twenty-four hours, as he said he would, but did a good twelve. He did not rise, however, like a giant refreshed; he was limp, weak, and pallid. He was a fair man, with light hair and blue eyes, and a drooping moustache. His smooth white hands and shapely nails indicated that he had never done hard manual labour, and he spoke like a man who was well educated. But there was a certain bloated appearance about him, as if he had been drinking heavily for a long time, and a certain wildness of the eyes and a twitching of the hands confirmed this.

Having procured the services of a servant, he demanded that a bottle of champagne might be brought to him, and as a demand for brandies and sodas was not unusual in Rutland House the first thing in the morning, the butler was not very much astonished at the order for champagne. And so a bottle was duly taken to the "seedy gent," as the servant described him, and when the cork had been drawn it was not long before the contents were disposed of.

A little later the "seedy gent," having performed his toilet, found his way down to the breakfast-room, where a cheerful fire was blazing; and when he had warmed himself he proceeded to an exploration of the drawing and other rooms; though, apparently, he was not much impressed nor much interested; and returning to the breakfast-room, he rang the bell and asked for some hot brandy and water, which was duly supplied to him.

After the night's revels the inmates of Rutland House were in no hurry to get up, and the strange visitor had the breakfast-room to himself till noon had passed, when Mrs. Glindon, looking faded and tired, appeared, clad in a wonderful tea-gown of bright green, while her raven tresses were loosely confined by a handkerchief of brilliant scarlet; and this remarkable combination of colours, which made her sallow complexion look infinitely sallower, had a very striking effect. The stranger was dozing on the sofa: but the entrance of the lady disturbed him, and he sat up. She was evidently not prepared for the presence of any one in the room, and she looked a little startled.

"Ex—excuse me," she stammered, "I—I did not know there was any one here. You are a friend of my husband's, I suppose?"

"Who is your husband, madam?"

"I am the wife of Mr. Glindon," she said haughtily.

A smirking, half-imbecile smile spread itself over the stranger's chalky face as he answered—

"Well—yes. I'm a good friend to your husband. But I did not know he was married. How long have you been his wife?"

He stared so fixedly and rudely at Mrs. Glindon that she felt quite uneasy, although she was pretty well used to the queer ways of some of the queer Bohemians who frequented the house.

"Well, really, sir, that's a strange question to ask," she said. "Perhaps you will inform me who you are first of all."

"Oh, your husband will do that, I dare say," answered the stranger, with a grin; and Mrs. Glindon felt so uncomfortable and uneasy that she excused herself and beat a hasty retreat.

Half an hour later Glindon himself put in an appearance. He was surly, and looked out of sorts.

"I say," exclaimed the stranger, "where did you pick that old woman up? I suppose she's your wife?"

"Beyond all manner of doubt."

"Well, dear boy, I'm sorry for you. After dear

little Vesta Florence, she is—well, I won't say what; but I thought you would have done better than that."

"Yes; so did I," growled Glindon. "But, as you said last night, we are creatures of circumstance."

"Oh ho! I see. It's that way, is it? Well, you ought to survive her," he added, with a strange look in his eyes.

The two men partook of breakfast, the stranger flavouring his coffee with brandy; and after breakfast they adjourned to the smoking-room, and Glindon suggested to his friend that it would be advisable for him to provide himself with quarters somewhere else; but the friend said—

"I'm very comfortable, dear boy, and intend to pull myself together here for a while. The missus and I will no doubt get on all right."

"I wish to the Lord you would take the missus and strangle her," growled Glindon savagely.

The stranger whistled and put his finger to his nose; and while the imbecile smile came into his face again, he said—

"Mum, mum. A wink is as good as a nod to a blind ass. But why, oh! why, dear boy, did you let such a siren bewitch you?"

Glindon did not offer any explanation. He was moody and sullen, and for some time they smoked their cigars in silence; and then they went out together.

In the course of a few days, thanks to the liberality of Mr. Glindon, the stranger had attired himself in a

manner more becoming the fine house in which he
had taken up his quarters. But it was very evident
that he had a fatal weakness in the shape of a craving
for stimulants. He was one of those peculiarly con-
stituted men who can imbibe an enormous amount
of alcohol without exhibiting the common symptoms
of intoxication. He soaked it in, as it were, until it
oozed out again through his skin; but though his
voice became husky, his eyes bleared, and his manner
strange, he was enabled to preserve a steadiness of
gait and a semblance of intelligence. Glindon was
not slow to note his weakness, but he did nothing
to counteract it. On the contrary, he encouraged it,
and fostered it with an obvious purpose.

For a whole fortnight the strange guest kept his
room on the plea of ill health, and during the time
his principal diet was champagne. But at last he
seemed to recover somewhat, and he reappeared, very
pallid, very blear-eyed, and very shaky. Then he
swore off for the time, and could be persuaded to take
nothing but tea. Mrs. Glindon avoided him. His
presence in the house filled her with alarm, and led
to some very strong scenes between herself and her
husband. She insisted on his being sent away, and
her husband insisted that he would have whom he
liked in his own house. The stranger was not un-
mindful of these matrimonial squabbles, nor was he
ignorant of the fact that he was the immediate cause
of them.

It chanced one evening that the stranger and Glindon

sat together in the drawing-room. An elegant roor
it was; and being very large, it was divided by massiv
curtains of purple velvet that could be drawn in col
weather. The room could be entered by four differen
doorways—two at either end. Being "Liberty Hall,
as Glindon termed it, he and his guests smoked in th
drawing-room when it so pleased them.

It was a bitterly cold night, and he and the strange
sat before the cheerful fire that blazed in the gree
steel grate. They were both smoking, and on a sma
round table near each was a little polished coffee-po
with sugar-basin and cups. The curtains were draw
and the gentlemen were taking their ease.

It chanced that afternoon that the matrimonial sk
had been unusually cloudy, and as evening drew c
a storm burst and for some time raged with unusu
fury. This storm had for a time been the subject
conversation between the two men, but a silence he
fallen upon them. Then suddenly the stranger, wl
had evidently been pondering on the conversatio
started up in his chair, and leaning towards his con
panion, said—

"Look here, Glindon, if that woman was my wife,
should have an undertaker's bill to pay for her in le
than a month."

"Pshaw! I'm not such a fool as to run a risk of th
kind," answered Glindon languidly.

"There need be no risk."

"What do you mean?" asked the other, with
display of animation.

" Well, old fellow, you are obtuse. There are more
ways of killing a cat than one. When I was in
Moscow I had a chum. He was a student in the
Government laboratory, at the school of experimental
chemistry."

" Well ? " cried Glindon, showing awakened interest
and sitting upright, with his head inclined towards his
guest; and so absorbed were they both that they did
not observe that the velvet curtains were agitated, and
where they met in the centre a face appeared, but
quickly withdrew again.

" Well, my chum told me once that he had a drug
in his possession a dozen drops of which, given to a
human being, produced symptoms identical with apoplexy, and death would ensue in from one to two days,
and all the medical skill in the world could not tell
that the victim had not died of apoplexy."

" Would to heaven I had a dozen drops ! " said
Glindon, with a sigh, as he fell back in his chair
again.

" Would you give them to her if you had ? "

" No, dear old boy ; I would get you to do it for me,"
answered Glindon sarcastically.

" What would you stand ? " asked the " dear old
boy."

" I should say it would be cheap at five thousand,"
was the answer, with a sneering laugh.

But the stranger was terribly serious, and springing
up, he exclaimed—

" **Give me your hand on it !** "

A pallor spread over Glindon's face, and he became excited.

" Do you mean to say that you have some of those drops? " he asked hoarsely.

" Yes.   I brought a small phial from Russia."

The curtains moved again, and the tips of fingers were just visible.   Somebody was evidently listening. But the men were all-unconscious of it.   Glindon grasped the proffered hand, and he said in a rough, raspy voice—

"Do it, and I will place in your hand brand-new Bank of England notes for five thousand pounds, on condition that you go away and never come back again."

" It's a bargain.   It shall be done this very night. Pick a quarrel with the missus.   Excite her, so that when she is seized with illness it will seem but the natural outcome of passion.   Do you understand? "

"I do," answered Glindon, with a grim smile. Then he added, "You are a pleasant sort of fiend to have in the house, but when once a fellow has gone wrong in this world he is glad enough sometimes to make friends even with the devil."

The tips of the fingers were suddenly withdrawn from the curtains, and half an hour later a woman, clad in a heavy sealskin cloak, clandestinely left the house, and securing a cab, she told the cabman to drive her to Fulham.

CHAPTER XXI.

THE STRANGE LETTER.

WHEN Mr. Calvin Sugg arrived home after his interview with Mobbs, the humpbacked lawyer's clerk, he
shut himself up in his sanctum, and proceeded to open
the letters which he had got from Mobbs, and which
were addressed to Perley Beck. Two of them were of
no interest, at any rate not to the detective, one being
a tailor's bill, and the other from a racing tipster
peremptorily demanding immediate payment of a large
sum due to him for "tips."

But the third was a remarkable document as well as
a puzzle. It was written on large letter-paper, with a
black border nearly quarter of an inch deep. It bore
no address, but had stamped on it for heading a skull
and cross-bones, and the motto *Heu!* The following
is a literal copy of the letter :—

"COMRADE IN DARKNESS,

"I take your hand. Ten thousand thanks
for your last and your advice. I am letting the latter simmer
in my brain, which is all aflame with torturing thoughts. Sometimes I think I am dead and the worms revel on me. But at
others I drink in life, until, like brandy, it sets my blood on fire,
and then comes upon me the craving of the ghoul. Bah! Why

should I talk thus to you, who are saturated with the law's jargon —you, who are incapable of a thought beyond the flesh? Your philosophy goes no deeper than mouldy parchment and red tape.

"I soar upward into the region of speculation and dream dreams. I revel amongst the air-drawn fiends of a mind that knows no rest. With me life is a passion, a poem of wildness and frenzy. With you it is a tame thing in which the only problem that vexes you is how to vary your dinner. I grant you that he who can cater successfully for the appetite of the epicure is an artist. But while ortolans and quails would not satisfy me, you would fatten on a vulgar steak; while I could laugh in mine enemy's ear as he lay a-dying, you would faint if you crushed a snail.

"What is it that constitutes the difference in men? We all have hearts and stomachs, livers and lungs. But these things are dust. There is something else that is not dust. Ah! therein is the great secret. It is that something that makes us fool or philosopher; which enables us to soar to heaven or plunge to hell; which enables us to see life either as a curse or a blessing. To me it has been a curse, and I have resented the gift which I asked not for. But since I live I live. Yet I hate life, though fear to die. Why should one fear? Fear what? Not the worms, for what matters it that they feed upon your senseless dust? Not the cold earth that surrounds you and seals you down, for your wretched clay is not conscious of it; not the torture of the damned, for life is a more exquisite torture than the fiends could possibly devise; and death is but as a kindly draught that closes the tired eyes in sleep, and deafens the ears to the groans that go up for ever to the stars from maddened humanity.

"What *is it*, then, we fear? Do any of your mouldy tomes of law answer the question? Or must it be sought for in the mystic writings of the ancient Egyptians? No; neither will give it. The dead alone can answer, but the dead are voiceless. The world is composed of dead men's dust. More men have died than there are sands on the sea-shore, yet we who live fear to die. This is a problem over which the Sphinx is dumb. The world is beautiful, but we hate it; life is a fever, and we cling to it; death is rest, and we fear it. Here be matter, my masters, for wonder. Will *no one* read me the riddle?

"You will say I rave. Well, better to rave than to live like

A worm in the earth. Some men have no more minds than worms; but others can gaze into the sun and clutch at the stars. I am of this class.

"But, my dear comrade, all the foregoing will be to you like pictures to a blind man, or like music to him who hath no ears.

"You are of the earth earthy. As for me, I am a child of the sun. This cold-blooded country freezes my marrow; but in a few days I, shall have shaken its accursed dust from my feet. You bid me go North to the land of the Czar; but I have had enough of it. Its dreariness, its sordidness, are worse than this. There, the millions are slaves who bow down and worship the Czar on his throne, and think him a god. They should rise in their might and hurl him to destruction; then they could shout 'Hosanna! We are free!' But FEAR keeps thirty millions of them in chains. Fear! How hateful the word! Fear is the primeval curse. No; I go to the sun—to where the air is dreamy and languid with the scent of flowers which will destroy the scent of blood; where colour dazzles the eye and the richness of nature ravishes the senses. There, and there only, shall I feel life again thrilling through my veins. And yet I am suffering from an embarrassment of riches; for the sun lands are many, and where should I go? I think it will be to the glorious Antilles, that float in seas of shimmering gold, and where the skies are aflame with amethyst and ruby. There one may enjoy the essence of life; here naught but the dregs.

"Here I am mad; there I shall be sane. Here there is a grave in my heart; there I can root it out. Will you not go with me? Come and join me at the old place two nights from this, when the hand of time points to the eighth hour. Then over an æsthetic feast, with draughts of amber and ruby wine, we'll thrash the subject out. What say you, my comrade? Shall it be so? Send me a message ere the sun goes down after you receive this. But if it cannot be, and we meet no more until we reach the Plutonian shore, farewell! We have known some glorious delirium together, but men's hands are against us, and we must be silent and watchful; one might tolerate dying the death of a gentleman, but to die the death of a dog—Pshaw! How the flesh creeps at the thought of it! But the lights grow dim and my familiar demons are round me again.—Yours as ever,   "THE PRINCE OF DARKNESS."

As Calvin Sugg finished reading this truly **extra-ordinary** document his brain was almost in a whirl. Cool and clear-headed as he usually was, he felt that the puzzle was getting more abstruse. The letter was hardly the letter of a sane man; and if written by a mad one, there was method in his madness. What did it point to? Was it not perfectly evident that there was much to read between the lines? And Sugg asked himself what bearing, if any, it had upon the dark mystery he was trying to clear up.

It bore no date, but it must have been written many months before, and it left no doubt that between the writer and Perley Beck there had been intimacy, and there was some secret bond between them. What was that bond? A very much less shrewd and clever man than Sugg could not have failed to jump to the conclusion that the bond was some guilty knowledge in common. "Men's hands are against us," the writer wrote. What did that mean if it did not mean guilt?

From the information supplied to him by Charles Mobbs, Mr. Sugg had learnt that Perley Beck had been well acquainted with Ricardo. Now, Ricardo was Ivan Glindon, and Glindon was the late Mr. Glindon's son. Between the father and son was some secret which led to the son changing his name and the father disowning him. Therefore, was it possible that the writer of that letter was Ivan Glindon? Hardly. And yet the writer implied that he had been in Russia. So had Glindon.

But the gentleman who facetiously styled himself "The Prince of Darkness" spoke of being a child of

the sun, and of going to the Antilles. It was certain
that Glindon had not gone to the Antilles, because
Sugg had seen him in Rutland House but recently.
But there was another very remarkable thing which
could not escape so sharp a man as Calvin Sugg. It
was the heading of the paper—the cross-bones and
skull, and the motto, *Heu!* Was that a mere coincidence, or was there some strange connection between
that and the antique ring in Sugg's possession?

He rose, and going to a small iron strong-box, he
took out the ring which he had so carefully guarded
since finding it on the sofa at Linda Villa after the
murder of Vesta Florence. He carried the ring to
the window and examined it carefully, as, indeed, he
had done before, but somehow it seemed to have a
new interest for him now. It was altogether a unique
ring. The stone on which the unusual symbol was
cut was broad, but oblong and convex, instead of flat.
The gold was exceedingly massive and chased with a
scroll-work. Presently the detective procured a powerful magnifying-glass and brought it to bear on the
ring, and then he almost uttered a cry of surprise, for
underneath the symbol, cut in characters so fine and
small as to be invisible to the naked eye, was the
motto—*Heu!*

Here, then, was another important discovery. That
motto had hitherto escaped Sugg's notice, and possibly
would have continued to do so had it not been for the
letter heading. The heading and the design on the
ring, therefore, were no mere coincidence. It was

evidently a family motto and symbol, strange and
gruesome as it was. And what was the inference to
be drawn. There could be but one, which was that
the writer of the letter was the owner of the ring.
The fact of Ivan Glindon having advertised for the
ring seemed *primâ facie* evidence that he was the
owner. But Sugg had satisfied himself that Glindon
did not murder Vesta Florence. And yet, how was it
that he was interested in the ring?

Calvin Sugg threw himself in his big chair, covered
his eyes with his hand, and mentally set to work to
put the various pieces of the mystery puzzle together
to see what he could make of it. During a long and
very varied career he had had to deal with many strange
and complicated cases, but they all sank into insignifi-
cance when compared with this startling mystery.

Nevertheless, he was convinced that in that letter
which had failed to reach Perley Beck, owing to
that gentleman having deemed it advisable to dis-
appear, he had got another link, and he was sanguine
that he would add link by link until the chain was
complete and he had tracked the criminal or criminals
to doom. But before that was accomplished there was
much to do.

Having pondered over the matter for some time,
he proceeded to compare the letter he had received
from Ivan Glindon about the restoration of the ring
with the handwriting of the letter signed "The
Prince of Darkness." But the writing of the two
was totally different. Glindon's was a small, cramped

hand, essentially foreign in its style and character. The other was a clear, small, round hand, exceedingly easy to read.

"No," thought Sugg, "the same hand never penned those two letters."

He next sketched neatly on a half-sheet of note-paper the design of the skull and cross-bones, with the motto *Heu !* underneath, and folding this up and placing it in his pocket-book, he hurried to Fulham to have an interview with Muriel Glindon. He, fortunately, found her at home, and she eagerly inquired if he had got any news.

"Well, I think I may venture to say that I have. But I want you now to tell me whether you ever saw in your father's possession any article, such as a ring or signet, marked with that design."

Here he took the half-sheet of note-paper from his pocket-book and handed it to her for inspection.

"Never," she unhesitatingly exclaimed.

"Would you ask your aunt to come here ?"

Mrs. Romanoff was called, and Sugg inquired if she had ever heard that such a design as that had ever been used by any member of her family. But she was equally emphatic in saying no, she had not. Of course, that did not disprove that the ring belonged to Ivan Glindon, but it did away with the idea that the design and motto were peculiar to the Glindon family.

As Muriel was very pressing in her desire to know what news he had got, he gave the letter signed by "The Prince of Darkness" to her to read, and asked what she thought of it, and her opinion was, that the writer was out of his mind. But the fact of the letter bearing the same design and motto as the ring was too much for her altogether, and seemed to quite bewilder her.

"And now," she said, "I have an extraordinary thing to tell you. A few nights ago I received a most unexpected visit from my old teacher, Ita Prokoff."

"Ita—Prokoff!"

"Yes; she drove up here in a cab. She was greatly excited, and I thought at first she had been drinking, and afterwards I thought she must be mad, for she asked me if I would give her two hundred pounds for some information that might be of use to me. I told her that the two hundred pounds was out of the question, as I could not command such a sum. But I pointed out that if she was in possession of any information that would be of service it was her duty to let me know it. She then seemed to break down and become hysterical, laughing and crying in turns, and while in this state she startled me by saying that she was my sister-in-law—that is, she was Ivan Glindon's wife."

CHAPTER XXII.

A CHANGE OF FRONT.

"ANOTHER revelation!" exclaimed Sugg, "and the light is breaking now. But why did Ita come here?"

"She said that her husband had treated her badly, and that her life was threatened."

"Then in offering to supply you with information she was inspired by motives of revenge."

"Probably so; but the fact is, I did not question her very closely, I was so utterly astounded and she was so excited."

"But did she give you no particulars?"

"No. She said she wanted to return to her people in Russia, and if I would give her two hundred pounds she could do so."

"Did you not induce her to intimate the nature of the information she was so anxious to sell?"

"Yes, I did; but she declined to tell me anything. The fact is, she behaved so strangely that I did think, and still think, there was something the matter with her. I asked her if she was still living with my brother at Rutland House, and she said she had left him for ever."

"Did you ask her where she was to be found?"

" Yes."

" And you have her address ? "

" No."

" That is unfortunate," answered Sugg thoughtfully.

" She told me she was going to take lodgings somewhere, and as soon as she had an address she would call and let me know."

" And have you seen her since ? "

" No."

" This is a very important matter," Sugg observed, after some considerable reflection ; " and I cannot help thinking that the woman, Ita Prokoff, or Mrs. Ivan Glindon, as she asserts she is, may be of use to us. Inferentially, it seems more than probable that when your father accused her of knowing something of the robbery that took place at his house he was correct, although she so stoutly and indignantly denied it. I shadowed her at the time, but failed to get anything that would have justified me in charging her with having been a party to the theft of your father's papers. However, we must try not to lose sight of her again. We will wait a few days, and see if she communicates with you; if not, I shall have to make an attempt to discover her."

A week passed after this interview, and nothing further had been heard of Ita Prokoff, and it seemed as if she had made up her mind to keep silent.

Sugg had taken steps in the meantime to ascertain that Mrs. Ivan Glindon was no longer at Rutland House, and nobody there seemed able to give any information as to where she had gone to. She had disappeared suddenly, much to the astonishment of all the servants, and—so it was said—"to the great grief" of her husband. He, indeed, seemed to be inconsolable; but having regard to the way that he and his wife quarrelled and the bitter things they said about each other, he regretted her departure, not because he loved her, but because he feared her.

At last Muriel received a note from her sister-in-law asking her to call upon her, as she was too ill to leave the house, and the address she gave was a street in Kentish Town. This was at once communicated to Sugg, who lost no time in calling at the address, which was a poor house in a somewhat poor street, and must have been a very disagreeable change to Ita after the grandeur of The Priory and Rutland House. The detective found that she was suffering severely from bronchitis, and was confined to her room, though not in bed.

She was thunderstruck on beholding Sugg, and said angrily—

"I suppose this is due to Muriel? Well, she is a fool for her pains—that is all I've got to say. My business was with her—for she is my sister-in-law—not with you, for you are a spy, a villain, and I hate you!"

"Ah, just so," answered Sugg imperturbably. "You are complimentary; but, you see, Mrs. Glindon, I am acting on her behalf. By the way, I suppose you have really a just claim to be addressed as Mrs. Glindon?"

The woman's dark eyes seemed to blaze out like

N

living coal at this suggestion that she was not what she represented herself to be. But she had obviously —in flying from Rutland House—felt the necessity of having documentary evidence in her possession that she was Glindon's wife; for she took from the bosom of her dress a small leather case, and from the case a marriage certificate, which she flung at Sugg with the remark—

"That is sufficient answer to you."

He picked up the certificate, opened it out, and read it, and there was no longer room to doubt that Ivan Glindon, widower, and Ita Prokoff, spinster, had been legally married at a church in Kensington.

"That's all right, Mrs. Glindon," he observed, as he handed the paper back to her; "but it justifies me in asking you why you have left your husband's roof."

"Because I don't agree with him; that is why," she growled.

"Why did you marry him?" asked Sugg abruptly, and looking her full in the face.

"Because I loved him."

"For no other reason?"

"What other reason do you suppose there was?" she demanded warmly, and beginning to get excited.

"I might suggest many reasons," he answered coolly.

"So you might, and they would all be wrong."

"Possibly. But there is one that, in all probability, would not be far from the truth?"

"And what is that, pray?"

"Some guilty knowledge that gave you power over him."

Although Calvin Sugg's keen eyes were fixed on the woman's as he said this, she did not seem disturbed, but met his gaze unflinchingly, and when she answered him a withering sneer spread itself over her swarthy face, and she said freezingly—

"If you think so, you can enjoy your opinion. There are some people who consider themselves so clever that it is a mere waste of time to try to convince them they are in error when once they have conceived an idea."

"True," said Sugg, with a smile; "but I don't think I am one of those people. If I am in the wrong, I am quite open to conviction; but I like to have it clearly demonstrated that I am in the wrong. Your bare denial doesn't convince me."

"Perhaps not; but I have no desire to convince you. You are free to think as you like."

"Of course I am, Mrs. Glindon. But it is no use our bandying words. You offered to sell some information to your sister-in-law. Although I can be no party to the compounding of a felony, I have this to say: if you are in a position to throw any light on the mystery surrounding Mr. Glindon's death, and so long as you were not a party directly or indirectly to a foul deed, you may rely upon being well paid for your services."

"Mr. Sugg!" she cried, with remarkable energy, "I declare before my Maker that I know nothing whatever about that crime."

Her whole manner suggested that she spoke the truth, and the detective asked—

"What is the nature of the information, then, that you are prepared to supply?"

Once more she became cynical and sneering, as she answered—

"What I had to tell Muriel does not concern you in any way. And the motives that prompted me were a desire to spite my husband. But now I decline to tell her anything."

"Why?"

"Because she has set you to act the part of a spy."

"But you forget that I have a duty to perform."

"I don't care what you have to do; I will tell you nothing."

"Is that your unalterable decision?"

"It is."

"Very well," said Sugg, rising and preparing to go. "Your obstinacy can serve you but little. Depend upon it, the mystery will be unravelled without your assistance."

Then he took his leave, and when he had gone Mrs. Glindon ground her teeth with anger, as she muttered—

"We shall see—we shall see. I hate spies; and you played the spy on me at The Priory, but you learnt nothing; and you shall learn nothing now."

Sugg made known to Muriel the result of his visit to Mrs. Glindon, and they mutually agreed that some diplomacy must be used, for Muriel knew Ita to be of an extraordinarily obstinate nature, and not likely to be

turned from a thing that she had made up her mind
to do. It was therefore decided that Muriel herself
should go out to Kentish Town; and this she did two
days later. Ita was slightly better, but still very ill.
She did not receive Muriel graciously by any means,
and was as obstinate with her as she had been with
Sugg.

"I could have told you something that might have
been of use to you," she said; "but now my lips are
sealed."

Muriel brought all the power of persuasion she could
to bear, but without effect. With strange inconsistency,
Ita exclaimed—

"Ivan Glindon is my husband; and though you, as
his sister, have thrown him over, I am not going to
do so."

This change of front on her part was extraordinary
—or, at any rate, it seemed so—when it is remembered
that she had fled from her husband's house to save
her life. But she saw matters in a different light now
from what she did on that night when she stood behind
the curtain and overheard the plot for her taking off.
Like most of her countrywomen, she was of an ex-
citable disposition; and when she rushed off to Muriel
at Fulham she might have been persuaded into almost
anything, for she was bitterly enraged against her husband. But she had had time for reflection; and she
had probably come to the conclusion that, whatever it
was she had to tell, she could make nothing out of it,
for Muriel had no money. And her evident desire was

to obtain money; for in her precipitate flight she had
only brought away with her a few pounds and her
jewellery. But, in spite of that, she was inflexible;
and Muriel made no more of her than Calvin Sugg
had done; and feeling angry, which, under the circumstances, was natural, she exclaimed—

"You are ungrateful, and evidently forget that at
the time of the robbery at The Priory, when my father
accused you of knowing something about it, I took
your part, even against him."

"You did," said Ita. "But your brother is now
my husband; and though he has treated me shamefully, I still love him. Of course, women are fools, I
know, in this respect; and I am one of the biggest,
but I can't help it; and I am not going to say one
word that will reflect upon my husband's character.
And since you are hand and glove with Mr. Calvin
Sugg, who thinks himself so clever, if there is anything to find out, let him find it out."

"You may depend upon it," answered Muriel
quietly, "he will do so."

"Will he?" exclaimed Ita, with a coarse laugh.
"Don't make too sure of that, or you may be disappointed."

Muriel had no desire to continue the argument with
a woman who was capable of such sudden changes of
mind and humour as was Ita, and who, moreover, was
so insincere; and so she left her—glad, indeed, to
get away. And she reported her failure to Sugg.

During a typical London fog one afternoon a week

later—when the atmosphere was almost the consistency of pea-soup and the darkness so intense that all the gas was lighted in shops and streets—Mrs. Ivan Glindon left her lodgings at Kentish Town in a cab and drove to Rutland House. When the door was opened to her by that superior being, John Thomas, she demanded peremptorily to know where his master was. John Thomas was so used to the vagaries and strange doings of the inmates of his master's dwelling that he was not greatly surprised at Mrs. Glindon's sudden and unexpected return, no more than he had been by her sudden and unexpected flight; and without showing that he was disturbed in the least, he said—

"He's hin the drawing-room, mum, a-playing cards with some of his friends."

"I will go to my room, then; and tell him to come to me immediately."

As the lady had told the cabman to wait for her, it was evident she had no intention of remaining long. Two hours, however, elapsed before she reappeared; and a little man, muffled in a big coat, and with his face almost concealed by a wideawake hat, who had followed in a hansom from Kentish Town, grew impatient, and stamped up and down the pavement to keep himself warm.

At last the great door of Rutland House swung open, and John Thomas and some of the other servants piled a large quantity of luggage on the cab; and, that done, Mrs. Glindon reappeared. She was now enveloped in a great Russian *shuba*. When she had taken her seat the cab drove away; and the little man in the big coat and slouched hat followed in the hansom.

The lady's destination was Charing Cross Station. Her luggage was taken on to the platform, and the little man who was shadowing her heard her tell the porter that the luggage was to be labelled for Paris. There were two hours yet before the train would start, and Mrs. Glindon went into the hotel, while the little man rushed to the telegraph-office opposite and wired some messages. Then he went into a hosier's and bought some odds and ends, including a couple of shirts; and into a trunk-maker's, where he provided himself with a hand-bag.

And when the Continental train steamed out of the station, carrying Mrs. Ivan Glindon, who travelled first-class, the little man was a fellow-passenger, and was snugly ensconced in a corner of the next compartment.

CHAPTER XXIII.

BY no means the least remarkable trait in Calvin Sugg's character was that of patience. No detective who does not possess this virtue in a greater or lesser degree can hope to be successful in dealing with criminal problems, but in Sugg it seemed to have no limit where he thought its full display was called for. Added to this patience was a power of observation that enabled him to see detail that an ordinary person would have passed over. And nothing was too small for Sugg that promised even an infinitesimal assistance in his work.

In dealing with what had come to be known as the St. John's Wood and Richmond mysteries his patience and his observation had been put to the severest test. The St. John's Wood tragedy was by this time out of the public memory, and such people as did remember it considered it a foregone conclusion that it would for ever be numbered amongst London's undetected crimes, and they did not hesitate to say, spitefully, that Sugg had been baffled.

It is, unfortunately, a painful truth that every successful man, no matter what his calling, is bound to make a certain number of enemies, for envy and jealousy seem inseparable from some natures. Of course, they are ignoble natures, but they very far out-number the noble ones. Sugg had been no excep-tion to this general rule, and it might almost be said that every success—and he had had many—had made him a new enemy. It was sad as depicting the mean-ness of human-kind, but Sugg was not affected by it, and the spiteful things that were said might have been left unsaid so far as he was concerned.

It was a noteworthy thing that, after his investiga-tions of the murder of Vesta Florence, when he called upon Mr. Glindon he said that the ring and the hand-kerchief he had secured would help him to solve the mystery. Now, after this length of time the ring had enabled him to determine that Ivan Glindon was aware of its existence, and was anxious to recover it.

If Sugg had not so clearly proved that Glindon had had nothing to do with the murder of his wife, his suspicions against him would have been aroused. But as it was, he was prepared to stake his very existence on the statement that Glindon was innocent. At his examination before the coroner it had been brought out that he and Vesta Florence lived on fairly amicable terms. Sometimes they had a little squabble, but nothing serious.

At the time of her death she had been married to Glindon about a year and a half. He had met her first in Manchester, where he had been attending the races. He saw her perform at the Theatre Royal there, and fell in love with her at first sight. Many men did that, for on the stage she was, as it were, a poem, the ideal of all that was graceful and beautiful in woman, but none were as fortunate as Glindon. By some means he obtained an introduction to her, and in six weeks she had become his wife. What magic or charm he used to charm her was not stated. He had succeeded where others had failed, but how he did it must be left to the reader's own imagination. Vesta Florence evidently saw in him much to admire, or she surely would never have married him.

When they came to London after their marriage they settled down at St. John's Wood, and each seemed to follow the bent of his and her inclination. They lived extravagantly—outrageously so; and though she had a large salary, not much of it was saved; and whatever his income was, it was all required to support the position he aimed at as a "man about town."

All this and much more was known to Sugg, and he had been unable to discover one single little reason why Glindon should have wished his wife out of the way. On the contrary, her death must have been a positive loss to him, because he certainly had the advantage of her position and her earnings, and she seemed to have been recklessly liberal and good-natured.

Now, the contrast between Vesta Florence and Ita Prokop was very striking, and any comparison instituted must have been greatly against the latter.

Besides that, she was impecunious; and though a clever linguist, that accomplishment did no more than enable her to earn the salary of a governess. What, then, was the attraction that induced Glindon to marry her, notwithstanding that on his father's death he became a rich man? Was it not in accord with common-sense to say that, as she was not rich and had no personal attractions, she had obtained some power over him which enabled her to sway him to her will? That she was in possession of a secret was made evident by her offer to sell her knowledge to Muriel. But the strange fact of her going back to her husband's house in spite of her life having been threatened, and of her having removed her luggage and started for Paris, suggested that she had got a much higher price from him to hold her tongue, and probably on condition that she left the country.

Sugg was not blind to these points; and so far as the lady was concerned his mind was easy, for she was being shadowed by one of his ablest assistants, who had telegraphed for instructions, and was told to travel to Paris with her and watch her closely.

And the part of the problem Sugg now set himself to solve was—whether there was any connection between the writer of the extraordinary letter signed "The Prince of Darkness" and Ivan Glindon. If so, what? That there was connection between Perley Beck and Glindon was unquestionable, and Perley Beck would have to be discovered. But a very care-

ful weighing of all facts led Sugg to the conclusion
that it might afford him very valuable aid if he went
to Russia and endeavoured to trace the past career
of Ivan Glindon. Up to then he had set great hopes
on the possible recovery of Mr. Thorne, but that gentleman's condition remained precisely the same; and the
doctors were silent as to what the issue might be. If
the secret locked up in that shattered brain could but
have been learned, the knowledge might have been
of enormous service; but the chances of that were
an utterly unknown quantity, and so Sugg decided to
start for Russia without further delay.

In order that his movements might be kept secret,
which was very important, he told no one where he
was going to; but he sent a little note to Muriel
saying he should be out of town for a few weeks,
and he telegraphed to his assistant in Paris telling him
to meet him there and report.

The report that Sugg did receive on reaching the
French capital was, that Mrs. Glindon was staying at
a small hotel in the Rue St. Honoré, and that she was
seriously ill with bronchitis, which had been rendered
worse by the journey in such inclement weather. He
found that she was staying there as "Madame Petro-
skowitch," and that she had stated her intention of
proceeding to Russia to join her friends. This made
Sugg pause and consider whether he should not wait
and follow her; but he ascertained that she was so
very ill indeed that she would not be able to travel
for some time, and the chances were she would not

recover. He therefore decided to lose no time, but continue his journey alone.

He knew that Ivan Glindon had been born in the little town of Yarensk, in the province of Vologda, and to this place he made his way, in order that he might start at the fountain-head.

Calvin Sugg spent ten weeks in Russia, but it is not necessary that we should follow all his movements during that time. Suffice to say that, so far as his main object was concerned, he was eminently successful.

Perhaps in no country in the world is it so easy to trace the movements of a person who has once brought himself under the notice of the police as in Russia. The system of espionage obtains there to a degree of absolute perfection; and when once the police have got their eye on a man or a woman, they may, in a sense, be said to never take it off.

Now, it will be remembered that, in briefly recounting his history to his half-sister, Ivan Glindon had confessed that he had been mixed up in a conspiracy which had led to his imprisonment for six months. Sugg had learnt this fact from Muriel herself, and it· was of great importance to him. He found that he had been registered in the police books as a Nihilist, and his history was not only known from that point onward to the moment when he quitted his native country for London, but it had been traced backward to his birth.

In St. Petersburg he had allied himself with a band

of treasonable students; but as he was a mere boy, and
nothing serious was proved against him, he escaped
with the light punishment of six months' imprisonment, although some of his companions were sent to
Siberia. On his release he seemed to have led a very
wild life, plunging into all sorts of dissipation, until at
last he became penniless, and a friend of his father's,
compassionating him, took him into his office as a clerk.

He did not remain long, however, for his habits and
style of life did not meet with the approval of his employer, who found that his kindness was being thrown
away, and so he discharged him.

For some time after that he led a very questionable
kind of existence, though he did nothing that brought
him into antagonism with the law. About this time
he became very intimate with a foreigner—supposed
to be an Englishman—who was known by the name
of Robert Hinton, though the police had reason to
believe that was not his right name, notwithstanding
he had a passport bearing that name. For a long
time Hinton and Glindon apparently made a living
by gambling, and for about six months they resided
in Cronstadt.

One night a man, who was carrying a tray of vege-
tables on his head, happened in passing to accidentally
strike Hinton as he was walking along the street.
This seemed to arouse him to a pitch of demoniacal
fury, and turning on the man, he knocked him down,
and so brutally ill-used him that he was picked up
unconscious and carried to the hospital. Hinton

managed to effect his escape; it is supposed that he
stowed himself away on board an English steamer
which sailed that very night for Liverpool. At any
rate he entirely disappeared, and the victim of his
brutality, after suffering severely for two months,
succumbed to his injuries.

What became of Hinton was never known. The
police were in possession of a photograph of him, a
copy of which was given to Sugg. Strangely enough,
according to the portrait, Hinton seemed to bear some
resemblance to Glindon himself. He had a dark,
swarthy complexion, intensely dark eyes and hair;
but the lines of his face suggested to the student of
the human face an innate and ferocious cruelty of
disposition.

Although Glindon was not with his friend when the
outrage occurred, considerable feeling was manifested
against him owing to his intimacy with Hinton, and
deeming it advisable to shift his quarters, he went to
Moscow.

Soon after that he joined the ranks of a travelling
theatrical company. He was known to be very fond of
the theatre, and had frequently taken part in amateur
theatricals. In his capacity as an actor he travelled
through most of the Russian provinces. One day,
while he and his company were performing at Viatka,
he and some brother-actors were mixed up in a riot
that occurred in a gambling-house, and it resulted in
Glindon suffering another term of imprisonment, owing
to his resisting and assaulting the police.

On his release he repaired once more to St. Petersburg, where he remained for a few months in a state
of poverty. But at last, by means of a forged bank
draft, he got possession of a considerable sum of
money, and before the forgery was discovered he had
left the country, and, as was believed, went to London.

Such was the story of Ivan Glindon's career down
to the time that he appeared in England.

It was not difficult to understand that, with such a
record against him as this, his father should feel dis-
inclined to own him and to bring him in contact with
his half-sister, who was a model of all that was good
and true in womanhood. But this did not explain Mr.
Glindon's intense bitterness against his son—indeed, it
might be referred to as positive hatred; for had he not
expressed a wish at the time of Vesta Florence's murder
that her husband—his own son—might be convicted of
the crime, his explanation of that desire being that he
would be relieved of an incubus? Surely a man could
hardly be so inhuman as to wish his son to die a
felon's death, unless that son had goaded him almost
into madness?

As Calvin Sugg dwelt upon this, he was convinced
that, though he had learned much and proved beyond
doubt that Ivan Glindon was a scoundrel, he was still
as far off as ever from the secret that had enabled
that son to wield such terrible power over his father
—a power that turned his father into a misanthrope,
that took the sunshine out of his life, and which was
powerful enough to cause him or compel him to leave

o

his daughter, upon whom he doted, practically penniless, while his worthless and scapegrace son was enriched. Nor, as it seemed then to Sugg, was he any nearer solving the mystery of the St. John's Wood and Richmond crimes. As a matter of fact, however, although he did not know it then, he had really got the key to the mystery.

After an absence of ten weeks Sugg commenced his return journey, feeling somewhat disappointed with the results of his efforts.

When he reached Paris a new surprise awaited him, for he learnt that, just a month before, the illness from which Ita Glindon was suffering had proved fatal, and she had been buried in Père la Chaise cemetery. He had received two or three letters from his assistant, who had informed him that the woman was dangerously ill; and news had also been sent announcing her death, but the latter letter had failed to reach him.

CHAPTER XXIv

WHEN Calvin Sugg returned to London he found brightness and light where he had left fog and gloom. Winter had fled, and spring had come in with blue skies and brilliant sunshine. There are times when our fickle climate seems to make up its mind—if it can be said, even in a figurative sense, to have a mind—to give us a taste of the balmy airs of the more favoured South.

On this occasion it more than justified all the poetic effusions that have been penned about vernal April and gladsome May. April had just gone out, tearful and coy, like a timid maiden; but so genial had the month been, that May came in with a gladsomeness that found a joyful echo in the great heart of Nature. London—the mighty, teeming, smoky world of London —was transfigured. Her squares were like patches of sweet woodland set down amongst the bricks and mortar, while the parks were glories of green, and all aflame with the brilliant colours of the early flowers. The cuckoo was already making his notes heard in the suburbs, and letters had appeared in the papers saying that the pioneer nightingales had been trilling their love-notes in Bushey and Windsor Parks and in the delightful woods of Surrey. Primroses, violets, daffodils, crocuses, narcissi, and early lilies filled the florists' windows with a mass of floral beauty, and lent a charm even to the crowded streets of the city, as they were hawked about the streets by the flower-girls, who, perhaps, are the dirtiest and most un-picturesque specimens of their tribe to be found in any part of the world.

And yet even these ragged vagrants, somehow, looked brighter and cleaner and more cheerful than is their wont. If London were only blessed with a greater amount of sunshine than is usually accorded it, how infinitely would its beauty be enhanced! For, let grumblers and foreigners scoff as they may, London is a most beautiful city. If it has its foul spots where human nature festers in the sight of heaven, and its flaunting and seductive hells, yclept gin-palaces, which are at once a disgrace and a curse, it has also a grandeur which is all its own, and fair stretches of almost sylvan beauty, that refresh the eye and re-joice the heart.

When Calvin Sugg left Russia that country was still in the hard grip of the White Frost King, and was cold, sterile, and monotonous; so that London, clothed in sunshine as it was and bright with flowers, was a most agreeable contrast.

During his absence there had been no change in Muriel Glindon's affairs. The days and weeks had gone by, each day very much like another. She had seen but little of Raymond Penoyre, as he had been away for several weeks staying with an uncle in Wales, who was very fond of him, and who had promised to help him in his career. But he had been a most diligent correspondent, and his letters glowed with the love he bore for her. In those letters she found much to comfort her, and also something to sadden, because it seemed to her that his hopes would never come to fruition. Every throb of her heart told her how truly this great love of his was returned by her, and yet when she wrote to him her expressions were studiously guarded; she felt as if she dare not give full vent to her feelings, lest she should allow herself to be carried away, and show him how she had set him on a pinnacle, as it were, and worshipped him as one may worship some bright star in the far-off heavens.

It was very pitiable for one of her sensitiveness, her refined and truly womanly nature, to have to crush her own heart, and to mourn with scalding tears over the flowers of her life that had bloomed so sweetly for a time, but which now seemed withered and dead. Her youth had been a delightful dream, from which she had been cruelly and rudely awakened, to find how stern life is, how full of bitterness, how dark with shadows. She did not and could not bring herself to believe that the strange mystery of her dear father's life and cruel death would ever be chased away by the light of revelation, and so an ineffable sadness had settled upon her; and though she longed with a wordless longing for her lover's return, she was glad he was away, because it was relatively easier for her to endure her sorrow in his absence than in his presence. When he was there she yearned for his strong arms to shield her, for his lips to meet hers in the passionate kisses of love; to lean on him, to look up to him, to be guided by him, to sink back once more into her blissful dream-state, when the world seemed so very, very beautiful and life an idyllic poem.

But with the sternness of a determined will she had to conquer herself, to condemn herself to the exquisite torture that Tantalus suffered; and so, in a paradoxical sense, she was glad that he was away. And at this time she did really hope—for his sake, not hers; for God knew how hard it was for her to tear herself from him —that his love for her might grow cold, but bloom and revive again under the burning glances of some other woman, who could make him happier and more contented than she could ever do. Such self-abnegation, such a negation of her own wishes and longings, could only be the outcome of a nature that was no less true and honourable than it was sensitive.

But if she really ever deemed it likely that Raymond Penoyre's love for her would grow cold, she must have formed a very mistaken estimate of him. It is not intended to represent him as being in any way perfect. He was a healthily-minded young man, with a fair share of man's faults and failings; but he had a very high regard for honour in its best sense; and to have deserted her in her changed fortunes, and while sorrow's

clouds enwrapped her, would have seemed to him so dis-
honourable, so dastardly, so repugnant to his feelings,
that he would rather have yielded up his life. No!
he was true to her, and would remain true to her,
come what might; and his temperament and disposition
were such that it was safe to predict, that if he failed
to secure her for his wife his bachelor state would
never be changed.

There are some men and women—and well it is for
poor humanity that it is so—who prize much higher
than mere worldly happiness the sacredness of a troth
given, a promise made. If this is not the case, how
is it that we occasionally come across people whose
lives are a silent sorrow, who look back regretfully
and tearfully to the past, but forward with a yearning
hopefulness, believing, with a beautiful and simple
faith, that there will be a reunion when the fever
called life shall end? Of such people it may fittingly
be said they—

> " Know what love is—that it draws
> Into itself all passion, hope, and thought ;
> The heart of life, to which all currents flow
> Through every vein of being, which if chilled
> The streams are ice for ever ! "

Undoubtedly the sentiments so aptly expressed in these
lines by Westland Marston were peculiarly applicable
to Muriel Glindon, for she had poured out to Penoyre
the full strength of her love; and though, with that
patience and resignation inseparable from such a disposition as hers, she would be able to bury her disap-

pointment in her own heart, where the gaze of the
vulgar and the curious could not reach it, her sorrow
would, nevertheless, be unending.

At length Penoyre returned to London, after many
weeks' absence, and he lost not a moment in going out
to see Muriel. Of course, she welcomed him warmly,
though she did not attempt to conceal that the shadows
still hung heavily upon her. He talked hopefully of
the future, for his uncle had undertaken to allow him
an income for two years to enable him to go to Italy,
that he might study art in that country. She expressed her gratification at this, and she really was
glad that he was going away, for reasons that have
been already explained—that is, glad for his own
sake, not for hers. Then he asked her if she had
any news.

"I have news of a kind," she said. "I have not
seen Mr. Sugg for nearly three months, as he has been
abroad, but he wrote me a few days ago announcing
his return, and also informing me that my sister-in-
law, Ita Glindon, was dead."

"Ita dead!"

"Yes; she died in Paris, from bronchitis. Sugg is
to see me shortly, but he says that just now he is
overwhelmed with work, for he is trying to overtake
an accumulation of arrears."

"Has he been abroad in connection with your case,
do you know?"

"I do not know. He does not tell me anything;
and I quite despair now of ever learning anything.

Ita was in possession of some secret that might have aided us; but she refused to make it known unless well paid, and I suppose her secret has died with her."

"I am surprised," remarked Penoyre thoughtfully, "that Calvin Sugg is not a little more communicative."

"I suppose he has nothing to communicate. I am sure he has done his best, but very likely he has come to the conclusion that it is a hopeless case. If Mr. Hilkiah Thorne could only be restored to reason, he might be able to afford valuable information; but I called on Mrs. Thorne some weeks ago, and she said her husband's condition was never likely to be changed, and that, though he might live for years, he was liable to die suddenly at any moment. It is terribly sad, for he was such a nice man, and knew so much of papa's affairs. No doubt that is the reason why the assassin wished to kill him as well as papa."

"Well, I tell you what it is, Muriel," exclaimed Raymond; "I shall go out, any way, and see Sugg. I don't think it is fair that he should keep us in suspense. If he has decided to abandon the case altogether, he had better say so at once, for to keep one fluttering between hope and despair is not kind."

"You do him an injustice, dear," said Muriel. "He is kindness itself; and I am convinced, from what I know of him, that he will never abandon the case as long as he thinks there is even a remote possibility of unravelling the mystery. But go and see him, by all means. It can do no harm."

The result of this conversation was, that Penoyre,

when he parted from Muriel, went out to Clapham
and called at the detective's house. When he arrived
it chanced that Sugg was engaged, and Penoyre had
to wait some time in a pleasant little room that was
filled with books and nicknacks, and was quite a
museum of trifles that the detective had picked up in
his extensive travelling abroad. In the examination
of these things Penoyre found plenty to interest
him. At last he began to examine some things on
the mantelpiece, and suddenly his eye was arrested
by a photograph in an oxydised frame. He caught
it up and scrutinised it keenly, and a strange look of
surprise swept over his face. It was the photograph
of a dark man, with a strikingly cruel expression of
mouth, and dark, staring eyes that peered at one
from under scowling brows.

At this moment Sugg entered the room. Penoyre
turned and greeted him, still holding the photograph
in his hand.

"I say, Sugg," he exclaimed, "whose likeness is this?"
Sugg looked surprised now.

"That! Oh, that is a likeness I got in Russia, from
whence I have just returned. It is the photograph of
a man who was known as Robert Hinton. But why
do you ask. Have you ever met the man?"

"Yes; I am certain of it."

"Where?"

"In the West Indies."

CHAPTER XXV

MARTHA AND HER YOUNG MAN.

THE news of his wife's death in Paris caused Ivan Glindon no concern or sorrow. On the contrary, he really rejoiced, and considered himself well rid of her. On condition that she returned to Russia and never troubled him again, he had given her a considerable sum of money, and allowed her to take all her things away. When she became conscious of the fact that the disease she had contracted was likely to prove fatal, she wrote to him begging him to go and see her. But he, fearing this was a trap, declined, and so she died a miserable death, and without a friend near her.

As soon as her husband heard that she was dead, he applied to the hotel-keeper to return him any money she had in her possession at the time of her death, as well as all her luggage. But in this he had been anticipated, for Sugg's assistant sent in a re-presentation to the chief of the police that the woman was suspected of having, directly or indirectly, been guilty of some offence against the law; and it was desirable, in the interests of justice, that all her effects should be detained pending further investigation.

This request was complied with; an official police visit was paid to the hotel, and the luggage was sealed up. Glindon was not informed of these facts, but he was told that in order to claim her luggage it would be necessary for him to apply for it personally, and furnish undoubted proof that he was entitled to receive it. It will be readily guessed that he did not put himself to the trouble to do this. He preferred to let the things go. In Rutland House there was not the slightest sign of mourning for the unhappy woman whose career had so suddenly come to an end. If the widower was disconsolate, he took good care that nobody should know anything about it, and he and his mysterious guest abandoned themselves to enjoyment. At least he did; but it is doubtful if the guest's capacity for enjoyment had not entirely passed. He spent much of his time in his room, and his principal diet was of an alcoholic nature. His craving for stimulants was insatiable, and though he would drink anything, he preferred champagne. With not altogether disinterested motives, his host allowed him unlimited supplies, and the wretched man had become little better than a drivelling imbecile. He was known to the servants as "Mr. Arthur Goodeve," and they were not slow to express an opinion that "he was a-killing of hisself with drink."

Soon after Mrs. Glindon's death a new servant took service at Rutland House. She was a young, smart, good-looking woman under thirty. Her position was that of chambermaid, and she had replaced one who had suddenly left. The new servant was known as Martha Gibbs, and though she was considered to be rather a duffer at her duties, she became a general favourite, for she was willing to turn her hand to anything, and would help any of the other servants without a murmur. She seemed to be greatly interested in Mr. Goodeve, and frequently expressed her sympathy with him. Indeed, she had not been many days in the house before her fellow-domestics said she was "making eyes" at the master's friend. Perhaps this was not true; but if it was, the master's friend, although a young man, seemed too dazed to appreciate her efforts to attract his attention.

One evening the master and his friend were seated together after dinner. The friend had consumed more than his ordinary quantity of wine, and was now trying to "pull himself together" with strong black coffee, largely diluted with cognac. He had been endeavouring for some time to light a cigar, but having failed to accomplish his purpose, he gave it up as a bad job. Suddenly he exclaimed in a maudlin, hiccoughing tone—

"I say, dear chappie, it was a deuced lucky thing for you the old woman slipped off the hooks so quickly. It saved me experimentalising on her, too, don't you know. But you always were a lucky dog. I suppose you were born under a lucky star—eh?"

"Possibly. But I don't think you've any cause to complain. You are in pretty comfortable quarters."

"Yes, dear boy. I say nothing about that. But

you know I've been a good friend to you, and you'd be ungrateful if you didn't treat me well. But there, there's no such thing as gratitude in this world. Ita Prokop was a good friend to you, but you treated her badly."

"What the devil do you mean?" asked Glindon hotly.

"Now, don't lose your temper, old fellow, for you can't say you were exactly an angel to her, were you?"

"Well, I married her, didn't I?"

"Ah! just so. Well, you know a man is an angel to a woman before marriage, but a devil afterwards. However, you are well rid of her—well rid of her—and I congratulate you. She might have proved a very awkward customer, for a woman bursts if she has to keep a secret over-long. But a dead woman tells no tales."

"Nor a dead man either," answered Glindon, with some significance in his tone and manner.

"Do you mean that for me?" asked Goodeve.

"No, of course not."

"Ah! I thought you couldn't be so ungrateful as that, for you know how I love you," was Goodeve's sarcastic answer.

"Yes, certainly I do. But have some more brandy, and let us talk about something else."

This fragment of conversation had been overheard by a very diligent listener in the person of Martha Gibbs. One of the parlour-maids being out, Martha was doing duty for her, and having brought in some hot water, she remained just outside the door, with the door ajar, when she retired, and seemed very eager to catch every word that was said.

A few days later Mr. Glindon went down to Doncaster, to attend the races there. He wished his friend Goodeve to accompany him; but Goodeve was in such a state of nervous prostration that he pleaded inability to travel, and said he preferred to remain in bed.

The old proverb says, "When the cat's away the mice will play," and Mr. Glindon's servants verified the truth of the adage, for in their master's absence they gave themselves up to a life of ease and enjoyment. The sick guest did not trouble them, nor did they, with one exception, concern themselves about him. The exception was Martha Gibbs. She displayed a very kindly interest, and tried to persuade him to drink beef-tea instead of brandy and champagne.

She was not altogether successful, although, yielding to her persuasion, he did consent to take a little of the beef-tea; but it only seemed to make him worse, as his weakened stomach would not retain food.

Like most sots, he alternated between maudlin sentimentality and imbecile mirth. When in the former condition he fretted like a child, and constantly referred in an incoherent way to his "poor mother." Martha did all she could to soothe him, and asked him where his mother was, and if she should send her any message, but he exclaimed with a passionate wail—

"No, no, my God! She must never know where I

am. She believes me dead. Let her think so." Then
he suddenly added, with a display of much irritation,
"What am I talking about? I'm a fool. I'm going
mad, I think," and he peremptorily ordered Martha
out of the room. But she had scarcely got downstairs,
when, evidently repenting of his hastiness, he rang
his bell violently, and when she went up to him again
he drawled out in a whining tone—

"Martha, forgive me. I didn't mean to be unkind
to you. But my poor head is all wrong. My brain
is giving way. You've been very good to me, and I
want to make you a little present. Put your hand
into the breast-pocket of that coat—there, hanging
behind the door. Yes, that's the one. There's a
pocket-book there, isn't there?"

"Yes."

"Just give it to me."

She did as he desired. It was a large Russian
leather pocket-book much worn. He fumbled for
some time trying to open it, but his hands trembled
like aspen leaves, and at last he held it out to her
and asked her to open it. She did so, and all but
uttered a cry of astonishment as she caught sight
of a name stamped in gold letters on the inside flap
of the book. The gold had partly worn off, but still
the name was quite legible. She controlled herself,
however, and gave him the open book, and from one
of the pockets he took two or three Bank of England
notes, and selecting one for five pounds, he held it out
to her, saying—

"Here; that will buy you a dress, or a brooch, or something."

"Oh! thank you, sir," she answered; "you are very kind, but I really couldn't think of taking it."

"Why not?" he asked sharply, as though he was offended.

"I don't know what I've done to deserve it," she said.

"Oh, nonsense! you've done plenty. There, take it. If you don't I'll tear it in pieces."

Thus urged she accepted the note, and then restored the book to his coat-pocket from whence she had taken it.

That evening the servants had a dance among themselves, and Martha Gibbs had asked the housekeeper in the course of the afternoon if she might have her young man, Bob Williams, in. The housekeeper gave permission, providing that he went away early, and Martha promised that he should not stay after half-past ten.

When Bob arrived all Martha's fellow-servants were disposed to burst out laughing at him; for he looked such a clumsy, awkward hobbledehoy, and he had a fiery-red head of hair, and a fiery moustache and a stubbly beard, and he talked with a broad Hertfordshire accent. Martha apologised for him by saying that he had not been long in London, and would improve, no doubt, when he got some of the roughness rubbed off him; and as he turned out to be rather an amusing sort of fellow, the servants tolerated him.

P

It was a very jolly evening. John Thomas was in
fine form, and so was Jeames, the butler. These two
gentlemen were very *distingué*, both as to their calves,
and as to their hair, and they considered themselves
to be perfect lady-killers. Perhaps they were justified
in this, for the ladies of the household below stairs
seemed to admire them greatly. A very excellent
supper had been provided by the thoughtful housekeeper, consisting of delicious oysters, a prime salmon,
roast lamb, and peas and new potatoes; and there were
some little *et cœteras* to follow, including lobster salad
and aspic jelly. Jeames was particularly liberal with
his master's champagne, and showed his refined taste
by choosing the best brands. Bob Williams turned
out to be a splendid fellow in spite of his uncouth
looks; he could sing a capital song in the Hertfordshire dialect, and he had quite a fund of stories at
his command.

When half-past ten struck no one suggested it was
time for Bob to go; and midnight still found him
there, and he appeared to be pretty mellow, though
not so bad as the other gentlemen. Jeames had quite
succumbed, and John Thomas's speech was so thick
that it was absolutely impossible to make out what
he said, so some of his fellow-servants managed to
lug him off to bed.

Then the good and faithful housekeeper, who was
not quite as steady on her legs as she might have been,
ordered Bob Williams to depart. But Bob was in a
happy state of don't-careism; he had ensconced him-

self on the kitchen sofa, and said he was blarmed if
he was a-going to leave that night. As all the influence of the ladies was incapable of bringing him
to reason, Martha pleaded that he might be allowed
to stay. Seeing that he refused to go, and that any
attempt to forcibly remove him might lead to an un-
desirable scene, the housekeeper consented to his remaining; so a rug was thrown over him, the lights were
turned out, and the household retired to their beds.

Two hours passed, and the proverbial pin might
have been heard to drop in Rutland House, for the
silence was profound; but a few minutes later a
figure carrying a shaded lantern noiselessly descended
the stairs. The figure was that of a woman, and the
woman was Martha Gibbs. She had no shoes on her
feet, and she moved cautiously, stopping now and
again to listen if anything else was astir. But all
was still. She descended to the kitchen, where Bob
Williams was sitting bolt upright on the sofa, looking
as fresh as a daisy, and as if a glass of wine had never
passed his lips—and, indeed, but very little had. He
had simply been playing a part.

"It's all right now," whispered Martha. "Come."

They went upstairs again with the utmost caution.
Bob had also divested himself of his boots, so that
his footfalls might be soundless. They made their way
to Mr. Glindon's room, on the second floor. He had
a spacious bedchamber, a dressing-room, and a writ-
ing-room *en suite.*

To this latter room Martha and her young man

went, closing the door behind them. Then Bob set
to work on the desks and drawers with a bunch of
peculiar keys he carried with him. They seemed
capable of opening every drawer and every desk with
little difficulty, and wherever papers were discovered
they were carefully overhauled and scrutinised, though
they were evidently of no importance—at least not to
Bob, for he put them back.

But at last he came across a packet that appeared
to have an absorbing interest for him. He seized it
eagerly and examined it. It had been carefully done
up and sealed in a wrapper, but the seals were broken
and the wrapper was torn.

"Fortune has favoured us," said Bob, as he carefully
put the packet between his bosom and his waistcoat
and buttoned his coat over. Two hours had been consumed in the search, and there was a glimmer of daylight in the east. "You let me out," he continued,
"and then go to your bed. You need rest."

The two of them went down to the hall. He put on
his boots, and in a few minutes, after some whispered
conversation, he left the house, and the great door
closed behind him.

CHAPTER XXVI.

It has already been stated that, owing to the peculiar physiological features of Mr. Hilkiah Thorne's case, it had excited unusual interest in the medical profession. There were plenty of cases on record where a man had lived for years with a bullet in his brain; but the entire loss of memory was almost without a parallel. Nor was this all, for with Mr. Thorne the mental powers were so destroyed that he seemed incapable of acquiring any fresh knowledge or relearning what he had forgotten. The result was, he was reduced to a state of absolute imbecility, as he could not express his wishes and did not know the meaning of signs.

Dr. Blewitt and Sir Wilfred Weir had tended the patient with unflagging zeal, and all that science could do for him had been done; but nothing had proved of any avail in restoring the memory. The unfortunate gentleman did not suffer in any way. He was in fairly good health and took nourishment well, but, of course, he had to be waited on hand and foot. Sir Wilfred had expressed an opinion that in the process of time, perhaps a long time, the bullet might make its way out by the ear or the palate, and if so there would probably be a partial restoration of the mental faculties. This, however, was all a mere matter of speculation; and, on the other hand, there was always the danger of an abscess on the brain forming, which, sooner or later, would prove fatal. If the exact position of the bullet could have been determined, some further attempt to abstract it might have been made. But the surgeons had been unable to localise it, and as indiscriminate exploration of the brain could not be made, in spite of the advancement of science, they had to leave the bullet in the unfortunate man's head.

It chanced that Sir Wilfred Weir was spending a brief holiday in Paris, and was introduced to the eminent specialist, Dr. Cavizette, who had recently made a great stir in the scientific world by his remarkable experiments in hypnotism. Cavizette had studied the subject for years, and being attached to the chief hospital for epileptic patients, he had had opportunities of practically carrying out his theories.

Like most people who have hobbies, he was perhaps inclined to attach too much importance to his.

But there was no doubt that he had produced some very wonderful results; and even the most biassed sceptic had to admit that a new power had been added to therapeutics, though the knowledge of it was exceedingly limited. Dr. Cavizette, however, spoke of it with enthusiasm, and said it was almost capable of restoring the dead to life.

Sir Wilfred Weir found Cavizette to be a man of high scientific attainments, but modest and unpretending withal. It was but natural that they should discuss the remarkable case of Hilkiah Thorne. Sir Wilfred told his French colleague that everything had been tried that could possibly be tried, but the patient was as far off recovery as ever.

"Everything except hypnotism," answered Cavizette.

"Well," said Sir Wilfred, "if I thought there was the slightest chance of that effecting a cure I should invite you to accompany me to England, for it is likely that Mr. Thorne might be able to clear up the mystery of a great crime."

"It occurs to me," said Cavizette, "that it is just one of those cases where the new science might be of considerable advantage. At any rate, with your permission, I should certainly like to see your patient."

The result of this conversation was, that Sir Wilfred gave his colleague a very cordial invitation to the British metropolis, and the invitation was as cordially accepted. It was not, however, until three weeks later that Dr. Cavizette was able to start for London, where he was the guest of Sir Wilfred Weir, and the day following his arrival the two eminent men journeyed down to The Crags at East Sheen, where they were joined by Dr. Blewitt and one or two other doctors, and after an examination of the patient a consultation was held, at which Dr. Cavizette expressed a firm opinion that by hypnotising the patient some striking results might be obtained. As there was a general desire that the experiment should be tried, the principal members of Mr. Thorne's family were approached, and as they offered no opposition, the morrow was fixed for the trial of Cavizette's skill.

The following day, accordingly, found a large assembly of medical and scientific men at the lawyer's house, and amongst one or two laymen who had been invited to be present was Calvin Sugg, whose face were an unusually anxious look.

The day was very fine and balmy, and the patient had been brought down to the large drawing-room and placed upon the sofa. He was thin and pale from long confinement and inactivity, and there was a peculiar, vacant expression in the eyes. But it was a remarkable thing that, a few minutes after Dr. Cavizette had taken means to throw the lawyer into a hypnotic sleep, the vacant expression gave place to one of keen intelligence and the patient sighed heavily.

Presently it became perfectly evident that he was under the hypnotic influence, and then, prompted by Sir Wilfred Weir, the hypnotiser put a series of questions, which elicited perfectly intelligible answers, that were given deliberately, but in a monotone, without the slightest variation.

"Do you remember how you met with your injury?" was the first question asked.

"Yes."

"How?"

"I was shot."

"Do you know by whom?"

"No."

"Did you not see any one?"

"No."

"Was the attack sudden?"

"Very sudden."

"You had been to The Priory?"

"Yes."

"What for?"

"To draw up my poor friend's will in favour of his daughter."

"Had he requested you to go for that purpose?"

"Yes. He wrote to me."

"Had he not made a will before that?"

"No."

"Why?"

"Because he was under the influence of his son, who exercised some remarkable power over him."

"Then if he had not made a will the son could have taken everything?"

"Yes; but he promised the son to make a will leaving all to him, and to place that will in the hands of the son's lawyers. But he put off making the will from day to day."

"And at last, owing to some cause or other, he decided to make a will and leave all his property to his daughter?"

"Yes."

"Why did he do that?"

"Because a manuscript that he attached great importance to was stolen."

"What was the substance of the manuscript?"

"It was the story of my friend's life, and was intended for his daughter."

"Who was supposed to have stolen it?"

"The son."

"How did the son know of its existence?"

"It was thought that he had a spy in the house by the name of Ita Prokop, who gave him the information."

"What was the object in stealing the manuscript?"

"In it Mr. Glindon was supposed to have confessed to some error in his life, and the son would probably be under the impression that if he possessed that document he would have a still greater power over his father; that is, documentary evidence."

"Did you draw up a will for Mr. Glindon?"

"I did."

"Where is it?"

"I don't know. It was in my pocket when I left the house."

During this extraordinary scene no one save Dr. Cavizette—who spoke English admirably—and the hypnotised man uttered a word, and as the various answers were given the sensation amongst the onlookers was extraordinary.

It was now deemed advisable to restore Mr. Thorne to the condition he was in before the *séance* began. This was done, and he immediately fell into a deep sleep.

Then Calvin Sugg, who had been by no means the least interested spectator, hurried away, for he had pressing work to do, and he felt that he now held the key to the problem that had so long puzzled him.

CHAPTER XXVII.

DOOM!

In the likeness Calvin Sugg had brought from Russia, and which, he had been told, was the photograph of an Englishman named Robert Hinton, his visitor, Raymond Penoyre, declared he recognised a remarkable person in Jamaica, who was known as Judge John Hosack. Hosack represented himself as a New York judge, and gave out that he was in the West Indies for the benefit of his health.

There was some reason to doubt the truth of his statement that he was an American; and he was considered to be something more than eccentric, for he was looked upon as being absolutely mad. As he did nothing outrageous, however, had plenty of money, and paid his way—in fact, was stupidly lavish in his expenditure—he was tolerated. Penoyre became rather familiar with him, and considered him to be singularly cold-blooded and cruel. He seemed to take especial delight in stories of violence and murder, and had a great partiality for anything weird and mysterious. He was easily excited, and when in that state he displayed a ferociousness that was alarming.

In support of this Penoyre instanced the following

which came under his own notice :— "Hosack was in
the market-place at Kingston one day, when a dog
growled at him. It seemed to convert the man into
a savage, and he suddenly drew from his pocket
a large red Tussore silk handkerchief, and with a
lightning-like movement he rolled the handkerchief
up rope-like, twisted it round the dog's neck, and
strangled the animal, remarking to an onlooker that
he had learnt the trick in India. He said it was the
way the Thugs strangled their victims."

When Sugg heard this he exclaimed—

"At last I triumph. The man who killed that dog
is the man who killed Vesta Florence and the man who
wrote the extraordinary letter to Perley Beck."

Penoyre added that he had repeatedly heard Hosack
say that he was going to end his days in the West
Indies, for he was a child of the sun, and could only
live in the sun, and that the only being he had ever
loved in the world was a sister. But she had died.
After that he had met a young woman who fascinated
him, but he did not love her.

On the strength of Penoyre's story Sugg applied
for a warrant for the arrest of the man calling himself
Judge Hosack on suspicion of his having committed
the St. John's Wood murder, and the execution of
the warrant was entrusted to another detective, who
left immediately for the West Indies. Then Calvin
Sugg applied himself diligently to obtaining other
links in the chain of evidence he was slowly but
surely forging; and in order to keep a watch on

the movements of Glindon and his besotted guest,
he introduced into Rutland House a very smart and
clever female assistant of his, who passed as Martha
Gibbs. And on the night of the servant's *soirée* Sugg
himself had assumed the character of Bob Williams,
and had thus been successful in recovering the late
Mr. Glindon's stolen manuscript.

But the ruse resulted in more than this, for the
name that "Martha Gibbs" had seen in the pocket-
book was Perley Beck. After Dr. Cavizette's experiment Sugg felt that he had nearly all the parts
of the puzzle in his hand, and that he would now
track to their doom the murderers or murderer of
Vesta Florence and Mr. Glindon.

A few days later a cab containing four men drove
up to Rutland House and inquired for Mr. Glindon.
They were shown into the reception-room, and in
the course of ten minutes or so Glindon entered.
As soon as he did so one of the four men stepped
forward. It was Calvin Sugg, and laying his hand
on Glindon's arm, he said—

"Ivan Glindon, I hold a warrant for your arrest!"

Every particle of colour fled from Glindon's face, and
his eyes seemed to bulge out with the terror he felt.
But this display of weakness was only momentary; and
recovering himself quickly, he said with a sneering
smile—"Really, Mr. Sugg, you must be mistaken.
Upon what charge, pray, do you arrest me?"

"On the charge of having murdered your father, the
late Ivan Peter Glindon, of The Priory, Richmond."

Glindon laughed contemptuously as he answered—

"You are certainly on a false scent this time, for I did not murder my father."

"I hope you will be able to prove that, for your own sake," said Sugg; "but it is my duty to arrest you."

"I shall not oppose you in your duty, but I hope you will give me half an hour at least to arrange my affairs."

"I cannot give you half a minute. You must go at once," said Sugg peremptorily.

Glindon shrugged his shoulders, took a silver cigarette-case from his pocket, selected a cigarette, and lighted it with enforced coolness, and puffing a volume of smoke in the detective's face, said—

"Come on, then; I'm ready."

"Where is your confederate, Perley Beck?" asked Sugg.

Again Glindon's countenance fell, as he grew a shade paler, if that was possible.

"Dead, for anything I know or care," he growled.

"Then he must have died very, very recently. Perhaps, then, you can tell me where Mr. Arthur Goodeve is?"

Glindon's eyes flashed fire, and grinding his white teeth, he answered—

"You seem to have posted yourself well up in my affairs. But you will find that, for once in your life, you have made a grand mistake. Arthur Goodeve is in a state of drivelling imbecility in his bedroom. Some of the servants will show you where the room is."

Telling two of his assistants to conduct the prisoner to the cab, Sugg and his companion went up to Beck's room, where they found him in a state of semi-unconsciousness. He was conveyed downstairs, and another cab procured, into which he was put; and while Sugg accompanied him, the fourth man was left in charge of the house, in order to protect the valuables from being pillaged by the servants as soon as they knew that their master was a prisoner. The two prisoners were driven at once to Bow Street, where Glindon was charged with the murder of his father and attempted murder of Mr. Thorne, while Beck was charged with being an accessory to the fact.

Of course, the news of the arrests soon flew over London, and the excitement in the public mind was as great as it had been when the St. John's Wood tragedy became known, and the people who had said the most spiteful things about Sugg were now the loudest in his praise.

As early as he could get away on the following day he hurried off to Fulham to see Muriel, who, of course, had heard the startling news. He found Penoyre with her and her aunt, and they were all much excited. Muriel greeted Sugg very warmly, but she was so overcome with emotion that she could scarcely find words wherein to express her feelings.

"It is altogether a sad business," she said, "but it at least ends the terrible and torturing suspense."

"Yes, Miss Muriel, it does; and I hope it will do something much more than that. I hope it will place you in the position your poor father evidently intended you to occupy as his heiress—a position you are so well fitted to adorn. And now it gives me very great pleasure indeed to be able to restore to you the manuscript that was stolen from your father's desk. I found it amongst your half-brother's papers. It has been opened, for the seals are broken and the wrapper torn; but I restore it to you exactly as I got it. I have never perused a line of it."

He handed her a neat brown-paper parcel, and she was so overcome that she was obliged to leave the room. What she had considered as impossible had now actually come to pass, and she saw the light breaking through the dark clouds that had so long hung over her. New hopes arose in her heart; a new life seemed stretching before her.

To return to the prisoners in Bow Street, Perley Beck was in such a condition that it was found necessary to place him at once in the hospital, but it was several days before he showed any real improvement. He was, however, a physical wreck, and the doctor expressed an opinion that he could not live long even under the most advantageous circumstances. When he had sufficiently recovered he was removed to the same cell as Glindon, and two officers were placed in such a position that they could overhear all that was said by the prisoners. At first Glindon preserved a sullen silence. But when Beck remarked that the bubble had burst he growled out—

" Yes, it has. But if you will keep your mouth closed

nothing whatever can be proved against us. How the devil can it, unless the dead come up out of their graves? And Thorne is as good as dead. Although the work might have been done better, it was done well, since it silenced him."

"But sometimes," answered Beck, with a sigh of pitiful despondency, "the dead do come up out of their graves to accuse those who have wronged them."

"Bah!" sneered Glindon, "you are a weak, pitiable fool. Why didn't you drink yourself to death? Then you would have been safe. As it is, I am doubtful about you. But even if you turn traitor you cannot do me much harm. Though, if the worst comes to the worst, I will checkmate you all. I have lived a free life; I have drunk my full of pleasure; and if my time is up, well—so be it." He snapped his fingers defiantly, but his face seemed to say that his cynicism and stoicism were assumed.

Beck was soon removed from the cell and placed alone, although a warder was appointed to constantly watch him, for now that he was deprived of drink he became a prey to the deepest melancholy.

In the meantime steps were taken to obtain possession of the late Ita Glindon's luggage, which was still retained by the French police; and after some formalities and red-tapeism, it was despatched to London and taken possession of by the authorities at Scotland Yard. The bulk of it was wearing apparel, some of it of a costly kind. There was also a quantity of valuable jewellery.

Q

But what was of far more importance for the purpose required was a rosewood writing-desk, containing a great number of letters, the larger portion of which were written in Russian. A careful perusal of all these letters revealed the fact that Ita Prokop had come from Russia at Glindon's instigation, and it appeared that he had known her in Russia for a long time. It was through him that she took service at The Priory, where she became a spy on all her master's movements, and she was thereby enabled to communicate to Glindon the existence of the manuscript story of his father's life. It was then decided that the manuscript should be secured, and it was Ita who admitted Ivan into the house on the night when Mr. Glindon and his family were absent at Eastbourne. With such consummate skill did she act her part, that she succeeded in completely deceiving Mr. Glindon when he accused her of having been a party to the robbery.

Soon after leaving The Priory she paid a hurried visit to Russia, and on her return was married to the man who had made her his victim, and with whom she seemed to have been madly infatuated.

Although so much was proved by the letters, which, by a strange and almost unaccountable oversight, Glindon had allowed his wife to retain, there was nothing whatever that would serve as legal evidence to fix the crime of the murder and attempted murder on Glindon, and it was predicted that the whole case for the prosecution would break down. Evidence, however, of a very startling nature came from another quarter.

Stricken with remorse or fear—perhaps both had something to do with it—Perley Beck expressed a desire to relieve his conscience, and he put into writing as startling a story as has ever been recorded in the annals of crime, the substance of which was as follows.

When Glindon came from Russia he soon found out who his father's lawyers were, and he made the acquaintance of Beck. They became very intimate indeed, and Beck being in difficulties, Glindon assisted him very considerably; and in return Beck was to keep him posted up in all that was done in his father's affairs. On the night that Vesta Florence was murdered her husband picked up in the room a small pocketbook that had evidently fallen from the pocket of the murderer. Glindon opened and examined this, when, to his amazement, he found by letters and cards in the book that he knew the man well. They had been chums in Russia, where the murderer was known as Robert Hinton, but whose real name was Jäel Parmiter, a native of Dutch Guiana.

Now, Glindon's wife's maiden name had been Mary Clara Rees, and before he married her she told him that she had had a lover by the name of Parmiter, who had treated her very badly, and at last left her suddenly, having to fly the country for some offence. Glindon's first impulse was to hand the pocket-book over to the police. But on reflection he decided not to do so, and, as would seem from inference, for a diabolically sinister motive. By means of a letter found in the book Glindon subsequently traced Parmiter out. As a matter of fact the murderer never left London.

His motive for the crime was an uncontrollable and fierce jealousy. He had returned from abroad, and had recognised in photographs of Vesta Florence, so freely displayed in the photographers' shop-windows, the beautiful Mary Clara Rees, whom he had so cruelly and shamefully wronged. He wished her to return to him, but as she resolutely declined to do that, he resolved to kill her. He obtained entrance to the house at St. John's Wood by means of a false key, and strangled his victim almost immediately after she entered.

The foregoing particulars, which were related to. Glindon by the murderer himself, were confided to Beck by Glindon, for at that time there was a very close intimacy between them.

Shortly after, Beck made Parmiter's acquaintance. One of his most striking traits was his utter callousness, and yet he was capable of exercising a strange fascination over those who associated with him. At any rate he did so over Beck, according to Beck's own account. When Mr. Glindon wrote to his friend Thorne, the lawyer, asking him to go down to The Priory to draft a will, Perley Beck surreptitiously read that letter, and immediately communicated its contents to Ivan, and it was decided that Mr. Glindon and Thorne were to be killed, and Jäel Parmiter was deputed to carry out the fiendish work. He undertook it with positive alacrity, for he seemed to revel in deeds of darkness. When he learnt by the papers that he had only half done his work and that Thorne still lived, he absolutely wanted to make some attempt to finish him off, but Ivan would not hear of it.

Such was the astounding story that Beck committed to writing, and subsequently Sugg was enabled to verify it in most of its details. Jäel Parmiter was a human monster of iniquity, incapable, as it seemed, of bearing love for any living thing, with one exception. That exception was his sister, and it presents one of the most interesting psychological studies in the whole range of human phenomena. And, lest the reader may be disposed to think Jäel Parmiter is simply a creation of a disordered imagination, it may be stated here in the most emphatic manner the man is a study from life.

When his sister was dying she gave him the strange ring, with its ghastly emblems of mortality and its peculiar motto. She bade him treasure it for her sake. It was a family heirloom, and had been handed down through generations. After his sister's death Jäel used the symbols and motto for his letter-heading; and the possibilities are, had the design of the ring been made known at the time of the murder, it might have led to his detection. But it was thought by Sugg, and justifiably so, that if it were made known that the ring had been found, it would put the murderer on his guard.

The loss of the ring seemed to have preyed very much on Jäel's mind. He knew that he lost it on the night of the crime, but had no idea where. At last he prevailed upon Glindon to advertise for it, in the hope that it might be recovered.   The result of that advertisement the reader already knows.   It played into the enemy's hands and gave Sugg his first clue.

When Glindon learnt that his partner in guilt had betrayed him he abandoned all hope ; for he knew that, though the death-penalty could hardly be inflicted, he would probably be condemned to a life-long imprisonment.   He must long before have prepared for some such contingency as this, for he received a letter in a woman's handwriting, but the writer was never discovered.   It was a few lines only, written on a sheet of notepaper, and ran as follows :—

"I, who have always loved you, and love you still, exhort you, in this hour of your mortal need, to turn your eyes to the only source whence you can hope for forgiveness and mercy.   For my sake do this.   HELEN."

As the authorities at the House of Detention where he was confined pending his trial thought this short note might be of advantage to him, it was decided that he should have it.   It was observed at the time it was given to him that a strange smile spread over his dark, pale face ; and when he had read the letter he tore the paper into fragments, put them into his mouth, chewed them into pulp, and swallowed it.   Half an hour later he was seized with violent convulsions, and in spite of all that was done he died in two hours, from poisoning by strychnine.   The paper had been soaked in a saturated solution of that poison, and thus Ivan Glindon escaped the justice of man, but having been tracked to doom, he preferred death to imprisonment.

When the detective who had been sent out with the warrant to Jamaica arrived there, he found that Jäel Parmiter was confined as a dangerous and criminal lunatic. It appeared that a native boatman with whom he had been out fishing in the bay offended him in some way, and he beat the poor fellow to death with an oar of the boat. For this he was tried and condemned to twenty years' imprisonment, and almost immediately afterwards he exhibited such an alarming form of insanity that he had been kept in a strait-jacket and carefully guarded ever since.

Under the circumstances he could not be removed, even if there had been no legal difficulties. But the common doom fell upon him in less than two years, as violent inflammation of the brain carried him off. About the same time, too, Perley Beck, who had been sentenced to seven years' penal servitude, succumbed in the prison infirmary to softening of the brain.

CHAPTER XXVIII.

"AFTER SORROW'S NIGHT COMES THE MORNING BRIGHT."

THE recovered packet that Calvin Sugg was enabled to place in Muriel Glindon's hands afforded her sad reading. It was the autobiography of her father's life. He commenced from his earliest boyhood, which seemed to have been very happy; but his happiness was not of long duration.

"When I was not yet twenty," he wrote, "I fell desperately in love with a woman who was much older than myself, and in spite of all the protests of my friends I married her. She was little better than an adventuress, and soon I proved the truth of the adage, that to marry in haste is to repent at leisure. In due course she bore me a son, and I fondly hoped that pledge of our union might bring us peace and joy.

"But, unfortunately, my wife had the temper of a fiend, and so morbidly jealous was she, that she would scarcely ever let me out of her sight if she could help it. I can solemnly avow, however, that there was not one atom of justification for this jealousy. Heaven knows I endeavoured to do my duty to her, but not even a saint could have pleased her. Fain would I speak well of the dead, but the truth must be told. A man who undertakes to write the story of his own life is ever under a disadvantage, for if he speaks much of himself—and how can he avoid doing so?—he is accused of egotism, or of viewing himself too favourably, or of suppressing facts. As this narrative, however, is meant for your eyes alone, I would express a hope that you will accept what I tell you as strictly accurate; for, while I will extenuate nothing, I will set naught down in malice. I am conscious that I had many faults, but they were not such faults as should have caused unending misery between a man and his wife. But, unfortunately, my wife was endowed with a temperament that would hardly permit her to see good in anything. At any rate, as far as I was concerned, nothing I did, nothing I said, or nothing that I expressed a wish to do pleased her.

"In trying to convey even a faint notion of what I suffered during those bitter, dark years I feel the poverty of language. My life was a torture to me; she made it so. Even the very child that had been born to us proved a curse instead of a blessing; for when I expressed my opinion as to how he should be trained, she accused me of wishing to blast the boy's future, and so I allowed her to control him entirely. Of course, that was weakness on my part—pitiable weakness. I did not know it then, but I know it now. And yet I did it in the hope that it would ensure peace and quietness.

"Alas! it failed to accomplish its purpose, as everything else would have failed. I was by nature a peaceful man, with a capacity for love and gratitude for any kindness done, any service rendered. I was deeply impressed with a sense of duty, and humbly strove to do my duty. I clearly recognised that life involved grave responsibilities that no right-thinking and honest-minded man would attempt to ignore. And in saying this I wish you distinctly to understand that I was not under the impression that my existence would be one round of unruffled calm and pleasure. Sunshine and clouds alternate, and I should have been quite prepared to have endured the clouds without a single murmur had I been favoured with but a little sunshine. But the sunshine was all blotted out by my wife's conduct. She tried to blast my reputation; she tried to ruin my business; and I believe she tried to drive me mad. In very truth I think she did, or the terrible sequel to those years of sadness would not have happened.

"If I seek for the cause of all that misery, I am driven to the one conclusion, that it was entirely due to my wife's ungovernable temper, which, in turn, was caused by a strange nervous irritability, which was nothing less than a mild form of insanity. It is quite unnecessary for me to dwell on all the petty details of our daily life. One day was very like another, and the days became weeks, weeks months, months years. It was a monotonous, melancholy round of carking care. She would recognise none of my friends, and so wretched did she make my home that I could entertain nobody. I was isolated; and even my business relations suffered.

"I should like to reiterate here, with all the emphasis I am capable of, that during these years, during which I struggled with my cruel fate, I did all that I could possibly think of to bring peace to my unhappy household. I denied her nothing, and I sacrificed myself in order to appease her. I have not the slightest doubt now that this display of weakness on my part —for weakness it assuredly was—was nothing more than a concession to the enemy which was taken every advantage of. I should have ruled her with a rod of iron, instead of trying to curb her with gentleness. But the time was approaching when my patience was to reach its extremest limits. There had been moments in my married life when I had, with a shudder, seen as through a glass darkly the possibilities of the limit being reached. I had generally been accounted an exceptionally patient man, and I had endeavoured to cultivate the virtue—if virtue it was—in all my dealings with my wife. But even had I been endowed with the patience of Job, the wisdom of Solomon, and the gentleness of St. Paul, it must all have come to an end under the infliction I was called upon to endure. After all, I was only human—very human—and therefore let me be judged from the human standpoint.

"At the period I am now coming to I occupied an important and confidential position in a large general trading firm, with headquarters in St. Petersburg. I had been with the firm for a number of years, and had hoped ultimately to secure a partnership in the

firm. It chanced one year—it was just at the commencement of winter—that a fur depôt of ours, situated
at Petropavlovski, on the western slopes of the Ural
Mountains, was destroyed by fire. The warehouse at
the time was stored with costly furs, and it became
necessary that some one should go from headquarters
to salvage the burnt goods and make arrangements
for another depôt. This business was entrusted to
me. I accepted it joyfully, as I counted upon a few
months' release from the miseries of my home.

"But, alas! I left one important factor out of the
calculation. When my wife heard of my intended
journey she insisted on going with me, and go she did.
We travelled by a covered sleigh, and I was attended
by a faithful and valued servant, a man named Schaml.
When we reached the Urals it was snowing heavily.
Our horses had fallen lame, and could scarcely walk.
In order to ease them on the steepest part of the pass,
my wife and I alighted. Some little time before, she
had been finding fault about something, and when I
ventured to remonstrate she flew into a temper and
abused me. As we slowly toiled up the pass, with the
sleigh in front, the quarrel was renewed, until she
irritated me into madness, and turning upon her I
pushed her suddenly over a precipice. It was the
facility of committing the crime that led to the crime
being committed. She uttered one cry as she fell, and
in that moment, I declare before my Maker, I would
have given my life to have saved hers. But it was too
late. Her time had come.

"There had been a witness to the deed in the person of Schaml, who, as I stood almost turned to stone with horror, moved close to me, and touching me lightly on the shoulder, said, 'Master, it was an accident. You are well rid of her. Let us proceed.'

"His words recalled me to my senses, and yet the rest of the journey was a sort of dream to me. On reaching our destination I reported the circumstance, and said my wife had fallen over the precipice by accident. Schaml corroborated this, and the story was believed. Men were sent out to look for the body. They succeeded in recovering it, and she was buried in Petropavlovski.

"If I could only have deadened my conscience I might now have been happy, but it was not to be; and as soon after that fatal day as possible I placed my boy at school, settled a pension on Schaml, gave him instructions to look after the boy, and I set out for London. What my life has been in London you know pretty well. On my son I set great hopes, but they were all doomed to be early blighted. Inheriting his mother's infirmity of temper and obdurate will, he rebelled against all authority; and for years his career was one of shame and disgrace. At last Schaml, being old and lying on his deathbed, imparted the secret of my wife's death to my unworthy son, and armed with this secret he came to London. I had then disowned him, and refused to assist him in any way; but with this powerful weapon in his possession he threatened to utterly ruin me.

"I ought to have defied him, but for your dear sake

I could not—dare not. I know I have been pitiably weak and a moral coward; but it was the dread of darkening your life, destroying your happiness, that kept me silent; but latterly I have felt as if I could not go down into my grave with this terrible secret, and therefore I have resolved to commit the wretched story to paper, so that when I am no more you may know how I have suffered—how my heart has been broken. I have tried, with sincere tears of repentance, to atone for my crime, and perhaps the suffering I have endured will beget me pardon.

"For you I have suffered, for you I have endured persecution, for you I have been silent; and when the grass waves green over my grave, you perhaps will think kindly and tenderly of your unhappy father."

It was all known now; the mystery was ended, and the light shone in the dark places. To say that Muriel wept would but poorly express the passion of her grief as she learnt the terrible secret that had blighted her dear father's life. Whatever uncharitable people might say, whatever the world might think, she would always revere his memory. To her he had acted the part of a noble-minded man, a tender father, a loving guardian. He had endeavoured to make her life bright with flowers and one long dream of summer pleasure. If he had failed, it was because it was in the natural order of things that he should fail. There is no life in this world but what is chequered with sadness.

For long months Muriel kept that pitiable story to

herself. She was rich now, for though Ivan Glindon had squandered many thousands of pounds, there was still much left, to say nothing of the splendid business that was still carried on. People who knew of Raymond Penoyre's devotion to her wondered why she still refused to become his wife. And he wondered too, but he held his peace for a long time, lest it might be said by the envious and uncharitable that he coveted her riches. But at length the time came when he could no longer keep silent, and he asked her—

"Is it ever to be thus, Muriel? Is the happiness I have prayed for, yearned for, never, never to be mine?"

"Raymond," she answered, "between us is a gulf that I fear can never be bridged. But you have been true and faithful to me, and I will not keep the secret from you."

Then she gave him the story of her father's life to read, and when he had read it he said—"Muriel, my beloved, may I burn this document, so that there may be no written record of your father's misfortune?"

"Yes," she answered, after a long pause.

So he thrust the manuscript into the fire and watched it consume, and when the last morsel had turned to ashes he took her hands, saying—

"Muriel, I will keep that secret as well as the fire will keep it. Will you be my wife?"

How could she deny him? How say "No"? She would have been less than woman had she done so. With a great sob she let her head sink upon his breast, and murmured softly and low, "Yes!"

Three months later his hopes were fulfilled. People expressed surprise that the "wealthy Miss Glindon" should have been content with such a quiet and unpretentious wedding. But she and her husband derived no pleasure in ostentatious display and outward show; and though they found true happiness in each other's love, the memory of what had been could never be wholly effaced; and to them, somehow, it seemed that mere pomp and ceremony were discordant and out of harmony with their lives.

After a few months' travelling abroad, in company with Mrs. Romanoff, they returned to England, and settled down in the dear old Priory, where Muriel had known so many happy years, and where she was destined to know many more with one of the most devoted of husbands and some of the most affectionate children. And among their large circle of friends there is none for whom they have a greater respect, or who is a more welcome guest at The Priory, than the famous detective, Calvin Sugg. By patience and perseverance he had tracked the wrong-doers to doom and righted those who had been so cruelly wronged.

THE END.

PRINTED BY BALLANTYNE, HANSON AND CO.
EDINBURGH AND LONDON.

[*March*, 1893.

𝔄 𝔏𝔦𝔰𝔱 𝔬𝔣 𝔅𝔬𝔬𝔨𝔰
PUBLISHED BY
CHATTO & WINDUS
214, Piccadilly, London, W.
Sold by all Booksellers, or sent post-free for the published price by the Publishers.

ABOUT.—THE FELLAH: An Egyptian Novel. By EDMOND ABOUT. Translated by Sir RANDAL ROBERTS. Post 8vo, illustrated boards, 2s.

ADAMS (W. DAVENPORT), WORKS BY.
A DICTIONARY OF THE DRAMA. Being a comprehensive Guide to the Plays, Playwrights, Players, and Playhouses of the United Kingdom and America. Crown 8vo half-bound, 12s. 6d. [*Preparing.*
QUIPS AND QUIDDITIES. Selected by W. D. ADAMS. Post 8vo, cloth limp, 2s. 6d.

AGONY COLUMN (THE) OF "THE TIMES," from 1800 to 1870. Edited, with an Introduction, by ALICE CLAY. Post 8vo, cloth limp, 2s. 6d.

AIDE (HAMILTON), WORKS BY. Post 8vo, illustrated boards, 2s. each.
CARR OF CARRLYON. | CONFIDENCES.

ALBERT.—BROOKE FINCHLEY'S DAUGHTER. By MARY ALBERT. Post 8vo, picture boards, 2s.; cloth limp, 2s. 6d.

ALDEN.—A LOST SOUL. By W. L. ALDEN. Fcap. 8vo, cl. bds., 1s. 6d.

ALEXANDER (MRS.), NOVELS BY. Post 8vo, illustrated boards, 2s. each.
MAID, WIFE, OR WIDOW? | VALERIE'S FATE.

ALLEN (F. M.).—GREEN AS GRASS. By F. M. ALLEN, Author of "Through Green Glasses." Frontispiece by J. SMYTH. Cr. 8vo, cloth ex., 3s. 6d.

ALLEN (GRANT), WORKS BY. Crown 8vo, cloth extra, 6s. each.
THE EVOLUTIONIST AT LARGE. | COLIN CLOUT'S CALENDAR.
Crown 8vo, cloth extra, 3s. 6d. each; post 8vo, illustrated boards, 2s. each.

PHILISTIA.	FOR MAIMIE'S SAKE.	THE TENTS OF SHEM.
BABYLON.	IN ALL SHADES.	THE GREAT TABOO.
STRANGE STORIES.	THE DEVIL'S DIE.	DUMARESQ'S DAUGHTER.
BECKONING HAND.	THIS MORTAL COIL.	

Crown 8vo, cloth extra, 3s. 6d. each.
THE DUCHESS OF POWYSLAND. | BLOOD ROYAL.
IVAN GREET'S MASTERPIECE, &c. With a Frontispiece. [*Shortly.*

AMERICAN LITERATURE, A LIBRARY OF, from the Earliest Settlement to the Present Time. Compiled and Edited by EDMUND CLARENCE STEDMAN and ELLEN MACKAY HUTCHINSON. Eleven Vols., royal 8vo, cloth extra, £6 12s.

ARCHITECTURAL STYLES, A HANDBOOK OF. By A. ROSENGARTEN. Translated by W. COLLETT-SANDARS. With 639 Illusts. Cr. 8vo, cl. ex., 7s. 6d.

ART (THE) OF AMUSING: A Collection of Graceful Arts, GAMES, Tricks, Puzzles, and Charades. By FRANK BELLEW. 300 Illusts. Cr. 8vo, cl. ex., 4s. 6d.

ARNOLD (EDWIN LESTER), WORKS BY.
THE WONDERFUL ADVENTURES OF PHRA THE PHŒNICIAN. With Introduction by Sir EDWIN ARNOLD, and 12 Illustrations by H. M. PAGET. Crown 8vo, cloth extra, 3s. 6d.; post 8vo, illustrated boards, 2s.
THE CONSTABLE OF ST. NICHOLAS. Crown 8vo, cloth, 3s. 6d. [*Shortly.*
BIRD LIFE IN ENGLAND. Crown 8vo, cloth extra, 6s.

ARTEMUS WARD'S WORKS. With Portrait and Facsimile. Crown
8vo, cloth extra, **7s. 6d.**—Also a POPULAR EDITION, post 8vo, picture boards, **2s.**
THE GENIAL SHOWMAN: Life and Adventures of ARTEMUS WARD. By EDWARD
P. HINGSTON. With a Frontispiece. Crown 8vo, cloth extra, **3s. 6d.**

ASHTON (JOHN), WORKS BY. Crown 8vo, cloth extra, **7s. 6d.** each.
HISTORY OF THE CHAP-BOOKS OF THE 18th CENTURY. With 334 Illusts.
SOCIAL LIFE IN THE REIGN OF QUEEN ANNE. With 85 Illustrations.
HUMOUR, WIT, AND SATIRE OF SEVENTEENTH CENTURY. With 82 Illusts.
ENGLISH CARICATURE AND SATIRE ON NAPOLEON THE FIRST. 115 Illusts.
MODERN STREET BALLADS. With 57 Illustrations.

BACTERIA.— A SYNOPSIS OF THE BACTERIA AND YEAST
FUNGI AND ALLIED SPECIES. By W. B. GROVE, B.A. With 87 Illustrations.
Crown 8vo, cloth extra, **3s. 6d.**

BARDSLEY (REV. C. W.), WORKS BY.
ENGLISH SURNAMES: Their Sources and Significations. Cr. 8vo, cloth, **7s. 6d.**
CURIOSITIES OF PURITAN NOMENCLATURE. Crown 8vo, cloth extra, **6s.**

BARING GOULD (S., Author of "John Herring," &c.**), NOVELS BY.**
Crown 8vo, cloth extra, **3s. 6d.** each; post 8vo, illustrated boards, **2s.** each.
RED SPIDER. | EVE.

BARRETT (FRANK, Author of "Lady Biddy Fane,"**) NOVELS BY.**
Post 8vo, illustrated boards, **2s.** each; cloth, **2s. 6d.** each.
FETTERED FOR LIFE. | A PRODIGAL'S PROGRESS.
THE SIN OF OLGA ZASSOULICH. | JOHN FORD; and HIS HELPMATE.
BETWEEN LIFE AND DEATH. | A RECOILING VENGEANCE.
FOLLY MORRISON. | HONEST DAVIE. | FOUND GUILTY.
LIEUT. BARNABAS. | FOR LOVE AND HONOUR.
LITTLE LADY LINTON.

BEACONSFIELD, LORD: A Biography. By T. P. O'CONNOR, M.P.
Sixth Edition, with an Introduction. Crown 8vo, cloth extra, **5s.**

BEAUCHAMP.—GRANTLEY GRANGE: A Novel. By SHELSLEY
BEAUCHAMP. Post 8vo, illustrated boards, **2s.**

BEAUTIFUL PICTURES BY BRITISH ARTISTS: A Gathering of
Favourites from our Picture Galleries, beautifully engraved on Steel. With Notices
of the Artists by SYDNEY ARMYTAGE, M.A. Imperial 4to, cloth extra, gilt edges, **21s.**

BECHSTEIN.—AS PRETTY AS SEVEN, and other German Stories.
Collected by LUDWIG BECHSTEIN. With Additional Tales by the Brothers GRIMM,
and 98 Illustrations by RICHTER. Square 8vo, cloth extra, **6s. 6d.**; gilt edges, **7s. 6d.**

BEERBOHM.—WANDERINGS IN PATAGONIA; or, Life among the
Ostrich Hunters. By JULIUS BEERBOHM. With Illusts. Cr. 8vo, cl. extra, **3s. 6d.**

BENNETT (W. C., LL.D.), WORKS BY. Post 8vo, cloth limp, **2s.** each.
A BALLAD HISTORY OF ENGLAND. | SONGS FOR SAILORS.

BESANT (WALTER), NOVELS BY.
Cr. 8vo, cl. ex., **3s. 6d.** each; post 8vo, illust. hds., **2s.** each; cl. limp, **2s. 6d.** each.
ALL SORTS AND CONDITIONS OF MEN. With Illustrations by FRED. BARNARD.
THE CAPTAINS' ROOM, &c. With Frontispiece by E. J. WHEELER.
ALL IN A GARDEN FAIR. With 6 Illustrations by HARRY FURNISS.
DOROTHY FORSTER. With Frontispiece by CHARLES GREEN.
UNCLE JACK, and other Stories. | CHILDREN OF GIBEON.
THE WORLD WENT VERY WELL THEN. With 12 Illustrations by A. FORESTIER.
HERR PAULUS: His Rise, his Greatness, and his Fall.
FOR FAITH AND FREEDOM. With Illustrations by A. FORESTIER and F. WADDY.
TO CALL HER MINE, &c. With 9 Illustrations by A. FORESTIER.
THE BELL OF ST. PAUL'S.
THE HOLY ROSE, &c. With Frontispiece by F. BARNARD.
ARMOREL OF LYONESSE: A Romance of To-day. With 12 Illusts. by F. BARNARD.
ST. KATHERINE'S BY THE TOWER. With 12 page Illustrations by C. GREEN.
Crown 8vo, cloth extra, **3s. 6d.** each.
VERBENA CAMELLIA STEPHANOTIS, &c. Frontispiece by GORDON BROWNE.
THE IVORY GATE: A Novel. *[Shortly.*
FIFTY-YEARS AGO. With 144 Plates and Woodcuts. Crown 8vo, cloth extra, **5s.**
THE EULOGY OF RICHARD JEFFERIES. With Portrait. Cr. 8vo, cl. extra, **6s.**
THE ART OF FICTION. Demy 8vo, **1s.**
LONDON. With 124 Illustrations. Demy 8vo, cloth extra, **18s.**
THE REBEL QUEEN: A Novel. Three Vols., crown 8vo. *[Shortly.*

BESANT (WALTER) AND JAMES RICE, NOVELS BY.
Cr. 8vo, cl. ex., **3s. 6d.** each ; post 8vo, illust. bds., **2s.** each; cl. limp, **2s. 6d.** each.

READY-MONEY MORTIBOY.	BY CELIA'S ARBOUR.
MY LITTLE GIRL.	THE CHAPLAIN OF THE FLEET.
WITH HARP AND CROWN.	THE SEAMY SIDE.
THIS SON OF VULCAN.	THE CASE OF MR. LUCRAFT, &c.
THE GOLDEN BUTTERFLY.	'TWAS IN TRAFALGAR'S BAY, &c.
THE MONKS OF THELEMA.	THE TEN YEARS' TENANT, &c.

*** There is also a LIBRARY EDITION of the above Twelve Volumes, handsomely set in new type, on a large crown 8vo page, and bound in cloth extra, **6s.** each.

BEWICK (THOMAS) AND HIS PUPILS. By AUSTIN DOBSON. With 95 Illustrations. Square 8vo, cloth extra, **6s.**

BIERCE.—IN THE MIDST OF LIFE: Tales of Soldiers and Civilians, By AMBROSE BIERCE. Crown 8vo, cloth extra, **6s.**; post 8vo, illustrated boards, **2s.**

BLACKBURN'S (HENRY) ART HANDBOOKS.
ACADEMY NOTES, separate years, from 1875-1887, 1889-1892, each **1s.**
ACADEMY NOTES, 1893. With Illustrations. **1s.**
ACADEMY NOTES, 1875-79. Complete in One Vol., with 600 Illusts. Cloth limp, **6s.**
ACADEMY NOTES, 1880-84. Complete in One Vol. with 700 Illusts. Cloth limp, **6s.**
GROSVENOR NOTES, 1877. **6d.**
GROSVENOR NOTES, separate years, from 1878 to 1890, each **1s.**
GROSVENOR NOTES, Vol. I., 1877-82. With 300 Illusts. Demy 8vo, cloth limp, **6s.**
GROSVENOR NOTES, Vol. II., 1883-87. With 300 Illusts. Demy 8vo, cloth limp, **6s.**
THE NEW GALLERY, 1888-1892. With numerous Illustrations, each **1s.**
THE NEW GALLERY, 1893. With Illustrations. **1s.**
THE NEW GALLERY, Vol. I, 1888-1892. With 250 Illusts. Demy 8vo, cloth, **6s.**
ENGLISH PICTURES AT THE NATIONAL GALLERY. 114 Illustrations. **1s.**
OLD MASTERS AT THE NATIONAL GALLERY. 128 Illustrations. **1s. 6d.**
ILLUSTRATED CATALOGUE TO THE NATIONAL GALLERY. 242 Illusts. cl., **3s.**
THE PARIS SALON, 1893. With Facsimile Sketches. **3s.**
THE PARIS SOCIETY OF FINE ARTS, 1893. With Sketches. **3s. 6d.** [Shortly.

BLAKE (WILLIAM): India-proof Etchings from his Works by WILLIAM BELL SCOTT. With descriptive Text. Folio, half-bound boards, **21s.**

BLIND (MATHILDE). Poems by. Crown 8vo, cloth extra, 5s. each.
THE ASCENT OF MAN.
DRAMAS IN MINIATURE. With a Frontispiece by FORD MADOX BROWN.
SONGS AND SONNETS. Fcap. 8vo, vellum and gold.

BOURNE (H. R. FOX), WORKS BY.
ENGLISH MERCHANTS: Memoirs in Illustration of the Progress of British Commerce. With numerous Illustrations. Crown 8vo, cloth extra, **7s. 6d.**
ENGLISH NEWSPAPERS: The History of Journalism. Two Vols., demy 8vo, cl., **25s.**
THE OTHER SIDE OF THE EMIN PASHA RELIEF EXPEDITION. Crown 8vo, cloth extra, **6s.**

BOWERS.—LEAVES FROM A HUNTING JOURNAL. By GEORGE BOWERS. Oblong folio, half-bound, **21s.**

BOYLE (FREDERICK), WORKS BY. Post 8vo, illustrated boards, **2s.** each.
CHRONICLES OF NO-MAN'S LAND. | CAMP NOTES.
SAVAGE LIFE. Crown 8vo, cloth extra, **3s. 6d.**; post 8vo, picture boards, **2s.**

BRAND'S OBSERVATIONS ON POPULAR ANTIQUITIES; chiefly illustrating the Origin of our Vulgar Customs, Ceremonies, and Superstitions. With the Additions of Sir HENRY ELLIS, and Illustrations. Cr. 8vo, cloth extra, **7s. 6d.**

BREWER (REV. DR.), WORKS BY.
THE READER'S HANDBOOK OF ALLUSIONS, REFERENCES, PLOTS, AND STORIES. Fifteenth Thousand. Crown 8vo, cloth extra, **7s. 6d.**
AUTHORS AND THEIR WORKS, WITH THE DATES: Being the Appendices to "The Reader's Handbook," separately printed. Crown 8vo, cloth limp, **2s.**
A DICTIONARY OF MIRACLES. Crown 8vo, cloth extra, **7s. 6d.**

BREWSTER (SIR DAVID), WORKS BY. Post 8vo cl. ex. **4s. 6d.** each.
MORE WORLDS THAN ONE: Creed of Philosopher and Hope of Christian. Plates.
THE MARTYRS OF SCIENCE: GALILEO, TYCHO BRAHE, and KEPLER. With Portraits.
LETTERS ON NATURAL MAGIC. With numerous Illustrations.

BRILLAT-SAVARIN.—GASTRONOMY AS A FINE ART. By BRILLAT-SAVARIN. Translated by R. E. ANDERSON, M.A. Post 8vo, half-bound, **2s.**

BRET HARTE, WORKS BY.
LIBRARY EDITION. In Seven Volumes, crown 8vo, cloth extra, **6s.** each.
BRET HARTE'S COLLECTED WORKS. Arranged and Revised by the Author.
Vol. I. COMPLETE POETICAL AND DRAMATIC WORKS. With Steel Portrait.
Vol. II. LUCK OF ROARING CAMP—BOHEMIAN PAPERS—AMERICAN LEGENDS.
Vol. III. TALES OF THE ARGONAUTS—EASTERN SKETCHES.
Vol. IV. GABRIEL CONROY. | Vol. V. STORIES—CONDENSED NOVELS, &c.
Vol. VI. TALES OF THE PACIFIC SLOPE.
Vol.VII. TALES OF THE PACIFIC SLOPE—II. With Portrait by JOHN PETTIE, R.A.

THE SELECT WORKS OF BRET HARTE, in Prose and Poetry With Introductory
Essay by J. M. BELLEW, Portrait of Author, and 50 Illusts. Cr.8vo, cl. ex., **7s. 6d.**
BRET HARTE'S POETICAL WORKS. Hand-made paper & buckram. Cr.8vo, **4s.6d.**
THE QUEEN OF THE PIRATE ISLE. With 28 original Drawings by KATE
GREENAWAY, reproduced in Colours by EDMUND EVANS. Small 4to, cloth, **5s.**

Crown 8vo, cloth extra, **3s. 6d.** each.
A WAIF OF THE PLAINS. With 60 Illustrations by STANLEY L. WOOD.
A WARD OF THE GOLDEN GATE. With 59 Illustrations by STANLEY L. WOOD
A SAPPHO OF GREEN SPRINGS, &c. With Two Illustrations by HUME NISBET
COLONEL STARBOTTLE'S CLIENT, AND SOME OTHER PEOPLE. With a
Frontispiece by FRED. BARNARD.
SUSY: A Novel. With Frontispiece and Vignette by J. A. CHRISTIE.
SALLY DOWS, &c. With 47 Illustrations by W. D. ALMOND, &c.

Post 8vo, illustrated boards, **2s.** each.
GABRIEL CONROY. | THE LUCK OF ROARING CAMP, &c.
AN HEIRESS OF RED DOG, &c. | CALIFORNIAN STORIES.
Post 8vo, illustrated boards, **2s.** each; cloth limp, **2s. 6d.** each.
FLIP. | MARUJA. | A PHYLLIS OF THE SIERRAS.
Fcap. 8vo. picture cover, **1s.** each.
THE TWINS OF TABLE MOUNTAIN. | JEFF BRIGGS'S LOVE STORY.
SNOW-BOUND AT EAGLE'S.

BRYDGES.—UNCLE SAM AT HOME. By HAROLD BRYDGES. Post
8vo, illustrated boards, **2s.**; cloth limp, **2s. 6d.**

BUCHANAN'S (ROBERT) WORKS. Crown 8vo, cloth extra, **6s.** each.
SELECTED POEMS OF ROBERT BUCHANAN. With Frontispiece by T. DALZIEL.
THE EARTHQUAKE; or, Six Days and a Sabbath.
THE CITY OF DREAM: An Epic Poem. With Two Illustrations by P. MACNAB.
THE WANDERING JEW: A Christmas Carol. Second Edition.
THE OUTCAST: A Rhyme for the Time. With 15 Illustrations by RUDOLF BLIND,
PETER MACNAB, and HUME NISBET. Small demy 8vo, cloth extra, **8s.**
ROBERT BUCHANAN'S COMPLETE POETICAL WORKS. With Steel-plate Por-
trait. Crown 8vo, cloth extra, **7s. 6d.**

Crown 8vo, cloth extra, **3s. 6d.** each; post 8vo, illustrated boards, **2s.** each.
THE SHADOW OF THE SWORD. | LOVE ME FOR EVER. Frontispiece.
A CHILD OF NATURE. Frontispiece. | ANNAN WATER. | FOXGLOVE MANOR.
GOD AND THE MAN. With 11 Illus- | THE NEW ABELARD.
trations by FRED. BARNARD. | MATT: A Story of a Caravan. Front.
THE MARTYRDOM OF MADELINE. | THE MASTER OF THE MINE. Front.
With Frontispiece by A. W. COOPER. | THE HEIR OF LINNE.

BURTON (CAPTAIN).—THE BOOK OF THE SWORD: Being a
History of the Sword and its Use in all Countries, from the Earliest Times. By
RICHARD F. BURTON. With over 400 Illustrations. Square 8vo, cloth extra. **32s.**

BURTON (ROBERT).
THE ANATOMY OF MELANCHOLY: A New Edition, with translations of the
Classical Extracts. Demy 8vo, cloth extra, **7s. 6d.**
MELANCHOLY ANATOMISED Being an Abridgment, for popular use, of BURTON'S
ANATOMY OF MELANCHOLY. Post 8vo, cloth limp, **2s. 6d.**

CAINE (T. HALL), NOVELS BY. Crown 8vo, cloth extra, **3s. 6d.** each;
post 8vo, illustrated boards, **2s.** each; cloth limp, **2s. 6d.** each.
SHADOW OF A CRIME. | A SON OF HAGAR. | THE DEEMSTER.

CAMERON (COMMANDER).—THE CRUISE OF THE "BLACK
PRINCE" PRIVATEER. By V. LOVETT CAMERON, R.N., C.B. With Two Illustrations by P. MACNAB. Crown 8vo, cloth extra, **5s.**; post 8vo, illustrated boards, **2s.**

CAMERON (MRS. H. LOVETT), NOVELS BY. Post 8vo, illust. bds., **2s.** each.
JULIET'S GUARDIAN. | DECEIVERS EVER.

CARLYLE (THOMAS) ON THE CHOICE OF BOOKS. With Life
by R. II. SHEPHERD, and Three Illustrations. Post 8vo. cloth extra, **1s. 6d.**
CORRESPONDENCE OF THOMAS CARLYLE AND R. W. EMERSON, 1834 to 1872.
Edited by C. E. NORTON. With Portraits. Two Vols., crown 8vo, cloth, **24s.**

CARLYLE (JANE WELSH), LIFE OF. By Mrs. ALEXANDER IRELAND.
With Portrait and Facsimile Letter. Small demy 8vo, cloth extra, **7s. 6d.**

CHAPMAN'S (GEORGE) WORKS. Vol. I. contains the Plays complete,
including the doubtful ones. Vol. II., the Poems and Minor Translations, with an
Introductory Essay by ALGERNON CHARLES SWINBURNE. Vol. III., the Translations
of the Iliad and Odyssey. Three Vols., crown 8vo, cloth extra, **6s.** each.

CHATTO AND JACKSON.—A TREATISE ON WOOD ENGRAVING,
Historical and Practical. By WILLIAM ANDREW CHATTO and JOHN JACKSON. With
an Additional Chapter by HENRY G. BOHN, and 450 fine Illusts. Large 4to, hf.-bd., **28s.**

CHAUCER FOR CHILDREN: A Golden Key. By Mrs. H. R. HAWEIS.
With 8 Coloured Plates and 30 Woodcuts. Small 4to, cloth extra, **6s.**
CHAUCER FOR SCHOOLS. By Mrs. H R. HAWEIS. Demy 8vo, cloth limp, **2s. 6d.**

CLARE.—FOR THE LOVE OF A LASS: A Tale of Tynedale. By
AUSTIN CLARE. Post 8vo, picture boards, **2s. ;** cloth limp, **2s. 6d.**

CLIVE (MRS. ARCHER), NOVELS BY. Post two, illust. boards, **2s.** each.
PAUL FERROLL. | WHY PAUL FERROLL KILLED HIS WIFE.

CLODD.—MYTHS AND DREAMS. By EDWARD CLODD, F.R.A.S.
Second Edition, Revised. Crown 8vo, cloth extra, **3s. 6d.**

COBBAN (J. MACLAREN), NOVELS BY.
THE CURE OF SOULS. Post 8vo, illustrated boards, **2s.**
THE RED SULTAN. Three Vols., crown 8vo. [Shortly.

COLEMAN (JOHN), WORKS BY.
PLAYERS AND PLAYWRIGHTS I HAVE KNOWN. Two Vols., 8vo, cloth, **24s.**
CURLY: An Actor's Story. With 21 Illusts. by J. C. DOLLMAN. Cr. 8vo, cl., **1s. 6d.**

COLERIDGE.—THE SEVEN SLEEPERS OF EPHESUS. By M. E.
COLERIDGE. Fcap. 8vo, cloth, **1s. 6d.**

COLLINS (C. ALLSTON).—THE BAR SINISTER. Post 8vo, 2s.

COLLINS (MORTIMER AND FRANCES), NOVELS BY.
Crown 8vo, cloth extra, **3s. 6d.** each ; post 8vo, illustrated boards, **2s.** each.
FROM MIDNIGHT TO MIDNIGHT. | BLACKSMITH AND SCHOLAR.
TRANSMIGRATION. | YOU PLAY ME FALSE. | A VILLAGE COMEDY.
Post 8vo, illustrated boards, **2s.** each.
SWEET ANNE PAGE. | FIGHT WITH FORTUNE. | SWEET & TWENTY. | FRANCES.

COLLINS (WILKIE), NOVELS BY.
Cr. 8vo. cl. ex., **3s. 6d.** each ; post 8vo. illust. bds., **2s.** each; cl. limp, **2s. 6d.** each.
ANTONINA. With a Frontispiece by Sir JOHN GILBERT, R.A.
BASIL. Illustrated by Sir JOHN GILBERT, R.A., and J. MAHONEY.
HIDE AND SEEK. Illustrated by Sir JOHN GILBERT, R.A., and J. MAHONEY.
AFTER DARK. Illustrations by A. B. HOUGHTON. | THE TWO DESTINIES.
THE DEAD SECRET. With a Frontispiece by Sir JOHN GILBERT, R.A.
QUEEN OF HEARTS. With a Frontispiece by Sir JOHN GILBERT, R.A.
THE WOMAN IN WHITE. With Illusts. by Sir J. GILBERT, R.A., and F. A. FRASER.
NO NAME. With Illustrations by Sir J. E. MILLAIS, R.A., and A. W. COOPER.
MY MISCELLANIES. With a Steel-plate Portrait of WILKIE COLLINS.
ARMADALE. With Illustrations by G. H. THOMAS.
THE MOONSTONE. With Illustrations by G. DU MAURIER and F. A. FRASER.
MAN AND WIFE. With Illustrations by WILLIAM SMALL.
POOR MISS FINCH. Illustrated by G. DU MAURIER and EDWARD HUGHES.
MISS OR MRS.? With Illusts. by S. L. FILDES, R.A., and HENRY WOODS, A.R.A.
THE NEW MAGDALEN. Illustrated by G. DU MAURIER and C. S. REINHARDT.
THE FROZEN DEEP. Illustrated by G. DU MAURIER and J. MAHONEY.
THE LAW AND THE LADY. Illusts. by S. L. FILDES, R.A., and SYDNEY HALL.
THE HAUNTED HOTEL. Illustrated by ARTHUR HOPKINS.
THE FALLEN LEAVES. | HEART AND SCIENCE. | THE EVIL GENIUS.
JEZEBEL'S DAUGHTER. | "I SAY NO." | LITTLE NOVELS.
THE BLACK ROBE. | A ROGUE'S LIFE. | THE LEGACY OF CAIN.
BLIND LOVE. With Preface by WALTER BESANT, and Illusts. by A. FORESTIER.

COLLINS (JOHN CHURTON, M.A.), BOOKS BY.
ILLUSTRATIONS OF TENNYSON. Crown 8vo, cloth extra, **6s.**
JONATHAN SWIFT: A Biographical and Critical Study. Cr. 8vo, cl. ex., **8s.** [Shortly

COLMAN'S HUMOROUS WORKS: "Broad Grins," "My Nightgown and Slippers," and other Humorous Works of GEORGE COLMAN. With Life by G. B. BUCKSTONE, and Frontispiece by HOGARTH. Crown 8vo, cloth extra, **7s. 6d.**

COLMORE.—A VALLEY OF SHADOWS. By G. COLMORE, Author of "A Conspiracy of Silence." Two Vols., crown 8vo.

COLQUHOUN.—EVERY INCH A SOLDIER: A Novel. By M. J. COLQUHOUN. Post 8vo, illustrated boards, **2s.**

CONVALESCENT COOKERY: A Family Handbook. By CATHERINE RYAN. Crown 8vo, **1s.;** cloth limp, **1s. 6d.**

CONWAY (MONCURE D.), WORKS BY.
DEMONOLOGY AND DEVIL-LORE. 65 Illustrations. Two Vols., 8vo, cloth **28s.**
A NECKLACE OF STORIES. 25 Illusts. by W. J. HENNESSY. Sq. 8vo, cloth, **6s.**
PINE AND PALM: A Novel. Two Vols., crown 8vo, cloth extra, **21s.**
GEORGE WASHINGTON'S RULES OF CIVILITY. Fcap. 8vo, Jap. vellum, **2s. 6d.**

COOK (DUTTON), NOVELS BY.
PAUL FOSTER'S DAUGHTER. Cr. 8vo, cl. ex, **3s. 6d.;** post 8vo, illust. boards, **2s.**
LEO. Post 8vo, illustrated boards, **2s.**

COOPER (EDWARD H.)—GEOFFORY HAMILTON. Two Vols.

CORNWALL.—POPULAR ROMANCES OF THE WEST OF ENG- LAND; or, The Drolls, Traditions, and Superstitions of Old Cornwall. Collected by ROBERT HUNT, F.R.S. Two Steel-plates by GEO. CRUIKSHANK. Cr. 8vo, cl., **7s. 6d.**

COTES.—TWO GIRLS ON A BARGE. By V. CECIL COTES. With 44 Illustrations by F. H. TOWNSEND. Crown 8vo, cloth extra, **3s. 6d.**

CRADDOCK.—THE PROPHET OF THE GREAT SMOKY MOUN- TAINS. By CHARLES EGBERT CRADDOCK. Post 8vo, illust. bds., **2s.;** cl. limp, **2s. 6d.**

CRIM.—ADVENTURES OF A FAIR REBEL. By MATT CRIM. With a Frontispiece. Crown 8vo, cloth extra, **3s. 6d.;** post 8vo, illustrated boards, **2s.**

CROKER (B.M.), NOVELS BY. Crown 8vo, cloth extra, **3s. 6d.** each; post 8vo, illustrated boards, **2s.** each; cloth limp, **2s. 6d.** each.
PRETTY MISS NEVILLE. | DIANA BARRINGTON.
A BIRD OF PASSAGE. | PROPER PRIDE.
A FAMILY LIKENESS. Three Vols., crown 8vo.

CRUIKSHANK'S COMIC ALMANACK. Complete in Two SERIES: The FIRST from 1835 to 1843; the SECOND from 1844 to 1853. A Gathering of the BEST HUMOUR of THACKERAY, HOOD, MAYHEW, ALBERT SMITH, A'BECKETT, ROBERT BROUGH, &c. With numerous Steel Engravings and Woodcuts by CRUIK-SHANK, HINE, LANDELLS, &c. Two Vols., crown 8vo, cloth gilt, **7s. 6d.** each.
THE LIFE OF GEORGE CRUIKSHANK. By BLANCHARD JERROLD. With 84 Illustrations and a Bibliography. Crown 8vo, cloth extra, **7s. 6d.**

CUMMING (C. F. GORDON), WORKS BY. Demy 8vo, cl. ex., **8s. 6d.** each.
IN THE HEBRIDES. With Autotype Facsimile and 23 Illustrations.
IN THE HIMALAYAS AND ON THE INDIAN PLAINS. With 42 Illustrations.
TWO HAPPY YEARS IN CEYLON. With 28 Illustrations.
VIA CORNWALL TO EGYPT. With Photogravure Frontis. Demy 8vo, cl., **7s. 6d.**

CUSSANS.—A HANDBOOK OF HERALDRY; with Instructions for Tracing Pedigrees and Deciphering Ancient MSS., &c. By JOHN E. CUSSANS. With 408 Woodcuts and 2 Coloured Plates. New edition, revised, crown 8vo, cloth, **6s.**

CYPLES(W.)—HEARTS of GOLD. Cr. 8vo, cl., **3s. 6d.;** post 8vo, bds., **2s.**

DANIEL.—MERRIE ENGLAND IN THE OLDEN TIME. By GEORGE DANIEL. With Illustrations by ROBERT CRUIKSHANK. Crown 8vo, cloth extra, **3s. 6d.**

DAUDET.—THE EVANGELIST; or, Port Salvation. By ALPHONSE DAUDET. Crown 8vo, cloth extra. **3s. 6d.;** post 8vo, illustrated boards, **2s.**

DAVENANT.—HINTS FOR PARENTS ON THE CHOICE OF A PRO- FESSION FOR THEIR SONS. By F. DAVENANT, M.A. Post 8vo, **1s.;** cl., **1s. 6d.**

DAVIES (DR. N. E. YORKE-), WORKS BY.
Crown 8vo, **1s.** each; cloth limp, **1s. 6d.** each.
ONE THOUSAND MEDICAL MAXIMS AND SURGICAL HINTS.
NURSERY HINTS: A Mother's Guide in Health and Disease.
FOODS FOR THE FAT: A Treatise on Corpulency, and a Dietary for its Cure.
AIDS TO LONG LIFE. Crown 8vo, **2s.;** cloth limp, **2s. 6d.**

DAVIES' (SIR JOHN) COMPLETE POETICAL WORKS, for the first
time Collected and Edited, with Memorial-Introduction and Notes, by the Rev. A. B.
GROSART, D.D. Two Vols., crown 8vo, cloth boards, **12s.**

DAWSON.—THE FOUNTAIN OF YOUTH : A Novel of Adventure.
By ERASMUS DAWSON, M.B. Edited by PAUL DEVON. With Two Illustrations by
HUME NISBET. Crown 8vo, cloth extra. **3s. 6d.** ; post 8vo, illustrated boards, **2s.**

DE GUERIN.—THE JOURNAL OF MAURICE DE GUERIN. Edited
by G. S. TREBUTIEN. With a Memoir by SAINTE-BEUVE. Translated from the
20th French Edition by JESSIE P. FROTHINGHAM. Fcap, 8vo, half-bound, **2s. 6d.**

DE MAISTRE.—A JOURNEY ROUND MY ROOM. By XAVIER DE
MAISTRE. Translated by HENRY ATTWELL. Post 8vo, cloth limp, **2s. 6d.**

DE MILLE.—A CASTLE IN SPAIN. By JAMES DE MILLE. With a
Frontispiece. Crown 8vo, cloth extra, **3s. 6d.**; post 8vo, illustrated boards, **2s.**

DERBY (THE).—THE BLUE RIBBON OF THE TURF : A Chronicle
of the RACE FOR THE DERBY, from Diomed to Donovan. With Brief Accounts of
THE OAKS. By LOUIS HENRY CURZON Crown 8vo, cloth limp, **2s. 6d.**

DERWENT (LEITH), NOVELS BY. Cr.8vo,cl., **3s.6d.** ea.; post 8vo,bds.,**2s.**ea.
OUR LADY OF TEARS. | CIRCE'S LOVERS.

DICKENS (CHARLES), NOVELS BY. Post 8vo. illustrated boards, **2s.** each.
SKETCHES BY BOZ. | NICHOLAS NICKLEBY.
THE PICKWICK PAPERS. | OLIVER TWIST.
THE SPEECHES OF CHARLES DICKENS, 1841-1870. With a New Bibliography.
    Edited by RICHARD HERNE SHEPHERD. Crown 8vo, cloth extra, **6s.**—Also a
    SMALLER EDITION, in the *Mayfair Library*, post 8vo, cloth limp, **2s. 6d.**
ABOUT ENGLAND WITH DICKENS. By ALFRED RIMMER. With 57 Illustrations
    by C. A. VANDERHOOF, ALFRED RIMMER, and others. Sq. 8vo, cloth extra, **7s. 6d.**

DICTIONARIES.
A DICTIONARY OF MIRACLES : Imitative, Realistic, and Dogmatic. By the Rev.
    E. C. BREWER, LL.D. Crown 8vo, cloth extra, **7s. 6d.**
THE READER'S HANDBOOK OF ALLUSIONS, REFERENCES, PLOTS, AND
    STORIES. By the Rev. E. C. BREWER, LL.D. With an ENGLISH BIBLIOGRAPHY.
    Fifteenth Thousand. Crown 8vo, cloth extra, **7s. 6d.**
AUTHORS AND THEIR WORKS, WITH THE DATES. Cr. 8vo, cloth limp, **2s.**
FAMILIAR SHORT SAYINGS OF GREAT MEN. With Historical and Explana-
    tory Notes. By SAMUEL A. BENT, A M. Crown 8vo, cloth extra, **7s. 6d.**
SLANG DICTIONARY : Etymological, Historical, and Anecdotal. Cr. 8vo, cl., **6s. 6d.**
WOMEN OF THE DAY : A Biographical Dictionary. By F. HAYS. Cr. 8vo, cl., **5s.**
WORDS, FACTS, AND PHRASES : A Dictionary of Curious, Quaint, and Out-of-
    the-Way Matters. By ELIEZER EDWARDS. Crown 8vo, cloth extra, **7s. 6d.**

DIDEROT.—THE PARADOX OF ACTING. Translated, with Annotations, from Diderot's " Le Paradoxe sur le Comédien," by WALTER HERRIES POLLOCK.
With a Preface by HENRY IRVING. Crown 8vo, parchment, **4s. 6d.**

DOBSON (AUSTIN), WORKS BY.
THOMAS BEWICK & HIS PUPILS. With 95 Illustrations. Square 8vo, cloth, **6s.**
FOUR FRENCHWOMEN. Fcap. 8vo, hf.-roxburghe, with a Portrait, **2s. 6d.**—
    Also, a Library Edition, with 4 Portraits, crown 8vo, buckram, gilt top, **6s.**
EIGHTEENTH CENTURY VIGNETTES. Crown 8vo, buckram, gilt top, **6s.**

DOBSON (W. T.)—POETICAL INGENUITIES AND ECCENTRICI-
TIES. Post 8vo, cloth limp, **2s. 6d.**

DONOVAN (DICK), DETECTIVE STORIES BY.
Post 8vo, illustrated boards, **2s.** each; cloth limp, **2s. 6d.** each.
THE MAN-HUNTER. | WANTED! | A DETECTIVE'S TRIUMPHS.
CAUGHT AT LAST! | IN THE GRIP OF THE LAW.
TRACKED AND TAKEN. | FROM INFORMATION RECEIVED.
WHO POISONED HETTY DUNCAN?
    Crown 8vo, cloth extra, **3s. 6d.** each ; post 8vo, illustrated boards, **2s.** each;
                                cloth limp, **2s. 6d.** each.
THE MAN FROM MANCHESTER. With 23 Illustrations.
TRACKED TO DOOM. With 6 full-page Illustrations by GORDON BROWNE.

DOYLE (CONAN).—THE FIRM OF GIRDLESTONE. By A. CONAN
DOYLE, Author of " Micah Clarke." Crown 8vo, cloth extra, **3s. 6d.**

MATISTS, THE OLD. With Vignette Portraits. Cr. 8vo, cl. ex., 6s. per Vol.
EN JONSON'S WORKS. With Notes Critical and Explanatory, and a Biographical Memoir by WM. GIFFORD. Edited by Col. CUNNINGHAM. Three Vols.
HAPMAN'S WORKS. Complete in Three Vols. Vol. I. contains the Plays complete; Vol. II., Poems and Minor Translations, with an Introductory Essay by A. C. SWINBURNE; Vol. III., Translations of the Iliad and Odyssey.
ARLOWE'S WORKS. Edited, with Notes, by Col. CUNNINGHAM. One Vol.
ASSINGER'S PLAYS. From GIFFORD'S Text. Edit by Col. CUNNINGHAM. One Vol.

CAN (SARA JEANNETTE), WORKS BY.
Crown 8vo, cloth extra, 7s. 6d. each.
SOCIAL DEPARTURE: How Orthodocia and I Went round the World by Ourselves. With 111 Illustrations by F. H. TOWNSEND.
N AMERICAN GIRL IN LONDON. With 80 Illustrations by F. H. TOWNSEND.
HE SIMPLE ADVENTURES OF A MEMSAHIB. Numerous Illusts. [Preparing.

R.—THE FOLK-LORE OF PLANTS. By Rev. T. F. THISELTON VER, M.A. Crown 8vo, cloth extra, 6s.

RLY ENGLISH POETS. Edited, with Introductions and Annotations, by Rev. A. B. GROSART, D.D. Crown 8vo, cloth boards, 6s. per Volume.
LETCHER'S (GILES) COMPLETE POEMS. One Vol.
AVIES' (SIR JOHN) COMPLETE POETICAL WORKS. Two Vols.
ERRICK'S (ROBERT) COMPLETE COLLECTED POEMS. Three Vols.
DNEY'S (SIR PHILIP) COMPLETE POETICAL WORKS. Three Vols.

CUMBE.—ZEPHYRUS : A Holiday in Brazil and on the River Plate.
y E. R. PEARCE EDGCUMBE. With 41 Illustrations. Crown 8vo, cloth extra, 5s.

VARDES (MRS. ANNIE), NOVELS BY:
POINT OF HONOUR. Post 8vo, illustrated boards, 2s.
RCHIE LOVELL. Crown 8vo, cloth extra, 3s. 6d.; post 8vo, illust. boards, 2s.

VARDS (ELIEZER).—WORDS, FACTS, AND PHRASES: A
ictionary of Curious, Quaint, and Out-of-the-Way Matters. By ELIEZER EDWARDS.
rown 8vo, cloth extra, 7s. 6d.

VARDS (M. BETHAM-), NOVELS BY.
ITTY. Post 8vo, illustrated boards, 2s.; cloth limp, 2s. 6d.
ELICIA. Post 8vo, illustrated boards, 2s.

RTON.—SUSSEX FOLK & SUSSEX WAYS. By Rev. J. C. EGERTON.
Vith Introduction by Rev. Dr. H. WACE, and 4 Illustrations. Cr. 8vo, cloth ex., 5s.

LESTON (EDWARD).—ROXY : A Novel. Post 8vo, illust. bds., 2s.

LISHMAN'S HOUSE, THE: A Practical Guide to all interested in
electing or Building a House; with Estimates of Cost, Quantities, &c. By C. J.
ICHARDSON. With Coloured Frontispiece and 600 Illusts. Crown 8vo, cloth, 7s. 6d.

ALD (ALEX. CHARLES, F.S.A.), WORKS BY.
HE LIFE AND TIMES OF PRINCE CHARLES STUART, Count of Albany
(THE YOUNG PRETENDER). With a Portrait. Crown 8vo, cloth extra, 7s. 6d.
TORIES FROM THE STATE PAPERS. With an Autotype. Crown 8vo, cloth, 6s.

S, OUR : How to Preserve Them from Infancy to Old Age. By
OHN BROWNING, F.R.A.S. With 70 Illusts. Eighteenth Thousand. Crown 8vo, 1s.

MILIAR SHORT SAYINGS OF GREAT MEN. By SAMUEL ARTHUR
BENT, A.M. Fifth Edition, Revised and Enlarged. Crown 8vo, cloth extra, 7s. 6d.

RADAY (MICHAEL), WORKS BY. Post 8vo, cloth extra, 4s. 6d. each.
THE CHEMICAL HISTORY OF A CANDLE: Lectures delivered before a Juvenile
Audience. Edited by WILLIAM CROOKES, F.C.S. With numerous Illustrations.
ON THE VARIOUS FORCES OF NATURE, AND THEIR RELATIONS TO
EACH OTHER. Edited by WILLIAM CROOKES, F.C.S. With Illustrations.

RRER (J. ANSON), WORKS BY.
MILITARY MANNERS AND CUSTOMS. Crown 8vo, cloth extra, 6s.
WAR: Three Essays, reprinted from "Military Manners." Cr. 8vo, 1s.; cl., 1s. 6d.

N (J. MANVILLE), NOVELS BY.
IHP NEW MISTRESS. Cr. 8vo, cloth extra, 3s. 6d.; post 8vo, illust. boards, 2s.
WITNESS TO THE DEED. Three Vo's., crown 8vo,

FIN-BEC.—THE CUPBOARD PAPERS: Observations on the Art of Living and Dining. By Fin-Bec. Post 8vo, cloth limp, 2s. 6d.

FIREWORKS, THE COMPLETE ART OF MAKING; or, The Pyrotechnist's Treasury. By Thomas Kentish. With 267 Illustrations. Cr. 8vo, cl., 5s.

FITZGERALD (PERCY, M.A., F.S.A.), WORKS BY.
THE WORLD BEHIND THE SCENES. Crown 8vo, cloth extra, 3s. 6d.
LITTLE ESSAYS: Passages from Letters of Charles Lamb. Post 8vo, cl., 2s. 6d.
A DAY'S TOUR: Journey through France and Belgium. With Sketches. Cr. 4to, 1s.
FATAL ZERO. Crown 8vo, cloth extra, 3s. 6d.; post 8vo, illustrated boards, 2s.

Post 8vo, illustrated boards, 2s. each.
BELLA DONNA. | LADY OF BRANTOME. | THE SECOND MRS. TILLOTSON.
POLLY. | NEVER FORGOTTEN. | SEVENTY-FIVE BROOKE STREET.
LIFE OF JAMES BOSWELL (of Auchinleck). With an Account of his Sayings, Doings, and Writings; and Four Portraits. Two Vols., demy 8vo, cloth, 24s.

FLAMMARION.—URANIA: A Romance. By Camille Flammarion. Translated by Augusta Rice Stetson. With 87 Illustrations by De Bieler, Myrbach, and Gambard. Crown 8vo, cloth extra, 5s.

FLETCHER'S (GILES, B.D.) COMPLETE POEMS: Christ's Victorie in Heaven, Christ's Victorie on Earth, Christ's Triumph over Death, and Minor Poems. With Notes by Rev. A. B. Grosart, D.D. Crown 8vo, cloth boards, 6s.

FLUDYER (HARRY) AT CAMBRIDGE: A Series of Family Letters. Post 8vo, picture cover, 1s.; cloth limp, 1s. 6d.

FONBLANQUE (ALBANY).—FILTHY LUCRE. Post 8vo, illust. bds., 2s.

FRANCILLON (R. E.), NOVELS BY.
Crown 8vo, cloth extra, 3s. 6d. each: post 8vo, illustrated boards, 2s. each.
ONE BY ONE. | QUEEN COPHETUA. | A REAL QUEEN. | KING OR KNAVE?
OLYMPIA. Post 8vo, illust. bds., 2s. | ESTHER'S GLOVE. Fcap. 8vo, pict. cover, 1s.
ROMANCES OF THE LAW. Crown 8vo, cloth, 6s.; post 8vo, illust. boards, 2s.
ROPES OF SAND. 3 vols., crown 8vo.

FREDERIC (HAROLD), NOVELS BY.
SETH'S BROTHER'S WIFE. Post 8vo, illustrated boards, 2s.
THE LAWTON GIRL. Cr. 8vo, cloth ex., 6s.: post 8vo, illustrated boards, 2s.

FRENCH LITERATURE, A HISTORY OF. By Henry Van Laun. Three Vols., demy 8vo, cloth boards, 7s. 6d. each.

FRERE.—PANDURANG HARI; or, Memoirs of a Hindoo. With Preface by Sir Bartle Frere. Crown 8vo, cloth, 3s. 6d.; post 8vo, illust. bds., 2s.

FRISWELL (HAIN).—ONE OF TWO: A Novel. Post 8vo, illust. bds., 2s.

FROST (THOMAS), WORKS BY. Crown 8vo, cloth extra, 3s. 6d. each.
CIRCUS LIFE AND CIRCUS CELEBRITIES. | LIVES OF THE CONJURERS.
THE OLD SHOWMEN AND THE OLD LONDON FAIRS.

FRY'S (HERBERT) ROYAL GUIDE TO THE LONDON CHARITIES. Showing their Name, Date of Foundation, Objects, Income, Officials, &c. Edited by John Lane. Published Annually. Crown 8vo, cloth, 1s. 6d.

GARDENING BOOKS. Post 8vo, 1s. each; cloth limp, 1s. 6d. each.
A YEAR'S WORK IN GARDEN AND GREENHOUSE: Practical Advice as to the Management of the Flower, Fruit, and Frame Garden. By George Glenny.
HOUSEHOLD HORTICULTURE. By Tom and Jane Jerrold. Illustrated.
THE GARDEN THAT PAID THE RENT. By Tom Jerrold.
OUR KITCHEN GARDEN: The Plants we Grow, and How we Cook Them. By Tom Jerrold. Crown 8vo, cloth, 1s. 6d.
MY GARDEN WILD, AND WHAT I GREW THERE. By Francis G. Heath. Crown 8vo, cloth extra, gilt edges, 6s.

GARRETT.—THE CAPEL GIRLS: A Novel. By Edward Garrett. Crown 8vo, cloth extra, 3s. 6d.; post 8vo, illustrated boards, 2s.

GENTLEMAN'S MAGAZINE, THE. 1s. Monthly. In addition to Articles upon subjects in Literature, Science, and Art, "TABLE TALK" by Sylvanus Urban, and "PAGES ON PLAYS" by Justin H. McCarthy, appear monthly.
⁎ Bound Volumes for recent years kept in stock, 8s. 6d. each; Cases for binding, 2s.

GENTLEMAN'S ANNUAL, THE. Published Annually in November. 1*s.*
The 1892 Annual, written by T. W. SPEIGHT, is entitled "**THE LOUDWATER TRAGEDY.**"

GERMAN POPULAR STORIES. Collected by the Brothers GRIMM and Translated by EDGAR TAYLOR. With Introduction by JOHN RUSKIN, and 22 Steel Plates after GEORGE CRUIKSHANK. Square 8vo, cloth, 6s. 6d.; gilt edges, 7s. 6d.

GIBBON (CHARLES), NOVELS BY.
Crown 8vo, cloth extra, 3s. 6d. each; post 8vo, illustrated boards, 2s. each.
ROBIN GRAY. | LOVING A DREAM. | THE GOLDEN SHAFT.
THE FLOWER OF THE FOREST. | OF HIGH DEGREE.
Post 8vo, illustrated boards, 2s. each.
THE DEAD HEART. | IN LOVE AND WAR.
FOR LACK OF GOLD. | A HEART'S PROBLEM.
WHAT WILL THE WORLD SAY? | BY MEAD AND STREAM.
FOR THE KING. | A HARD KNOT. | THE BRAES OF YARROW.
QUEEN OF THE MEADOW. | FANCY FREE. | IN HONOUR BOUND.
IN PASTURES GREEN. | HEART'S DELIGHT. | BLOOD-MONEY.

GIBNEY (SOMERVILLE).—SENTENCED! Cr. 8vo, 1s. ; cl., 1s. 6d.

GILBERT (WILLIAM), NOVELS BY. Post 8vo, illustrated boards, 2s. each.
DR. AUSTIN'S GUESTS. | JAMES DUKE, COSTERMONGER.
THE WIZARD OF THE MOUNTAIN. |

GILBERT (W. S.), ORIGINAL PLAYS BY. Two Series, 2s. 6d. each.
The FIRST SERIES contains: The Wicked World—Pygmalion and Galatea—Charity—The Princess—The Palace of Truth—Trial by Jury.
The SECOND SERIES: Broken Hearts—Engaged—Sweethearts—Gretchen—Dan'l Druce—Tom Cobb—H.M.S. " Pinafore "—The Sorcerer—Pirates of Penzance.

EIGHT ORIGINAL COMIC OPERAS written by W. S. GILBERT. Containing: The Sorcerer—H.M.S. "Pinafore"—Pirates of Penzance—Iolanthe—Patience—Princess Ida—The Mikado—Trial by Jury. Demy 8vo, cloth limp, 2s. 6d.
THE "GILBERT AND SULLIVAN" BIRTHDAY BOOK: Quotations for Every Day in the Year, Selected from Plays by W. S. GILBERT set to Music by Sir A. SULLIVAN. Compiled by ALEX. WATSON. Royal 16mo, Jap. leather, 2s. 6d.

GLANVILLE (ERNEST), NOVELS BY.
Crown 8vo, cloth extra, 3s. 6d. each ; post 8vo, illustrated boards, 2s. each.
THE LOST HEIRESS: A Tale of Love, Battle, and Adventure. With 2 Illusts.
THE FOSSICKER: A Romance of Mashonaland. With 2 Illusts. by HUME NISBET.

GLENNY.—A YEAR'S WORK IN GARDEN AND GREENHOUSE: Practical Advice to Amateur Gardeners as to the Management of the Flower, Fruit, and Frame Garden. By GEORGE GLENNY. Post 8vo, 1s.; cloth limp, 1s. 6d.

GODWIN.—LIVES OF THE NECROMANCERS. By WILLIAM GODWIN. Post 8vo, cloth limp, 2s.

GOLDEN TREASURY OF THOUGHT, THE: An Encyclopædia of QUOTATIONS. Edited by THEODORE TAYLOR. Crown 8vo, cloth gilt, 7s. 6d.

GOODMAN.—THE FATE OF HERBERT WAYNE. By E. J. GOODMAN, Author of "Too Curious." Crown 8vo, cloth, 3s. 6d.

GOWING.—FIVE THOUSAND MILES IN A SLEDGE: A Midwinter Journey Across Siberia. By LIONEL F. GOWING. With 30 Illustrations by C. J. UREN, and a Map by E. WELLER. Large crown 8vo, cloth extra, 8s.

GRAHAM. — THE PROFESSOR'S WIFE: A Story By LEONARD GRAHAM. Fcap. 8vo, picture cover, 1s.

GREEKS AND ROMANS, THE LIFE OF THE, described from Antique Monuments. By ERNST GUHL and W. KONER. Edited by Dr. F. HUEFFER. With 545 Illustrations. Large crown 8vo, cloth extra, 7s. 6d.

GREENWOOD (JAMES), WORKS BY. Cr. 8vo. cloth extra, 3s. 6d. each.
THE WILDS OF LONDON. | LOW-LIFE DEEPS.

GREVILLE (HENRY), NOVELS BY:
NIKANOR. Translated by ELIZA E. CHASE. With 8 Illustrations. Crown 8vo, cloth extra, 6s.; post 8vo, illustrated boards, 2s.
A NOBLE WOMAN. Crown 8vo, cloth extra, 5s. ; post 8vo, illustrated boards, 2s.

GRIFFITH.—CORINTHIA MARAZION: A Novel. By CECIL GRIFFITH, Author of " Victory Deane," &c. Crown 8vo, cloth extra, 3s. 6d.

HABBERTON (JOHN, Author of "Helen's Babies"), NOVELS BY.
Post 8vo, illustrated boards **2s.** each; cloth limp, **2s. 6d.** each,
BRUETON'S BAYOU. | COUNTRY LUCK.

HAIR, THE: Its Treatment in Health, Weakness, and Disease. Translated from the German of Dr. J. PINCUS. Crown 8vo, **1s.**; cloth, **1s. 6d.**

HAKE (DR. THOMAS GORDON), POEMS BY. Cr. 8vo, cl. ex., **6s.** each.
NEW SYMBOLS. | LEGENDS OF THE MORROW. | THE SERPENT PLAY.
MAIDEN ECSTASY. Small 4to, cloth extra, **8s.**

HALL.—SKETCHES OF IRISH CHARACTER. By Mrs. S. C. HALL.
With numerous Illustrations on Steel and Wood by MACLISE, GILBERT, HARVEY, and
GEORGE CRUIKSHANK. Medium 8vo, cloth extra, **7s. 6d.**

HALLIDAY (ANDR.).—EVERY-DAY PAPERS. Post 8vo, bds., 2s.

HANDWRITING, THE PHILOSOPHY OF. With over 100 Facsimiles
and Explanatory Text. By DON FELIX DE SALAMANCA. Post 8vo, cloth limp, **2s. 6d.**

HANKY-PANKY: Easy Tricks, White Magic, Sleight of Hand, &c.
Edited by W. H. CREMER. With 200 Illustrations. Crown 8vo, cloth extra, **4s. 6d.**

HARDY (LADY DUFFUS). — PAUL WYNTER'S SACRIFICE. 2s.

HARDY (THOMAS). — UNDER THE GREENWOOD TREE. By
THOMAS HARDY, Author of "Far from the Madding Crowd." With Portrait and 15
Illustrations. Crown 8vo, cloth extra, **3s. 6d.**; post 8vo, illustrated boards, **2s.**

HARPER.—THE BRIGHTON ROAD: Old Times and New on a Classic
Highway. By CHARLES G. HARPER. With a Photogravure Frontispiece and 90 Illustrations. Demy 8vo, cloth extra, **16s.**

HARWOOD.—THE TENTH EARL. By J. BERWICK HARWOOD. Post
8vo, illustrated boards, **2s.**

HAWEIS (MRS. H. R.), WORKS BY. Square 8vo, cloth extra, **6s.** each.
THE ART OF BEAUTY. With Coloured Frontispiece and 91 Illustrations.
THE ART OF DECORATION. With Coloured Frontispiece and 74 Illustrations,
CHAUCER FOR CHILDREN. With 8 Coloured Plates and 30 Woodcuts.
THE ART OF DRESS. With 32 Illustrations. Post 8vo, **1s.**; cloth, **1s. 6d.**
CHAUCER FOR SCHOOLS. Demy 8vo, cloth limp, **2s. 6d.**

HAWEIS(Rev. H. R.,M.A.).—AMERICAN HUMORISTS: WASHINGTON
IRVING, OLIVER WENDELL HOLMES, JAMES RUSSELL LOWELL, ARTEMUS WARD,
MARK TWAIN, and BRET HARTE. Third Edition. Crown 8vo, cloth extra, **6s.**

HAWLEY SMART.—WITHOUT LOVE OR LICENCE: A Novel. By
HAWLEY SMART. Crown 8vo, cloth extra, **3s. 6d.**; post 8vo, illustrated boards, **2s.**

HAWTHORNE. —OUR OLD HOME. By NATHANIEL HAWTHORNE.
Annotated with Passages from the Author's Note-book, and Illustrated with 31
Photogravures. Two Vols., crown 8vo, buckram, gilt top, **15s.**

HAWTHORNE (JULIAN), NOVELS BY.
Crown 8vo, cloth extra, **3s. 6d.** each; post 8vo, illustrated boards, 2s. each.
GARTH. | ELLICE QUENTIN. | BEATRIX RANDOLPH. | DUST.
SEBASTIAN STROME. | DAVID POINDEXTER.
FORTUNE'S FOOL. | THE SPECTRE OF THE CAMERA.
Post 8vo, illustrated boards, **2s.** each.
MISS CADOGNA. | LOVE—OR A NAME.
MRS. GAINSBOROUGH'S DIAMONDS. Fcap. 8vo. illustrated cover, **1s.**

HEATH.—MY GARDEN WILD, AND WHAT I GREW THERE.
By FRANCIS GEORGE HEATH. Crown 8vo, cloth extra, gilt edges, **6s.**

HELPS (SIR ARTHUR), WORKS BY. Post 8vo, cloth limp, **2s. 6d.** each.
ANIMALS AND THEIR MASTERS. | SOCIAL PRESSURE.
IVAN DE BIRON: A Novel. Cr. 8vo, cl. extra, **3s. 6d.**; post 8vo, illust. bds., **2s.**

HENDERSON.—AGATHA PAGE: A Novel. By ISAAC HENDERSON.
Crown 8vo cloth extra, **3s. 6d.**

HENTY.—RUJUB, THE JUGGLER. By G. A. HENTY. Three Vols.

HERMAN.—A LEADING LADY. By HENRY HERMAN, joint-Author
of "The Bishops' Bible." Post 8vo, illustrated boards, **2s.**; cloth extra, **2s. 6d.**

**HERRICK'S (ROBERT) HESPERIDES, NOBLE NUMBERS, AND
COMPLETE COLLECTED POEMS.** With Memorial-Introduction and Notes by the
Rev. A. B. GROSART, D.D.; Steel Portrait, &c. Three Vols., crown 8vo, cl. bds., 18s.

HERTZKA.—FREELAND: A Social Anticipation. By Dr. THEODOR
HERTZKA. Translated by ARTHUR RANSOM. Crown 8vo, cloth extra, 6s.

HESSE-WARTEGG.—TUNIS: The Land and the People. By Chevalier
ERNST VON HESSE-WARTEGG. With 22 Illustrations. Cr. 8vo, cloth extra, 3s. 6d.

HILL.—TREASON-FELONY: A Novel. By JOHN HILL. Two Vols.

HINDLEY (CHARLES), WORKS BY.
 TAVERN ANECDOTES AND SAYINGS: Including Reminiscences connected with
 Coffee Houses, Clubs, &c. With Illustrations. Crown 8vo, cloth, 3s. 6d.
 THE LIFE AND ADVENTURES OF A CHEAP JACK. Cr. 8vo. cloth ex., 3s. 6d.

HOEY.—THE LOVER'S CREED. By Mrs. CASHEL HOEY. Post 8vo, 2s.

HOLLINGSHEAD (JOHN).—NIAGARA SPRAY. Crown 8vo, 1s.

**HOLMES.—THE SCIENCE OF VOICE PRODUCTION AND VOICE
PRESERVATION.** By GORDON HOLMES, M.D. Crown 8vo, 1s.; cloth, 1s. 6d.

HOLMES (OLIVER WENDELL), WORKS BY.
 THE AUTOCRAT OF THE BREAKFAST-TABLE. Illustrated by J. GORDON
 THOMSON. Post 8vo, cloth limp, 2s. 6d.—Another Edition, in smaller type, with
 an Introduction by G. A. SALA. Post 8vo, cloth limp, 2s.
 THE AUTOCRAT OF THE BREAKFAST-TABLE and THE PROFESSOR AT THE
 BREAKFAST-TABLE. In One Vol. Post 8vo, half-bound, 2s.

HOOD'S (THOMAS) CHOICE WORKS, in Prose and Verse. With Life
of the Author, Portrait, and 200 Illustrations. Crown 8vo, cloth extra, 7s. 6d.
 HOOD'S WHIMS AND ODDITIES. With 85 Illustrations. Post 8vo, printed on
 laid paper and half-bound, 2s.

HOOD (TOM).—FROM NOWHERE TO THE NORTH POLE: A
Noah's Arkæological Narrative. By TOM HOOD. With 25 Illustrations by W. BRUNTON
and E. C. BARNES. Square 8vo, cloth extra, gilt edges, 6s.

HOOK'S (THEODORE) CHOICE HUMOROUS WORKS; including his
Ludicrous Adventures, Bons Mots, Puns, and Hoaxes. With Life of the Author,
Portraits, Facsimiles, and Illustrations. Crown 8vo, cloth extra, 7s. 6d.

HOOPER.—THE HOUSE OF RABY: A Novel. By Mrs. GEORGE
HOOPER. Post 8vo, illustrated boards, 2s.

HOPKINS.—"'TWIXT LOVE AND DUTY:" A Novel. By TIGHE
HOPKINS. Post 8vo, illustrated boards, 2s.

HORNE.—ORION: An Epic Poem. By RICHARD HENGIST HORNE.
With Photographic Portrait by SUMMERS. Tenth Edition. Cr. 8vo, cloth extra, 7s.

HORSE (THE) AND HIS RIDER: An Anecdotic Medley. By "THOR-
MANBY." Crown 8vo, cloth extra, 6s.

HUNGERFORD (MRS.), Author of "Molly Bawn," **NOVELS BY.**
 Post 8vo, illustrated boards, 2s. each; cloth limp, 2s. 6d. each.
 A MAIDEN ALL FORLORN. | IN DURANCE VILE. | A MENTAL STRUGGLE.
 MARVEL. | A MODERN CIRCE.
 LADY VERNER'S FLIGHT. Two Vols., crown 8vo.

HUNT.—ESSAYS BY LEIGH HUNT: A TALE FOR A CHIMNEY CORNER,
&c. Edited by EDMUND OLLIER. Post 8vo, printed on laid paper and half-bd., 2s.

HUNT (MRS. ALFRED), NOVELS BY.
 Crown 8vo, cloth extra, 3s. 6d. each; post 8vo, illustrated boards, 2s. each.
 THE LEADEN CASKET. | SELF-CONDEMNED. | THAT OTHER PERSON.
 THORNICROFT'S MODEL. Post 8vo, illustrated boards, 2s.
 MRS. JULIET. Three Vols., crown 8vo.

HUTCHISON.—HINTS ON COLT-BREAKING. By W. M. HUTCHISON.
With 25 Illustrations. Crown 8vo, cloth extra, 3s. 6d.

HYDROPHOBIA: An Account of M. PASTEUR's System; Technique of
his Method, and Statistics. By RENAUD SUZOR, M.B. Crown 8vo, cloth extra, 6s.

IDLER (THE): A Monthly Magazine. Edited by JEROME K. JEROME
and ROBERT E. BARR. Profusely Illustrated. Sixpence Monthly.—Vols. I. and
II. now ready, cloth extra, 5s. each; Cases for Binding, 1s. 6d.

INGELOW (JEAN).—FATED TO BE FREE. Post 8vo, illustrated bds., **2s.**

INDOOR PAUPERS. By ONE OF THEM. Crown 8vo, 1s.; cloth, 1s. 6d.

INNKEEPER'S HANDBOOK (THE) AND LICENSED VICTUALLER'S MANUAL. By J. TREVOR-DAVIES. Crown 8vo, **1s.**; cloth, **1s. 6d.**

IRISH WIT AND HUMOUR, SONGS OF. Collected and Edited by A. PERCEVAL GRAVES. Post 8vo, cloth limp, **2s. 6d.**

JAMES.—A ROMANCE OF THE QUEEN'S HOUNDS. By CHARLES JAMES. Post 8vo, picture cover, **1s.**; cloth limp, **1s. 6d.**

JANVIER.—PRACTICAL KERAMICS FOR STUDENTS. By CATHERINE A. JANVIER. Crown 8vo, cloth extra, **6s.**

JAY (HARRIETT), NOVELS BY. Post 8vo, illustrated boards, **2s.** each.
THE DARK COLLEEN. | THE QUEEN OF CONNAUGHT.

JEFFERIES (RICHARD), WORKS BY. Post 8vo, cloth limp, **2s. 6d.** each.
NATURE NEAR LONDON. | THE LIFE OF THE FIELDS. | THE OPEN AIR.
. Also the HAND-MADE PAPER EDITION, crown 8vo, buckram, gilt top, **6s.** each.

THE EULOGY OF RICHARD JEFFERIES. By WALTER BESANT. Second Edition. With a Photograph Portrait. Crown 8vo, cloth extra, **6s.**

JENNINGS (H. J.), WORKS BY.
CURIOSITIES OF CRITICISM. Post 8vo, cloth limp, **2s. 6d.**
LORD TENNYSON: A Biographical Sketch. With a Photograph. Cr. 8vo, cl., **6s.**

JEROME.—STAGELAND. By JEROME K. JEROME. With 64 Illustrations by J. BERNARD PARTRIDGE. Square 8vo, picture cover, **1s.**; cloth limp, **2s.**

JERROLD.—THE BARBER'S CHAIR; & THE HEDGEHOG LETTERS. By DOUGLAS JERROLD. Post 8vo, printed on laid paper and half-bound, **2s.**

JERROLD (TOM), WORKS BY. Post 8vo, 1s. each; cloth limp, **1s. 6d.** each.
THE GARDEN THAT PAID THE RENT.
HOUSEHOLD HORTICULTURE: A Gossip about Flowers. Illustrated.
OUR KITCHEN GARDEN: The Plants, and How we Cook Them. Cr. 8vo, cl., **1s. 6d.**

JESSE.—SCENES AND OCCUPATIONS OF A COUNTRY LIFE. By EDWARD JESSE. Post 8vo, cloth limp, **2s.**

JONES (WILLIAM, F.S.A.), WORKS BY. Cr. 8vo, cl. extra, **7s. 6d.** each.
FINGER-RING LORE: Historical, Legendary, and Anecdotal. With nearly 300 Illustrations. Second Edition, Revised and Enlarged.
CREDULITIES, PAST AND PRESENT. Including the Sea and Seamen, Miners, Talismans, Word and Letter Divination, Exorcising and Blessing of Animals, Birds, Eggs, Luck, &c. With an Etched Frontispiece.
CROWNS AND CORONATIONS: A History of Regalia. With 100 Illustrations.

JONSON'S (BEN) WORKS. With Notes Critical and Explanatory, and a Biographical Memoir by WILLIAM GIFFORD. Edited by Colonel CUNNINGHAM. Three Vols., crown 8vo, cloth extra, **6s.** each.

JOSEPHUS, THE COMPLETE WORKS OF. Translated by WHISTON. Containing "The Antiquities of the Jews" and "The Wars of the Jews." With 52 Illustrations and Maps. Two Vols., demy 8vo, half-bound, **12s. 6d.**

KEMPT.—PENCIL AND PALETTE: Chapters on Art and Artists. By ROBERT KEMPT. Post 8vo, cloth limp, **2s. 6d.**

KERSHAW.— COLONIAL FACTS AND FICTIONS: Humorous Sketches. By MARK KERSHAW. Post 8vo, illustrated boards, **2s.**; cloth, **2s. 6d.**

KEYSER.— CUT BY THE MESS: A Novel. By ARTHUR KEYSER. Crown 8vo, picture cover, **1s.**; cloth limp, **1s. 6d.**

KING (R. ASHE), NOVELS BY. Cr. 8vo, cl., **3s. 6d.** ea.; post 8vo, bds., **2s.** ea.
A DRAWN GAME. | "THE WEARING OF THE GREEN."
Post 8vo, illustrated boards, **2s.** each.
PASSION'S SLAVE. | BELL BARRY.

KNIGHTS (THE) OF THE LION: A Romance of the Thirteenth Century. Edited, with an Introduction, by the MARQUESS of LORNE, K.T. Cr. 8vo, cl. ex., **6s.**

KNIGHT.—THE PATIENT'S VA——————————————— st
Benefit from Medical Advice. By WILLIAM KNIGHT, M.R.C.S., and EDWARD KNIGHT, L.R.C.P. Crown 8vo, 1s.; cloth limp, 1s. 6d.

LAMB'S (CHARLES) COMPLETE WORKS, in Prose and Verse, including "Poetry for Children" and "Prince Dorus." Edited, with Notes and Introduction, by R. H. SHEPHERD. With Two Portraits and Facsimile of a page of the "Essay on Roast Pig." Crown 8vo, half-bound, 7s. 6d.
THE ESSAYS OF ELIA. Post 8vo, printed on laid paper and half-bound, 2s.
LITTLE ESSAYS: Sketches and Characters by CHARLES LAMB, selected from his Letters by PERCY FITZGERALD. Post 8vo, cloth limp, 2s. 6d.
THE DRAMATIC ESSAYS OF CHARLES LAMB. With Introduction and Notes by BRANDER MATTHEWS, and Steel-plate Portrait. Fcap. 8vo, hf.-bd., 2s. 6d.

LANDOR.—CITATION AND EXAMINATION OF WILLIAM SHAKS-
PEARE, &c., before Sir THOMAS LUCY, touching Deer-stealing, 19th September, 1582. To which is added, A CONFERENCE OF MASTER EDMUND SPENSER with the Earl of Essex, touching the State of Ireland, 1595. By WALTER SAVAGE LANDOR. Fcap. 8vo, half-Roxburghe, 2s. 6d.

LANE.—THE THOUSAND AND ONE NIGHTS, commonly called in England THE ARABIAN NIGHTS' ENTERTAINMENTS. Translated from the Arabic, with Notes, by EDWARD WILLIAM LANE. Illustrated by many hundred Engravings from Designs by HARVEY. Edited by EDWARD STANLEY POOLE. With a Preface by STANLEY LANE-POOLE. Three Vols., demy 8vo, cloth extra, 7s. 6d. each.

LARWOOD (JACOB), WORKS BY.
THE STORY OF THE LONDON PARKS. With Illusts. Cr. 8vo, cl. extra, 3s. 6d.
ANECDOTES OF THE CLERGY: The Antiquities, Humours, and Eccentricities of the Cloth. Post 8vo, printed on laid paper and half-bound, 2s.
Post 8vo, cloth limp, 2s. 6d. each.
FORENSIC ANECDOTES. | THEATRICAL ANECDOTES.

LEIGH (HENRY S.), WORKS BY.
CAROLS OF COCKAYNE. Printed on hand-made paper, bound in buckram, 5s.
JEUX D'ESPRIT. Edited by HENRY S. LEIGH. Post 8vo, cloth limp, 2s. 6d.

LEYS (JOHN).—THE LINDSAYS : A Romance. Post 8vo, illust. bds., 2s.

LIFE IN LONDON; or, The History of JERRY HAWTHORN and COR-
INTHIAN TOM. With CRUIKSHANK's Coloured Illustrations. Crown 8vo, cloth extra, 7s. 6d. [*New Edition preparing.*

LINTON (E. LYNN), WORKS BY. Post 8vo, cloth limp, 2s. 6d. each.
WITCH STORIES. | OURSELVES: ESSAYS ON WOMEN.

Crown 8vo, cloth extra, 3s. 6d. each; | post 8vo, illustrated boards, 2s. each.
SOWING THE WIND. | UNDER WHICH LORD?
PATRICIA KEMBALL. | "MY LOVE!" | IONE.
ATONEMENT OF LEAM DUNDAS. | PASTON CAREW, Millionaire & Miser.
THE WORLD WELL LOST.

Post 8vo, illustrated boards, 2s. each.
THE REBEL OF THE FAMILY. | WITH A SILKEN THREAD.
FREESHOOTING : Extracts from the Works of Mrs. LYNN LINTON. Post 8vo, cloth, 2s. 6d.

LONGFELLOW'S POETICAL WORKS. With numerous Illustrations on Steel and Wood. Crown 8vo, cloth extra, 7s. 6d.

LUCY.—GIDEON FLEYCE : A Novel. By HENRY W. LUCY. Crown 8vo, cloth extra, 3s. 6d.; post 8vo, illustrated boards, 2s.

LUSIAD (THE) OF CAMOENS. Translated into English Spenserian Verse by ROBERT FFRENCH DUFF. With 14 Plates. Demy 8vo, cloth boards, 18s.

MACALPINE (AVERY), NOVELS BY.
TERESA ITASCA. Crown 8vo, cloth extra, 1s.
BROKEN WINGS. With 6 Illusts. by W. J. HENNESSY. Crown 8vo, cloth extra, 6s.

MACCOLL (HUGH), NOVELS BY.
MR. STRANGER'S SEALED PACKET. Crown 8vo, cloth extra, 5s.; post 8vo, illustrated boards, 2s.
EDNOR WHITLOCK. Crown 8vo, cloth extra, 6s.

MACDONELL.—QUAKER COUSINS : A Novel. By AGNES MACDONELL. Crown 8vo, cloth extra, 3s. 6d. ; post 8vo, illustrated boards, 2s.

McCARTHY (JUSTIN, M.P.), WORKS BY.

A HISTORY OF OUR OWN TIMES, from the Accession of Queen Victoria to the General Election of 1880. Four Vols. demy 8vo, cloth extra, **12s.** each.—Also a POPULAR EDITION, in Four Vols., crown 8vo, cloth extra, **6s.** each.—And a JUBILEE EDITION, with an Appendix of Events to the end of 1886, in Two Vols., large crown 8vo, cloth extra, **7s. 6d.** each.

A SHORT HISTORY OF OUR OWN TIMES. One Vol., crown 8vo, cloth extra, **6s.** —Also a CHEAP POPULAR EDITION, post 8vo, cloth limp, **2s. 6d.**

A HISTORY OF THE FOUR GEORGES. Four Vols. demy 8vo, cloth extra, **12s.** each.   [Vols. I. & II. _ready._

Cr. 8vo, extra, **3s. 6d.** each; post 8vo, illust. bds., **2s.** each; cl. limp, **2s. 6d.** each.

THE WATERDALE NEIGHBOURS.	**MISS MISANTHROPE.**
MY ENEMY'S DAUGHTER.	**DONNA QUIXOTE.**
A FAIR SAXON.	**THE COMET OF A SEASON.**
LINLEY ROCHFORD.	**MAID OF ATHENS.**
DEAR LADY DISDAIN.	**CAMIOLA:** A Girl with a Fortune.

THE DICTATOR. Three Vols., crown 8vo.   [_Shortly_

"THE RIGHT HONOURABLE." By JUSTIN McCARTHY, M.P., and Mrs.CAMPBELL PRAED. Fourth Edition. Crown 8vo. cloth extra, **6s.**

McCARTHY (JUSTIN H.), WORKS BY.

THE FRENCH REVOLUTION. Four Vols., 8vo, **12s.** each.   [Vols. I. & II. _ready._
AN OUTLINE OF THE HISTORY OF IRELAND. Crown 8vo, **1s.**; cloth, **1s. 6d.**
IRELAND SINCE THE UNION : Irish History, 1798-1886. Crown 8vo, cloth, **6s.**
HAFIZ IN LONDON : Poems. Small 8vo, gold cloth, **3s. 6d.**
HARLEQUINADE : Poems. Small 4to, Japanese vellum, **8s.**
OUR SENSATION NOVEL. Crown 8vo, picture cover, **1s.**; cloth limp, **1s. 6d.**
DOOM! An Atlantic Episode. Crown 8vo, picture cover, **1s.**
DOLLY : A Sketch. Crown 8vo, picture cover, **1s.**; cloth limp, **1s. 6d.**
LILY LASS: A Romance. Crown 8vo, picture cover, **1s.**; cloth limp, **1s. 6d.**
THE THOUSAND AND ONE DAYS: Persian Tales. Edited by JUSTIN H. McCARTHY. With 2 Photogravures by STANLEY L. WOOD. Two Vols., crown 8vo, half-bound, **12s.**

MACDONALD (GEORGE, LL.D.), WORKS BY.

WORKS OF FANCY AND IMAGINATION. Ten Vols., cl. extra, gilt edges, in cloth case, **21s.** Or the Vols. may be had separately, in grolier cl., at **2s. 6d.** each.

Vol. I. WITHIN AND WITHOUT.—THE HIDDEN LIFE.
  ,, II. THE DISCIPLE.—THE GOSPEL WOMEN.—BOOK OF SONNETS.—ORGAN SONGS.
  ,, III. VIOLIN SONGS.—SONGS OF THE DAYS AND NIGHTS.—A BOOK OF DREAMS.—
          ROADSIDE POEMS.—POEMS FOR CHILDREN.
  ,, IV. PARABLES.—BALLADS.—SCOTCH SONGS.
  ,, V. & VI. PHANTASTES: A Faerie Romance. | Vol. VII. THE PORTENT.
  ,, VIII. THE LIGHT PRINCESS.—THE GIANT'S HEART.—SHADOWS.
  ,, IX. CROSS PURPOSES.—THE GOLDEN KEY.—THE CARASOYN.—LITTLE DAYLIGHT.
  ,, X. THE CRUEL PAINTER.—THE WOW o' RIVVEN.—THE CASTLE.—THE BROKEN
          SWORDS.—THE GRAY WOLF.—UNCLE CORNELIUS.

POETICAL WORKS OF GEORGE MACDONALD. Collected and arranged by the Author. 2 vols., crown 8vo, buckram, **12s.**
A THREEFOLD CORD. Edited by GEORGE MACDONALD. Post 8vo, cloth, **5s.**
HEATHER AND SNOW: A Novel. 2 vols., crown 8vo.   [_Shortly._

MACGREGOR. — PASTIMES AND PLAYERS: Notes on Popular

Games. By ROBERT MACGREGOR. Post 8vo, cloth limp, **2s. 6d.**

MACKAY.—INTERLUDES AND UNDERTONES; or, Music at Twilight.

By CHARLES MACKAY, LL.D. Crown 8vo, cloth extra, **6s.**

MACLISE PORTRAIT GALLERY (THE) OF ILLUSTRIOUS LITER-

ARY CHARACTERS: **85 PORTRAITS;** with Memoirs — Biographical, Critical, Bibliographical, and Anecdotal—illustrative of the Literature of the former half of the Present Century, by WILLIAM BATES, B.A. Crown 8vo, cloth extra, **7s. 6d.**

MACQUOID (MRS.), WORKS BY. Square 8vo, cloth extra, **7s. 6d.** each.

IN THE ARDENNES. With 50 Illustrations by THOMAS R. MACQUOID.
PICTURES AND LEGENDS FROM NORMANDY AND BRITTANY. With 34 Illustrations by THOMAS R. MACQUOID.
THROUGH NORMANDY. With 92 Illustrations by T. R. MACQUOID, and a Map.
THROUGH BRITTANY. With 35 Illustrations by T. R. MACQUOID, and a Map.
ABOUT YORKSHIRE. With 67 Illustrations by T. R. MACQUOID.

Post 8vo, illustrated boards, **2s.** each,
THE EVIL EYE, and other Stories. | **LOST ROSE.**

MAGIC LANTERN, THE, and its Management: including full Practical Directions for producing the Limelight, making Oxygen Gas, and preparing Lantern Slides. By T. C. HEPWORTH. With 10 Illustrations. Cr. 8vo. **1s.;** cloth. **1s. 6d**

MAGICIAN'S OWN BOOK, THE: Performances with Cups and Balls, Eggs, Hats, Handkerchiefs, &c. All from actual Experience. Edited by W. H. CREMER. With 200 Illustrations. Crown 8vo. cloth extra, **4s. 6d.**

MAGNA CHARTA: An Exact Facsimile of the Original in the British Museum, 3 feet by 2 feet, with Arms and Seals emblazoned in Gold and Colours, **5s.**

MALLOCK (W. H.), WORKS BY.
THE NEW REPUBLIC. Post 8vo, picture cover, **2s.;** cloth limp, **2s. 6d.**
THE NEW PAUL & VIRGINIA: Positivism on an Island. Post 8vo, cloth, **2s. 6d.**
POEMS. Small 4to, parchment, **8s.**
IS LIFE WORTH LIVING? Crown 8vo, cloth extra, **6s.**
A ROMANCE OF THE NINETEENTH CENTURY. Crown 8vo, cloth, **6s.**

MALLORY'S (SIR THOMAS) MORT D'ARTHUR: The Stories of King Arthur and of the Knights of the Round Table. (A Selection.) Edited by B. MONTGOMERIE RANKING. Post 8vo, cloth limp, **2s.**

MARK TWAIN, WORKS BY. Crown 8vo, cloth extra, **7s. 6d.** each.
THE CHOICE WORKS OF MARK TWAIN. Revised and Corrected throughout by the Author. With Life, Portrait, and numerous Illustrations.
ROUGHING IT, and INNOCENTS AT HOME. With 200 Illusts. by F. A. FRASER.
MARK TWAIN'S LIBRARY OF HUMOUR. With 197 Illustrations.
Crown 8vo, cloth extra (illustrated), **7s. 6d.** each; post 8vo, illust. boards, **2s.** each.
THE INNOCENTS ABROAD; or, New Pilgrim's Progress. With 234 Illustrations.
(The Two-Shilling Edition is entitled MARK TWAIN'S PLEASURE TRIP.)
THE GILDED AGE. By MARK TWAIN and C. D. WARNER. With 212 Illustrations.
THE ADVENTURES OF TOM SAWYER. With 111 Illustrations.
A TRAMP ABROAD. With 314 Illustrations.
THE PRINCE AND THE PAUPER. With 190 Illustrations.
LIFE ON THE MISSISSIPPI. With 300 Illustrations.
ADVENTURES OF HUCKLEBERRY FINN. With 174 Illusts. by E. W. KEMBLE.
A YANKEE AT THE COURT OF KING ARTHUR. With 220 Illusts. by BEARD
MARK TWAIN'S SKETCHES. Post 8vo, illustrated boards, **2s.**
THE STOLEN WHITE ELEPHANT, &c. Cr. 8vo, cl., **6s.;** post 8vo, illust. bds., **2s.**
THE AMERICAN CLAIMANT. With 81 Illustrations by HAL HURST and DAN BEARD. Crown 8vo, cloth extra, **3s. 6d.**

MARLOWE'S WORKS. Including his Translations. Edited, with Notes and Introductions, by Col. CUNNINGHAM. Crown 8vo, cloth extra, **6s.**

MARRYAT (FLORENCE), NOVELS BY. Post 8vo, illust. boards, **2s.** each.
A HARVEST OF WILD OATS.   FIGHTING THE AIR.
OPEN! SESAME!   WRITTEN IN FIRE.

MASSINGER'S PLAYS. From the Text of WILLIAM GIFFORD. Edited by Col. CUNNINGHAM. Crown 8vo. cloth extra, **6s.**

MASTERMAN.—HALF-A-DOZEN DAUGHTERS: A Novel. By J. MASTERMAN. Post 8vo, illustrated boards, **2s.**

MATTHEWS.—A SECRET OF THE SEA, &c. By BRANDER MATTHEWS. Post 8vo, illustrated boards, **2s.;** cloth limp, **2s. 6d.**

MAYHEW.—LONDON CHARACTERS AND THE HUMOROUS SIDE OF LONDON LIFE. By HENRY MAYHEW. With Illusts. Crown 8vo, cloth, **3s. 6d.**

MENKEN.—INFELICIA: Poems by ADAH ISAACS MENKEN. With Illustrations by F. E. LUMMIS and F. O. C. DARLEY. Small 4to, cloth extra, **7s. 6d.**

MERRICK.—THE MAN WHO WAS GOOD. By LEONARD MERRICK, Author of "Violet Moses," &c. Post 8vo, illustrated boards, **2s.**

MEXICAN MUSTANG (ON A), through Texas to the Rio Grande. By A. E. SWEET and J. ARMOY KNOX. With 265 Illusts. Cr. 8vo, cloth extra, **7s. 6d.**

MIDDLEMASS (JEAN), NOVELS BY. Post 8vo, illust. boards, **2s.** each.
TOUCH AND GO. | MR. DORILLION.

MILLER.—PHYSIOLOGY FOR THE YOUNG; or, The House of Life: Human Physiology, with its application to the Preservation of Health. By Mrs. F. FENWICK MILLER. With numerous Illustrations. Post 8vo, cloth limp, **2s. 6d.**

MILTON (J. L.), WORKS BY. Post 8vo, **1s.** each; cloth, **1s. 6d.** each.
THE HYGIENE OF THE SKIN. With Directions for Diet, Soaps, Baths, &c.
THE BATH IN DISEASES OF THE SKIN.
THE LAWS OF LIFE, AND THEIR RELATION TO DISEASES OF THE SKIN.
THE SUCCESSFUL TREATMENT OF LEPROSY. Demy 8vo, **1s.**

MINTO (WM.)—WAS SHE GOOD OR BAD? Cr. 8vo, 1s. ; cloth, 1s. 6d.

MOLESWORTH (MRS.), NOVELS BY.
HATHERCOURT RECTORY. Post 8vo, illustrated boards, **2s.**
THAT GIRL IN BLACK. Crown 8vo, cloth, **1s. 6d.**

MOORE (THOMAS), WORKS BY.
THE EPICUREAN; and ALCIPHRON. Post 8vo, half-bound, **2s.**
PROSE AND VERSE, Humorous, Satirical, and Sentimental, by THOMAS MOORE;
with Suppressed Passages from the MEMOIRS OF LORD BYRON. Edited by R.
HERNE SHEPHERD. With Portrait. Crown 8vo, cloth extra, **7s. 6d.**

MUDDOCK (J. E.), STORIES BY.
STORIES WEIRD AND WONDERFUL. Post 8vo, illust. boards, **2s.**; cloth, **2s. 6d.**
THE DEAD MAN'S SECRET; or, The Valley of Gold. With Frontispiece by
F. BARNARD. Crown 8vo, cloth extra, **5s.**; post 8vo, illustrated boards, **2s.**
FROM THE BOSOM OF THE DEEP. Post 8vo, illustrated boards, **2s.**
MAID MARIAN AND ROBIN HOOD: A Romance of Old Sherwood Forest. With
12 Illustrations by STANLEY L. WOOD. Crown 8vo, cloth extra, **5s.**

MURRAY (D. CHRISTIE), NOVELS BY.
Crown 8vo, cloth extra, **3s. 6d.** each; post 8vo, illustrated boards. **2s.** each.

A LIFE'S ATONEMENT.	HEARTS.	BY THE GATE OF THE SEA.
JOSEPH'S COAT.	WAY OF THE WORLD	A BIT OF HUMAN NATURE.
COALS OF FIRE.	A MODEL FATHER.	FIRST PERSON SINGULAR.
VAL STRANGE.	OLD BLAZER'S HERO.	CYNIC FORTUNE.

BOB MARTIN'S LITTLE GIRL. Crown 8vo, cloth extra, **3s. 6d.**
TIME'S REVENGES. Three Vols., crown 8vo.

MURRAY (D. CHRISTIE) & HENRY HERMAN, WORKS BY.
ONE TRAVELLER RETURNS. Cr. 8vo, cl. extra, **6s.**; post 8vo, illust. bds., **2s.**
Crown 8vo, cloth extra, **3s. 6d.** each; post 8vo, illustrated boards, **2s.** each.
PAUL JONES'S ALIAS. With 13 Illustrations. | THE BISHOPS' BIBLE.

MURRAY (HENRY), NOVELS BY.
A GAME OF BLUFF. Post 8vo, illustrated boards, **2s.**; cloth, **2s. 6d.**
A SONG OF SIXPENCE. Post 8vo, cloth extra, **2s. 6d.**

NEWBOLT.—TAKEN FROM THE ENEMY. By HENRY NEWBOLT.
Fcap. 8vo, cloth boards, **1s. 6d.**

NISBET (HUME), BOOKS BY.
"BAIL UP!" Crown 8vo, cloth extra, **3s. 6d.**; post 8vo, illustrated boards, **2s.**
DR. BERNARD ST. VINCENT. Post 8vo, illustrated boards, **2s.**
LESSONS IN ART. With 21 Illustrations. Crown 8vo, cloth extra, **2s. 6d.**
WHERE ART BEGINS. With 27 Illusts. Square 8vo, cloth extra, **7s. 6d.**

NOVELISTS.—HALF-HOURS WITH THE BEST NOVELISTS OF
THE CENTURY. Edit. by H. T. MACKENZIE BELL. Cr. 8vo, cl., **3s. 6d.** [Preparing.

O'HANLON (ALICE), NOVELS BY. Post 8vo, illustrated boards, **2s.** each.
THE UNFORESEEN. | CHANCE? OR FATE?

OHNET (GEORGES), NOVELS BY.
DOCTOR RAMEAU. 9 Illusts. by E. BAYARD. Cr. 8vo, cl., **6s.**; post 8vo, bds., **2s.**
A LAST LOVE. Crown 8vo, cloth, **5s.**; post 8vo, boards, **2s.**
A WEIRD GIFT. Crown 8vo, cloth, **3s. 6d.**; post 8vo, boards, **2s.**

OLIPHANT (MRS.), NOVELS BY. Post 8vo, illustrated boards, **2s.** each.
THE PRIMROSE PATH. | THE GREATEST HEIRESS IN ENGLAND
WHITELADIES. With Illustrations by ARTHUR HOPKINS and HENRY WOODS,
A.R.A. Crown 8vo, cloth extra, **3s. 6d.**; post 8vo, illustrated boards, **2s.**

O'REILLY (HARRINGTON).—FIFTY YEARS ON THE TRAIL: Ad-
ventures of JOHN Y. NELSON. 100 Illusts. by P. FRENZENY. Crown 8vo, **3s. 6d.**

O'REILLY (MRS.).—PHŒBE'S FORTUNES. Post 8vo, illust. bds., 2s.

O'SHAUGHNESSY (ARTHUR), POEMS BY.
LAYS OF FRANCE. Crown 8vo, cloth extra, **10s. 6d.**
MUSIC & MOONLIGHT. Fp. 8vo, **7s. 6d.** | SONGS OF A WORKER, Fp. 8vo, **7s. 6d.**

OUIDA, NOVELS BY. Cr. 8vo, cl., **3s. 6d.** each ; post 8vo, llust. bds., **2s.** each.

HELD IN BONDAGE.	FOLLE-FARINE.	MOTHS.
TRICOTRIN.	A DOG OF FLANDERS.	PIPISTRELLO.
STRATHMORE.	PASCAREL.	A VILLAGE COMMUNE.
CHANDOS.	TWO LITTLE WOODEN	IN MAREMMA.
CECIL CASTLEMAINE'S	SHOES.	BIMBI. | SYRLIN.
GAGE.	SIGNA.	WANDA.
IDALIA.	IN A WINTER CITY.	FRESCOES. | OTHMAR.
UNDER TWO FLAGS.	ARIADNE.	PRINCESS NAPRAXINE.
PUCK.	FRIENDSHIP.	GUILDEROY. | RUFFINO.

BIMBI. Presentation Edition, with Nine Illustrations by EDMUND H. GARRETT.
Square 8vo, cloth, **5s.**
SANTA BARBARA, &c. Square 8vo, cloth, **6s.**; crown 8vo, cloth, **3s. 6d.**
WISDOM, WIT, AND PATHOS, selected from the Works of OUIDA by F. SYDNEY
MORRIS. Post 8vo, cloth extra, **5s.** CHEAP EDITION, illustrated boards, **2s.**

PAGE (H. A.), WORKS BY.
THOREAU: His Life and Aims. With Portrait. Post 8vo, cloth limp, **2s. 6d.**
ANIMAL ANECDOTES. Arranged on a New Principle. Crown 8vo, cloth extra, **5s.**

PARLIAMENTARY ELECTIONS AND ELECTIONEERING, A HIS-
TORY OF, from the Stuarts to Queen Victoria. By JOSEPH GREGO. A New Edition,
with 93 Illustrations. Demy 8vo, cloth extra, **7s. 6d.**

PASCAL'S PROVINCIAL LETTERS. A New Translation, with His-
torical Introduction and Notes by T. M'CRIE, D.D. Post 8vo, cloth limp, **2s.**

PAUL.—GENTLE AND SIMPLE. By MARGARET A. PAUL. With Frontis-
piece by HELEN PATERSON. Crown 8vo, cloth, **3s. 6d.**; post 8vo, illust. boards, **2s.**

PAYN (JAMES), NOVELS BY.
Crown 8vo. cloth extra. **3s. 6d.** each; post 8vo, illustrated boards. **2s.** each.

LOST SIR MASSINGBERD.	A GRAPE FROM A THORN.
WALTER'S WORD.	FROM EXILE.
LESS BLACK THAN WE'RE	THE CANON'S WARD.
PAINTED.	THE TALK OF THE TOWN.
BY PROXY.	HOLIDAY TASKS.
HIGH SPIRITS.	GLOW-WORM TALES.
UNDER ONE ROOF.	THE MYSTERY OF MIRBRIDGE.
A CONFIDENTIAL AGENT.	THE WORD AND THE WILL.

Post 8vo, illustrated boards, **2s.** each.

HUMOROUS STORIES.	FOUND DEAD.
THE FOSTER BROTHERS.	GWENDOLINE'S HARVEST.
THE FAMILY SCAPEGRACE.	A MARINE RESIDENCE.
MARRIED BENEATH HIM.	MIRK ABBEY.|SOME PRIVATE VIEWS.
BENTINCK'S TUTOR.	NOT WOOED, BUT WON.
A PERFECT TREASURE.	TWO HUNDRED POUNDS REWARD.
A COUNTY FAMILY.	THE BEST OF HUSBANDS.
LIKE FATHER, LIKE SON.	HALVES. | THE BURNT MILLION.
A WOMAN'S VENGEANCE.	FALLEN FORTUNES.
CARLYON'S YEAR.|CECIL'S TRYST.	WHAT HE COST HER.
MURPHY'S MASTER.	KIT: A MEMORY.|FOR CASH ONLY.
AT HER MERCY.	A PRINCE OF THE BLOOD.
THE CLYFFARDS OF CLYFFE.	SUNNY STORIES.

IN PERIL AND PRIVATION; Stories of MARINE ADVENTURE. With 17 Illustrations. Crown 8vo, cloth extra, **3s. 6d.**
NOTES FROM THE "NEWS." Crown 8vo, portrait cover, **1s.**; cloth, **1s. 6d.**

PENNELL (H. CHOLMONDELEY), WORKS BY. Post 8vo, cl., **2s. 6d.** each.
PUCK ON PEGASUS. With Illustrations.
PEGASUS RE-SADDLED. With Ten full-page Illustrations by G. DU MAURIER.
THE MUSES OF MAYFAIR. Vers de Société, Selected by H. C. PENNELL.

PHELPS (E. STUART), WORKS BY. Post 8vo, **1s.** each; cloth, **1s. 6d.** each.
BEYOND THE GATES. By the Author | AN OLD MAID'S PARADISE.
of "The Gates Ajar." | BURGLARS IN PARADISE.
JACK THE FISHERMAN. Illustrated by C. W. REED. Cr. 8vo, **1s.**; cloth, **1s. 6d.**

PIRKIS (C. L.), NOVELS BY.
TROOPING WITH CROWS. Fcap. 8vo, picture cover, **1s.**
LADY LOVELACE. Post 8vo, illustrated boards, **2s.**

PLANCHE (J. R.), WORKS BY.
THE PURSUIVANT OF ARMS. With Six Plates, and 209 Illusts. Cr. 8vo, cl. **7s. 6d.**
SONGS AND POEMS, 1819-1879. Introduction by Mrs. MACKARNESS. Cr. 8vo, cl., **6s.**

PLUTARCH'S LIVES OF ILLUSTRIOUS MEN. Translated from the
Greek, with Notes Critical and Historical, and a Life of Plutarch, by JOHN and WILLIAM LANGHORNE. With Portraits. Two Vols., demy 8vo, half-bound, **10s. 6d.**

POE'S (EDGAR ALLAN) CHOICE WORKS, in Prose and Poetry. Intro-
duction by CHAS. BAUDELAIRE, Portrait, and Facsimiles. Cr. 8vo, cloth, **7s. 6d.**
THE MYSTERY OF MARIE ROGET, &c. Post 8vo, illustrated boards, **2s.**

POPE'S POETICAL WORKS. Post 8vo, cloth limp, 2s.

PRAED (MRS. CAMPBELL), NOVELS BY. Post 8vo, illust. bds., 2s. ea.
THE ROMANCE OF A STATION. | **THE SOUL OF COUNTESS ADRIAN.**
"THE RIGHT HONOURABLE." By Mrs. CAMPBELL PRAED and JUSTIN McCARTHY, M.P. Crown 8vo, cloth extra, **6s.**

PRICE (E. C.), NOVELS BY.
Crown 8vo, cloth extra, **3s. 6d.** each; post 8vo, illustrated boards. **2s.** each.
VALENTINA. | **THE FOREIGNERS.** | **MRS. LANCASTER'S RIVAL.**
GERALD. Post 8vo, illustrated boards, **2s.**

PRINCESS OLGA.—RADNA; or, The Great Conspiracy of 1881. By
the Princess OLGA. Crown 8vo, cloth extra, **6s.**

PROCTOR (RICHARD A., B.A.), WORKS BY.
FLOWERS OF THE SKY. With 55 Illusts. Small crown 8vo, cloth extra, **3s. 6d.**
EASY STAR LESSONS. With Star Maps for Every Night in the Year. Cr. 8vo, **6s.**
FAMILIAR SCIENCE STUDIES. Crown 8vo, cloth extra, **6s.**
SATURN AND ITS SYSTEM. With 13 Steel Plates. Demy 8vo, cloth ex., **10s. 6d.**
MYSTERIES OF TIME AND SPACE. With Illustrations. Cr. 8vo, cloth extra, **6s.**
THE UNIVERSE OF SUNS. With numerous Illustrations. Cr. 8vo, cloth ex., **6s.**
WAGES AND WANTS OF SCIENCE WORKERS. Crown 8vo, **1s. 6d.**

PRYCE.—MISS MAXWELL'S AFFECTIONS. By RICHARD PRYCE.
Frontispiece by HAL LUDLOW. Cr. 8vo, cl., **3s. 6d.**; post 8vo, illust. boards., **2s.**

RAMBOSSON.—POPULAR ASTRONOMY. By J. RAMBOSSON, Laureate
of the Institute of France. With numerous Illusts. Crown 8vo, cloth extra, **7s. 6d.**

RANDOLPH.—AUNT ABIGAIL DYKES: A Novel. By Lt.-Colonel
GEORGE RANDOLPH, U.S.A. Crown 8vo, cloth extra, **7s. 6d.**

READE (CHARLES), NOVELS BY.
Crown 8vo, cloth extra, illustrated, **3s. 6d.** each; post 8vo, illust. bds., **2s.** each.
PEG WOFFINGTON. Illustrated by S. L. FILDES, R.A.—Also a POCKET EDITION, set in New Type, in Elzevir style, fcap. 8vo, half-leather, **2s. 6d.**
CHRISTIE JOHNSTONE. Illustrated by WILLIAM SMALL.—Also a POCKET EDITION, set in New Type, in Elzevir style, fcap. 8vo, half-leather, **2s. 6d.**
IT IS NEVER TOO LATE TO MEND. Illustrated by G. J. PINWELL.
COURSE OF TRUE LOVE NEVER DID RUN SMOOTH. Illust. HELEN PATERSON.
THE AUTOBIOGRAPHY OF A THIEF, &c. Illustrated by MATT STRETCH.
LOVE ME LITTLE, LOVE ME LONG. Illustrated by M. ELLEN EDWARDS.
THE DOUBLE MARRIAGE. Illusts. by Sir JOHN GILBERT, R.A., and C. KEENE.
THE CLOISTER AND THE HEARTH. Illustrated by CHARLES KEENE.
HARD CASH. Illustrated by F. W. LAWSON.
GRIFFITH GAUNT. Illustrated by S. L. FILDES, R.A., and WILLIAM SMALL.
FOUL PLAY. Illustrated by GEORGE DU MAURIER.
PUT YOURSELF IN HIS PLACE. Illustrated by ROBERT BARNES.
A TERRIBLE TEMPTATION. Illustrated by EDWARD HUGHES and A. W. COOPER.
A SIMPLETON. Illustrated by KATE CRAUFURD.
THE WANDERING HEIR. Illust. by H. PATERSON, S. L. FILDES, C. GREEN, &c.
A WOMAN-HATER. Illustrated by THOMAS COULDERY.
SINGLEHEART AND DOUBLEFACE. Illustrated by P. MACNAB.
GOOD STORIES OF MEN AND OTHER ANIMALS. Illust. by E. A. ABBEY, &c.
THE JILT, and other Stories. Illustrated by JOSEPH NASH.
A PERILOUS SECRET. Illustrated by FRED. BARNARD.
READIANA. With a Steel-plate Portrait of CHARLES READE.
BIBLE CHARACTERS: Studies of David, Paul, &c. Fcap. 8vo, leatherette, **1s.**
THE CLOISTER AND THE HEARTH. With an Introduction by WALTER BESANT. Elzevir Edition. 4 vols., post 8vo, each with Front., cl. ex., gilt top, **14s.** the set.
SELECTIONS FROM THE WORKS OF CHARLES READE. Cr. 8vo, buckram, **6s.**

RIDDELL (MRS. J. H.), NOVELS BY.
Crown 8vo, cloth extra, **3s. 6d.** each; post 8vo, illustrated boards, **2s.** each.
THE PRINCE OF WALES'S GARDEN PARTY. | WEIRD STORIES.
Post 8vo, illustrated boards, **2s.** each.
THE UNINHABITED HOUSE. | HER MOTHER'S DARLING.
MYSTERY IN PALACE GARDENS. | THE NUN'S CURSE.
FAIRY WATER. | IDLE TALES.

RIMMER (ALFRED), WORKS BY. Square 8vo, cloth gilt, **7s. 6d.** each.
OUR OLD COUNTRY TOWNS. With 55 Illustrations.
RAMBLES ROUND ETON AND HARROW. With 50 Illustrations.
ABOUT ENGLAND WITH DICKENS. With 58 Illusts. by C. A. VANDERHOOF, &c.

RIVES (Amélie).—BARBARA DERING. By AMÉLIE RIVES, Author
of "The Quick or the Dead?" Crown 8vo, cloth extra, **3s. 6d.**

ROBINSON CRUSOE. By DANIEL DEFOE. (MAJOR'S EDITION.) With
37 Illustrations by GEORGE CRUIKSHANK. Post 8vo, half-bound, **2s.**

ROBINSON (F. W.), NOVELS BY.
WOMEN ARE STRANGE. Post 8vo, illustrated boards, **2s.**
THE HANDS OF JUSTICE. Cr. 8vo, cloth ex., **3s. 6d.**; post 8vo, illust. bds., **2s.**

ROBINSON (PHIL), WORKS BY. Crown 8vo, cloth extra, **6s.** each.
THE POETS' BIRDS. | THE POETS' BEASTS.
THE POETS AND NATURE: REPTILES, FISHES, AND INSECTS.

ROCHEFOUCAULD'S MAXIMS AND MORAL REFLECTIONS. With
Notes, and an Introductory Essay by SAINTE-BEUVE. Post 8vo, cloth limp, **2s.**

ROLL OF BATTLE ABBEY, THE: A List of the Principal Warriors
who came from Normandy with William the Conqueror, and Settled in this Country,
A.D. 1066-7. With Arms emblazoned in Gold and Colours. Handsomely printed, **5s.**

ROWLEY (HON. HUGH), WORKS BY. Post 8vo, cloth, **2s. 6d.** each.
PUNIANA: RIDDLES AND JOKES. With numerous Illustrations.
MORE PUNIANA. Profusely Illustrated.

RUNCIMAN (JAMES), STORIES BY. Post 8vo, bds., **2s.** ea.; cl., **2s. 6d.** ea.
SKIPPERS AND SHELLBACKS. | GRACE BALMAIGN'S SWEETHEART.
SCHOOLS AND SCHOLARS. |

RUSSELL (W. CLARK), BOOKS AND NOVELS BY:
Cr. 8vo, cloth extra, **6s.** each; post 8vo, illust. boards. **2s.** each; cloth limp, **2s. 6d.** ea.
ROUND THE GALLEY-FIRE. | A BOOK FOR THE HAMMOCK.
IN THE MIDDLE WATCH. | MYSTERY OF THE "OCEAN STAR."
A VOYAGE TO THE CAPE. | THE ROMANCE OF JENNY HARLOWE.

Cr. 8vo, cl. extra, **3s. 6d.** ea.; post 8vo, illust. boards, **2s.** ea.; cloth limp, **2s. 6d.** ea.
AN OCEAN TRAGEDY. | MY SHIPMATE LOUISE.
ALONE ON A WIDE WIDE SEA.
ON THE FO'K'SLE HEAD. Post 8vo, illust. boards, **2s.**; cloth limp, **2s. 6d.**

SAINT AUBYN (ALAN), NOVELS BY.
Crown 8vo, cloth extra, **3s. 6d.** each; post 8vo, illust. boards, **2s.** each.
A FELLOW OF TRINITY. Note by OLIVER WENDELL HOLMES and Frontispiece.
THE JUNIOR DEAN.
Fcap. 8vo, cloth boards, **1s. 6d.** each.
THE OLD MAID'S SWEETHEART. | MODEST LITTLE SARA.
THE MASTER OF ST. BENEDICT'S. Two Vols., crown 8vo.

SALA (G. A.).—GASLIGHT AND DAYLIGHT. Post 8vo, boards, 2s.

SANSON.—SEVEN GENERATIONS OF EXECUTIONERS: Memoirs
of the Sanson Family (1688 to 1847). Crown 8vo, cloth extra, **3s. 6d.**

SAUNDERS (JOHN), NOVELS BY.
Crown 8vo, cloth extra, **3s. 6d.** each; post 8vo, illustrated boards, **2s.** each.
GUY WATERMAN. | THE LION IN THE PATH. | THE TWO DREAMERS.
BOUND TO THE WHEEL. Crown 8vo, cloth extra, **3s. 6d.**

SAUNDERS (KATHARINE), NOVELS BY.
Crown 8vo, cloth extra, **3s. 6d.** each; post 8vo, illustrated boards, **2s.** each.
MARGARET AND ELIZABETH. | HEART SALVAGE.
THE HIGH MILLS. | SEBASTIAN.
JOAN MERRYWEATHER. Post 8vo, illustrated boards, **2s.**
GIDEON'S ROCK. Crown 8vo, cloth extra, **3s. 6d.**

SCIENCE-GOSSIP. Edited by Dr. J. E. TAYLOR, F.L.S., &c. Devoted t> Geology, Botany, Physiology, Chemistry, Zoology, Microscopy, Telescopy, Physiography, &c. **4d.** Monthly. Pts. 1 to 300, **8d.** each; Pts. 301 to date, **4d.** each. Vols. I. to XIX., **7s. 6d.** each; Vols. XX. to date, **5s.** each. Cases for Binding, **1s. 6d.**

SCOTLAND YARD: Experiences of 37 Years. By Chief-Inspector CAVANAGH. Post 8vo, illustrated boards. **2s.**; cloth, **2s. 6d.**

SECRET OUT, THE: One Thousand Tricks with Cards; with Entertaining Experiments in Drawing-room or "White Magic." By W. H. CREMER. With 300 Illustrations. Crown 8vo, cloth extra, **4s. 6d.**

SEGUIN (L. G.), WORKS BY.
THE COUNTRY OF THE PASSION PLAY (OBERAMMERGAU) and the Highlands of Bavaria. With Map and 37 Illustrations. Crown 8vo, cloth extra, **3s. 6d.**
WALKS IN ALGIERS. With 2 Maps and 16 Illusts. Crown 8vo. cloth extra. **6s.**

SENIOR (WM.).—BY STREAM AND SEA. Post 8vo, cloth, 2s. 6d.

SHAKESPEARE FOR CHILDREN: LAMB'S TALES FROM SHAKE-SPEARE. With Illustrations, coloured and plain, by J. MOYR SMITH. Cr. 4to, **6s.**

SHARP.—CHILDREN OF TO-MORROW: A Novel. By WILLIAM SHARP. Crown 8vo, cloth extra, **6s.**

SHARP, LUKE (ROBERT BARR), STORIES BY.
IN A STEAMER CHAIR. With 2 Illustrations. Crown 8vo, cloth extra, **3s. 6d.**
FROM WHOSE BOURNE? &c. With Fifty Illustratioos. [Shortly.

SHELLEY.—THE COMPLETE WORKS IN VERSE AND PROSE OF PERCY BYSSHE SHELLEY. Edited, Prefaced, and Annotated by R. HERNE SHEPHERD. Five Vols., crown 8vo, cloth boards, **3s. 6d.** each.
POETICAL WORKS, in Three Vols.:
Vol. I. Introduction by the Editor; Posthumous Fragments of Margaret Nicholson; Shelley's Correspondence with Stockdale; The Wandering Jew; Queen Mab, with the Notes; Alastor, and other Poems; Rosalind and Helen: Prometheus Unbound; Adonais, &c.
Vol. II. Laon and Cythna; The Cenci; Julian and Maddalo; Swellfoot the Tyrant; The Witch of Atlas; Epipsychidion; Hellas.
Vol. III. Posthumous Poems; The Masque of Anarchy; and other Pieces.
PROSE WORKS, in Two Vols.:
Vol. I. The Two Romances of Zastrozzi and St. Irvyne; the Dublin and Marlow Pamphlets; A Refutation of Deism; Letters to Leigh Hunt, and some Minor Writings and Fragments.
Vol. II. The Essays; Letters from Abroad; Translations and Fragments, Edited by Mrs. SHELLEY. With a Bibliography of Shelley, and an Index of the Prose Works.

SHERARD (R. H.).—ROGUES: A Novel. Crown 8vo, **1s.**; cloth, **1s. 6d.**

SHERIDAN (GENERAL). — PERSONAL MEMOIRS OF GENERAL P. H. SHERIDAN. With Portraits and Facsimiles. Two Vols., demy 8vo, cloth, **24s.**

SHERIDAN'S (RICHARD BRINSLEY) COMPLETE WORKS. With Life and Anecdotes. Including his Dramatic Writings, his Works in Prose and Poetry, Translations, Speeches and Jokes. 10 Illusts. Cr. 8vo, hf.-bound, **7s. 6d.**
THE RIVALS, THE SCHOOL FOR SCANDAL, and other Plays. Post 8vo, printed on laid paper and half-bound, **2s.**
SHERIDAN'S COMEDIES: THE RIVALS and THE SCHOOL FOR SCANDAL. Edited, with an Introduction and Notes to each Play, and a Biographical Sketch, by BRANDER MATTHEWS. With Illustrations. Demy 8vo, half-parchment, **12s. 6d.**

SIDNEY'S (SIR PHILIP) COMPLETE POETICAL WORKS, including all those in "Arcadia." With Portrait, Memorial-Introduction, Notes, &c. by the Rev. A. B. GROSART, D.D. Three Vols., crown 8vo, cloth boards, **18s.**

SIGNBOARDS: Their History. With Anecdotes of Famous Taverns and Remarkable Characters. By JACOB LARWOOD and JOHN CAMDEN HOTTEN. With Coloured Frontispiece and 94 Illustrations. Crown 8vo, cloth extra. **7s. 6d.**

SIMS (GEORGE R.), WORKS BY.
Post 8vo, illustrated boards, **2s.** each: cloth limp, **2s. 6d.** eaca.
ROGUES AND VAGABONDS. | MARY JANE MARRIED.
THE RING O' BELLS. | TALES OF TO-DAY.
MARY JANE'S MEMOIRS. | DRAMAS OF LIFE. With 60 Illustrations.
TINKLETOP'S CRIME. With a Frontispiece by MAURICE GREIFFENHAGEN.
ZEPH: A Circus Story, &c.
Crown 8vo, picture cover, **1s.** each; cloth, **1s. 6d.** each.
HOW THE POOR LIVE; and HORRIBLE LONDON.
THE DAGONET RECITER AND READER: being Readings and Recitations in Prose and Verse, selected from his own Works by GEORGE R. SIMS.
THE CASE OF GEORGE CANDLEMAS. | DAGONET DITTIES.

SISTER DORA: A Biography. By MARGARET LONSDALE. With Four Illustrations. Demy 8vo, picture cover, **4d.;** cloth, **6d.**

SKETCHLEY.—A MATCH IN THE DARK. By ARTHUR SKETCHLEY. Post 8vo, illustrated boards, **2s.**

SLANG DICTIONARY (THE): Etymological, Historical, and Anecdotal. Crown 8vo, cloth extra, **6s. 6d.**

SMITH (J. MOYR), WORKS BY.
THE PRINCE OF ARGOLIS. With 130 Illusts. Post 8vo, cloth extra, **3s. 6d.**
TALES OF OLD THULE. With numerous Illustrations. Crown 8vo, cloth gilt, **6s.**
THE WOOING OF THE WATER WITCH. Illustrated. Post 8vo, cloth, **6s.**

SOCIETY IN LONDON. By A FOREIGN RESIDENT. Crown 8vo, **1s.;** cloth, **1s. 6d.**

SOCIETY IN PARIS: The Upper Ten Thousand. A Series of Letters from Count PAUL VASILI to a Young French Diplomat. Crown 8vo. cloth, **6s.**

SOMERSET. — SONGS OF ADIEU. By Lord HENRY SOMERSET. Small 4to, Japanese vellum, **6s.**

SPALDING.—ELIZABETHAN DEMONOLOGY : An Essay on the Belief in the Existence of Devils. By T. A. SPALDING, LL.B. Crown 8vo, cloth extra, **5s.**

SPEIGHT (T. W.), NOVELS BY.
Post 8vo, illustrated boards. **2s.** each.
THE MYSTERIES OF HERON DYKE. | HOODWINKED; and THE SANDY-
BY DEVIOUS WAYS, &c. | CROFT MYSTERY.
THE GOLDEN HOOP. | BACK TO LIFE.
Post 8vo, cloth limp, **1s. 6d.** each.
A BARREN TITLE. | WIFE OR NO WIFE?
THE SANDYCROFT MYSTERY. Crown 8vo, picture cover, **1s.**

SPENSER FOR CHILDREN. By M. H. TOWRY. With Illustrations by WALTER J. MORGAN. Crown 4to, cloth gilt, **6s.**

STARRY HEAVENS (THE): A POETICAL BIRTHDAY BOOK. Royal 16mo, cloth extra, **2s. 6d.**

STAUNTON.—THE LAWS AND PRACTICE OF CHESS. With an Analysis of the Openings. By HOWARD STAUNTON. Edited by ROBERT B. WORMALD. Crown 8vo, cloth extra, **5s.**

STEDMAN (E. C.), WORKS BY.
VICTORIAN POETS. Thirteenth Edition. Crown 8vo. cloth extra, **9s.**
THE POETS OF AMERICA. Crown 8vo, cloth extra, **9s.**

STERNDALE. — THE AFGHAN KNIFE: A Novel. By ROBERT ARMITAGE STERNDALE. Cr. 8vo, cloth extra. **3s. 6d.**; post 8vo, illust. boards, **2s.**

STEVENSON (R. LOUIS), WORKS BY. Post 8vo, cl. limp, **2s. 6d.** each.
TRAVELS WITH A DONKEY. Seventh Edit. With a Frontis. by WALTER CRANE.
AN INLAND VOYAGE. Fourth Edition. With a Frontispiece by WALTER CRANE.

Crown 8vo, buckram, gilt top, **6s.** each.
FAMILIAR STUDIES OF MEN AND BOOKS. Sixth Edition.
THE SILVERADO SQUATTERS. With a Frontispiece. Third Edition.
THE MERRY MEN. Third Edition. | UNDERWOODS: Poems. Fifth Edition.
MEMORIES AND PORTRAITS. Third Edition.
VIRGINIBUS PUERISQUE, and other Papers. Seventh Edition. | BALLADS.
ACROSS THE PLAINS, with other Memories and Essays.

NEW ARABIAN NIGHTS. Eleventh Edition. Crown 8vo, buckram, gilt top, **6s.;** post 8vo, illustrated boards, **2s.**
THE SUICIDE CLUB; and THE RAJAH'S DIAMOND. (From NEW ARABIAN NIGHTS.) With Six Illustrations by J. BERNARD PARTRIDGE. Crown 8vo, cloth extra, **5s.**
PRINCE OTTO. Sixth Edition. Post 8vo, illustrated boards, **2s.**
FATHER DAMIEN: An Open Letter to the Rev. Dr. Hyde. Second Edition. Crown 8vo, hand-made and brown paper, **1s.**

STODDARD. — SUMMER CRUISING IN THE SOUTH SEAS. By C. WARREN STODDARD. Illustrated by WALLIS MACKAY. Cr. 8vo, cl. extra, **3s. 6d.**

STORIES FROM FOREIGN NOVELISTS. With Notices by HELEN and ALICE ZIMMERN. Crown 8vo, cloth extra, **3s. 6d.**; post 8vo, illustrated boards, **2s.**

STRANGE MANUSCRIPT (A) FOUND IN A COPPER CYLINDER.
With 19 Illustrations by GILBERT GAUL. Third Edition. Crown 8vo, cloth extra, 5s.

STRANGE SECRETS. Told by CONAN DOYLE, PERCY FITZGERALD, FLOR-
ENCE MARRYAT, &c. Cr. 8vo, cl. ex., Eight Illusts., 6s.; post 8vo, illust. bds., 2s.

STRUTT'S SPORTS AND PASTIMES OF THE PEOPLE OF
ENGLAND; including the Rural and Domestic Recreations, May Games, Mum-
meries, Shows, &c., from the Earliest Period to the Present Time. Edited by
WILLIAM HONE. With 140 Illustrations. Crown 8vo, cloth extra, 7s. 6d.

SUBURBAN HOMES (THE) OF LONDON : A Residential Guide. With
a Map, and Notes on Rental, Rates, and Accommodation. Crown 8vo, cloth, 7s. 6d.

SWIFT'S (DEAN) CHOICE WORKS, in Prose and Verse. With Memoir,
Portrait, and Facsimiles of the Maps in "Gulliver's Travels." Cr. 8vo. cl., 7s. 6d.
GULLIVER'S TRAVELS, and A TALE OF A TUB. Post 8vo, half-bound, 2s.
A MONOGRAPH ON SWIFT. By J. CHURTON COLLINS. Cr. 8vo, cloth, 8s. [Shortly.

SWINBURNE (ALGERNON C.), WORKS BY.

SELECTIONS FROM POETICAL WORKS
OF A. C. SWINBURNE. Fcap. 8vo, 6s.
ATALANTA IN CALYDON. Crown 8vo,
6s.
CHASTELARD: A Tragedy. Cr. 8vo, 7s.
POEMS AND BALLADS. FIRST SERIES.
Crown 8vo or fcap. 8vo, 9s.
POEMS AND BALLADS. SECOND SERIES.
Crown 8vo or fcap. 8vo, 9s.
POEMS AND BALLADS. THIRD SERIES.
Crown 8vo, 7s.
SONGS BEFORE SUNRISE. Crown 8vo,
10s. 6d.
BOTHWELL: A Tragedy. Crown 8vo,
12s. 6d.
SONGS OF TWO NATIONS. Cr. 8vo, 6s.
GEORGE CHAPMAN. (See Vol. II. of G.
CHAPMAN'S Works.) Crown 8vo, 6s.

ESSAYS AND STUDIES. Cr. 8vo, 12s.
ERECHTHEUS: A Tragedy. Cr. 8vo, 6s.
SONGS OF THE SPRINGTIDES. Crown
8vo, 6s.
STUDIES IN SONG. Crown 8vo, 7s.
MARY STUART: A Tragedy. Cr. 8vo, 8s.
TRISTRAM OF LYONESSE. Cr. 8vo, 9s.
A CENTURY OF ROUNDELS. Sm. 4to, 8s.
A MIDSUMMER HOLIDAY. Cr. 8vo, 7s.
MARINO FALIERO: A Tragedy. Crown
8vo, 6s.
A STUDY OF VICTOR HUGO. Cr. 8vo, 6s.
MISCELLANIES. Crown 8vo, 12s.
LOCRINE: A Tragedy. Cr. 8vo, 6s.
A STUDY OF BEN JONSON. Cr. 8vo, 7s.
THE SISTERS: A Tragedy. Cr. 8vo, 6s.

SYMONDS.—WINE, WOMEN, AND SONG: Mediæval Latin Students'
Songs. With Essay and Trans. by J. ADDINGTON SYMONDS. Fcap. 8vo, parchment, 6s.

SYNTAX'S (DR.) THREE TOURS: In Search of the Picturesque, in
Search of Consolation, and in Search of a Wife. With ROWLANDSON'S Coloured Illustrations, and Life of the Author by J. C. HOTTEN. Crown 8vo, cloth extra, 7s. 6d.

TAINE'S HISTORY OF ENGLISH LITERATURE. Translated by
HENRY VAN LAUN. Four Vols., small demy 8vo, cl. bds., 30s.—POPULAR EDITION,
Two Vols., large crown 8vo, cloth extra, 15s.

TAYLOR'S (BAYARD) DIVERSIONS OF THE ECHO CLUB: Bur-
lesques of Modern Writers. Post 8vo, cloth limp, 2s.

TAYLOR (DR. J. E., F.L.S.), WORKS BY. Cr. 8vo, cl. ex., 7s. 6d. each.
THE SAGACITY AND MORALITY OF PLANTS: A Sketch of the Life and Conduct
of the Vegetable Kingdom. With a Coloured Frontispiece and 100 Illustrations.
OUR COMMON BRITISH FOSSILS, and Where to Find Them. 331 Illustrations.
THE PLAYTIME NATURALIST. With 366 Illustrations. Crown 8vo, cloth, 5s.

TAYLOR'S (TOM) HISTORICAL DRAMAS. Containing "Clancarty,"
"Jeanne Darc," "'Twixt Axe and Crown," "The Fool's Revenge," "Arkwright's
Wife," "Anne Boleyn," "Plot and Passion." Crown 8vo, cloth extra, 7s. 6d.
*** The Plays may also be had separately, at 1s. each.

TENNYSON (LORD): A Biographical Sketch. By H. J. JENNINGS.
With a Photograph-Portrait. Crown 8vo, cloth extra, 6s.—Cheap Edition, post 8vo,
portrait cover, 1s.; cloth, 1s. 6d.

THACKERAYANA : Notes and Anecdotes. Illustrated by Hundreds of
Sketches by WILLIAM MAKEPEACE THACKERAY. Crown 8vo, cloth extra, 7s. 6d.

THAMES.—A NEW PICTORIAL HISTORY OF THE THAMES.
By A. S. KRAUSSE. With 340 Illustrations. Post 8vo, 1s.; cloth, 1s. 6d.

THOMAS (BERTHA), NOVELS BY. Cr. 8vo, cl., 3s. 6d. ea.; post 8vo, 2s. ea.
THE VIOLIN-PLAYER. | PROUD MAISIE.

C

THOMSON'S SEASONS, and CASTLE OF INDOLENCE. With Introduction by ALLAN CUNNINGHAM, and 48 Illustrations. Post 8vo, half-bound, 2s.

THORNBURY (WALTER), WORKS BY. Cr. 8vo, cl. extra, 7s. 6d. each.
THE LIFE AND CORRESPONDENCE OF J. M. W. TURNER. Founded upon Letters and Papers furnished by his Friends. With Illustrations in Colours.
HAUNTED LONDON. Edit. by E. WALFORD, M.A. Illusts. by F. W. FAIRHOLT, F.S.A.
     Post 8vo, illustrated boards, 2s. each.
OLD STORIES RE-TOLD. | TALES FOR THE MARINES.

TIMBS (JOHN), WORKS BY. Crown 8vo, cloth extra, 7s. 6d. each.
THE HISTORY OF CLUBS AND CLUB LIFE IN LONDON: Anecdotes of its Famous Coffee-houses, Hostelries, and Taverns. With 42 Illustrations.
ENGLISH ECCENTRICS AND ECCENTRICITIES: Stories of Delusions, Impostures, Sporting Scenes, Eccentric Artists, Theatrical Folk, &c. 48 Illustrations.

TROLLOPE (ANTHONY), NOVELS BY.
Crown 8vo, cloth extra, 3s. 6d. each; post 8vo, illustrated boards, 2s. each.
THE WAY WE LIVE NOW. | MARION FAY.
KEPT IN THE DARK. | MR. SCARBOROUGH'S FAMILY.
FRAU FROHMANN. | THE LAND-LEAGUERS.
     Post 8vo, illustrated boards, 2s. each.
GOLDEN LION OF GRANPERE. | JOHN CALDIGATE. | AMERICAN SENATOR.

TROLLOPE (FRANCES E.), NOVELS BY.
Crown 8vo, cloth extra, 3s. 6d. each; post 8vo, illustrated boards, 2s. each.
LIKE SHIPS UPON THE SEA. | MABEL'S PROGRESS. | ANNE FURNESS.

TROLLOPE (T. A.).—DIAMOND CUT DIAMOND. Post 8vo, illust. bds., 2s.

TROWBRIDGE.—FARNELL'S FOLLY: A Novel. By J. T. TROWBRIDGE. Post 8vo, illustrated boards, 2s.

TYTLER (C. C. FRASER-).—MISTRESS JUDITH: A Novel. By C. C. FRASER-TYTLER. Crown 8vo, cloth extra, 3s. 6d.; post 8vo, illust. boards, 2s.

TYTLER (SARAH), NOVELS BY.
Crown 8vo, cloth extra, 3s. 6d. each; post 8vo, illustrated boards, 2s. each.
THE BRIDE'S PASS. | BURIED DIAMONDS.
LADY BELL. | THE BLACKHALL GHOSTS.
     Post 8vo, illustrated boards, 2s. each.
WHAT SHE CAME THROUGH. | BEAUTY AND THE BEAST.
CITOYENNE JACQUELINE. | DISAPPEARED.
SAINT MUNGO'S CITY. | THE HUGUENOT FAMILY.
NOBLESSE OBLIGE.

VILLARI.—A DOUBLE BOND. By LINDA VILLARI. Fcap. 8vo, picture cover, 1s.

WALT WHITMAN, POEMS BY. Edited, with Introduction, by WILLIAM M. ROSSETTI. With Portrait. Cr. 8vo, hand-made paper and buckram, 6s.

WALTON AND COTTON'S COMPLETE ANGLER; or, The Contemplative Man's Recreation, by IZAAK WALTON; and Instructions how to Angle for a Trout or Grayling in a clear Stream, by CHARLES COTTON. With Memoirs and Notes by Sir HARRIS NICOLAS, and 61 Illustrations. Crown 8vo, cloth antique, 7s. 6d.

WARD (HERBERT), WORKS BY.
FIVE YEARS WITH THE CONGO CANNIBALS. With 92 Illustrations by the Author, VICTOR PERARD, and W. B. DAVIS. Third ed. Roy. 8vo, cloth ex., 14s.
MY LIFE WITH STANLEY'S REAR GUARD. With a Map by F. S. WELLER, F.R.G.S. Post 8vo, 1s.; cloth, 1s. 6d.

WARNER.—A ROUNDABOUT JOURNEY. By CHARLES DUDLEY WARNER. Crown 8vo, cloth extra, 6s.

WARRANT TO EXECUTE CHARLES I. A Facsimile, with the 59 Signatures and Seals. Printed on paper 22 in. by 14 in. 2s.
WARRANT TO EXECUTE MARY QUEEN OF SCOTS. A Facsimile, including Queen Elizabeth's Signature and the Great Seal. 2s.

WASSERMANN (LILLIAS), NOVELS BY.
THE DAFFODIL. Crown 8vo, 1s.; cloth, 1s. 6d.
THE MARQUIS OF CARABAS. By AARON WATSON and LILLIAS WASSERMANN. 3 vols., crown 8vo.

WALFORD (EDWARD, M.A.), WORKS BY.
WALFORD'S COUNTY FAMILIES OF THE UNITED KINGDOM (1893). Containing the Descent, Birth, Marriage, Education, &c., of 12,000 Heads of Families, their Heirs, Offices, Addresses, Clubs, &c. Royal 8vo, cloth gilt, **50s.**
WALFORD'S WINDSOR PEERAGE, BARONETAGE, AND KNIGHTAGE (1893). Crown 8vo, cloth extra, **12s. 6d.**
WALFORD'S SHILLING PEERAGE (1893). Containing a List of the House of Lords, Scotch and Irish Peers, &c. 32mo, cloth, **1s.**
WALFORD'S SHILLING BARONETAGE (1893). Containing a List of the Baronets of the United Kingdom, Biographical Notices, Addresses, &c. 32mo, cloth, **1s.**
WALFORD'S SHILLING KNIGHTAGE (1893). Containing a List of the Knights of the United Kingdom, Biographical Notices, Addresses, &c. 32mo, cloth, **1s.**
WALFORD'S SHILLING HOUSE OF COMMONS (1893). Containing a List of all Members of the New Parliament, their Addresses. Clubs, &c. 32mo, cloth, **1s.**
WALFORD'S COMPLETE PEERAGE, BARONETAGE, KNIGHTAGE, AND HOUSE OF COMMONS (1893). Royal 32mo, cloth extra, gilt edges, **5s.**
TALES OF OUR GREAT FAMILIES. Crown 8vo, cloth extra, **3s. 6d.**

WEATHER, HOW TO FORETELL THE, WITH POCKET SPECTROSCOPE.
By F. W. CORY. With 10 Illustrations. Cr. 8vo, **1s.**; cloth, **1s. 6d.**

WESTALL (William).—TRUST-MONEY.
Three Vols., crown 8vo.

WHIST.—HOW TO PLAY SOLO WHIST.
By ABRAHAM S. WILKS and CHARLES F. PARDON. New Edition. Post 8vo, cloth limp, **2s.**

WHITE.—THE NATURAL HISTORY OF SELBORNE.
By GILBERT WHITE, M.A. Post 8vo, printed on laid paper and half-bound, **2s.**

WILLIAMS (W. MATTIEU, F.R.A.S.), WORKS BY.
SCIENCE IN SHORT CHAPTERS. Crown 8vo, cloth extra, **7s. 6d.**
A SIMPLE TREATISE ON HEAT. With Illusts. Cr. 8vo, cloth limp, **2s. 6d.**
THE CHEMISTRY OF COOKERY. Crown 8vo, cloth extra, **6s.**
THE CHEMISTRY OF IRON AND STEEL MAKING. Crown 8vo, cloth extra, **9s.**

WILLIAMSON (MRS. F. H.).—A CHILD WIDOW.
Post 8vo, bds., 2s.

WILSON (DR. ANDREW, F.R.S.E.), WORKS BY.
CHAPTERS ON EVOLUTION. With 259 Illustrations. Cr. 8vo, cloth extra, **7s. 6d.**
LEAVES FROM A NATURALIST'S NOTE-BOOK. Post 8vo, cloth limp, **2s. 6d.**
LEISURE-TIME STUDIES. With Illustrations. Crown 8vo, cloth extra, **6s.**
STUDIES IN LIFE AND SENSE. With numerous Illusts. Cr. 8vo, cl. ex., **6s.**
COMMON ACCIDENTS: HOW TO TREAT THEM. Illusts. Cr. 8vo, **1s.**; cl., **1s. 6d.**
GLIMPSES OF NATURE. With 35 Illustrations. Crown 8vo, cloth extra, **3s. 6d.**

WINTER (J. S.), STORIES BY.
Post 8vo, illustrated boards, **2s.** each; cloth limp, **2s. 6d.** each.
CAVALRY LIFE. | **REGIMENTAL LEGENDS.**
A SOLDIER'S CHILDREN. With 34 Illustrations by E. G. THOMSON and E. STUART HARDY. Crown 8vo, cloth extra, **3s. 6d.**

WISSMANN.—MY SECOND JOURNEY THROUGH EQUATORIAL AFRICA.
By HERMANN VON WISSMANN. With 92 Illusts. Demy 8vo, **16s.**

WOOD.—SABINA: A Novel.
By Lady WOOD. Post 8vo, boards, 2s.

WOOD (H. F.), DETECTIVE STORIES BY.
Cr. 8vo, **6s.** ea.; post 8vo, bds. **2s.**
PASSENGER FROM SCOTLAND YARD. | **ENGLISHMAN OF THE RUE CAIN.**

WOOLLEY.—RACHEL ARMSTRONG; or, Love and Theology.
By CELIA PARKER WOOLLEY. Post 8vo, illustrated boards, **2s.**; cloth, **2s. 6d.**

WRIGHT (THOMAS), WORKS BY.
Crown 8vo, cloth extra, **7s. 6d.** each.
CARICATURE HISTORY OF THE GEORGES. With 400 Caricatures, Squibs, &c.
HISTORY OF CARICATURE AND OF THE GROTESQUE IN ART, LITERATURE, SCULPTURE, AND PAINTING. Illustrated by F. W. FAIRHOLT, F.S.A.

WYNMAN.—MY FLIRTATIONS.
By MARGARET WYNMAN. With 13 Illustrations by J. BERNARD PARTRIDGE. Crown 8vo, cloth extra, **3s. 6d.**

YATES (EDMUND), NOVELS BY.
Post 8vo, illustrated boards, **2s.** each.
LAND AT LAST. | **THE FORLORN HOPE.** | **CASTAWAY.**

ZOLA (EMILE), NOVELS BY.
Crown 8vo, cloth extra, 3s. 6d. each.
THE DOWNFALL. Translated by E. A. VIZETELLY. Third Edition.
THE DREAM. Translated by ELIZA CHASE. With 8 Illustrations by JEANNIOT.

LISTS OF BOOKS CLASSIFIED IN SERIES.

, *For fuller cataloguing, see alphabetical arrangement, pp. 1-25.*

THE MAYFAIR LIBRARY. Post 8vo, cloth limp, 2s. 6d. per Volume.

A Journey Round My Room. By XAVIER DE MAISTRE.
Quips and Quiddities. By W. D. ADAMS.
The Agony Column of "The Times."
Melancholy Anatomised: Abridgment of "Burton's Anatomy of Melancholy."
The Speeches of Charles Dickens.
Poetical Ingenuities. By W. T. DOBSON.
The Cupboard Papers. By FIN-BEC.
W. S. Gilbert's Plays. FIRST SERIES.
W. S. Gilbert's Plays. SECOND SERIES.
Songs of Irish Wit and Humour.
Animals and Masters. By Sir A. HELPS.
Social Pressure. By Sir A. HELPS.
Curiosities of Criticism. H. J. JENNINGS.
Holmes's Autocrat of Breakfast-Table.
Pencil and Palette. By R. KEMPT.
Little Essays: from LAMB's Letters.

Forensic Anecdotes. By JACOB LARWOO!
Theatrical Anecdotes. JACOB LARWOO!
Jeux d'Esprit. Edited by HENRY S. LEIG!
Witch Stories. By E. LYNN LINTON.
Ourselves. By E. LYNN LINTON.
Pastimes & Players. By R. MACGREGO!
New Paul and Virginia. W.H.MALLOC
New Republic. By W. H. MALLOCK.
Puck on Pegasus. By H. C. PENNE W
Pegasus Re-Saddl'. 3y H. C. PEN:
Muses of Mayfair. Ed. H. C. PENNELL.
Thoreau : His Life & Aims. By H. A. PA!
Puniana. By Hon. HUGH ROWLEY.
More Puniana. By Hon. HUGH ROV
The Philosophy of Handwriting.
By Stream and Sea. By WM. SENIO.
Leaves from a Naturalist's Note-Bo'
By Dr. ANDREW WILSON.

THE GOLDEN LIBRARY. Post 8vo, cloth limp, 2s. per Volume.

Bayard Taylor's Diversions of the Echo Club.
Bennett's Ballad History of England.
Bennett's Songs for Sailors.
Godwin's Lives of the Necromancers.
Pope's Poetical Works.
Holmes's Autocrat of Breakfast Table.

Jesse's Scenes of Country Life.
Leigh Hunt's Tale for a Chi. Corner.
Mallory's Mort d'Arthur: Selection-
Pascal's Provincial Letters.
Rochefoucauld's Maxims & Reflect.

THE WANDERER'S LIBRARY. Crown 8vo, cloth extra, 3s. 6d. eac...

Wanderings in Patagonia. By JULIUS BEERBOHM. Illustrated.
Camp Notes. By FREDERICK BOYLE.
Savage Life. By FREDERICK BOYLE.
Merrie England in the Olden Time. By G. DANIEL. Illustrated by CRUIKSHANK.
Circus Life. By THOMAS FROST.
Lives of the Conjurers. THOMAS FROST.
The Old Showmen and the Old London Fairs. By THOMAS FROST.
Low-Life Deeps. By JAMES GREENWOOD.

Wilds of London. JAMES GREENWOOD.
Tunis. Chev. HESSE-WARTEGG. 22 Illu'
Life and Adventures of a Cheap J
World Behind the Scenes. P.FITZGE.
Tavern Anecdotes and Sayings.
The Genial Showman. By E.P. HINGSTO!
Story of London Parks. JACOB LARWOO!
London Characters. By HENRY MAYHEW
Seven Generations of Executioners.
Summer Cruising in the South Sea'
By C. WARREN STODDARD. Illustrate

POPULAR SHILLING BOOKS.

Harry Fludyer at Cambridge.
Jeff Briggs's Love Story. BRET HARTE.
Twins of Table Mountain. BRET HARTE.
Snow-bound at Eagle's. By BRET HARTE.
A Day's Tour. By PERCY FITZGERALD.
Esther's Glove. By R. E. FRANCILLON.
Sentenced! By SOMERVILLE GIBNEY.
The Professor's Wife. By L. GRAHAM.
Mrs. Gainsborough's Diamonds. By JULIAN HAWTHORNE.
Niagara Spray. By J. HOLLINGSHEAD.
A Romance of the Queen's Hounds. By CHARLES JAMES.
Garden that Paid Rent. TOM JERROLD.
Cut by the Mess. By ARTHUR KEYSER.
Teresa Itasca. By A. MACALPINE.
Our Sensation Novel. J. H. McCARTHY.
Doom! By JUSTIN H. McCARTHY.
Dolly. By JUSTIN H. McCARTHY.

Lily Lass. JUSTIN H. McCARTHY.
Was She Good or Bad? By W. MINTO.
Notes from the "News." By JAS. PAYN
Beyond the Gates. By E. S. PHELPS.
Old Maid's Paradise. By E. S. PHELPS.
Burglars in Paradise. By E. S. PHELPS
Jack the Fisherman. By E. S. PHEI **
Trooping with Crows. By C. L. PIRK
Bible Characters. By CHARLES REAF
Rogues. By R. H. SHERARD.
The Dagonet Reciter. By G. R. SIM
How the Poor Live. By G. R. SIMS.
Case of George Candlemas. G. R. S...
Sandycroft Mystery. T. W. SPEIGHT.
Hoodwinked. By T. W. SPEIGHT.
Father Damien. By R. L. STEVENSON.
A Double Bond. By LINDA VILLARI.
My Life with Stanley's Rear Guard.]
HERBERT WARD.

HANDY NOVELS. Fcap. 8vo, cloth boards, 1s. 6d. each.

The Old Maid's-Sweetheart. A.ST.AUBYN
Modest Little Sara. ALAN'ST. AUBYN

Taken from the Enemy. H. NEWBOLT.
A Lost Soul. By W. L. ALDEN.

The Seven Sleepers of Ephesus. By M. E. COLERIDGE.